Stolen Lives

Intense, chilling, and ultimately redemptive, Stolen Lives *will have you flipping pages all the way to the end. Brian Reaves really delivers the goods in this thought-provoking novel.*

—JAMES SCOTT BELL
BEST-SELLING AUTHOR OF *PRESUMED GUILTY*

Stolen Lives *is a devious and intriguing thriller. Trapped in bitter loss and bad acts, the characters are beyond hope and redemption—but aren't we all without the love of a Savior? This chilling account of cyber-revenge, seasoned with grace, makes Brian Reaves an author to watch.*

—KATHRYN MACKEL
AUTHOR OF *THE HIDDEN*

With its timely spin on identity theft, Stolen Lives *is a first-rate thriller that is sure to steal readers' time and sleep. Brian Reaves never chooses sides between his characters, instead letting his audience determine where blame should fall. Reaves proves to be a worthy storyteller, weaving plot threads and multiple characters into a fast-paced tale of revenge—and ultimate redemption.*

—ERIC WILSON
AUTHOR OF *EXPIRATION DATE, DARK TO MORTAL EYES,*
AND THE UPCOMING *THE BEST OF EVIL*

Brian Reaves has crafted a modern-day Count of Monte Cristo, filled with the seduction of revenge and the hope of redemption!

—TIM FRANKOVICH
CHRISTIANFICTIONREVIEW.COM

With Stolen Lives, *author Brian Reaves has crafted a real page-turner. The characters are rich, the pace is frenetic, and the book grabs you from the outset and never lets go.*

—MATT CONNOR
REVIEWS EDITOR, INFUZEMAG.COM

A supreme tale of suspense. This brilliant young author weaves sorrow, vengeance, and redemption into a richly textured tapestry portraying people like you and me losing what's most precious. Mark my words, you'll be telling your friends about this book, that is, if they don't tell you first.

—JEFFREY L. CURRY
AUTHOR OF *THE PARABLE DISCOVERY*

STOLEN LIVES

A NOVEL

BRIAN REAVES

RIVEROAK®
Good News in Fiction

COOK COMMUNICATIONS MINISTRIES
Colorado Springs, Colorado • Paris, Ontario
KINGSWAY COMMUNICATIONS LTD
Eastbourne, England

RiverOak® is an imprint of
Cook Communications Ministries, Colorado Springs, CO 80918
Cook Communications, Paris, Ontario
Kingsway Communications, Eastbourne, England

STOLEN LIVES
© 2006 by Brian Reaves

Cover Design: Disciple Design

The Web addresses (URLs) mentioned throughout this book are fictional. The citation of these Web sites does not in any way imply an endorsement on the part of the author or the publisher, nor does the author or publisher vouch for their content for the life of this book.

This story is a work of fiction. All characters and events are the product of the author's imagination. Any resemblance to any person, living or dead, is coincidental.

First Printing, 2006
Printed in the United States of America

1 2 3 4 5 6 7 8 9 10 Printing/Year 11 10 09 08 07 06

All Scripture quotations are taken from the King James Version of the Bible. (Public Domain.)

ISBN-13: 978-1-58919-060-3
ISBN-10: 1-58919-060-2

LCCN: 2006925229

To Lisettet, Khristian, and Chase,
for believing it could happen

Be ye angry, and sin not: let not the sun go down upon your wrath.
—EPHESIANS 4:26

Man must evolve for all human conflict a method which rejects revenge, aggression and retaliation. The foundation of such a method is love.
—MARTIN LUTHER KING JR. (1929–1968)

PART
ONE

REVENGE

*Consider how much more you often suffer from your anger and grief, than from
those very things for which you are angry and grieved.*
—MARCUS AURELIUS ANTONIUS (121–180)

ONE

BY FIVE THIRTY, DEREK Morrison would be a murderer, but for now he was eating a tuna sandwich.

He sat in silence at a truck stop just off I-20 in Oxford, Alabama. His eyes were heavy, and his head hurt from a lack of sleep, but he couldn't afford to stop now to rest. He promised himself a good nap when he reached Birmingham in less than an hour. He had been driving since one that morning to make up for the time he'd lost when his Atlanta load was delayed in Oklahoma. Then he'd agreed to take one more load from Atlanta to Birmingham before resting.

Derek was paid by the mile, not by the hour. He couldn't afford to waste time. The radio over the counter played another country ballad as he crammed the last of the sandwich into his mouth. He turned up his glass of tea to help wash down the stale bread and walked to the cash register.

The pretty blonde behind the counter began to ring up the order. "Did you have the usual, Derek?"

He reached for his wallet. "Yeah. How about you fixing me a fresh sandwich next time I come through?"

The woman smiled and held out her hand. "How do you think we can afford to sell it so cheap? The bread's a day away from green when we get it. That's three dollars, and that doesn't include my tip."

He held out a five. "Debbie, if you can take this with a clear conscience, then go ahead."

She snatched the money from his hand and grinned. "Gorgeous, you think I could work in a place like this if I had a conscience?" Stuffing the money into the register, she looked at him. "Seriously though, you don't look good. How long have you been on the road?"

"About fifteen hours. But I haven't slept five hours together since Tuesday. Gotta keep going so I can be in Birmingham by six. I'll crash then."

Debbie shook her head. "I'm telling you, handsome, you need to stop now. I've seen those eyes on other truckers, and you're gonna crash long before Birmingham."

"Stop trying to seduce me, you evil woman. I know you just want to get me alone and helpless in the back of my rig."

She let out a short laugh. "I'd love to get you alone, but you'd better have a lot more rest before you invite me into your cab."

He winked and walked out as a Clint Black song about another lost woman he'd never see again started playing. Unlike most truckers, Derek hated country music. He stopped here because he was lonely. When a guy spends hours on the road alone, he needs to be with people who know him. The CB allowed him to talk to others, but a disembodied voice wasn't the same as another human being.

One day he might be tempted to take Debbie up on her offer. He glanced at the ring on his left hand and knew he couldn't—not again. He might not have a perfect marriage, but he wouldn't end it yet.

He walked to a nearby pay phone and dialed his home. After three rings, a boy answered. "Morrison residence."

Derek smiled, hearing the voice. "Hey, buddy. How're you doing?"

"That you, Dad? Boy, is Mom ticked at you. You were supposed to be home this morning, and she was waiting for you. Where're you at?"

"Right outside of Anniston, about ninety minutes from Birmingham. I've got to drop a load off, and then I'll be home. Is your mom around?"

"Yeah, hang on a sec." Derek heard the receiver being laid down, and then the boy's voice screaming at the top of his lungs for his mother. He dreaded what he knew was coming, but he had to call.

"Hello?"

"Hi, Rachel. I'm sorry I haven't called sooner, but—"

"I don't care anymore, Derek. I thought things were going to be different. I guess I was wrong. Who was she this time?"

His stomach tightened as he anticipated what would come next. "It's not like that. Listen, Rachel, I've been on the road all this time. I just stopped to get something to eat. I'll be home as soon as I drop off this load, then we can talk."

The beautiful voice on the other end of the line turned cold. "Derek, I don't know what's left for us to say. It's over, and we should both just face it."

Derek fought to keep his voice under control as he spoke. He wanted to shout until he was hoarse, but he knew that wouldn't do any good. He knew exactly where this conversation was heading, and there was nothing he could do about it. The past was too much for either of them to forget. But he still had to try.

"Rachel, don't talk like that. I've got to make money for us to live, baby. I've got to be able to put food on the table for you and Scott. I'll be home soon, I promise. We can talk it over then. I don't want to lose you."

There was a moment of silence on the line. "You lost me a long time ago. You just weren't man enough to face it."

He started to reply, but the dial tone in his ear told him it was useless. She had hung up after getting the last word, just as she always seemed to do. He clutched the receiver so tightly his knuckles turned white. He wanted to slam the phone down and knock it off the wall; instead, he gently replaced the receiver and closed his eyes. He desperately needed some aspirin, but he didn't have the time. He needed to hurry with the load and get home. Maybe he could still talk to her.

Robert Whitney had ten seconds to live.

He glared at the computer monitor before him. On-screen, a digital rendition of a short beaver with a gigantic tail stood there mocking him. Water rushed all around it as a timer in the top corner of the screen counted down the seconds. It was now down to five.

When an ugly brown log suddenly rose to the surface of the water, Robert pressed a button on the joystick.

And nothing happened.

"No!" he shouted and exploded from his chair. "No! Jump, you filthy rat! Move! Why won't that stupid beaver do what it's supposed to?" He turned back to the screen just as the huge tail disappeared into the virtual river around it. "Good riddance, you stupid rodent!"

Robert looked at the monitor and shook his head. It was hard to believe, but this digital animal had been a constant source of frustration and anxiety during the past seven months of programming. He leaned forward on his desk and rubbed the bridge of his nose.

"Well, what do you think?"

Robert turned to the source of the voice behind him. Charlie Bolton was in his early twenties and had the kind of baby face that made people wonder if he was old enough for a driver's license. As always, he was dressed in blue jeans and a black T-shirt with some obscure rock band on it. Robert had never officially had a "casual day" at the office, yet Charlie was never anything but casual.

"I have no idea, Charlie. We've been working on this stupid game for months now, and we're so close to finishing I can taste it. What are we missing? Haven't we gone over this stupid code a hundred times already?"

Charlie slid into the empty chair in front of the monitor and began typing. Within seconds, lines of computer code began to scroll along the screen. "One more time ... I just need to look through this one more time." After reading several lines, he started making corrections here and there, stubbornly refusing to give up.

Robert sighed. "Young man, one day you're going to realize what a genius you are. When that happens, you'll probably want to strike out on your own and start your own software company. Unfortunately, before I let you get away, I'll have to kill you."

Charlie nodded. "You'll miss me when I'm rich and famous."

Robert laughed. "Yes, I think I will. Did you call CyberCross?"

"I just got off the phone with them. I told them we're tweaking the game to their specs. If they call again, we're very happy with the results we have so far and are going to deliver a better game than we'd originally promised. They love that kind of talk."

Robert stared at the ceiling. "What are we going to do? If we don't get this program to them on time, we're in trouble. We need their business, and I don't even want to think about what they could tell other potential customers. The bottom line is that either we get this to them on time and working right, or we're through. If they pull the plug and go elsewhere—"

"Hey, chief, stop being so negative. I'm on the case. We haven't had a failure yet. A couple of close calls, yes, but no failures."

Robert looked at the office around them. It seemed that the walls had grown closer since morning. "Listen, I've fought this thing all I can for today. I thought I might call Tara and tell her I'll be home early, so would you mind ...?"

Charlie raised his hands. "I know. You want me to hold down the fort so you can go gallivanting around with that supermodel you married. No problem. Just remember this when I finally decide to settle down."

Robert shut down his computer and stood. His shoulders were aching from the tension he had been feeling for the past several days. The good news was that he knew an excellent masseuse, and she would be waiting at home for him with their daughter.

"If you ever decide to settle down, then you can officially have a vacation." Robert turned off his computer and began to straighten his desk. As he bent down, his eyes caught a glimpse of the picture sitting in the corner. Tara and Emily were on each side of him, their arms wrapped around his neck and their cheeks pressed tightly next to his. The expression on his face said it all: He was in love with these two beauties. The picture had been taken last year during a picnic at the zoo. It had been Emily's first trip to the zoo, and he'd kept the camera constantly poised, trying to catch her every expression as she saw the animals. At least a part of his life was good.

As he walked to the door, he turned one last time and saw Charlie bent over his keyboard, intently working on the faulty program. Robert smiled and left, quietly closing the door behind him.

Tara Whitney carefully checked the grocery list she had prepared, trying to think of anything that she might have overlooked. Her eyes darted around the kitchen, momentarily locking on each cabinet door and taking a mental inventory of what was behind it.

She glanced at the clock on the wall and smiled. In less than an hour she would be picking up her daughter at school, and then they would be off to the store. Emily was always thrilled at the prospect of grocery shopping. She would stand in the cart as her mother wheeled through each aisle, silent but missing nothing. Tara couldn't remember the last time she had gotten to the checkout line without something in her cart that Emily had managed to sneak in. For a five-year-old, she was pretty slick.

As Tara finally finished her rounds through the house, the phone rang. "Hello?"

"Hey, beautiful, has anyone ever told you what a sexy voice you have?" The voice on the other end of the line was deep and masculine. Even after all this time, it still made her heart leap.

"Only my husband. Of course, he's not home right now. Actually, he never gets here before seven, so if you want to come over ..." She bit her lower lip and grinned.

"Well, guess what? Your husband's going to surprise you this evening by coming home early. As a matter of fact, he'll be home by the time you get back there with your daughter."

Tara raised her eyebrows. "Well, this *is* a surprise. To what do I owe this honor?"

"My dear, I just need some good company." The troubled tone of his voice made Tara pull the phone closer.

"Is everything all right?"

"Yeah, everything's fine. Just been a long day, and I need to get out of the office."

"The game's still not working?"

Robert chuckled. "You know me too well, don't you? No, Barney the Battlin' Beaver still refuses to cooperate. I'm seriously considering a second game involving logging trucks and chainsaws, but that's a whole other story."

"Well, you come on home then. We'll see about making it a casual evening for you."

After several moments of silence, Robert said, "I love you, beautiful woman." He sounded so tired and deflated that it made her heart ache.

"I love you, too. You'll make that game work, baby. I have confidence in you."

She spoke her farewells and gently replaced the receiver. She would have to cut the grocery trip short. She would grab a few things for a special dinner, a little wine for a special dessert, and then they would be out of there. Tara raced to the bathroom and began to do her hair and touch up her makeup. She wanted everything to be perfect for Robert.

Derek walked over to his rig and circled it. It was a habit of his to check everything on his load before driving off. He checked the lock on his trailer and then looked over his tires. He glanced over four of them before finally giving up and getting in. His eyes were killing him. He looked in one of the truck's side mirrors at his reflection. Three days of beard stubble covered his face. His disheveled brown hair looked like it hadn't seen a decent cut in weeks. And his eyes ... the dark circles under them weren't good. Debbie had been right; he'd seen eyes like his before too.

But he couldn't afford to stop yet. He slid behind the wheel and cranked the engine. He loved the sound of the truck's motor starting up and the way the cab would shake as he set off on another road trip. Even through his tired haze, he appreciated his machine.

He slowly started up the entrance ramp onto I-20, all the while promising his body rest when he reached his destination. As he was pulling onto the highway, a small white car whizzed by him. Derek jerked the wheel to the side to avoid hitting the vehicle, cursing all the while.

"One day," he screamed, "I'm gonna have all I can take from you idiots, and I'm gonna just take one of you out! You wait and see."

He cursed some more and pulled onto the highway. He turned the radio up and let the music fuel his anger.

"One day ..." he muttered under his breath.

T W O

Robert was halfway home when he heard his cell phone ringing. He reached over to turn the radio down and flipped the phone open. "Hello?"

"Robert? Listen, I've got to pick up Emily from school and go to the grocery store. Why don't you just meet us at the store? It'll be a big help if you watch Em for me while I shop," Tara's voice turned low and seductive, "and I'll make it worth your while later."

He smiled. "Just tell me where, and I'll be on my way."

At thirty-three, Robert was still in good shape for a man who sat behind a computer all day. He always ate and drank sensibly, and he forced himself to exercise every morning so that his wife wouldn't have to wake up one day and see some fat guy sitting across the kitchen table. She had always kept herself looking good, so he felt he should do the same.

His black hair flew wildly in the wind as the Pathfinder sped along Interstate 20 from Hoover, the part of Birmingham where Robert kept his business. He pushed the SUV to eighty and turned up the radio. He slipped in an Aerosmith CD and sang along as they screamed the lyrics to "Angel," but his mind was on the digital beaver that threatened his company.

Derek's blood raced. He constantly glanced at his mirrors to see the flow of traffic around him.

As he passed another truck, a small sports car flew up behind him and started flashing its lights for him to move. He ignored it as best he could, but finally the driver of the car put his lights on high beam and left them there. Derek's lips tightened, but instead of speeding up, he started slowing down.

He grinned as he looked into his side mirror. "Yeah, pretty boy, what's your hurry? Let me show you what happens when you try to become king of the road. Let's just see how slow that little car of yours can go."

Derek continued to slow down until the front of his truck was just beyond the rear of the truck in the other lane. He could see the driver in the little car stick his fist out the window and wave it in his direction. Derek's smile widened.

"You want a piece of me, little boy?" he said to no one. "I'll give you a piece of me."

He began to speed up until he passed the other truck. As he started to pull into the right lane, the sports car whipped into the passing lane and flew up beside him. Derek jerked the wheel slightly to the left, and the car pulled onto the gravel at the side of the highway to avoid a collision. Finally, the driver punched the accelerator, pulling in front of Derek's truck and barely missing his left headlight. Now it was Derek's turn to dodge the impact. He cursed again and blew his horn as the car sped away, but the smile was still on his face.

"Scared you, didn't I?"

He glanced at his mirrors again and spoke in a low, menacing tone.

"Who's next?"

Tara waited patiently in the line of cars for her daughter. Finally, she saw Emily coming toward her holding her teacher's hand. Emily's short dark hair bounced with every step, and a huge grin crossed her face as she saw her mother.

"Mommy, look what I colored today." She held out the wrinkled piece of paper to her mother before jumping into the backseat of the Maxima. Tara opened the paper and saw three stick figures with huge heads standing on a green line. All three figures were holding hands and smiling. The smallest of the three was holding what appeared to be a bouquet of flowers.

Emily snapped on her seat belt and spoke from the back to her mother. "Well? Do you like it? It's a picture of you and me and Daddy at a picnic. I *like* picnics. Can we go on one again soon?"

Tara carefully folded the paper and handed it over her shoulder to her daughter. "It's beautiful, baby. Why don't you give that to your daddy? I'm sure he'd love to put that up on the wall at his office and show it to everyone. And I'll bet that you'll be able to talk him into a picnic pretty easily."

Emily tenderly held the picture on her lap and broke out into her contagious grin. "I'll call him when we get home."

Tara pulled out into the road and headed toward the grocery store. "Well, I have a little job for you. Daddy's not having a very good day, so we need to cheer him up. We're going to make tonight a fun one, okay? You are officially in charge of making him happy." She knew that if anyone could help Robert forget the problems he was having at work, it would be Emily. Tara understood how important it was to get this game out on time, and she knew they desperately needed to make the sale, but she also knew that Robert had been pushing himself too hard lately. He needed at least one night with no thoughts about programming or impending deadlines.

"And I have a surprise for you: Daddy's coming home early today. In fact, he's going to meet us at Food City."

Emily's little hands shot up as she shouted with glee. "Yeah!" Then she started her familiar chant of "Dad-ee, Dad-ee, Dad-ee," and kept it up until they were almost at the grocery store.

Derek was going over ninety in the passing lane when he saw the sign for Birmingham ahead. He was getting closer now. Soon he'd give Rachel exactly what was coming to her.

Thirty feet ahead, a minivan pulled into his lane. Slamming his fist into the steering wheel, Derek shouted, "What do you think you're doing? There's no one ahead of you!"

He slammed on his brakes and felt the trailer shake a little behind him as the tires caught. The rear of the minivan drew closer by the second. Bracing for the impact, he fought to keep the truck from jack-knifing. Curses flew from between clenched teeth.

Suddenly the minivan swerved back over into the right lane, its driver apparently noticing the impending collision coming up behind it. Derek eased off the brake and downshifted. Within seconds he had the rig back under control.

As he zoomed by the vehicle, he let out a long blast from his horn. With a sneer, he jerked the truck over into the right lane and watched as the minivan slammed on its brakes and swerved off the road. He laughed coldly.

"Stupid! What in the world were you thinking?"

As he wiped the sweat from his face, he saw the city limits of Birmingham.

THREE

Robert JUMPED FROM HIS car and opened the Maxima's door as his daughter began to reach for him. He unbuckled her seat belt and held her up high, spinning her around. She laughed and clapped. As he lowered her, she clamped her arms around his neck like a vice.

"How have my women been today?" he asked, trying to sound as if everything was all right. He put his free arm around his wife's shoulders and pulled her close. Emily rested her head on his shoulder and began to pat his back tenderly.

"I'm fine, Daddy. I'm glad you're here with us. Mommy doesn't know how to shop right."

Robert laughed. "What does Mommy do wrong?"

Emily peeked at her mother and whispered in his ear. Tara lightly punched Robert in the arm and faked a frown. "All right. You know the rules here: *no secrets*. What did she say?"

Robert glanced at his daughter and turned to Tara. "Apparently you put back all the good stuff that she sticks in the cart."

Tara patted Robert's stomach and smiled at Emily. "I have to, or else Daddy would start looking like Grandpa. We don't want that, do we?"

Emily laughed at the thought and then remembered something. "Daddy, I almost forgot your surprise. It's in the car. We've got to go back and get it."

"We'll get it on our way out, baby." The look on Emily's face made him realize that it was pointless to try to argue with her. He turned to Tara and raised his brows. She laughed. "I guess I'll see you two inside."

At the car Emily told him to put her down. After he had unlocked the door, she turned and pointed her tiny finger at him. "Now you close your eyes, Daddy. And no peeking."

Robert obeyed, but kept his eyes partially open to watch her. Emily reached into the car and then turned around and planted something into his hand. "Surprise, Daddy. Can we go on a picnic?"

He opened the paper and looked at the picture. "That's beautiful, baby." Then he frowned as he glanced from the picture to Emily and back again. "It's missing something."

Emily's mouth fell, and her bottom lip protruded.

"Oh, you did everything right, baby. Daddy's not the least bit disappointed. It's just that all great artists have to sign their work, and I don't see your name anywhere on here." He pulled a pen from his shirt pocket and handed it to her. "Will you autograph this for me?"

Emily's face brightened, and she giggled. "Sure." Her mouth puckered and her forehead creased as she slowly scrawled *EMILY* along the bottom of the picture. When she had inspected it, she turned to hand it back. "How's that?"

"Perfect, absolutely perfect. Now, why don't we try to catch up to your mom?"

Robert gently folded the picture and put it in his pocket as he stood. He took his daughter's hand and started walking back toward the store. She looked up at him and tugged his shirtsleeve. He looked down and smiled. "Yes, ma'am?"

"You never said we could take a picnic. Mommy said you'd take us, but you didn't say."

Robert thought about work, and the hours he still needed to put in there. He looked down into Emily's eyes and made his decision.

Guess I'll be working after everyone else has gone to bed, he thought.

Scooping her up, he said, "Young lady, we are going on the best picnic you've ever seen this weekend. We'll go wherever you want to go—within reason, of course."

She looked deep into his eyes. "Could we go to the zoo?"

He scrunched up his face as if in deep thought. "I don't see why not. The zoo it is."

She pulled her fist down as she exclaimed, "Yes!"

He spun her around again once more as they walked through the door. She reached down and wrapped her arms around his neck again. "I love you, Daddy."

Robert hugged her tight. "I love you, too, baby."

Twenty minutes later the threesome walked out carrying four bags of groceries. Tara had managed to keep most of the sweets away, though she allowed Robert to sneak in a couple so he wouldn't look bad in front of his daughter. Tara and Robert had passed little glances back and forth that expressed the silent messages only couples understand, and she had acquiesced to his unspoken requests.

After they had loaded everything into Tara's car, Robert buckled Emily into the back and shut her door. Tara walked around and kissed Robert for the first time that afternoon. It was a kiss that was worth waiting for.

"See you at home, handsome."

He smiled as he got into his car and started the engine. He saw Emily saying something to her mother, waving her hands in excitement and pointing toward him. He rolled down his window and motioned for Tara to do the same.

"I'll race you home," she said.

"You're on."

Robert laughed as he rolled up his window and put the car in reverse. He'd have to let her win, but there was no reason they couldn't have fun along the way. Tara pulled out of the parking lot with Robert right behind her. He honked his horn and waved as Emily looked back.

Without a second thought, they pulled onto the highway.

Window rolled down, the wind in his face, Derek drove on. He had finally made it to Birmingham. Now he just had another twenty minutes and he'd be through. He had gone over the conversation with Rachel again and again.

"Not man enough? Not man enough? I'll show you who's man enough. I'll walk in there and slap that stupid smirk off your face and show you who wears the pants in this family. You've been asking for it for years."

Derek had just pulled into the left lane to pass a car when he noticed the white Maxima speeding up behind him.

Emily squealed with delight as Robert pulled alongside of them and waved. Tara started to get nervous as she came up behind a big truck. She gave Robert a look that told him to back off. He caught the message. With a final wave to Emily, he slowed down and pulled back. Emily twisted to look behind her.

"Oh no, Daddy's getting too far behind." She turned back to her mother and pleaded, "We can't leave him."

Tara looked into the rearview mirror into her daughter's worried eyes. "We're not going to leave him, baby. We're just winning, that's all."

Emily looked up at her as if she didn't believe her, and then glanced back behind her again. "Mommy, please."

"Emily, everything is—" Tara looked back at the road. She'd inadvertently drifted to the right and into the next lane. The car beside her swerved a little, then the guy laid on his horn. Tara pulled back into her lane, waving apologetically, but the man kept honking. She glanced over and saw him screaming something at her.

Okay, okay, I get the message. I messed up, and I'm sorry. How about calming down over there?

She was embarrassed now, both for herself and for the way this man was acting in front of her little girl. His horn was one long blast now.

Derek turned down his radio and listened. There! The driver of the car behind him was honking its horn at him. She was trying to get him to hurry up and get out of her way, as if she owned the road.

"All right, honey. You want to play? We'll play."

Derek pushed the accelerator and shifted gears to speed past the car in the right lane. His eyes never left his side mirror as he pulled into the right lane again. He would wait for just the right moment, and then he'd show this little idiot who really owned the road.

Tara was relieved to see the big truck pull over. Now she could get away from the crazy man in the next lane.

Tara glanced in her rearview mirror and saw Robert well behind her. She began to pass the car in the other lane and then came up beside the eighteen-wheeler.

Derek smiled.

The car was in position.

He jerked the wheel to the left and let the truck slip over into the passing lane. Just as he'd expected, the driver panicked and pulled to the left, with the front wheel going into the gravel.

And then everything went wrong.

Robert screamed.

He watched in horror as the huge truck tractor-trailer pulled into the lane with Tara. He saw her car wrench off the side of the road and suddenly begin to spin as the front tire caught the gravel. He saw the car whirl around completely and could see Tara's horrified face for an instant before the car disappeared under the truck's trailer.

Derek felt his truck jerk and bounce as he glanced in the mirror. He fought the wheel to keep on the road. Then he heard a loud screech of metal being crushed and tires exploding. He slammed on his brakes and began to pray for the first time in his life.

"Oh, dear God, no!"

Robert stopped the car in the middle of the highway and yelled as he jumped out and ran toward the lump of white metal that had been his wife's car. He'd seen the trailer bounce twice before the twisted wreckage spun from under it and flipped over. His mind knew that there was no way Tara and Emily could have survived the wreck, but his heart wouldn't accept it.

He was vaguely aware of other cars stopping, of someone shouting something about 911, but his entire being was focused on what was ahead of him. He ran to what had been the driver's side of the car and tried to look in, but he couldn't see anything. The roof of the car was pushed down into the car itself. He screamed out their names, but there was no answer.

Robert frantically ran around to the other side and tried to see in. As he rounded the corner, he stepped in a growing dark-red puddle.

No! They're all right! They're going to make it!

If he could have, he would have ripped the car apart like an eggshell to pull his family out. He would have flipped it over and torn the doors off. But he could do nothing more than impotently bang his fists against the side of what had been the passenger door and cry.

Derek grabbed the fire extinguisher and jumped out of his truck. As he raced toward the car, he saw a man running around it in a desperate attempt to reach the people inside. Smoke was pouring from the engine, but the man seemed impervious to the imminent danger of an explosion.

Derek turned the extinguisher on the car and emptied it. He made his own circle around the car, but could see no way of getting in to help anyone who was still inside. Several people were gathering at a safe distance as traffic began to back up. There was glass all over the highway, along with several other parts of the car.

As Derek began to approach the man who still pounded on the car, he noticed for the first time that the man was crying and calling out two names again and again, his knees resting in a pool of blood.

This guy knew the people in the car. Oh man, he might have seen everything.

Derek walked up to the man and reached out to touch his arm. "Mister? The paramedics are coming. You need to get back in case the car explodes."

When the man looked up at him, Derek felt his blood freeze. Tears flowed down the man's twisted face as he spoke through clenched teeth. "You ... you were the one driving the truck?"

Derek closed his gaping mouth and swallowed before slowly nodding.

Without warning, the man exploded into him. "You monster! What did you think you were doing? You killed them!" The man's fist slammed into Derek's face, but Derek didn't try to stop him. He fell backward under the impact of the blow.

Two men came and pulled the man off of him as the paramedics arrived. The man continued to scream at him, but Derek lay silent on the pavement hearing those last words echo again and again in his mind.

You killed them!

FOUR

ROBERT STOOD IN SILENCE, watching the swarm of rescue workers pull the remains of his wife from the twisted wreckage that had been her car. At his feet lay a small covered figure that had less than an hour earlier been his laughing, beautiful baby girl. A strand of her brown hair stuck out from under the blanket that shrouded her. His expressionless face watched as it twisted slightly in the gentle breeze that seemed to caress him in his grief and loneliness.

He turned and looked at the truck driver, engrossed in a conversation with a state trooper. The trooper hadn't come for his side of the story, but Robert knew he would have to tell it. Several people who had been behind his car were prepared with their statements. The truck driver would probably lose his job, maybe pay a little fine. But it was an accident, so he said.

Robert had seen it all. It was no accident. The man had killed his family as surely as if he had put a gun to their heads and pulled the trigger himself, murdering them in cold blood.

Almost unconsciously, Robert began to move toward the man.

His hands balled into fists, and he felt the blood surging through his temples. His face was hard-set.

The trucker and the trooper were still in conversation, until they noticed his approach. At the sight of him, they both fell silent, and the trooper's hand moved casually to the baton hanging from his belt as he nonchalantly stepped between Robert and the truck driver.

Robert only glanced at him before his eyes locked onto the trucker and didn't let go. Finally, he stopped within a few feet of them both. All three were silent, waiting for one of the others to speak.

In a quiet voice that seemed to rely on nothing but sheer presence to relay his message, Robert spoke to the trucker.

"God himself can't protect you from me."

With a final glance at the trooper, daring him to make a move, Robert turned and walked back to the bodies of his family. His wife's still form was now lying next to his daughter's.

No one there could see it, no one else could know, but there were actually three bodies lying there on the paramedic gurneys. There was a beautiful woman named Tara, who had been the greatest wife and mother that any man could have dreamed of. There was a precious little girl named Emily, whose life had only begun. And lying beside them unseen by all but one was a man named Robert, who had wrapped his entire world around them. None of them had ever realized how incredibly cruel the world could be.

Three bodies.

Someone else standing and looking down at them.

Not the father.

Not the husband.

The avenging angel of death.

The one who would make sure their senseless deaths were not forgotten.

Robert glanced back one last time at the trucker and measured him. In his mind he tortured him in unspeakable ways and watched as he begged for death. He watched the life slowly ebb from his body until only the empty husk remained.

And then he destroyed that too.

But he would not kill him. Not yet.

The man would suffer. He would beg for an end to it all.

Robert stared hard at the scene around him, memorizing this moment in time.

He would never forget.

FIVE

Y OU WANT PROTECTION FROM that guy?"

Derek's attention snapped back to the tall black state trooper. It took him a second to realize what he'd said, and then he whispered his reply.

"No. I don't think I'll need it."

The trooper studied him and then glanced over at the man who had just walked away. He shook his head slowly. "It's a real tragedy. Nobody should have to watch his wife and kid die. That's gotta do something to a man."

He looked over his report again, then reached into his pocket and pulled out his business card. "My number is there. The name's Gold, Terrance Gold. If you think of anything else related to this incident, please call me. There's a little confusion in this whole business. None of the witnesses saw that other vehicle you said caused you to pull over onto that lady. I'll have to talk to that other guy, of course, but you appear to have had the only view of it. What was it again?"

Derek's eyes had wandered back to the two shrouded figures on the gurneys and the man standing alone watching over them. "It was a white truck … a small white pickup truck. It pulled over in front of me and made me swerve into the other lane. I wasn't anywhere near that woman enough to run her that far off the road though."

Gold looked at the white mass of metal that had been a car just an hour ago. "Don't worry about it. The lady probably overcompensated for your truck and just went into a spin. You know how these women drivers are. Don't lose my card now; you may need to contact me about this situation."

He winked at Derek and then walked to the man who stood guarding the bodies of his dead wife and child. Derek was sweating and shaking like a junkie. He looked at the scene one final time and walked to his truck.

He had lied. In his panic and fear, he had lied. He didn't want to go to jail, and after all, it had been an accident. He would never have killed that woman for anything. Blaming the wreck on another vehicle seemed like the only way to get out of this mess he had gotten into.

Traffic moved slowly past them as the people gawked from the passing cars, trying to get a good look at the covered corpses and the man who was with them. Derek wanted to shout at them to go away. He wanted to scream at them for being sick and sadistic, for wanting to watch as someone else suffered.

Instead, he climbed into his truck, now unhitched from its trailer, and started the engine. He closed his eyes and took a deep breath. He needed to call his company first, talk to the insurance guy. Then he'd have to stumble home and see if anyone was there waiting for him.

Derek jumped as someone rapped on his window. He looked out and saw a stocky man waving at him. Derek recognized him as one of the witnesses who had talked to the trooper. He rolled down his window.

"Hi," the short man said. "My name's Chris Rickles. I saw the whole thing, and like I was telling that trooper, I don't remember seeing any pickup truck." He slipped a folded piece of paper up to Derek, who took it with a questioning look on his face. "That's my name and address. My phone number's on the bottom of it. Give it to your boss or somebody and let them know I don't remember seeing any truck, but my memory has a way of coming and going. I'm sure you know what I mean." The little man smiled again and walked off.

Derek looked down at the paper. *I can't believe this. Vultures. Sick freaks who want to make a fast buck off of someone else's misfortune.*

He started to throw the paper away, but then thought better of it and stuffed it into his pocket. Like it or not, he might need that vulture if it came down to it. He put the truck in gear and pulled out into the traffic.

"Mr. Whitney?"

Robert had been watching the paramedics load up the bodies of his wife and child. He turned his head at the sound of the man's voice. It was the trooper he'd seen a few minutes earlier. "Yes?"

"I need to get a statement from you about your version of the accident. You saw everything, correct?"

He took a deep breath to get himself under control. He wished now that his threat had only been whispered to the trucker, but the heat of the moment had made him overzealous.

"Yes. I saw it all."

The trooper scribbled something on the report. "Did you see the other vehicle?"

Robert turned to face him. "What other vehicle?"

"The truck driver says that another vehicle," he lifted a page, "a white pickup truck, pulled in front of him and forced him to swerve to miss it. Did you see the vehicle?"

"There was no pickup truck. The lane was empty in front of that trucker. He purposely pulled over onto my wife and caused the accident."

"Why would he do that, Mr. Whitney?"

Robert fought to keep control. "I don't *know* why. I just know he did. I saw everything and he—"

"Now, Mr. Whitney, you were well behind the truck, isn't that correct? How could you say what the guy did or didn't do on purpose? Maybe you didn't notice the other vehicle. Maybe there really wasn't one. These things are so hard to write up."

Robert's eyes narrowed. "What do you mean?"

The trooper looked over at the wreckage. "I mean, I can't be certain what happened one way or another. I have witnesses who aren't sure whether there was another vehicle involved or not. I have conflicting versions from Mr. Morrison and yourself. I guess it'll just all boil down to what *I* think happened. What I put in my report will be the final say, and that report's not written yet, know what I mean?"

He pulled out a business card. "My number's on there if you think of anything important you want to tell me later. You never know when you might think of something you wished you'd said."

Robert took the card and looked down at it. Three phone numbers were listed. The top two were business numbers, with the final one listed as "Residence." He looked up at Officer Gold. "Don't you want the rest of my statement?"

"Why don't you take some time to recover from this trauma? You can contact me when you have a chance to think about what happened. Call me if you need me." He tipped his hat and walked off.

Robert looked at the card again. He was beginning to feel numb. When he looked up, the trooper was talking to the man operating the wrecker.

Robert looked around, surveying the scene. His wife and child's bodies had been put into an ambulance and taken away. The glass and metal had been swept up, and the mangled car was being loaded onto a wrecker to be removed. Within minutes, there would be no sign of the accident except a few skid marks on the road and a bloody stain. When those two things had been worn away, there would be nothing left to show that the two most important people in his life had died there.

"Excuse me."

He turned and looked down into the face of a fat little man who was smiling and holding out a small folded piece of paper. "My name's Chris Rickles. I was a witness to the accident. I think I saw a pickup truck cut the other man off, but I can't be certain. As I told the other gentleman, my memory comes and goes. Here's my number if you need to call me about anything for your case."

The fat man trotted to his car, and Robert watched him drive away without saying a word. He stuffed the trooper's card and the piece of paper into his pocket and went to his Pathfinder. He looked one last time at the spot where his wife and child had died.

A cold wind blew around him, but he didn't feel it.

He was beyond feeling anything.

SIX

WHEN DEREK ARRIVED AT the trucking company minus his trailer, everyone wanted every detail. More important, they wanted names.

"Who was the officer who filled out the report?" was the first question out of his employer's mouth. Derek's boss, Gordon James, was an older man with a round belly and no hair. If he decided to grow a mustache and beard, he would look like a wino version of Santa Claus. His nose, which had been broken several times in bar fights and at truck stops, was now red and bulbous. His manner and demeanor, however, totally dispelled the image of jolly old St. Nick.

"Did you get me names and phone numbers?"

Derek handed him the trooper's card. Then he thought of the fat man, and found the little scrap of paper that he'd given him. "Here's someone who was a witness to it. He seemed a little fuzzy on the details, but he said you'd know how to clear up his memory."

James smiled as he took the paper from him. "I think we can probably fix that. Did the officer say anything?"

Derek turned to leave. "Nothing important, but I'm sure his memory could use a little help too. I'm going home to get some sleep. Don't call me for a few days. I need some time to think."

Derek was still shaking as he walked through his front door. He needed a drink. But he had promised Rachel that his drinking days were over. At the thought of his wife, he realized how quiet the house was. "Rachel?"

Silence.

He walked into the hallway. "Rachel? Scott? Hey, Daddy's home."

More silence.

His heart began to pound in his chest until he could hear its every beat. He walked down the hall to his son's room to find it empty. He ran down the hall into the kitchen.

Empty.

She had finally left him.

He sat down at the kitchen table and put his hand on his forehead. He didn't need this now. His day had been bad enough already. He desperately wanted a drink and some sleep so that maybe this nightmare would go away. He rested his head on the table and closed his eyes, trying to sort everything out as simply as possible.

First, he was a murderer.

Maybe that was a little harsh. Manslaughter would probably be the most the law could stick him with. He'd probably spend time in prison, but the death penalty wasn't really something to worry about for this kind of thing.

Second, he was now alone.

In a time when he needed someone more than ever, he was alone. "Derek?"

His head jerked up, and he regretted it instantly. His headache worsened as the blood rushed to his brain, but what he saw made it worthwhile.

"Rachel."

She was standing there with two grocery bags in her arms. She was wearing a pair of shorts that accented her long, graceful legs. Her blonde hair was pulled back in a hastily made ponytail. Her blue eyes narrowed as she surveyed his condition.

"What's wrong? You look awful."

Before he could answer, he saw a little boy walk into the kitchen struggling with a grocery sack that was almost as big as he was. When he saw Derek sitting at the table, the boy dropped his load and ran to him. "Daddy!"

Derek scooped his son up in his arms and squeezed him tightly. "Hey, buddy. I've missed you."

The little boy looked up. "And Mommy?"

Derek looked at Rachel, who had walked to the counter to set down the groceries. "Yeah, and Mommy, too."

Rachel glanced over at him. "There's a few more bags in the trunk if you want to help."

Derek got up and walked toward the door. He wanted to grab Rachel and hold her. He wanted to tell her what had happened and ask her advice about what he should do next. He wanted to cry in her embrace until the fear left him. But her obvious indifference to him had already set the boundaries for the evening.

Even though she was there in the house with him, he was still alone.

That night, as he lay in bed next to Rachel, Derek felt as if he was suffocating. He couldn't breathe, and it seemed as if he had a metal band wrapped around his chest that was tightening with each second. Although his body craved sleep, it eluded him.

When he finally fell asleep, the nightmare came.

He can feel the rush of the wind through the open window, the rumbling of the truck around him.

Then he hears the horn.

He glances in his side mirror and sees the white car. He pulls into the right lane and carefully times his attack. As soon as it is next to him, he swerves into the passing lane. He watches as the car spins around once before disappearing under his rig. He feels the truck shudder at the sudden obstacle.

He stops and gets out, suddenly feeling the same nausea he felt the first time it happened. He runs toward the wreckage and the man who is running around it, screaming to the people inside.

He comes up behind the man and calls to him. When the man turns, it is Derek's turn to scream.

The man's face is a skull.

It is Death itself.

It points a finger at Derek and speaks in a cold, distant voice.

"God himself can't protect you from me."

Then it screams and reaches for him....

Derek bolted up in bed, but he was able to stifle the cry of terror while it was still in his throat. He was soaked in sweat and had started shaking again. He looked over and saw that Rachel was still asleep.

One thought was foremost in his mind: *I need a drink.*

He rolled out of bed and walked into the kitchen. He searched the cabinets, but they held none of the magical elixir for which he so desperately hungered. He quietly opened the back door and walked out to the shed behind the house.

Rachel had forced him to give up drinking because, in all honesty, he had become an alcoholic. It was only by her love and bulldog tenacity that he was able to give it up. She had consistently warned him that his next drink would end their marriage because she wouldn't put up with his drunken fits of rage any longer. He knew she was serious.

But he couldn't help it; this was more than anyone could bear.

Derek felt the cool night air swirl around him as he walked the short distance to the shed and the stash he'd kept hidden there for a rainy day.

And it was definitely pouring now.

He opened the door and walked into the small, dark building. Inside were his workbench, a few tools and assorted pieces of wood, and his lawn mower. He walked directly to the wood and lifted up a piece of plywood that was propped against the wall.

The bottle of whiskey was still there.

Along with a note attached to it.

He picked up the folded piece of paper and read it.

Derek,

    I've always known about this little secret place of yours. I haven't moved your liquor because the decision will ultimately have to be yours. I love you and hate to see you when you drink, but I can't be there to stop you all the time. You must decide to stop yourself.

    If you drink this, then we are through. When you wake up from your binge, you'll be alone. Scott and I will be gone. And I promise you, we will not be back.

    Think about it.

      I love you.
      Rachel

Derek leaned back on the workbench and closed his eyes. He took several deep breaths and thought about what the note said.

It would be so easy to go and wake her up. He could tell her everything, and then they could face it together. She would know what to do, and she would help him stand up to what he'd done.

But what if she didn't understand? What if she called him horrible things and then called the police? What then?

When he opened his eyes, he saw the bottle on the ground. Derek brought the note to his face and inhaled. He could smell her perfume on it. He gently folded the paper and put it in his pocket.

Then he reached for a drink.

SEVEN

W<small>E CAN'T KNOW THE</small> mind of God."

The man dressed in black spoke quietly over the caskets. In his hand a limp Bible flopped back and forth as he punctuated each sentence with a shake of the Holy Book.

The sky was overcast, and a steady, strong breeze blew around the group as they stood in the cemetery beside the new graves. Robert watched in silence, his long black overcoat billowing about his legs. There were no tears in his eyes. He'd cried all he could over the past three nights.

Those in the small crowd around him were also silent. Some of the women were crying and sniffling as their husbands tried to comfort them. Charlie stood behind him, obviously uncertain of what to do next. The only one speaking now was the thin preacher who was presiding over the ceremony.

"In his infinite wisdom, almighty God has taken unto himself the souls of Tara and Emily. We may not see why now, but we must believe that he is in control. We must know that he had a reason; one that we might not understand, but we cannot know the mind of God."

Robert was no longer listening to the droning voice. Tara had been the one to take Emily to church, while he'd hardly ever had time to go himself. But the way this preacher talked, the God who Tara had gone to worship all those Sundays was the same one who'd just killed her. What kind of God would do something like that? If there was a God, then how could he allow horrible things like this to happen? The answer was obvious: Either God was a sadist, or he didn't exist. It didn't matter which was true, it only mattered that there was no reason why anyone should want to serve such a God.

He watched the limp Bible flap around awhile longer before the man stopped talking and said a final prayer over the bodies. As soon as he said "Amen," the crowd changed. They moved away from the grave site, and their sad faces disappeared, to be replaced with smiles and even laughter. They bantered back and forth about how good someone's dress looked, or where they should go to eat, never noticing the lonely figure still standing over the caskets, watching them slowly disappear into the ground.

Charlie leaned forward and whispered, "I'm so sorry, man. If you need anything, just say the word." Then he squeezed his arm and walked away.

When the coffins were completely gone, Robert looked up. The crowd had dispersed so that only he and the preacher remained. Robert's eyes locked on him, but he didn't say a word. The preacher appeared uncomfortable with the silence.

"Robert, I want you to understand that we're here for you. I realize you don't know me that well, but please remember we're praying for you that God will give you peace in the coming weeks. If there's anything we can do, don't hesitate to call." He smiled sympathetically and gave Robert a reassuring pat on his arm before walking away.

Robert watched him go a few steps and then called to him.

"Reverend?"

The preacher stopped and turned around. "Yes?"

"Vengeance is mine."

The preacher looked quizzically at Robert for a moment before finishing the quote. "I will repay, saith the Lord."

Robert looked down at the graves one last time and began to walk away.

"Not if I get to him first."

Derek woke with a headache like none he had ever had before. He slowly opened his eyes and tried to acclimate himself to his surroundings. He had spent many mornings in similar situations—waking up in a strange bed with a strange woman—but not in a long time. He waited for his eyes to focus on the ceiling and realized immediately that it wasn't his bedroom. He slowly turned his head to the side and found that the slumbering form next to him was also definitely not his Rachel. He forced himself onto one elbow to see if his clothes were anywhere nearby, while at the same time trying to keep his unknown partner asleep.

As he swung his legs over the side of the bed, he had to stop for a second while the world went into a tailspin around him. His head throbbed with every heartbeat, and his eyes felt as if they were on fire, but he pushed himself to get dressed as quickly as possible. He glanced behind him one last time to see the steady breathing of the stranger in the bed. Her back was to him, but he didn't dare turn her over to identify her.

He found himself in a mobile home. It was relatively easy to locate the back door and to slip out quietly. He checked to make sure the door was locked before shutting it and turning to find his truck. He felt for his keys and made sure he still had his wallet, then got into the pickup and started it up. His ears were instantly assaulted by a loud blast of music from his radio. He wanted to black out, but found the volume knob and turned it off. He put the truck in gear and started out, wrestling with his emotions while trying to keep his head from exploding in pain.

After a few wrong turns, he found an area he recognized and slowly made his way onto the highway and toward home. He wasn't fooling himself into thinking Rachel would still be there, since he had no idea how long he'd been on this latest binge. The last thing he remembered was sitting in the shed with his empty liquor bottle and realizing that he wasn't drunk enough, so he'd gone to get a beer.

He stopped at a gas station and looked at the date on the newspaper in the stand outside. *Three days! I've been drunk and out of it for three days! What can I say to Rachel?* He knew without really thinking about it that no excuse would be good enough. His only hope was that she might forgive him if he told her the truth about the accident. Maybe she would understand how tired he'd been, how their argument had driven him to rage, how ...

But he knew it was too late to try the "honesty is the best policy" routine now.

Yet it was all he had left.

Feeling hopeless, Derek headed home.

"What? Why you lousy, stinking—"

"Now, Mr. Whitney," the deep, commanding voice on the other end of the line began, "I had told you before that there were witnesses."

Robert's face was a dark red as he fought to control the rage. His knuckles were white from his grip on the phone. "You told me that the witnesses didn't know what they'd seen."

"But, Mr. Whitney," Officer Gold's calm voice continued, "I told you to call me if you thought of anything else that you needed to tell me. I never heard from you, so I was forced to go with the testimony I had received. I'm afraid it was basically two against one as far as that was concerned. The truck driver and a witness both stated seeing a white pickup truck whip in front of Mr. Morrison's rig. I'm sorry, but that's the story I've put down."

"But you've put it down as my wife's fault. You've got the report saying she overcompensated for the truck pulling into her lane. You've got it saying she *purposefully* drove under the eighteen-wheeler." Robert was looking at the final report that Gold had faxed to him minutes earlier. It stated plainly that Morrison was not at fault, that there had been another driver who had caused the accident resulting in a tragic loss of life. And Morrison had been the innocent victim in all of it.

"I'm sorry, Mr. Whitney. But that's my report. It's the final version of it, and it's what will stand. Now I really don't think you need to worry about hearing from Mr. Morrison's trucking company about the damages to his truck, but I would retain a good lawyer just in case."

"What?" For the second time in five minutes, Robert was speechless. Those filthy animals that murdered his family were now thinking about possibly making him pay for the machine that killed them? Robert spoke into the phone in a voice that was almost a whisper.

"How much did they pay you, Gold? How much was my family worth?"

There was a moment's hesitation on the other end of the line, and then Officer Gold spoke in a cold voice. "It's only out of respect for the fact that you've been under a lot of stress in the past three days that I don't come down there and rip your head off for that remark, Whitney. This conversation is over." The line went dead.

Robert realized that he had struck a nerve with Gold, which just proved his theory.

He gently replaced the receiver, then reached down for a blank piece of paper and wrote down all the information on Officer Terrance Gold he could find on the police report. What else had he said ... something about a witness? Robert thought for a moment, and then remembered the little man who had come to him and slipped him the piece of paper with his name and number on it. Robert reached into his wallet for the paper and looked at it. Then he methodically added the name "Chris Rickles" directly under Gold's information and wrote down the man's phone number.

Then, almost as an afterthought, Robert wrote down the name of Morrison's trucking company and looked up their number in the phone book. If they truly had bought Gold and Rickles off, then they would pay too.

Finally, Robert wrote the name, address, and phone number of the one man he hated most in the world. In a slow, deliberate script he wrote "Derek Morrison," and the information below it. When he'd finished, Robert held up the piece of paper and looked again at the names on it.

He now had his list. These people would pay dearly. They would all beg for mercy before he was through with them, especially Morrison. He was special. He would be the only one to suffer to the point of welcoming death as a sweet relief from his torture.

And then Robert would end his suffering.

Forever.

A cold smile played across Robert's face. He slowly turned to his computer and opened his Internet browser.

It was time to begin.

Terrance Gold stared at the phone intently for several minutes, trying to slow his breathing and steady himself. He had not expected Whitney's accusation. Was he that transparent? He had been so careful in his dealings with the trucking company. He felt certain that there was nothing to tie him with them, but what had made Whitney think there was?

Finally, he whispered a response to the now-dead phone.

"What was your family worth? A lot more to me dead than they were alive, that's for sure." He chuckled at his joke, and then rose to return to his patrol.

Derek wheeled into his driveway and realized right away something was wrong. He got out and entered slowly through the front door. "Rachel?" he called softly.

No answer.

He went to the living room, and then he noticed it.

Things were different for some reason. It was hard to concentrate with his head pounding, but it was obvious that some things were missing or out of place. He stumbled to his bedroom and opened the closet door. His suspicions were confirmed. All of Rachel's things were gone. He moved as quickly as he dared to Scott's room. His things were gone too. The room was now abandoned with only a small, uncovered bed and an empty desk in it. Everything that suggested Derek had at one time had a family was now gone. He slammed his fist into the wall and let out a low wail that seemed to come from someone else. He slid into a crumpled heap on the floor, crying and calling for his wife and son.

Robert quickly used Gold's home phone number listed on the business card he'd given him at the accident to do a reverse lookup. Within seconds Robert had Gold's home address and used the information to set up a Web-based e-mail account in Gold's name. The Web-based accounts were the easiest to create with false information; and if someone decided to trace what would be happening in the next few weeks, they would go to the wrong person about it. He purposefully avoided the obvious accounts that were immediately relegated to an e-mail program's spam folder, going with a smaller one that had recently started up.

Robert smiled. This might be fun after all.

He looked at the small cell phone lying beside the computer's keyboard. It was a cheap one on a prepaid account, and one he only planned to use sparingly over the next few days. None of the information about the owner of the phone was correct though. While standing in line to purchase it, the woman in front of him had absentmindedly left her wallet open in her hand as she waited to reach the cashier. It had given Robert plenty of time to memorize her name, address, and driver's license number. Her license was an older one that actually still had her Social Security number on it too. She didn't know how lucky she was that he hadn't wanted the information for more sinister motives, like setting up a credit-card account in her name.

Picking up the cell phone, he dialed the number of the trucking company that Morrison worked for. A woman's voice answered in a deep Southern drawl. "Starline Trucking. How may I direct your call?"

Robert had been ready for this response. "Well, actually I need a little information. My name is Thomas Strickland, and I'm with the Highway Patrol. One of our officers filled out an accident report for an incident that happened a few days ago on I-20, and I need to confirm a piece of information on it. Who do I need to talk to?"

"Well, honey, I'll have to connect you to Gordon at home."

Within seconds, a gruff voice answered. "Gordon James."

Robert's voice lowered and hardened instantly. "Listen to me, you filthy scum. I know you paid off that trooper and probably Rickles too. I just want you to know that you will pay dearly for it."

The voice on the other end gasped, but then spewed out a response. "Who is this?"

Robert hung up the phone.

He looked down at his list of four names, and directly beside Starline Trucking he wrote "Gordon James."

James hadn't immediately denied the accusations, which is something an innocent man would do out of reflex. He was guilty, and that made what Robert was about to do next much easier.

He jumped back onto his computer and did a quick reference lookup on all listings for Gordon James in Alabama. He decided not to target his search to any specific area yet, since commuting was a way of life in the state. A person working in Birmingham could live an hour away in any direction to avoid the high rent in the metropolitan area apartments. His search turned up seven responses. He discarded four at once as too far away to seriously consider. That left three possibilities. He picked up the cell phone and began to dial the numbers listed. On the second number, he heard a familiar voice on an answering machine. He raised his voice several pitches and said, "Sorry, wrong number." He didn't want to give James any reason to get paranoid yet, outside of the phone call he'd just received a few minutes earlier.

He scribbled down the address and phone number now available to him on the screen. He had enough for now.

Well, almost.

As an afterthought, he used the information to check for an e-mail address. These days it was doubtful that anyone in business could afford to be without one. He was right. Gordon James' e-mail address was listed, and Robert added it to his list of information on James. He checked Starline Trucking's Web site and found more contact information and even a short bio on the members of upper management. It was a vanity bit done by a small company trying to seem more professional than they were, but it gave him what he needed.

Gordon James had no idea of it, but he was now at the mercy of someone who could destroy him—someone who *would* destroy him—slowly.

Robert turned his attention to the last name on the list. His expression turned to stone at the sight of the name.

He turned back to his computer, typed in *Derek Morrison,* and began his search.

EIGHT

Rachel Morrison sat lost in thought in a booth at Chappee's, a local restaurant known for its incredible selection of desserts. She'd spent the day at her lawyer's office preparing various papers for divorce proceedings, supplying him with the necessary documentation for calculating child support and possible alimony—though Rachel knew her chances of receiving it were slim. Alabama was strong on child support, but few wives ever received an alimony judgment. That left Rachel to contemplate a return to the job market, which was fine with her.

Scott was now at her parents' house, where she herself would have to stay for a while. It would've been easy to kick Derek out of the house and have it for Scott and herself, but she knew she didn't want to live there anyway. The memories would be too much for her.

She had to admit some concern for Derek. She hadn't heard from him in four days; and while that was nothing during one of his old binges, he hadn't gone on a binge in a very long time. She hoped he was all right, but in the same breath she cursed him for what he'd done to their lives.

She took a few bites from an exquisite piece of chocolate cake she'd ordered and looked around the room. People of all ages and nationalities were there. The only thing that distinguished her from the rest was the fact that she was alone.

Then she noticed the man looking at her.

When she locked eyes with him, he smiled and nodded his head slightly. He was an incredibly attractive man with deep blue eyes and black hair. He was one of those rare individuals blessed with a naturally dark complexion. She smiled back and looked down at her cake. She glanced up again and found that he was still grinning at her, but now the smile had gotten wider. Rachel couldn't remember the last time a strange man had made a pass at her. It was exciting. She felt like it had been years since she'd been noticed by anyone—even Derek. He'd become more of a roommate than a lover. But this man made her feel attractive.

She averted her gaze and stared out the window. She watched his reflection in the glass and took the chance to study him. He finished his drink and stood to leave. As he got up, she measured every inch of him in the image on the window. He was fit, that much was obvious from the slim jeans and the tailored button-down shirt he wore. They were casual, but they were tight enough to show a measure of the musculature beneath them. It made her feel good to know that a man like that would show interest in her. Maybe being single again wouldn't be so bad.

He turned to leave, but then Rachel's breath caught as she saw him turn back to her and walk toward her table. He waited patiently until she turned to face him. His smile and deep blue eyes melted her; and when he spoke, his voice was deeply masculine and sexy.

"Hi, my name's Robert. May I buy you a drink?"

"Please, Paul, I need to talk to her," Derek pleaded into the phone to his father-in-law.

"I'm sorry, Derek. I don't think that would be a good idea right now. Anyway, she's not here. She's gone to get some dinner. I'll let you talk to Scott if you give me your word you won't upset him or speak against Rachel."

Derek's voice softened. "You know me better than that, Paul. I don't want to drag Scott into the middle of all this and try to make him choose sides."

There was silence for a moment before the older man answered. "I know, Derek. I'm really sorry all this happened. I had high hopes for you and Rachel. I thought you'd licked that drinking problem, but I guess we all have our demons to face."

Derek's mind raced to the dream where he was facing death itself and the statement that still cut him to the core.

God himself can't protect you from me.

He cleared his throat. "Yeah, demons. Thanks for letting me speak to Scott, Paul."

Scott was on the line a few seconds later. "Hey, Dad."

"Hey, buddy. Are you having fun at Grandma and Grandpa's?" He tried to sound upbeat, although every second of hearing his son's voice was slicing him to his soul. He wanted to hold his boy, to tell him that he was so sorry for what he'd done.

"Yeah, Dad, it's fun, but I wish you were here to play with me. Mom took all our stuff and brought it here. She said that we were moving. Why? I like our house."

"I know, buddy. It's not permanent yet. You still might be coming back real soon." Derek's eyes watered, and his voice began to quiver. He had to be strong. He couldn't let his son know how bad things really were.

"Are you okay, Dad? You sound sick."

"Yeah, I'm fine. Listen, I've got to go, but I'll call you again very soon. Give my love to your grandparents."

"Okay, Dad. Bye. I love you."

"I love you too." He hung up quickly before his son could hear his voice falter completely. Tears streamed down his cheeks as he turned to his truck. Rachel was out eating dinner. He ran through the places nearest her parents' home, and then picked the most logical one.

Chappee's. She loved to eat there when they went to visit her folks.

He could be there in twenty minutes.

Rachel laughed again as the man across the table made another funny remark. He had an incredible sense of humor, and that smile just held her when she saw it. She couldn't remember the last time she'd had so much fun with someone. It had been too long, that was for sure.

She ran the tip of her finger idly along the stem of her wine glass. She looked up at him, as he sipped from his. "So, Robert Whitney, why isn't a catch like you taken already? Are you some sort of serial killer or something?"

He looked at her for only a moment then placed his glass back on the table. Leaning forward, he said, "Actually, I was about to ask you the same thing. You're an incredibly beautiful woman, Rachel. I just can't believe that you haven't been snatched up already by some lucky guy."

Rachel glanced at her ring finger and remembered she'd removed her wedding ring four days earlier when she'd left her home. At first her hand felt strange and empty, but now she had grown accustomed to the ring's absence. "I was married for quite some time. I guess he just wasn't the right guy ... but I'm still hopeful." She locked eyes with him. He didn't blink. He had a thoughtful look on his face, but he wasn't backing down. She liked that about him. In fact, she liked everything she'd seen about him so far. Something in the back of her mind told her to slow down, but she'd waited her whole life for a man like this to come along. Derek was a good father, but she needed a man who was in control of his own life and wouldn't be afraid to take charge of hers.

She noticed the time and said, "I'm sorry, but I've got to go. My son is with my parents, and I've got to be there to put him to bed."

"I understand." He stood and waited beside her seat until she did the same. He threw a twenty-dollar bill onto the table to cover their checks and a generous tip, and then walked her to her car.

Rachel noticed his easy stride that was confident while not being cocky. She felt an intense attraction to him, but she held herself in check for the time being.

When they reached her car, he said, "Well, I had a great time talking to you." He reached out to shake her hand, but when she put it in his, he brought it up and kissed the back of it. "Good night." Giving her hand a gentle squeeze, he released it and turned to walk away. Rachel touched his arm, and he turned to her again. He brought his hand up and stroked her cheek, then kissed her. It was wonderful. Rachel couldn't remember the last time a kiss had done so much to her. Then she thought back to the first time she'd kissed Derek, and suddenly felt ashamed for what she was doing.

They broke the kiss, and he brushed a lock of hair from her forehead. It sent shivers down her spine. He knew just where to touch her and how to do it.

He spoke, his voice low and seductive. "You are an incredible woman, Rachel. When can I see you again?"

Without a moment's hesitation, she gave him her parents' number.

Robert said, "I'm swamped with a project at work that has me staying late tomorrow, but I'll call you the day after. What time will you be home from work?"

She glanced down for a second, and then looked back up at him again. "I'll be spending the next couple of days looking for a new job. I ... I didn't like the one I had so I quit recently."

His eyes didn't judge her at all. He merely nodded. "I understand. What about if I call around seven? Will that be late enough?"

"Yes, that should be fine." She decided she would be home by six in case he called earlier.

With one last squeeze of her hand, he turned and walked away. She watched him as he walked, and he glanced over his shoulder at her before getting into his car.

She was so wrapped up in the moment she didn't notice the familiar pickup truck pulling into the lot.

Derek's headlights flashed onto the man walking toward the black SUV.

It's him! That guy from the wreck!

He ducked down a little and pulled into a space as far away from the man as he could. When the car pulled out of the parking lot, he stepped out of the truck to watch it drive off. Satisfied the man hadn't seen him, Derek scanned the lot to see if he could find Rachel's car. He noticed it just as the engine started up. The brake lights came on, and there was the quick flash of the taillights as she put it into reverse. He broke into a run, but she switched gears, stepped on the accelerator, and was gone before he could get to her. He'd parked far away to avoid the man from the accident, and it had cost him precious time in reaching her.

He went back to his truck and got in. He knew better than to try to go to her parents' house. Paul was a nice person, but if he felt his daughter was being upset, he could get very mean very quickly. Derek had missed his chance for now.

He glanced at Chappee's, then got out and went inside. Finding a table toward the back, he slid in and ordered a beer. When the waitress brought it, he went ahead and ordered another. By the time he left this place, he planned to be well on his way to drunk. It wouldn't help get Rachel back, but he no longer cared. The pain of losing his family was too much for him. He couldn't imagine who was feeling worse right now: the guy from the accident or himself. Sure, the accident had taken that man's family forever, but at least he could grieve and move on. Derek had to face the fact that his family was somewhere else, and would probably be with some*one* else before long. What could be worse than that?

He raised the beer to his mouth and felt its bitter taste burn as it slid down his throat. It would be a long night.

Robert drove home ecstatic over his change of fortune. Things were coming together even better than he'd planned.

He'd spent the past two days gathering information about Derek Morrison. First, he'd hacked into Starline Trucking's main server and found the personnel file on Morrison. Because very few people would ever have a reason to hack into a trucking company, the security had been almost nonexistent. They'd kept the same password that the majority of amateur system administrators in America use: *admin.* Robert had allowed himself to stay online with them for quite a while, which might have been a mistake with other companies, but not with this one.

The personnel file showed that Derek Morrison had two dependents. Further investigation into his company's life-insurance information revealed his primary beneficiary as Rachel Morrison, and his other dependent was a son named Scott, now seven years old.

Finding information about Scott had proved equally simple. All he had to do was call the local public schools around where Morrison lived and inquire about Scott. He struck pay dirt with his first call. He told the secretary who answered the phone that he was Scott's father and that someone had told him Scott was sick and needed to come home. The wonderfully helpful lady put him on hold while she checked on Scott's condition with his teacher, but then found that he was still in his classroom safe and sound. Robert thanked her and hung up. He now knew which school Scott went to and who his teacher was.

Tracking down Rachel had proved to be the challenge. He'd been forced to settle with finding her maiden name on one of the electronic forms Morrison's company had filed away on him. Using that data, he searched for information on Rachel Mason and hadn't been disappointed. He found her parents' names, looked them up in the phone book to confirm that they were indeed still living, and then called to check on Rachel as a fictitious concerned friend.

Robert figured on Rachel moving in with her parents—at least at the beginning. When he went to her house earlier in the day, no one was home. A quick glance in the windows showed several empty spaces in the living room where feminine knickknacks would have gone. There was a large family portrait on one of the walls that gave him his first look at Rachel and Scott. She was beautiful, and her smile was breathtaking. Scott showed the mischievous grin of a little boy with things to do on his mind. Robert grinned at the thought of the boy playing—and then his mind drifted to Emily. The pain returned in a wave that swept over him. He closed his eyes for a few seconds and continued his search of the house. A glance into the couples' bedroom window revealed equal emptiness, but it wasn't until he'd looked into what must have been the boy's bedroom, judging from the size of the bed, that his suspicions were confirmed. It was completely stripped bare. There was no doubt that Rachel was gone.

From that point, he'd located her parents' home and checked out the area around them. He'd been doing basic reconnaissance of the area, planning to drive by their house, when he stopped for a drink. It had been his incredible good fortune to see her sitting in the same restaurant. He couldn't believe his eyes at first; but when she looked at him and smiled, her identity had been confirmed.

After that, it had been easy. Robert had followed the flow with her. She was a very willing respondent to his overtures, and the whole scene had gone off beautifully. When she stopped him for the kiss at the end of the evening, he knew without a doubt that she was hooked. Everything was working out exactly as he'd planned so far—even ahead of schedule.

Now, if only it would stay that way.

Rachel was in tears by the time she arrived at her parents' house. Fortunately, her mother had already put Scott to bed, so Rachel went straight to the guest bedroom where she was staying and fell onto the bed without bothering to turn on the lights. Her mind was a swirl of emotions. On the one hand, she couldn't believe how fortunate she was to have met someone who seemed as wonderful as Robert. He would have been the answer to her prayers if she'd been a praying woman.

On the other hand, however, there was Derek. Try as she might, she knew that there was a part of her that still loved him. Despite his recent actions and strange behavior—not to mention the fact that she had been gone for several days now without his trying to contact her—she couldn't just turn off her feelings for him so easily. They'd been married for a long time and been blessed with a wonderful son from their union. She knew without a doubt that Derek would never change though. He would always be Derek, for better or worse. He would get off his drinking binges, then back onto them again. He'd never gotten violent with either Scott or her, but he always scared her when he was drunk. She didn't like living in fear.

Her mind played games with her for the next half hour, trying to debate the pros and cons of returning to Derek. For every reason to return, there were three reasons not to. And then there was Robert. She couldn't get his smile out of her mind. The way he looked at her, not judging her or looking down at her or looking at her as a piece of meat to bed and abandon, but looking at her as a woman of worth. Almost looking at her like a prize to be won. It made her feel good about herself. Maybe she'd been wrong to flirt with him so much, but it wasn't like Derek hadn't strayed a few times since they'd been married. Then she thought of the kiss, and a pang of guilt settled over her. What had she been thinking? Why had this charming man whom she knew nothing about so easily swayed her? Was she really so lonely that she would throw herself at the first stranger who showed an interest in her?

But it wasn't that. Other men had showed an interest in her, but Robert had been different. No man had ever looked at her the way he did.

No other man except Derek.

The guilt returned. She cried until late in the night, never realizing exactly when she finally fell asleep.

NINE

THE NEXT MORNING, ROBERT sat in his SUV three houses down from the address he'd found for Gordon James. The street was quiet for the most part, with occasional cars leaving.

Steam rose and billowed like a curtain of fog over the cup of coffee he held in his hand. He'd been there for twenty minutes, but he knew he wouldn't have much longer to wait.

At eight-fifteen, the garage door opened, and a beat-up Cadillac pulled out. The yellow paint was gone in some spots, replaced by the dark coppery color of rust. When the car reached the end of the driveway, it stopped, and a ruddy-faced man struggled out. He waddled to the mailbox and slid something inside, raising the bright red plastic flag next to it. Without even a glance around the neighborhood, the man slid back into the car. It bounced a little as his portly frame filled the seat.

Robert watched until the car turned at the end of the street and disappeared. He pulled up next to the mailbox and opened it. Inside were three envelopes, one of which was a utility bill. He tossed it onto the seat next to him and closed the mailbox. He drove to the next street and pulled over to the curb. Tearing open the envelope, he was rewarded with a check made out to Alabama Power. Along its bottom were the nine digits he was searching for.

Gordon James' checking-account number.

Scribbling the information down, he stuck the bill and check into another envelope and addressed it to Alabama Power. Finding a public mailbox nearby, he dropped it inside. The bill would be paid on time, and James would have no reason to think anyone had intercepted it.

Robert glanced down at the other item on the seat next to him: a piece of junk mail addressed to Chris Rickles. It was a simple credit card application, one that would have probably been overlooked and thrown away. Now the "preapproved" notice on the envelope almost glowed at Robert. He'd fished it out of Rickles' mailbox the previous afternoon. Now he'd use it to open an account for the dirty little man, after changing the address it was to come to and making it an anonymous post office box, of course.

It was almost too easy.

Charlie Bolton walked into the office promptly at eight thirty. He prided himself on never being late. Though they didn't keep any specific office hours, he tried to show up before nine. On very rare occasions he would beat his boss to the office—but those days were few and far between.

Until now.

Since Tara and Emily's deaths, Robert hadn't been in the office for any length of time. He came sporadically, staying for a few hours without saying a word, then leaving again. Their customers were sympathetic, and projects were postponed without a complaint. But now time was running out, and they needed to resume work. Charlie felt the pressure. It was time for Robert to join the real world again.

He passed Robert's desk and found his computer running. That wasn't like Robert. He glanced around the office to see if he was there, but he was alone.

What are you up to, Robert? Mind if I see?

Charlie settled into Robert's chair and turned on the monitor. He waited for it to warm up, and soon the image started to appear.

It was a database of some sort. Had Robert accepted another project without telling him? The names were unfamiliar to him, but they were all relatively local numbers. Only one was a business, and it was a trucking company.

He rested his fingers on the keyboard, preparing to type in a few commands. Surely it wouldn't hurt to see what else was on the agenda for the week.

"Can I help you?"

Charlie jumped and spun around in the chair. Robert stood near the door, staring at him. The smile that always lived on his face was gone. The man looking at Charlie now was as expressionless as a statue, his easy demeanor replaced with a hard edge. He wore a black sweater and jeans, his briefcase by his side.

"Hey, boss." Charlie stumbled to his feet and smiled. "I was just seeing if you'd made any progress on that new file-integration program for Uptech. They called about it yesterday, and I told them I'd get back to them today."

Robert walked toward him slowly, his expression never changing and his eyes never leaving his. At the last second, Robert brushed past him and flicked the monitor off, then reached into his briefcase and pulled out a CD.

"Here's the file they wanted. Upload it to them and tell them it does everything they asked for and more." He tossed the CD to Charlie and turned to sit down. Charlie stayed glued to his spot, and for a moment he thought that Robert was going to ignore him. Before he turned the monitor back on, he looked up at Charlie. "Is there something else?"

"Well, yes," Charlie stammered. He wasn't used to this nonchalant tone from Robert, and it unnerved him. "I don't know if you know it or not—and I don't blame you for not noticing—but we're falling a little behind schedule with a couple of projects. I'm doing all I can, but we're going to have to start making some phone calls if things don't change. Some of our customers are starting to wonder when we're going to get their programs to them and—"

"I'm fully aware of how impatient everyone is. I called the paper yesterday and had them post a job opening in the classifieds. Your name is there as the contact. When applicants call, you interview them. If you like them and can work with them, hire them. I'm going to be busy on other things for a while, so get one or two people who can take care of things with you."

"But, Robert—"

"There's nothing to discuss. I'm giving you a little more responsibility. Can you handle it?"

Charlie couldn't read anything in Robert's expressionless face, but there was something going on—and he was going to find out what it was.

"No problem, Robert. I'll set up the interviews, and I'll talk to the applicants. When I find some people who can handle the job, I'll start hiring. Thanks for the vote of confidence in me."

Robert's eyes softened a bit. "Listen, Charlie, I know this seems strange to you. I understand that. I just need you to understand that my mind isn't on the business right now. I miss the girls, and I just have something I have to do. Please trust me."

Charlie stepped toward him and slowly put his hand on Robert's shoulder. "I can only imagine what you're going through. If you need me, I'm here. Otherwise, I'll just back off and run the business until you feel like getting into it again. Hey, it's not like you were actually doing any of the work around here anyway."

Robert took his seat behind his desk. Charlie watched him for a second and then went to a computer near the back where he could upload the program to Uptech.

Robert watched his monitor as it warmed up. The information on the screen wasn't that important, and it wasn't something that Charlie would easily put together. Still, it had been a mistake to leave it on when he'd left yesterday. He would have to be more careful in the future or he could be asking for trouble.

He reached inside his briefcase and pulled out another CD. This one would not prove to be as helpful as the one he'd produced a few minutes ago, but it would serve its purpose. He inserted it into the drive and began to read off of it.

He'd spent the better part of the evening at home on his computer writing a program that would gather the information he needed so he wouldn't have to waste time. He decided on using a variation of a virus called a "sniffer." Hackers used them to find credit-card numbers by sitting silently in a server and watching for particular strings of numbers. He'd modified this one, however, so now it looked for a specific list of names. For the next week, all activity pertaining to Robert's list would raise a red flag, and a log file would be sent to the e-mail account Robert had set up for Terrance Gold. When checking it, he would simply disguise his tracks and then delete the mail. If it wasn't checked within forty-eight hours, the mailbox was set to delete the messages.

There would not be any evidence left when he was through. But for now, any book, video, grocery item, article of clothing, or dirty magazine those on his list ordered online, Robert would know about. He doubted the trucker had much of a presence online, but the rest could produce a harvest.

He sent his program into cyberspace and turned his attention to the next matter on his agenda.

Picking up the phone, he dialed the number he'd found for Chris Rickles. After two rings a familiar voice answered.

"Hello?"

Robert changed the pitch and cadence of his voice slightly. "Yes, this is David Johnson with Primetime Video. Our computer randomly chooses customers from our database for a weekly free rental drawing, and your name came up this week. Congratulations!"

There was a momentary pause as the meaning of the message sank in. "I won? Free rentals?"

"Yes, sir. You'll get ten free movie rentals at the store of your choice. I just need to know the location that you visit most often."

"Oh, all right. There's one about two blocks from my house that I go to pretty regularly. It's on Sixth Street in Birmingham."

Robert wrote down the information. "Ah yes, that's store number six-one-eight. All right, sir, I have it. You'll be set up within the next two days to receive your free rentals, and thanks for being a Primetime customer."

Robert hung up and grabbed the phone book to look up the number for the video store Rickles had mentioned. Dialing the number, he waited patiently for someone to answer.

"Primetime Video." It sounded like a tired teenager who wanted desperately to be elsewhere. Robert smiled. It was perfect.

Robert did his best to sound frustrated. "Yes, this is Bob, manager at the Anniston store. Are you guys having computer trouble out there?"

"No, I don't think so."

"Good. Listen, I have a customer here named Chris Rickles who wants to buy some movies, but he's left his credit card at home. Our computers are down because of some network problem or something, and I can't access his information. Can you look up his number and give it to me?"

There was a long pause on the other end of the line, and Robert began to get worried. Then the teenager spoke again. "Who did you say this was?"

"My name is Bob Reynolds, and I'm the manager of the store in Anniston."

"Why is a customer from our store shopping in Anniston?"

Robert let a tinge of anger slip into his voice. "I have no idea, kid, and it's none of my business. All I know is that this guy wants an arm-load of movies and doesn't have his card. He's got his license, though, but I can't look up the information because our computers are down."

After several tense seconds, the kid said, "Okay, read me his license number."

Robert quickly gave him the number he'd found earlier with a quick search of an online DMV database. Within seconds the boy gave him the account number of the credit card Rickles used when he registered with them for membership. Robert thanked him and hung up.

Now it was time to get creative.

"Flowers?"

The look of surprise on Rachel's face was quickly replaced with a pleasant smile as she signed for the delivery. It was a huge arrangement, filled with a variety of flowers in vibrant colors that seemed to have been splashed from an artist's canvas.

"Who are they from, Mom?" Scott's eyes were wide at the sight of the floral blessing.

Rachel couldn't keep the excitement out of her voice as she set the flowers down and opened the card. "Well, baby, your father is the only person who would be sending Mommy flow—" She stopped short as she read the card.

> Rachel,
>   I hope you don't think this forward of me, but I was hoping you'd do me the honor of having dinner with me this evening. I enjoyed talking to you the other night, and would love to get to know you better. I could pick you up at seven. Good luck on your job hunt today. Knock 'em dead!

The card was simply signed *Robert*. Below the name was a phone number. Rachel read the card again and felt a flood of emotions wash over her. Disappointment that they weren't from Derek, but excitement that she'd found a man who felt she was special enough to send them to her.

"Well, Mom? Did Daddy send them?" Scott gently stroked a bright pink rosebud that pointed toward him as if to shake his hand. Rachel watched him for a second, lost in thought.

"Uh, yeah. Of course, sweetie. Who else would send flowers to Mommy?" She closed the card and inhaled deeply the beautiful scent of her gift. Then she walked back to her bedroom and sat down on her bed. She heard her mother's voice down the hall as she suddenly found the bouquet, and listened as Scott excitedly talked about how his daddy had sent them.

Then Rachel closed her eyes and quietly began to sob. She didn't know what she was feeling, nor what she should do next.

On the one hand, she had Derek. He had his faults, and yes, it appeared that they had reached the glass ceiling on their standard of living—but Derek was a wonderful father and a loving husband for the most part. Every time he came home, regardless of how long he'd been on the road, he'd never complained about it. He'd just walked in like he'd worked a short shift and started playing with Scott. It was hard to imagine anyone else doing that.

And when they had their good times, they were very good. Derek had a romantic side to him. It didn't come out very often, but he could be a real charmer when he wanted to be. And Valentine's Day was always special for them because he'd do his yearly stint in the kitchen for her. The meal was barely edible, but it was the thought that mattered.

Many other good things came to mind, and Rachel didn't stop the sudden flood of memories. But then she began to think about Derek's drinking problem, and the memories took a different turn. She remembered the nights she sat alone with Scott, making up excuses as to where his father was, having no idea herself. She thought about times she had locked herself in her bathroom and cried over the bills that she couldn't find the money to pay after Derek had spent everything on his liquor. She remembered the many evenings sleeping alone when she wanted to be held more than anything else in the world. And she remembered where he'd been—and whom he'd been with—while she'd been alone.

Slowly, the tears stopped. She looked down at the card in her hands and gently ran her fingers over the shiny gold foil picture on the front of it. Then she slowly opened it and began to reread the message that she'd already memorized.

She thought about this wonderful mystery man named Robert who had strolled into her life at just the moment she'd needed him. It had to be fate. She remembered the feeling of being wrapped gently but securely in his arms as he kissed her.

Taking a deep breath, she reached for the phone.

Officer Terrance Gold checked his mail as usual. In it he found the usual assortment of junk mail and bills that he had grown to expect. He also saw something extra in this delivery. He opened the black plastic bag with his name and address on it and found the latest issue of a popular adult magazine.

I don't subscribe to any magazines. Where did this come from?

A quick call to the subscription department listed inside the magazine revealed that it was a gift subscription, paid for by credit card. The sender, however, wished to remain anonymous. None of Terrance's threats could force the name out of the lady on the phone.

But what harm had been done? He thought to himself that he deserved a little relaxation.

Hey, it's free. Who cares who paid for it?

And with that, he settled into his favorite chair with a cold beer and began to enjoy his newest hobby.

By the time Derek showered and got out the door, it was already noon. His head was hurting again, but he was getting used to it. Every step was labored, but his abused body knew all too well what to do.

He fumbled with his keys and got into his truck, but this time he made sure the radio was turned off before starting it up. Derek slowly began the long drive to his in-laws' house. He had to talk to Rachel.

Yes, he had messed up—twice now—but he had learned his lesson and had a very good reason for all of it. He just needed her now, and needed her to understand what was going on in his head. She would feel just as overwhelmed in his position, no matter how perfect she thought she was.

Derek drove along I-20, picking up speed as he went. He kept a careful eye out for state troopers, who were known to be plentiful down this stretch of highway, but he wanted to make good time. Every second away from Rachel was torture. He'd never really realized how much he loved her until she was gone.

And Scott. Derek's stomach twisted with a huge knot as he thought of his son. The knot tightened as he thought about the possibility of getting to see him only on alternating weekends. He would die without Scott, he knew it.

The fear of loneliness pushed him, and he stepped on the accelerator, forcing more speed from the old pickup. He stopped at a flower shop right off the highway and bought a single red rose. He had given one to Rachel on the night of their first date, and he hoped it would help her remember happier times.

By the time he pulled into Pell City and found his way to Logan Martin Lake, he'd been on the road for almost forty minutes. He wheeled into the driveway of the Masons' home, searching for Rachel's car, but it was gone.

Derek slowly got out of his truck and checked his appearance. His headache was slowly starting to subside, and for that he was thankful. He walked to the door and hesitated, unsure of what to do next. How would the Masons treat him? What would they think?

Before he could turn and walk away, the door opened, and Scott bounded into him.

"Dad!" The boy smiled and grabbed Derek's waist in a death grip. Derek pulled free long enough to kneel down and take his son into his arms. He squeezed tightly and didn't want to let go, but the boy broke away and said, "Where've you been? Wanna play catch? I've got the football out here in the yard somewhere." His little eyes eagerly scanned the grass for the familiar oval-shaped ball, as he darted out on a quest for it. Derek watched him go, and then heard the door open again behind him.

"Derek? I didn't hear you knock. I'm sorry, come in." He turned to see Rachel's mother, Sarah. She was a lovely woman who had aged incredibly well. Though she was in her late fifties, people usually guessed her to be ten years younger. Her easygoing way and pleasant smile had a way of making anyone feel at home, and Derek relaxed a little seeing it.

"Hello, Sarah. Is Rachel here?"

"No, she went out a little while ago. I'm not sure where she was going, but I know that she'll be back soon. But, Derek, I don't know if it's a good time to be talking to her or not." Sarah stepped back and held out her hand, motioning for Derek to enter. The accommodating look on her face was now replaced with a slightly worried one, and he noticed.

"It's okay. I'll just leave her a note, if that'll be all right. I've got to talk to Gordon about a new route I'm supposed to run this week, and then I can check back to see if she's here."

Derek's heart was pounding as he stepped into the Masons' home. He had been there on many holidays, but had never felt the sense of dread and finality he experienced as he crossed their threshold this time.

His senses were overwhelmed by a beautifully fragrant scent that reminded him of his mother's flower garden. It was then that he noticed the huge floral arrangement on the kitchen table.

"The flowers are beautiful, Sarah. Special occasion?"

Sarah opened the cabinet above the sink and chose two glasses. She opened the refrigerator and pulled out a gallon pitcher of tea before turning around. "Oh, those are the ones you sent her. Very nice, and a wonderful gesture, I might add."

Derek looked at her for a moment. "The ones I sent her?"

Sarah crossed the kitchen and handed him a glass of tea. "Yes, that's what Scott said. He said that they had come from you. That's what Rachel told him, anyway."

Derek took a long drink and thought. He hadn't sent flowers, and the look on Sarah's face said that she hadn't either. Still, apparently *someone* had sent them to Rachel in his name. It was hard to sort things out, and he wished his head would quit hurting.

"Derek? Are you all right?" The tone of Sarah's voice was soft and concerned. The bags under his bloodshot eyes and his sallow look wouldn't fool anyone.

Derek locked eyes with her and swallowed. A part of him wanted to pour out the whole story and hold nothing back, to unload the huge weight from his chest—but another part realized how dangerous that would be. If he was ever going to get Rachel back, he had to be able to tell her himself.

He glanced past Sarah to the array of beautiful blooms on the kitchen table. He thought about the simple rose that he had awaiting his wife in the truck, and lowered his face again. He didn't know what to think, but someone had apparently done him a favor with the flowers, and he wouldn't waste that chance.

He set his glass quietly down on the counter and spoke with his back to his mother-in-law, unable to look her in the eye. "I've got to go now. I'll be back by in a little while. Please tell Rachel to wait for me so we can talk, if she will."

Derek quickly walked out the front door and toward his truck. He looked up in time to see Scott catch his football and throw it up into the air again. When Scott saw his father leaving, he waved and tossed the ball again. Derek waved back and smiled, then turned and got into his truck before his son could see the tears.

Chris Rickles was shopping.

Not just anyplace, but at one of the finest stores at the Summit. The Summit was a huge series of shops located on top of a hill overlooking one of the more elite areas of Birmingham, and the clothes in some of the designer stores were well into the three- and four-figure price range.

Chris had never been one to splurge. He'd always been extremely careful with his money and how he chose to spend it. But he'd never been afraid to window-shop. And like most folks, he dreamed of the day when he would be able to buy those expensive outfits he saw on display.

And now that day had arrived.

No one would ever have believed how easy it would turn out to be. He pulled up to an accident that had already happened, milled around the accident scene like a concerned citizen, and eavesdropped on the truck driver giving his statement. Chris had always prided himself on being a shrewd businessman, and he knew an opportunity when he saw it. There had been no white pickup truck; of this he was certain. He didn't know why the trucker had pulled into the passing car, and frankly, he didn't care. All he cared about was the fact that he was able to be of some small assistance in settling the matter.

Well, that and the five-thousand-dollar "gift" he'd received. That had been a wonderful motivation to embellish his story to the state trooper. For that much cash, he'd have sworn in court that an alien spacecraft had pushed the truck over.

Now, he was here, shopping with the affluent and getting ready to sit pretty.

He went into one of the custom shops and ordered a tailor-made suit. He'd always wanted one, though he very seldom dressed up. The salesman acted too snooty for Chris's tastes, but he didn't care—he had money now.

"And how will you be paying for this, sir?" The salesman almost seemed to sneer at him.

Chris reached into his wallet and retrieved the first card he saw. The salesman picked it up without a comment and swiped it through the reader. The high-pitched squeal of the computer connecting split the reverent air of the store. The display changed, but the angle of the screen didn't allow Chris to get a good look at what it said. However, the expression on the salesman's face was not a pleasant one.

"I'm sorry, sir, but your card has been declined. Do you have another method of payment?" With a smirk on his face, he handed the card back to Chris as if it were an old smelly sock.

Chris was stunned. He knew he had mailed in a payment, and he knew that he was nowhere near the limit on that card. What was going on?

He replaced the card in his wallet and pulled out a second card. His hands were less sure this time as he handed it to the salesman, who glanced at the card and then at Chris before swiping it.

Chris heard the squealing noise again and began to get irritated. *Good grief! Why has that thing got to be so loud?*

The display changed again, and Chris studied the face of the salesman to try to get a read on what was coming. He said nothing, but merely handed the card back to Chris along with a receipt the register had spit out.

"Please sign the top copy, and the bottom copy is yours. The suit will be ready in three days. Sorry for the unpleasantness over your first card, sir." There was no sympathy in his voice at all.

"No problem." Chris managed to smile again as he replaced the second card in his wallet. "Stupid credit-card people. I pay my bills on time, and they still don't keep up with the account."

"I'm sure, sir." The salesman's nostrils seemed to flare as he spoke, and it made Chris uneasy, so he gave a nervous laugh and left the store in a hurry.

What was that all about? I guess they just didn't post my check yet on that card, but they should have by now. I sent the payment in a long time ago.

He made a mental note to look at that statement very carefully when it came in next month, and started walking toward a nearby shoe store.

TEN

Robert put the finishing touches on his newest computer virus. It was a simple one, actually. This time, he'd created a program that was attached to another smaller one. Technically it was a Trojan Horse, so called because when the smaller program activated, the larger one would go into effect without anyone's knowledge. It was safely hidden inside a JPEG file so as not to alert any antivirus programs installed on James' computer.

Robert logged into the Terrance Gold e-mail account he'd created and sent the file as an e-mail attachment to Gordon James. When James opened the e-mail, a short advertisement would pop up, while another program went into effect. This program was more malicious than the harmless ad. Its purpose was to begin copying financial records within a specific search string, compressing them for later delivery. It would also seek out the numeral "2" in the "hundreds" column of any spreadsheet and immediately change it to a "1," effectively siphoning off a hundred dollars each time. After it had finished its tasks, it had one last job to perform—and it would be an impressive one.

Robert then logged off and turned to some printouts on his desk. Everything he needed was at his fingertips. Most people never realized how naked they were in cyberspace, but information could be gathered on anyone with a minimal amount of knowledge. And when a person's information rested in the hands of someone as computer knowledgeable as Robert, that individual was helpless.

So far that afternoon, he'd been able to set three phases of his plan in motion. Now it was time to rest for a while and let things take their course.

He glanced over at Charlie, seated behind his desk tapping away at his keyboard. Charlie was happiest in this environment, and his dedication to his job was impressive. Robert had no doubt that Charlie would run his own software company one day.

The phone rang, and Charlie answered it without missing a beat in his typing. Robert heard him set up another job interview for that afternoon, and then hang up with a hasty good-bye. Charlie was trying to get caught up with most of the projects they had waiting, while at the same time trying to hire some help. Robert knew he'd succeed.

He scanned the list of waiting projects and chose the hardest one, then logged onto his terminal again. Before he left, he planned to finish two pressing jobs for Charlie, and then he'd be finished with his company for a while.

He reached into his briefcase for a printout and pulled out a folded piece of plain paper. When he opened it, he found a crayon drawing of three stick figures having a picnic, and the signature of the budding Picasso.

Emily.

Robert ran his fingers along the picture and stroked the face of the smallest figure. Then, before his eyes could water and betray his thoughts, he gently pushed it back into his briefcase and found the printout.

Oh, how he missed her. And how he missed Tara. He would lie awake at night and listen for the sound of Tara breathing next to him. He would go to Emily's door and stand quietly, searching for any noise that would betray her presence there. But all that ever greeted him was silence. And sometimes the silence could be too loud for him to stand.

More than anything else, he wished he'd been the one to die in that wreck. No, that was wrong. More than anything else, he wished that *Derek Morrison* had been the one to die in it. The world wouldn't have missed one less lying scumbag.

But it hadn't happened that way. Morrison's family was still alive, while Robert was alone. Now Morrison's house was as quiet as Robert's. And before it was all over, Robert wouldn't be alone anymore. He smiled at that thought.

After he left work tonight, he had dinner plans.

Gordon James checked his e-mail from work. As usual, there was the smattering of junk e-mail peppered in among his important messages. One had a subject heading simply saying: *Gordon, read this*. It caught his eye first.

I don't recognize who it's from, but who the devil else would know my name? Might as well see who this is, but if it's just another piece of spam, I'll …

He opened the message and saw a simple banner ad for an Internet bookstore. Mumbling under his breath, he deleted it and moved on to the next message without giving it another thought.

He was totally oblivious to the fact that he had just compromised his entire network.

Before he could finish his next message, Derek Morrison walked in. He was dressed in a plaid flannel shirt and faded jeans, and he looked as if he'd had a hard night. His face was pale, and his eyes had dark circles under them. One look told Gordon all he needed to know.

"When did you start drinking again?"

Gordon watched as Derek opened his mouth to speak and then paused. He sighed. "A few days ago. Right after the accident, actually."

Gordon's eyes narrowed as he let out a low hiss. "You sure? So help me, if you were drinking when you hit those—"

"I wasn't drinking then!"

"Don't you ever raise your voice to me like that again. Do you hear me?" Gordon slammed his hand on his desk and rose to his feet. His voice lowered several decibels as he spoke again. "I fixed your little mistake, and no one is the wiser. Now I want you to listen to me good. You do something stupid like you did the other day, and you'll be in manure so deep you'll need an airlift to get you out, you got it? I ought to fire you now—and given your history, I'd be justified in doing it—but we need drivers, so you're safe for the moment." He glanced at his watch. "It's almost five. What are you doing here so late?"

Morrison cleared his throat and swallowed. "I ... I had some errands to run today, and I got a late start of it."

Gordon leaned in closer to try to catch the scent of alcohol on Morrison's breath, but he was clean. Whatever had held him up, it had nothing to do with liquor.

He looked down at his desk and found a yellow invoice, then shoved it in Morrison's chest. "You've got a load. Now hit the road and get it delivered."

Morrison snatched the paper from his hand. "I'll leave first thing in the morning."

"You'll leave tonight. The load is expected early tomorrow." Gordon sat back down and turned to his terminal again.

Morrison looked at the invoice, then back at the fat man behind the desk. "Tonight? I can't leave tonight. I have business to take care of. I have to talk to Rachel, and—"

Gordon exploded from behind his desk.

"You will get your sorry carcass out of my office and plant it in that run-down truck, or you're fired—driver shortage or not!"

Morrison's hand tightened into fists, and he looked as if he was fighting the urge to jump over the desk and pound his boss into a greasy lump. Instead, he turned and left in silence.

Gordon called out to him before he left. "And, Morrison, no casualties this time, okay?"

ELEVEN

WHEN SARAH MASON OPENED her door, there were a couple of people she expected to see. First and foremost, she expected to see her husband, Paul. He'd been out working all day and should have been home already. Second, she expected Derek, who had promised to come back by later that afternoon. Sarah had given Rachel his message, but she could tell by that solid reserve behind her blue eyes that Rachel was not giving in this time. She'd gone up to her bedroom with a couple of packages and shut the door, and Sarah hadn't seen her since.

But the man waiting for her when she opened the door was a complete surprise. He was strikingly handsome. His black hair was neatly trimmed and styled, and his smile caught her completely off guard. He was dressed in a dark suit, with a shirt and beautiful silk tie that combined blue and black in a stunning array of intricate designs.

But it was his eyes that caught her attention. They were a rich azure, and when they locked onto hers there was an intensity behind them that almost frightened her. She wasn't scared of the man as much as she was intimidated by the sheer confidence he radiated. Her hands quickly smoothed her hair and clothes.

"Hello. Is Rachel here?" His voice was masculine, yet warm. It put her at ease almost instantly. Still, she was confused as to why this unfamiliar albeit handsome man was asking about her daughter.

For several seconds, she stared mutely at him, before finally replying. "Yes. But who, may I ask …" Sarah silently berated herself for being so girlish. She was a stronger woman than this. Why had this man affected her so?

"Oh, how terribly rude of me. My name is Robert … Robert Whitney. I had made arrangements with Rachel tonight to—"

"It's all right, Mother. I've been expecting him."

Robert and Sarah both turned to look up at the top of the stairs where Rachel began to descend. She was dressed in a black sleeveless blouse and a skirt that stopped directly above her knees. The entire outfit perfectly accented her figure. Her beautiful blonde hair cascaded down her shoulders. She smiled at Robert as she walked.

"You're a little early, aren't you?" She was breathtaking, and Sarah couldn't remember the last time her daughter had looked so radiant.

"Why, yes," Robert answered, "but I just couldn't wait any longer."

Sarah was dumbstruck. Surely Rachel wasn't going out on a date so soon. She was still married, for heaven's sake.

Rachel seemed to notice the look in her mother's eyes, for as she leaned in to kiss her good-bye on the cheek, she whispered, "He's just a friend taking me to dinner at City Lights. We're discussing my divorce."

She pulled back and winked at her mom. "I've already given Scott his bath; I just need you to make sure he's in bed by nine. Thanks, Mom."

As they turned to leave, Robert looked back and said, "Nice to meet you, ma'am." He smiled at her again, and shut the door behind them, checking to make sure it was locked.

Sarah stood looking at the door for a moment before finally finding her voice to offer a quiet prayer.

"Dear Lord, watch over my daughter. Please don't let her do anything stupid."

Robert and Rachel pulled into City Lights, one of the local restaurants overlooking Logan Martin Lake. He mentioned driving her into Birmingham for something a little more substantial, but she wanted to stay close tonight; besides, she'd just met this mystery man.

They were seated near the window. The moonlight reflected on the water and danced on the gentle waves as they lapped the shore-line. The room was dimly lit with a small lantern on each table giving off an amber glow. Since it was a weeknight, it wasn't crowded, so they were able to talk freely with little interruption. With Rachel's consent, Robert ordered for both of them.

"So," he started, leaning closer, "I'm so glad you agreed to have dinner with me. I was a little nervous you'd say no. I hope you don't mind that I chose this route rather than a simple phone call."

"Not at all," Rachel answered. "Truthfully, I haven't been out to a place like this in a while. And I'd much rather get to know someone in person. You know, they say the eyes are the window to the soul and all that. I believe it." Rachel toyed with a loose strand of hair as she spoke.

Robert leaned back in his chair, and his whole body seemed to relax. "What a coincidence. Has anyone ever told you what incredible eyes you have?"

Coming from any other man, this would have seemed an outright come-on, but Rachel realized that he genuinely meant it as a compliment. This was the same charming man who'd kissed her last night. She was impressed.

"Thank you." She smiled at him and continued to pull nervously at her hair.

Robert reached across the table and gently took her hand from her hair. He held it softly, stroking the back of it with his thumb. He leaned closer, and in a low voice said, "Rachel, since my eyes are the windows to my soul, what do you see when you look into them?"

Once more she was overcome with a wave of emotions as she looked deeply into his captivating eyes. She could see a million things, all of them fascinating. She felt so safe, so secure with him.

Then for a brief instant she suddenly felt like she was looking into the eyes of a cobra, poised and ready to strike. She felt trancelike in his almost hypnotic stare, and the cold hand of fear grabbed her stomach.

And then, as quickly as it had appeared, it was gone. Rachel was again looking into the warm, intense eyes of an incredible man. But that second of fear shook her, and she pulled her hand away slowly.

Before she could answer him, the waiter brought their salads and set them down. The mood was broken, and they both laughed nervously.

But when she looked up at him again, she felt she was missing something.

And it frightened her.

When Sarah Mason went to answer her door this time, she had no preconceived notions as to who might be waiting for her. She had already had enough surprises for one night. As she opened the door, a part of her was relieved to see her son-in-law standing there; but another part was suddenly nervous about what she would have to tell him.

Derek stood there with a disheveled air about him. She could tell that he hadn't had a good day since they'd last talked that afternoon. Still, he managed a smile as he tried to fix his hair with his hand.

"Hi, Sarah. Can I talk to Rachel? I saw her car outside."

Robert watched Rachel as she ate. She had a grace and elegance to her movements that seemed alien to the surroundings in which shc'd lived for the past few years. This was a woman who would have been at home in a much more elegant environment than the modest home of a truck driver. There was no doubt that she was a strong woman, and could easily adapt to situations quickly. For a moment, he allowed himself to consider what he might have to offer her; what kind of life he might be able to provide for her.

Then, he stifled those thoughts. By the time all this was over, she would never want to see him again. In that instant his hatred and thirst for revenge fought against his loneliness and desire to be with someone who could love him the way his beloved Tara had. In the end hate won over love, as it always does. It is the natural flow of life.

Suddenly, there was the familiar chirp of a cell phone. Both of them glanced at their phones to see who was the lucky winner.

"It's me," Rachel announced with a smile as she pulled out her small phone. "Hello?" There was a brief pause as her face suddenly darkened. "What do you want?" Her eyes narrowed. "Dinner with a friend. Just a minute." Robert watched as she lowered the phone and leaned toward him. "Sorry, it's ... excuse me, I'll be right back."

She got up and walked toward the ladies' restroom. As she was almost at the door, Robert saw her talking animatedly into her phone, obviously agitated at the person she was talking to. Most likely, it was her husband—but since Robert wasn't supposed to know yet that she was married, he decided he'd have to act innocent when she returned.

A few minutes later, Rachel returned to the table. She tried to smile and seem at ease, but Robert could tell she was upset. He leaned forward and inquired, "Is everything all right?"

"Fine," Rachel quipped, reaching for her wine glass. After she took a sip, she closed her eyes for a moment and took a deep breath. When she opened them, she seemed to have calmed considerably. She spoke again, her voice quieter and more subdued. "I'm sorry. We shouldn't have any more interruptions tonight."

Robert smiled. "That's all right. Business is business." He pulled his coat open to show her his cell phone. "Even I can't get away from it totally."

Rachel glanced up as she placed her glass back on the table. "That reminds me. I don't even know what kind of work you do."

"I'm sorry," he said. "I'm a computer programmer. I own a small software-development company in Birmingham. We're not on a par with Microsoft yet, but give us time."

Rachel played with her food. "I don't suppose you need some help with accounting, do you?"

Robert paused, his fork midway to his mouth. *Could it be this easy?*

"Well, as a matter of fact, we are doing some hiring right now. I have a ... special project I'm working on and need some people to help my assistant. It would take a tremendous load off us if someone would take over our books for a while. Would you be interested?"

Rachel looked up at him as a grin creased her face. "As a matter of fact, I'd be very interested."

"Great. Why don't you come by Monday morning, and we'll get you started?"

Rachel's eyebrows went up as her head cocked a little. "Well, that was definitely the easiest job interview I've ever been through. Don't you even want to see my résumé?"

Robert laughed. "No, I'm the kind of guy who goes with what his instinct tells him."

Rachel's voice lowered into a sexy tone. "Oh really? A spontaneous kind of guy, eh? Kind of dangerous to be that way sometimes, you know."

He winked at her and returned his attention to his fork. "That's me. Aren't you ever like that?"

"Sometimes," she answered quietly.

"So what is your instinct telling you now?" he asked, as he reached for his wine glass.

"Oh, no . . . not now."

"Excuse me?" Robert's hand froze as he reached for the glass. When he looked at her, he noticed that her eyes were not on him, but rather were looking past him at a point over his shoulder. He swiveled in his seat to see what had drawn her attention.

Derek Morrison was coming toward their table.

TWELVE

As DEREK THREADED HIS way through the tables to reach Rachel, he noticed a man sitting with her. His anger boiled with every step he took. His attention went from Rachel to the back of the man's head, at about the point where Derek planned to start punching. The man seemed to notice Rachel's expression and turned toward him. When Derek saw his face, he froze, his nightmares coming back to him ...

> He runs toward the wreckage and the man who is running around it, screaming to the people inside.
>
> He comes up behind the man and calls to him. When the man turns, it is Derek's turn to scream.
>
> The man's face is a skull.
>
> It is Death itself.
>
> It points a finger at Derek and speaks in a cold, distant voice.
>
> "God himself can't protect you from me."
>
> Then it screams and reaches for him ...

Derek squeezed his eyes shut and forced his feet to continue. He tore his eyes from the man and back to his wife. Rachel was already standing up, and the look on her face was one of red-hot fury tinged with embarrassment.

"Rachel, what's going on?" Derek's voice didn't have any of the anger he'd come in with, but instead sounded nervous or scared. He could have kicked himself for the childlike way it sounded.

She ignored his question. "I told you on the phone I didn't want to see you right now. Now leave."

"Rachel, what are you doing here? And why are you with him? We need to talk."

Rachel leaned closer. "We have nothing to talk about, Derek. I told you that. And it is none of your business who I'm with. You have nothing to do with my life anymore."

Every patron at the restaurant was now watching in rapt attention the drama unfolding before them.

Derek looked into his wife's eyes, trying to find that center of balance that he'd seen in happier times, but it was gone. Now there was nothing but hurt and hatred looking back at him. "But, Rachel, this guy ..."

"... is here offering her a job." Derek and Rachel both looked down at Robert. "I don't think there's a law against it, or any reason for you to get all upset over it, sir."

"Don't worry, Robert," Rachel said, glowering at her husband, "there's nothing to explain to this man."

Derek glanced up at her, then down to Robert. "I want to talk to you."

Rachel's voice became hard again. "No you don't. You're leaving."

"It's okay, Rachel. I don't mind," Robert said in the same friendly, soothing tone he'd used since Derek had walked up to them. It was a hypnotic rhythm of speech that seemed to captivate them.

Derek's gaze never left Robert. "Alone."

Rachel glanced at Robert, as if asking permission. Robert looked over at her and shrugged slightly. She looked back at Derek. "Fine. But if you cause any trouble, I'll—"

"Don't worry, Rachel," Robert said, "we'll be fine."

With a final glance at both of them, she walked to the door.

Both men watched her leave, then their eyes locked again. It was Robert who spoke first.

"Sit down, Derek."

"Listen, I want you to—"

Robert's low voice spoke again, with a harsh, cold edge. "Sit ... down."

Derek glanced around the room and noticed that he was the center of attention, then slid into the seat his wife had just vacated.

Robert smiled, and his voice softened a little. "Thank you. No need to be the dinner show for all these nice folks, now is there?"

Derek leaned forward. "Listen, I'm sorry for what happened to your family. I feel terrible about—"

"You feel *nothing*. You haven't even begun to feel a *fraction* of what I've gone through."

Derek was taken aback by the man's harsh tone. "Yeah, you're right. I'm sorry. But stay away from my wife."

A smile touched the corners of Robert's mouth. His hands moved to his lap under the table. "I don't think I want to do that, Derek. She's quite a charming woman. I like her."

Derek lowered his voice and leaned forward, fists on the table. "You stay away from her, or I'll rip you apart."

Robert let out a scornful snicker. "Violence, Derek? You think that by using harsh tones and dirty looks you can scare me away? How stupid."

Derek's eyes narrowed. "You calling me stupid? What's to stop me from reaching across this table right now and pulling your lungs out?"

Robert cocked his head and smiled. "I suppose it would be the fact that I have a gun pointed at you under this table."

Derek froze. His eyes widened as it dawned on him what had just been said. He glanced down and noticed for the first time that Robert's hands were under the table, out of sight. He looked into the man's eyes, and hatred as cold as death stared back. He swallowed, cleared his throat, and spoke. "You're lying."

Robert's eyebrows raised. "You never know."

Derek stared at his unblinking gaze. "What if I yell for help?"

"Well then," Robert answered, in a friendly tone, "the management comes or calls the cops. If I have a gun, you're saved. If I'm bluffing, then I deny ever saying anything to you about it, and you look like a real idiot to everyone—including Rachel."

God himself ...

"Why would you have a gun?"

Robert rolled his eyes. "I should think the answer would be obvious. I'm going out with your wife ... we might run into you, the jealous husband ... who knows how you'll react? I'm a very smart man, Derek. Very smart, and very prepared."

... can't protect you ...

Derek looked into his eyes, searching for any signs of falsehood.

... from me.

It was no good. The man had a perfect poker face. Derek settled back into his chair, and unclasped his fists.

"Very good, Derek. Smart move."

"What are you doing here, you freakin' psycho? What are you doing with my wife?"

"Not a very friendly tone you have there. I mean, what have you got to be mad about? You are the one who killed my wife and child, while yours are still alive and happy."

Derek closed his eyes and took a deep breath. "I told you I was sorry. How many times do I have to apologize? If your wife hadn't—"

Robert leaned in again and hissed through clenched teeth, "Don't you even think about blaming my wife. I saw the whole thing, and it was your own stupidity that took them from me. And what happened to you? You're not even getting a day's jail time for it."

"Then let's step outside and settle this right now."

Robert settled back in his chair. "If I killed you now, I'd go to jail and you'd be out of your misery. You haven't even begun to suffer yet. Before it's settled, you'll wish you were dead."

Derek tried to stay calm. He could feel his heart pounding in his ears. He wasn't getting anywhere. He needed time alone with Rachel. He looked to the door where she stood, watching. He hoped that she saw Robert's hands and noticed whether there was a gun in them, but the tablecloth probably hung too low. He was at a dead end.

Taking a deep breath, he stood. "There's nothing more to say. I'm sorry about your family, but please leave mine alone. It's over." He turned to go.

"It's not over, Derek," Robert said in a cold, distant voice. "As long as both of us are drawing breath, it'll never be over."

Before he could reply, Rachel was there. "Let's go, Derek. You've talked long enough." She grabbed his arm and pulled him away. "Wait for me in the truck. You can take me home. I'm going to say some things to you, and you're going to listen. Understand?"

With a final glance at Robert, Derek walked toward the door. Anger fueled his every step, and hatred began to grow. Maybe he could talk some sense into Rachel on their short ride home.

Robert and Rachel watched Derek leave. "I'm sorry, Robert. It's just a personal matter. I'll have it cleared up tonight. Please give me a chance to make this up to you."

Robert smiled. "There's nothing to make up; just a little misunderstanding, that's all."

"Can I still come by about the job?"

He laughed. "Of course you can. I'll be looking forward to seeing you on Monday."

"Thanks."

Robert studied her again as she left, and then settled in to finish his meal. Things hadn't gone exactly as he'd planned, but some things had progressed better than he'd dreamed. It would all come together. It was just a matter of time.

On the way home in the truck, Rachel began the conversation. "What in the world were you doing back there? What gives you the right to come and humiliate me like that?"

"What are you talking about? You're my wife. That's all the right I need."

Rachel's eyes narrowed, and a sneer came over her face. "Your *wife?* No, I stopped being your *wife* a long time ago. You made your choice, Derek. I told you what would happen when you made your decision, but you didn't care. Now accept the fact that it's finally over and *move on,* Derek."

Derek continued undaunted. "I saw the flowers at Sarah's."

Rachel's gaze went forward, and she smiled. "Yes, they were beautiful, weren't they?"

"Yeah, I thought you'd like them."

Rachel stiffened. "Don't you dare try to take credit for that. I didn't mean enough for you to send me flowers, so don't try to steal the credit from someone who thinks I'm special."

They pulled into Sarah's yard, and Derek shut off the engine. Rachel opened the door, but he grabbed her arm.

"Wait a minute, baby. I'm sorry for yelling, and I'm sorry for my decisions, but I've had good reason to act the way I've acted. I'm not excusing what I've done, but I want you to know what's going on."

Rachel glared at his hand until he removed it. Then her eyes locked onto his. "Derek, it is over. Do you understand me? I don't mind you seeing Scott or calling him, but don't call me anymore. I have nothing more to say to you."

She got out of the truck and started to close the door.

"Rachel, please, whatever you do, don't go to work for that man. You don't know him. He's crazy."

She huffed and slammed the truck door. Derek watched as she disappeared into the house. To follow her would serve no purpose, since he would only feed her fury. He glanced at the seat next to him. The rose he had brought for Rachel lay in pieces, forgotten when they'd been sitting together and crushed under their weight.

He knew how it felt.

THIRTEEN

MONDAY MORNING, DEREK SAT on a loading dock in Mobile, waiting as workers unloaded his rig. He decided to write a note to Rachel. If she wouldn't talk to him, then maybe she'd read something.

He couldn't believe how bad his life had become. A little over a week ago he'd still had a clear conscience and a family at home waiting on him. Now he was alone, a murderer, and an adulterer.

To make matters worse, he was forced to watch as his wife walked into a trap set by Robert Whitney. She was completely innocent, yet he seemed dead-set on making her the prize in some twisted contest of wills.

Derek looked at the note. He'd written two pages, but all he could do was explain his side of things. If only he had solid proof of Whitney's intentions. If only he had something—

And then it hit him. He ran to his truck and scrambled into the back. Scott had ridden with him on a short trip about a month ago and hadn't been able to get a good look out the windows. Derek, wanting to help, had snatched a Birmingham phone directory from the office for him to sit on. After a frantic search, he found it under a stack of junk-food wrappers behind his seat. He flipped through the yellow pages until he found the listing he was looking for. He scribbled the number down on the pad he'd been using for his letter, and looked for a pay phone.

Maybe he could save his family after all.

When Charlie arrived at work on Monday morning, a slender blonde stood at the door, waiting. He began to feel self-conscious about what he was wearing and was glad he'd changed into a new pair of jeans that morning.

"Um, can I help you?"

She smiled at him and reached out to shake his hand. "Hi, I'm Rachel Mason. I'm here to see Robert about the accounting position."

Charlie shook her hand and returned her smile, but cocked his head to one side. "Accounting position? I know we're in desperate need of programmers, but I had no idea he was bringing on an accountant. Well, let's get inside and wait for him. Shouldn't be much longer."

He opened the door and watched her walk in.

Maybe there's hope for this job yet, Charlie thought with a grin.

"Rachel. Glad to see you made it."

They both glanced back, seeing Robert at the door. Charlie noticed that he was in khakis and a pullover, a dressier look than usual.

Rachel walked over and spoke to Robert in low tones. Charlie heard her apologize for something, but the rest was lost. He turned to his computer and began his busy day.

As he started to type, he heard the door open again. He let out a sigh of frustration and twisted around to see who had entered. A gorgeous brunette in her early twenties, wearing blue jeans and a light-gray button-down shirt, stood in the doorway. Her dark eyes caught his as he stood. She had the most breathtaking smile he'd ever seen.

For the second time that morning, he hated what he was wearing.

"Hi, I'm Amy. I'm here about the programming job."

It took a moment for Charlie to remember that it was his turn to talk. He blinked and cleared his throat.

"Um, hi. I'm Charlie, your new boss."

Robert glanced up and saw Charlie working with the new girl, Amy, at a table with two workstations. One worked on animation and the other on database processing. Since earlier that morning when she'd walked in, Charlie, who'd always been a hard worker, had gone at it harder than Robert could ever remember. He smiled at this budding romantic possibility. Charlie had already talked to two other applicants that morning who were slated to begin work tomorrow, so it wouldn't be long before they were back up to speed and ahead of schedule.

His eyes moved across the room to a desk in the front corner. Rachel sat behind it under a flood of paperwork, looking content as she worked through various calculations and profit margins or whatever it was she was supposed to be doing.

He'd been forced to create the position for her and honestly didn't have that much work for her to do. True, it would take a couple of weeks to get the books into perfect shape as she wanted them, but after that she'd be twiddling her thumbs. Yet Robert couldn't afford to let the opportunity pass him by. He was now in daily contact with her, and this arrangement would help speed things along.

He looked at his computer screen and began to work again. It was time to send another anonymous present to a deserving friend.

Chris Rickles sat at a booth in the Bombay Café. He smiled across the table at the shapely redhead sitting with him. Her name was Denise, and up until today she'd never looked at him twice. Recently, however, he'd made it a habit to mention the sudden influx of cash he'd received "from a good stock-market deal." Her interest had immediately risen.

It had been his idea to take her to lunch at one of the most expensive restaurants in town. One way or another, he planned to win her over.

Their meal progressed with a bit of small talk. Chris planned on working slowly. A casual date here, some drinks after work there, and eventually he'd have her where he wanted her.

The waiter brought the bill in a black leather wallet. Chris slid a credit card in with the bill, not missing a beat in the meaningless conversation he was having with Denise.

A few moments later, the waiter returned. Chris could tell from the stricken look on his face that he was the bearer of bad news.

It can't be. Not again. I know my cards are paid up and nowhere near the credit limit.

His thoughts raced as he tried to figure out how he would be able to save face in front of Denise.

The waiter started to speak, but Chris spoke first, pulling two one-hundred-dollar bills out of his wallet. "Excuse me, but if you haven't already put the bill on my card, I'd like to pay in cash. I don't really want to add any unnecessary charges to my credit cards."

The waiter smiled and glanced over at Denise, then back, obviously understanding what Chris was trying to do. "Very well, sir. It's not a problem. Here is your card. Will you be needing change?"

Chris looked at the knowing smile of the waiter and realized he was being blackmailed on a small scale. Still, it wouldn't hurt for Denise to see him as a good tipper. "No, thank you. You did an excellent job today."

The waiter smiled and bowed his head before turning and leaving.

"Wow, that was some tip you gave him." Denise looked at Chris with a curious expression. Chris just winked and put the card back into his wallet.

Officer Terrance Gold answered the phone with a curse on the third ring. He had been sound asleep in preparation for working the night shift, and the interruption irritated him.

"What?" he grumbled.

"Mr. Gold?" The voice was male with a slightly English accent.

Terrance glanced at the clock and cleared his throat. "Who is this?"

The man on the other end of the line began to speak rapidly. "You've won a free dinner for two at Marigold's here in Birmingham. Are you familiar with our establishment, sir?"

Terrance's eyes opened wide. He was very familiar with Marigold's. It was a posh restaurant in the heart of downtown Birmingham, far too expensive for him to consider on his salary. Even with his recent "gift" from Starline Trucking, he wouldn't go there on any normal night.

Terrance had been smart with the gift. He'd had it sent in cash, and then he'd hidden it in his bedroom. There would be no sudden large deposits in his accounts that could attract attention. It wasn't the first payoff he'd taken, and wouldn't be the last. He'd become quite a pro at taking bribes over the years.

"Yeah, I've heard of you. How did I win something?" he asked.

"Well, sir, apparently someone dropped one of your business cards in for a drawing. We only offer one a week, so consider yourself fortunate."

Terrance rubbed his eyes and sat up. "Thanks. What do I have to do?"

"Oh, there's nothing to do except make your reservations, sir. We'll take care of the rest."

He thought for a moment. "Okay, how about tomorrow night?"

The voice on the other end of the line hesitated a moment as if consulting an appointment book and spoke again. "Tomorrow night is not a problem, sir. Shall we say two people at eight o'clock?"

"Yeah, eight's fine."

"Good. We'll see you then, sir. Congratulations again."

"Hey, who am I speaking to?" Terrance asked, but the line was dead. He got up and started across the room, kicking an empty box at his feet. He looked on his dresser and saw the contents of the box.

Three adult videotapes.

Since the middle of last week, he'd received several packages in the mail. Some contained movies, some contained books, and others contained various other paraphernalia that he was unsure about.

Whoever had started the joke was going too far. Terrance decided it was time to talk to the guys at work and see about getting it all stopped before it got out of hand.

Robert chuckled as he hung up the phone. The drama class in high school had paid off.

"See you tomorrow, sir," he said with a light English accent, as he dialed a new number. When the other party picked up, he lowered his voice and developed an edgier tone.

"Hello? Marigold's? Yes, I'd like to make a reservation for two for tomorrow evening. My name is Terrance Gold."

Sarah Mason sat in her living room with her Bible in her lap. She'd tried to read it, but her mind was on her daughter. Rachel had left that morning in high spirits, and Sarah had been happy to see her daughter in such an upbeat mood. But she worried that her daughter's job would end up costing her in the end.

Sarah couldn't excuse Derek's behavior. Rachel had given him more than enough opportunities to fly right. In truth she'd given Derek far more opportunities than he deserved.

Still, Derek seemed sincerely repentant this time. And there was something behind his actions that disturbed her. What was going on that he couldn't talk to his own wife about? Sarah started to reach for the phone to call him, but hesitated.

She got up and turned on the radio. In a few seconds the familiar strands of Rachmaninoff's "Rhapsody on a Theme by Paganini" flowed through the room. She sat down and picked up her Bible, trying to read once more. As she turned the pages, she offered a quick prayer for her daughter.

Rachel glanced up from the papers spread before her and noticed Robert engrossed in whatever was on his computer screen. She smiled, thinking of how happy she was to have someone like him in her life. Fortune had been kind to her.

As she stared, Robert's eyes suddenly cut from the screen to hers. For one moment the depth and warmth was gone from them. Instead, she saw a cold edge that caused her smile to vanish.

But then, when he noticed she was watching him, he grinned at her. She blinked a few times to stir herself, then waved. He glanced at his watch, then got up and started walking toward her.

"Time for lunch," he said, perching on the edge of her desk. "I don't want to work you to death on your first day."

Rachel glanced at her watch to collect herself. Had she imagined that look?

"You're right. I have a few errands I have to run, but I shouldn't be long."

Robert glanced at Charlie and Amy. "We don't keep strict office hours here, so feel free to take as long as you need. We'll be here when you get back."

He stood and spoke to Charlie. "Hey, whiz kid, it's time for a lunch break. I'll be back in an hour or so, and Rachel's got things to do too. The company is yours for the next little while, so work out some multimillion-dollar merger for me while I'm gone, okay?"

Charlie raised his hand without taking his eyes from the program.

"I'll see you in a while, Rachel. Have a nice lunch," Robert said as he shut the door behind him and headed down the street.

In a small alleyway in downtown Birmingham, a dirty man in ragged clothes dug through the dumpster off Twenty-second Street. He pulled four bags out before tearing them open and going through them.

Finally, as if finding secret treasure, the man pulled out several pieces of paper and skimmed over them before stuffing them in his shirt. He went through two other bags, then threw them all back and looked for new ones. He glanced at the garbage cans sitting next to the dumpster and realized that he had a good amount of work ahead of him.

"What you think you're doin', man?"

The vagrant turned to see three rough-looking teenagers standing at the alleyway's entrance. Two were tall and thin, while the third, obviously the leader of the group, was short and fat. The fat one spoke again.

"I asked you a question, man. You don't belong here." With that, the trio began to amble forward.

"Leave me alone," the vagrant replied, turning back to the garbage.

"Hey, man, who you think you givin' orders to? Sounds to me like you need to be taught some manners."

"Shouldn't you be in school?" the dirty man asked, not even looking back at the threesome as he began to tear into the contents of a nearby trash can.

The fat teenager balled his fists as he closed the gap between himself and the tramp. "You think you funny? I'm gonna show you what's funny!" He swung his fist at the back of the vagrant's head.

It never connected.

The vagrant kicked backward with his right leg and caught the surprised assailant in the knee. A loud crack filled the alley, followed by an anguished scream. As the boy collapsed, the vagrant spun around and whirled a trash-can lid at one of the other boys. It caught him on the bridge of his nose, and he yelled, grabbing his face as he fell backward. The third turned right as the man was on top of him. The dirty man punched him in the throat and the boy hit the ground, gagging.

Taking a moment to study the three, he returned to the leader and knelt beside him. "You're right, that *was* funny."

Satisfied that the other two were in no condition to cause any more trouble, he headed out of the alley. He heard a door opening behind him into the alleyway and picked up his step.

"What … Hey, you! Stop!"

He glanced over his shoulder to find a muscular man standing open-mouthed over the three punks. The vagrant recognized him immediately.

Fred Spencer.

It was time to get out of there.

As he reached the street, he felt a familiar vibration at his side. He pulled up his dirty shirt to expose a cell phone. Checking the number, he sighed. It was the office. There was just no way to get any work done without their calling.

"Yeah?" He looked around to make certain no one was watching him.

"Mr. Richardson? If you think you can fit it in, I have a potential client who sounds pretty urgent." The female voice on the line was direct and professional.

The man listened as he pulled out a key chain and pointed the black controller on it at a blue Mustang parked nearby. He heard the familiar chirp of the car alarm being deactivated and the pop of the doors unlocking. Once inside the car, he spoke into the phone.

"Okay, Linda, call Mrs. Spencer and tell her I found the print-outs from her husband's company. The second account is there, just as she'd suspected. Fred's a bit richer than she knows. I would have gotten more, but I had some friends drop by, and I couldn't stick around."

The woman sounded pleased. "Really? She should be able to tear into him in court then. Good job, Ian."

"Thanks. Now, who's this new client?"

"His name is Derek Morrison, and it's a pretty interesting case."

FOURTEEN

WHEN IAN FINISHED HIS conversation with Linda, he started planning as he drove home. The new case was simple enough. It sounded like a day or two of digging around in the guy's personal business, then a couple of weeks of surveillance or tailing. Nothing hard. Just the way he liked it. To make it even easier, Linda had already gotten the preliminary work started.

Ian Richardson had been a private investigator for almost eight years, and he loved his work. He wasn't incredibly muscular or a championship gymnast, two common misconceptions couch potatoes thought absolute necessities to being a PI. He kept in shape, but wasn't a fanatic about it. And after losing his fair share of fights over the years, he had worked on that area of his life by studying various styles of martial arts.

But for the most part, real investigative work never involved anything athletic. The thing he needed most in his work was stamina. He'd endured hours of watching a husband go about his daily duties blissfully unaware that his wife suspected him of infidelity and was having him tailed. He'd matched phone records and accounts-payable statements until the mere thought of numbers gave him a headache. He'd worked thirty-six hours straight with no breaks on more than one occasion. And then there were the glamorous times like today when he was forced to go dumpster-diving in search of that forgotten phone bill or profit statement that should have been shredded. Such little things often spelled life or death to someone's court case.

He pulled into the parking lot of his apartment complex in Pelham and got out. Once inside, he found his roommate waiting for him by the door.

"Hey there, Sam."

A large German shepherd stood up, tail wagging. The dog followed Ian into the kitchen where Ian filled its bowl with scraps from lunch. He'd adopted the retired police dog after Sam's partner and trainer was killed in the line of duty. Sometimes Sam had gone with him on jobs and proved invaluable. Though he was harmless most of the time, Sam knew how to protect his owner.

Ian went to his bedroom, stripped, and showered. If the trio of muggers had paid attention, they would have noticed something very different about the bum they were approaching. He looked the part, but didn't smell it. Even though he always strived for as much realism as possible when he worked, he couldn't stand the thought of going without a shower for a few days. His clothes were torn and dirty, but it was all cosmetic. And even though he'd showered that morning, he still felt like pounds of dirt and grime were pouring off his flesh under the spray of the water.

After he felt clean, he shaved and walked into the bedroom, water still glistening in his jet-black hair. Half of his bed was covered with various books and printouts of Web sites he had visited. His thirst for knowledge was voracious. Any seemingly minor comment or anecdote he came across could make or break a case when the time came.

Ian sat down at his laptop and waited as it connected to the Internet. It was time to begin digging into the life of Robert Whitney.

Robert stopped by the mall for lunch. He always enjoyed a few mindless minutes in the bookstore whenever he could squeeze them in. He found a new novel, managed to grab a comfortable chair near the children's section, and settled in to begin reading.

After about ten minutes, his subconscious started to notice noise around him. He looked up from the book to see a small girl sitting on the floor ten feet away with her back to him. She was sobbing, her brown curls shaking. An electric chill shot through his chest at the sight.

"Emily?"

He rose, the novel he'd been reading now lying forgotten on the floor. Never taking his eyes from her, he moved to the girl. Was this some ghost of his daughter come back to haunt him? Was he starting to lose his mind? How could Emily be sitting here?

When he reached her, he knelt and spoke softly. "Emily?"

When the girl looked up, he saw his mistake. She was about Emily's age, and had the same hairstyle and color, but it was not his daughter. Robert felt his heart settling down in his chest as the truth became apparent. Tears streamed down her face, and her lower lip was protruding.

Robert tilted his head, trying not to appear threatening. "What's wrong?"

"I can't find my mommy," she said, sniffling.

Robert smiled. "That's all right. I'm sure she's somewhere close. Let's find her together, okay?" Robert stood and held out a hand. The girl nodded and took his hand, rising.

Glancing around the room, Robert looked back at the girl. "My name's Robert. Do you know your mommy's name?"

She nodded. "Mommy."

"That's good. Does your daddy call your mommy a name too? Something besides Mommy?"

The girl's face brightened, as she nodded again emphatically. "Yes, he calls her honey."

Robert sighed. "Not a lot to go on, but let's give it a shot." Walking with the girl into the main aisle, he started yelling, "Mommy, Mommy, are you here?"

The child caught the idea and joined in the loud chorus. "Mommy! Mom-ee!"

Every head in the room turned toward them. Robert ignored their upset expressions and kept calling out. "Mommy, we're lost!"

"Meghan?"

Robert turned to see a crying woman rushing toward them. She knelt down beside the girl and wrapped her arms around her. "Where did you go? I was so worried about you."

The girl hugged her mother and then broke away. "You got lost, Mommy."

The woman smiled and then looked up at Robert. "Thank you. I turned my back for just a second while I was paying for my coffee, and she was gone."

"I understand. I'm just glad I was near enough to help." Looking down at the girl, he said, "Well, Meghan, thanks for a great adventure. You stay close to Mommy from now on, okay? I might not be there next time."

Meghan nodded, and then tugged on Robert's hand, pulling him down. When he knelt beside her, she wrapped her tiny arms around his neck and kissed him on the cheek. "Thanks, Robber."

"You're welcome, Emily."

The child's brows furrowed. Jerking her thumb toward her chest, she said, "Meghan."

Robert closed his eyes tightly and shook his head. "I'm sorry. You're welcome, *Meghan.*"

The woman thanked him again and, taking her daughter's hand, began to walk away. Meghan turned one last time and waved. Robert smiled and returned the gesture, watching them until they disappeared out the door and into the crowd.

After Robert returned from lunch, he decided to spend time on a project for one of his clients. He was caught up in his "extra activities," and now he was just letting things happen. He'd received a couple of e-mails from his various viruses throughout the day and was keeping a steady record of the information they conveyed to him.

Charlie and Amy had pizza delivered for lunch, so they'd never left their posts throughout the day. Robert thought they were probably having an unspoken endurance contest to see who could outlast the other in constant work. He was thankful Charlie had managed to find someone so compatible to the position they'd needed.

That would be very important in just a short while.

He glanced over at Rachel, typing away at her computer. She was a beautiful woman, and had the tenacity that made her even more attractive. He considered again the possibility of just letting her go, trying to move on and forget about everything that had been done to his family.

But then he looked at the photograph on his desk of his beloved wife and child, now dead, and his resolve hardened. Derek Morrison would pay, as would all those who had tried to wrong him and deny him justice for his family's death.

He got up and walked to Rachel's desk. The stack of papers on it had shrunk considerably since that morning, and she'd entered a large amount of information into the computer. She'd learned fast and had found her way around in an admirable amount of time.

Rachel stopped typing as he approached and took a deep breath. "How are things going?"

"Well, everything's really in pretty good shape. Honestly, I don't think you needed a full-time bookkeeper around here," she answered with a smile.

At that, Robert noticed Charlie glance over at them as if agreeing with her comment. Before anything could be said, he turned back to his computer.

Robert's gaze returned to Rachel. "Well, we'll see how it goes."

She rubbed her eyes and blinked hard a couple of times. "I've got to get used to working with a computer all day though. I've never really dealt with one for any length of time."

Rachel explained to him the figures she had accumulated, and they examined the work together for several minutes. Finally, Robert knelt down next to her desk and locked eyes with her.

"Rachel, I don't want you to feel like you have to do this—and I know some people might consider it inappropriate—but I was wondering if you'd like to have dinner again tonight? I mean, we didn't really get to finish Friday night, did we?"

"You're right. I don't think it's at all improper for you to ask. I can't tonight, but I'm free tomorrow evening."

"Tomorrow night would be great. I'll pick you up at seven thirty."

He rose to go, but she touched his arm.

"Where are we going?"

Robert put his hand on hers, still resting on his arm. "It's a surprise."

He winked at her and then returned to his desk. As he walked, he noticed Charlie casting a questioning glance at him.

Five thirty was quitting time. Charlie set his workstation to compile code, and then checked on Amy. She was still working like crazy to get them caught up. She was a godsend, and a pretty one at that.

She smiled as she put the final commands into the system and crossed her arms triumphantly. Charlie looked at the screen, and his jaw dropped.

"You … you just finished up the whole thing in one day? That program modification had three days marked on my calendar, and you finished it up in one?"

Amy stood and gathered her things to leave. Leaning near Charlie, she whispered, "It's called being good. See you in the morning, boss."

She grinned and turned to go. When she reached the door, she tossed a casual good-bye to Robert. Charlie's eyes never left her until the door shut behind her.

"Marry me?" he whispered wistfully.

He turned and saw Robert still at his terminal. The light from the monitor gave his face a cadaverous glow, and it made Charlie a little nervous. It was time to confront Robert about his conduct the past few days.

"Boss? Do you have a minute?"

Robert rubbed his eyes. He looked rough, and Charlie was concerned about him. For all he knew Robert was drowning himself in his work to avoid facing his obvious grief.

Robert opened his eyes wide and blinked a couple of times before settling back in his chair. "Sure. What's up?"

Charlie pulled a chair from a nearby workbench and sat down beside Robert's desk. "Well, I wanted to ask you about Rachel. She seems like a nice girl and all, but do you mind me asking why we hired a full-time bookkeeper? Most of our transactions are run through the accounting program we have, so everything's automated. I mean, we needed to get caught up and straightened up, but she'll be through in a few days. What happens then?"

"Then I'll find her something else to do. We'll teach her how to use the work-order program, and she can answer phones and make the clients happy. You said before that we could use someone to intercept the calls that come through here, so here she is." Robert closed his eyes for a few seconds and then sighed. "Look, Charlie, she's a nice lady I met a few days ago who's going through a hard time right now. She's planning on going back to night school soon to finish her degree. We're just helping her and her son out for a little while until she can get back on her feet. She'll be gone before you know it."

Charlie sat back in his chair. "So is that why you offered to take her to dinner tomorrow night?"

Robert's face turned to stone. "It is none of your business who I ask out and why. My private life is my own. Do you understand?"

Charlie was startled. "I ... I didn't mean anything bad, I just think it's a little soon after Tara's accident for you to be dating again."

Robert's gaze stayed locked on Charlie for a few seconds. Charlie was worried that he might actually punch him. After several moments of uncomfortable silence, a very small smile touched the edges of Robert's mouth. When he spoke again, his tone was friendly, and he seemed back to normal again. "I'm sorry about that, Charlie. I've been a little tense lately. You've been nothing but helpful to me, and I appreciate that. If it'll make you feel any better, I'm not taking her out romantically; I just want to help her, that's all."

Charlie tried to read Robert, but could tell nothing. If Robert was lying to him, he was doing a really good job of it.

"Okay, boss, I understand. Sorry I bothered you."

Robert shut down his computer and stood. "I really appreciate you, Charlie. I promise everything will be back to normal soon." Then his brows rose. "By the way, I noticed that you may have finally met your match on the programming front. Amy appears to be as gifted as you are, my young protégé."

Charlie chuckled as he stood and turned to go. "She's good, but let's just see if she can keep it up."

Robert laughed, and Charlie liked the sound of it. It was more like the man he used to know, and it made him relax a little to hear it. Maybe things weren't quite as bad as he'd imagined them to be.

"Now, if you'll excuse me, I have to do some shopping before the stores close." Robert picked up his briefcase and held the door open for Charlie.

They left together, and Charlie's mind was so preoccupied with his newest employee that he only glanced at the man standing across the street before getting into his car.

Ian watched Whitney get into his Pathfinder and drive off. After giving him a few seconds head start, he got into his car and followed. Tailing Whitney was easy because the small transmitter he had put on Whitney's car signaled his position every few seconds. It only had a five-mile range, so he needed to stay close—but he was still able to leave some breathing room between them.

Ian tailed him for two hours while Whitney went to several shops before finally deciding to go home. As he turned the car to return to his own apartment, Ian dialed a number on his cell phone. After two rings, a deep but friendly voice answered.

"Yes?"

"Bishop? I think I'm going to need your help on something."

FIFTEEN

T HE NEXT MORNING, CHARLIE had two inter-
views for more help. He hired both applicants and told them to
come back after lunch to start. That gave him time to set up extra
workstations.

Tom Wilson was fresh out of college and hungry for work. Charlie
set him up near the front window with Rachel. He planned to give him
the tedious task of double-checking their work from the night before.
He didn't expect Tom to find anything wrong, but he wanted to be certain before they sent the program to prospective buyers.

Jonathan March was in his midthirties and had enough experience
to work without too much supervision. His workstation was set up
near the back. Charlie planned on giving him a custom programming
job that had been due last week. He had high hopes for both new
recruits.

He stood back and looked over the shop. They had gone from two
guys in an empty room to an office full of folks who were seriously eating up space. Rachel was answering the phones, and it seemed that a
steady stream of work had been pouring in over the past few days.

Amy had even managed to fix the glitch with the "Barney the Battlin' Beaver" game, and CyberCross was ecstatic.

Charlie glanced down and noticed that his office wasn't the only thing going through changes. He was wearing slacks and a pullover. He was the boss now, and should start dressing like it. His days of writing vicious computer viruses in a college dorm were over. Time to grow up.

He settled into his spot next to Amy and glanced at her monitor. She seemed to notice the attention and smiled.

"About time you decided to get some work done. I thought you were just going to prance around here all day."

"Well, I thought I'd give you a head start before coming back to cream your record time today. I know yesterday was just beginner's luck."

She laughed and returned her attention to her monitor. As she typed, she said, "I like you. You've got spunk. You're slow, mind you, but you've got spunk. I can work with that."

Charlie tried to act nonchalant, but he could feel his heart racing.

Derek sat in Ian Richardson's outer office biting his fingernails. The woman behind the receptionist's desk was typing away on the keyboard before her, oblivious to him. He didn't know why they'd wanted him to come down, but he hoped they had something he could give Rachel to show her what kind of person Robert Whitney really was.

When Richardson arrived, he apologized for running late and led Derek into his office. As Derek walked in, he studied Richardson. This was his first look at the man he'd previously talked to by phone only. He was a little taller than six feet, with short dark hair. He looked to be about thirty-five and in good shape.

Richardson shut the door behind them and sat down at his desk. There were two chairs in front of it, so Derek settled down into one and waited while Richardson opened a small notebook he'd brought in with him. Derek looked around the room and saw several old posters advertising various magicians of the past. On one wall sat a framed pair of rusted handcuffs.

"They were Houdini's," said Richardson. "One of his later sets, so it's not as valuable as some of the earlier ones, but it's still one of the highlights of my collection." He motioned to a display case in one corner of his office filled with various objects of different sizes and colors. Derek recognized some of them as cups and balls, along with some ropes and rings, but other things were foreign to him.

"Those are another part of my collection. They're old magic tricks I've collected over the years. Sleight of hand is a hobby of mine."

Richardson glanced at his watch. "I'm expecting someone to join us here any minute."

Derek started to ask another question when he heard the door behind him open again. He turned and found himself staring at a walking wall. The ebony-skinned giant before him stood at least six and a half feet tall and looked as big as any pro football linebacker Derek had ever seen. He was carrying a manila folder that had several papers sticking out of it. He was dressed totally in black—an expensive-looking black suit over a tight-fitting black shirt.

Richardson smiled as he spoke. "Bishop, glad to see you made it."

Bishop's deep voice was friendly. "Sorry for my tardiness, gentlemen. I had to drop by and see a young man who decided to make a very big mistake last night and is now incarcerated. His mother is a member of my congregation, and I promised her I'd look in on him."

Richardson turned to Derek, who stood there with his mouth open. "Derek Morrison, I'd like you to meet Levi Franklin Bishop."

The giant smiled warmly and shook Derek's hand. "Nice to meet you, Mr. Morrison."

Oh great, I've been turned over to a priest from the NFL. Maybe I can still get my retainer back.

Bishop sat down in the chair opposite Derek and opened the folder he'd been carrying. Derek lowered himself into his chair. Richardson rolled a coin across his knuckles and looked at a stack of papers.

"I called Levi in because, despite his serene exterior, he used to be a rather shady character," Richardson explained. "I thought maybe he could give me his opinion."

Bishop's expression was one of dead seriousness as he spoke. "You did the right thing in hiring Ian to look into this; and I come at no extra charge to you, so don't worry about that. I'm doing this because of the nature of your case."

Derek's eyes narrowed slightly. "What? You ever had your family stalked by a computer psycho before?"

Bishop leaned forward and lowered his voice. "You can't begin to imagine what I've been through, Mr. Morrison. I lost my family too, and I know how it feels to need revenge. The road Robert Whitney's traveling has one destination, and I'd like to think there's a chance I can reach him before it gets to that point."

Again, there was awkward silence as Bishop's words sank in. Derek looked at both men and sat back in his seat. "So let me get this straight: I hire you to get me something on Whitney I can use against him for my wife, and maybe you can do a little pushing to get him to back off, and instead you're using this as a chance to preach to the guy? Yeah, he lost his family, and it's sad and all that, but I'm the one he's terrorizing here. Did you guys forget who's paying you?"

Derek shot to his feet. "I want my money back. You go preach your sermons behind someone else's pulpit."

Bishop stood and towered over Derek. He looked down at him with a steady gaze. "I wasn't finished, Mr. Morrison. If you'd allowed me to complete my thought, you'd understand why I'm here. May I continue before you leave? If you don't like what you hear after that, I'm sure Mr. Richardson will be happy to refund your money—minus his expenses, of course."

Derek glanced at Richardson, who was still sitting behind his desk. Richardson shrugged and gave him a half smile. After a few seconds, Derek sat back down.

"Thank you," Bishop said, as he lowered himself back into his seat. "I'm not here heading up the 'Robert Whitney Pity Party,' Mr. Morrison. You need to understand that if he continues on the path he's going now, he isn't endangering just himself. He appears to have set himself rather nicely into your wife's daily routine now, and shows signs of pursuing a relationship with her. If he decides at some point to strike out at you, who do you think would be the easiest targets? Who do you think he would go after if he were truly trying to hurt you?"

Derek's eyes widened as he understood the gravity of those words. "You mean you think he's going to hurt Rachel and Scott? I thought he was doing all that stuff to make me feel bad about him being with her."

Richardson picked up a pencil from his desk and began to move it in his hands as he spoke. "You see, Mr. Morrison, we're still looking out for you as our client. Your family is also a concern though, and after you spoke with my secretary the first time, we started the wheels rolling to get a good idea of Whitney's frame of mind. We even have someone on the inside now feeding us information. It's not a lot at the moment, but if something happens, we'll know about it."

Richardson looked down at one of the papers in front of him. "We know he's planning on taking your wife to dinner tonight. We have no idea where, but I promise you that we'll be following along wherever he goes."

Derek sat up. "I want to go with you. I want to see what he's doing."

Richardson shook his head. "No, I'm afraid that's not an option. Besides, it's long and tedious work to tail someone, and I don't think you'd enjoy it."

Derek leaned forward and put his arm on Richardson's desk. "I believe I'm the one paying for all this. I think that entitles me to a few privileges, don't you? I'm a truck driver, Mr. Richardson, and if there's one thing I know how to do, it's sit for long periods of time. I'm not going to go busting out of the car and punch the guy out or anything. I need information if I'm going to change my wife's opinion of him. If I go out there swinging, she'll see him as the poor victim and hate me even more. I just want to see what's going on."

Richardson stared at Derek for several tense seconds. "Okay, Mr. Morrison, you can ride along with Levi and watch—but if you give us any trouble or compromise us in any way, we're out of there, and you can find someone else to take the case."

Derek glanced at Bishop and back at Richardson. "I'm riding with Levi? Why aren't you going to be there? Shouldn't you be doing something too?"

Richardson smiled. "I'll be there, Mr. Morrison. I just prefer to do things a little differently, that's all. I'll still be hard at work earning those big bucks you're paying me. Now if you'll excuse me, I have someplace to be in a few minutes."

Bishop chuckled and patted Derek's shoulder. "Looks like we'll be riding together. I'll meet you in front of this office at six, and we'll be waiting when Mr. Whitney leaves work."

Derek stood and turned to go. Before he could reach the door, Richardson spoke. "Mr. Morrison? One more thing."

Richardson's voice was quiet, but firm. "You need to understand that no matter what happens, I won't be 'pushing him around,' as you mentioned. We're not thugs. I'm not going to 'lean on him' or 'meet him in a dark alley' or anything remotely resembling that. I'm an investigator, not a bully. If you want him slapped around, you'll have to do it yourself. Understood?"

Derek stood silent for a moment and then nodded. He looked at Bishop, still seated quietly in his chair, and cleared his throat. "I'll see you tonight, Mr. Bishop. I promise you won't even know I'm there."

Bishop smiled and winked. With one final glance at Richardson, Derek opened the door and left.

After lunch, Charlie helped his two newest employees get settled in. It appeared that both Jonathan and Tom would be working on new projects by the next day. Jonathan was extremely quiet and set about doing his work after the briefest of direction. His eyes never missed anything that happened around the office, and Charlie had caught him more than once staring at Robert throughout the day.

Tom, on the other hand, started the shift with a little small talk, and then worked like a madman. Charlie thought he needed to get him a new chair, though, because it seemed like he was leaning back to stretch and look around the office quite often. Both men were amazing workers, and Charlie couldn't be more pleased with the way things were going.

Robert had arrived earlier that morning, and—after speaking briefly with Rachel—settled in to work. Charlie had never noticed how much work Robert was capable of doing until he'd been forced to hire two guys to take his place. It was obvious Robert was more talented than he'd given him credit for.

As Charlie sat at his workstation to pull up the work orders Rachel had entered from the day before, he felt Amy lean toward him.

"Psssst."

He smiled and ignored her. After a few seconds, he heard her again, louder this time.

"Pssst."

He looked over at her, a sly grin on his face. "Either you've sprung an air leak or you want my attention."

Amy gave him a quick, sarcastic smile. "Very funny. I hear the boss is taking our pretty receptionist out to dinner, and I understand it's someplace nice."

Charlie's eyes narrowed as he lowered his voice to match hers. "And just where did we hear this little tidbit of information?"

Amy winked. "Girl talk. Since Rachel and I are the only two ladies in this room full of sweaty men, we have to stick together. She shares things with me, and I do likewise."

Charlie raised his eyebrows. "Oh really? And what valuable knowledge do you pass on to our receptionist-slash-bookkeeper?"

Amy smiled wryly. "Girl stuff. Do you know where they're going? Rachel's dying to know, and so am I. I'll never tell, I promise."

Charlie sighed. "Marigold's."

She gently laid a hand on his arm. "How do you know that?"

He rubbed his neck. He could smell her perfume, and was momentarily lost in the sweet fragrance. Her touch, and now this—he was in heaven. He cleared his throat. "Because I heard him making the reservations by phone yesterday. It sounded like there was something wrong with his voice, but I could hear clearly enough. You can't tell her, all right?"

Amy's dark eyes looked deep into his. She sat back in her chair, her hand falling from Charlie's arm. "Marigold's. That's a really wonderful place. I've always wanted to eat there."

Charlie's arm felt naked with the loss of her touch. Staring forward at his monitor again, he swallowed hard and decided to dive in. "Would you like to go tonight? I'm sure Robert wouldn't mind if we joined them. And if he does want to be alone, we could always eat at another table. I mean, there would be a lot of people around, so you wouldn't have to feel like you were on a date or anything. It wouldn't be a date, really … just a company dinner or something."

Charlie felt like an idiot, and he wished he could find some way to straighten out the mess he'd made. When he glanced over at her, however, she was smiling. Her voice rose in mock surprise as she said, "Are you asking me out?"

The office seemed to grow silent and he could feel all eyes on him. Charlie took a deep breath and decided that he'd come too far to back out now. "Yes, I am asking you out ... to dinner. You and me, food, you know, all that. What do you think?"

She laughed. "I think your delivery needs a bit more polish before you try to go professional, but I'm flattered. I'd love to go to dinner with you tonight."

Charlie sighed in relief and nodded. "Okay, I'll pick you up at six thirty."

Amy leaned over and kissed his cheek. "I'll be ready and looking foxy, you sexy beast you." With a wink, she began to work.

Charlie felt a huge, stupid grin growing on his face. He decided to see if anyone else had noticed his little victory. With a quick glance around the room, he received a smile from Tom, a wink from Robert, and a brief wave from Rachel. Jonathan watched him also, but his face remained expressionless.

Chris Rickles was furious.

For the third time in one day, he'd been on the phone with one of his credit-card companies, trying to talk to a human being rather than a computer. He was able to get two or three levels into the directory tree, but then he would press the wrong button and find himself in the wrong department. After a brief conversation with whatever live voice he finally connected with, he'd be put on hold until he gave up.

His attempt to access his bill online had proved equally fruitless. He stared at the computer monitor before him, still not sure what to make of the things he saw. For some reason his credit card was completely maxed out because of several online orders he hadn't made. Someone had been ordering adult books and products using his card. And the really upsetting thing was the fact that this wasn't the only card he'd found that way. After checking his other billing statements online, he found a dozen other fraudulent purchases.

Chris slammed down the phone in frustration and decided to try a different approach. He opened his e-mail program and composed a blistering message for the issuers of his Visa. He also included the list of items that he disputed buying and let them know in no uncertain terms that he wasn't paying for them. If they couldn't stop people from using his card, he wasn't going to be the one penalized for it.

After finishing up his three-page tome, he hit *send* and got up to grab a soda.

Unseen, a second message left Chris's computer with the first.

Gordon James cursed as he waited for his computer to bring up the logs from the previous day. For some reason, the computers had been slower lately, which frustrated him. He eyed the keyboard and debated using it as a bat to knock his monitor onto the floor.

The company's resident "computer guy," Larry, had been unable to fix the problem. The fact that he'd never really been formally trained could have been a factor; but if he was too lazy to read the books the company had purchased, that was his own fault. If he didn't watch his step, he'd be back driving a truck again.

When the spreadsheet finally opened, Gordon studied it and began to assign routes. He was in a bad mood because of the computer harassment he'd just had to endure, and was brutal with a couple of the drivers. When he got to Derek Morrison's name, he smiled. With a few keystrokes, he mapped out a lengthy haul that would keep Morrison behind the wheel for a long time.

Feeling pleased with himself, he hit *print* and leaned back in his chair with his hands folded behind his head. He stared at the ceiling for a moment, listening to the printer behind him as it rolled paper after paper from its tray, then he lit up a cigar and took a leisurely drag from it.

He couldn't wait to see the looks on the faces of his drivers when they came in over the next two days—especially Morrison's. A wicked grin crossed his face at the thought.

Unknown and unseen, the virus on the network server corrupted a few more files, copied a couple, and discreetly sent off a message to its creator.

Robert sat at his terminal and read the messages on the screen. A half smile formed on his lips as he saw what the day's work had brought him.

His fingers settled on the keyboard in front of him, and he began to type.

Time to turn up the heat.

SIXTEEN

DEREK WAS STANDING OUTSIDE Ian Richardson's office fifteen minutes early. His eyes scanned the streets for any signs of a car holding a gargantuan driver. After five minutes of unsuccessful searches, he was rewarded by the sound of a horn as a gray Camry pulled up next to him. The driver's side window rolled down, and Bishop's smiling face greeted him.

"How we doing, partner? Hop in, and let's get going. I was hoping you'd be early so we could get a head start on things."

Derek went around the car, opened the door, and settled into the passenger seat. Derek listened to the music coming from the car stereo. After a few seconds, his fears were confirmed: It was all religious. The beat was good, and the singer was great, but it still wasn't his preference. He reached for the radio. "Mind if I change stations?"

Bishop smiled and placed his gigantic hand over the dial. "I would prefer you didn't. I'm eating right now." After noticing Derek's obviously confused look, he continued. "I'm feeding my spirit, and it sure tastes good." He settled back into his seat with a rich laugh.

Derek looked out the window and tried to drown out the music with thoughts of Rachel. He knew tonight could be very important in his efforts to win her back. If anything went wrong, however, he could be in serious trouble.

As Charlie walked up to Amy's apartment, he checked his outfit again. He wanted to make sure he hadn't missed anything. He held a single white rose.

The only suit he owned was the one that he'd bought for Tara and Emily's funeral. That held too many memories to consider, so he'd left work early enough to grab a tan sport coat and some dark-brown slacks on the way home. After a quick ironing, they were ready to go.

Charlie rang the doorbell and waited. He couldn't remember the last time he'd been this nervous. He heard the sound of footsteps, and then the door opened.

Though he'd heard the term "breathtaking" before, Charlie had never actually seen anyone who fit that description. Sure, the movie stars and models looked great from time to time, but no woman had ever actually taken his breath away.

Until now.

Amy answered the door in a red dress that ended right above her knees, and she wore no hose or stockings. Her legs had a dark hue that suggested time spent in a tanning bed or outside soaking up the ultraviolet rays. Her hair was pulled up except for two strands that fell on either side of her face, framing it provocatively. Her face was barely touched with makeup, and it had been applied only enough to highlight her natural beauty. She smiled when she saw him, and her smile made him forget his name. Charlie stood there openmouthed, the single rose grasped in his hand.

After an awkward moment of silence, Amy pointed to the flower. "Is that for me?"

Charlie blinked a couple of times and glanced down at the rose as if noticing it for the first time. "Uh, yeah."

She smiled again and gently took it, bringing it to her face and breathing its fragrance. She took his hand and led him inside.

"I'll be ready in just a few minutes. I'm sorry I'm running a little late, but I'm trying my best to look good for you."

Charlie followed her inside. "You've succeeded already."

"Why, Mr. Bolton, if I didn't know better I'd say you were trying to flatter me." She winked at him and headed back toward her bedroom. "I'll be right out. Just make yourself comfortable on the couch."

Charlie glanced around the apartment. In one corner of the living room sat a small gas fireplace with a painting hanging over the mantle of two people dancing on a windy beach while being serenaded by a man in a tuxedo and covered by a maid with an umbrella.

"Nice painting," he called to her.

She peeked around the corner of her doorway. "What?"

Charlie pointed to the framed print on the wall. "Nice painting."

She gazed at it and smiled. "It's called *The Singing Butler* and was done by Jack Vettriano. I'm a sucker for the romantic. Have you ever danced on the beach at night?"

Charlie shook his head.

Amy sighed. "Me, neither. But it seems like it would be incredibly romantic, doesn't it?" She disappeared down the hall once more.

Off to one side in the room sat a small computer desk with a black LCD monitor on it. Charlie walked to the desk and noticed the computer sitting next to it. It was a workhorse. It was apparent that she didn't use it just to check her e-mail and surf the Web. He knew that the stock model of this computer was top-of-the-line, and if she'd made any upgrades to it, then it would smoke. He also knew that it wasn't cheap, so this meant Amy hadn't bought it on a modest salary like Robert was paying her.

A bookshelf sat near the computer desk with an eclectic array of books on it. Everything from classic literature and romance novels to mysteries and computer programming were combined to create the odd library.

As he continued his casual scan of her room, he continued to peel away more layers of Amy's life like an onion. She had several training videos on hacking and computer security, and two framed diplomas on her wall added the icing to the cake. She held a bachelor's degree in computer sciences and a second in programming. She also had several certifications.

All of this began to nag at Charlie's mind. There was no reason in the world a woman with this much talent and training should ever be working at the kind of job Robert was offering.

Amy glided beside him and gently put her arm into his. "Okay, enough snooping around. If you want to know more, you'll have to ask me yourself. Besides, I'm hungry, and you're supposed to be filling my stomach with overpriced goodies. Let's get going."

Charlie smiled and turned toward the door. "Well, let it never be said I allowed my date to starve."

Robert arrived five minutes early and was allowed in by Sarah. He took a seat in the living room across from Rachel's father, and they sat in awkward silence for several seconds. Paul gazed at Robert intently, while Robert continued to keep a smile on his face throughout the obvious scrutiny. Finally, Paul broke the silence.

"Robert, are you aware of the fact that Rachel's a married woman?"

Robert smiled and let his gaze fall to the floor for a few moments, then leaned forward. It was important to keep the ruse going. "Well, I had suspected as much, but I didn't have anything concrete until you mentioned it just now. She hasn't seen fit to share that part of her life with me yet, so I'm not going to push her. When she's ready to open up to me, I'll listen. Otherwise, I think it's best if we honor her silence."

Paul stirred uncomfortably. "I'm not trying to do anything behind her back. I'm just saying that she and Derek have a young son together, and if there's any way they can work out their problems, they should. You appear to be a very good man, and I really appreciate what you've done for Rachel with the job. It's helped her tremendously. It's just that she doesn't need the added distraction of a relationship to finish off her marriage. Derek's a good man. Something's disturbed him recently, but he's still a good man at heart. Everyone deserves a second chance."

The smile on Robert's face stayed the same, but his eyes turned hard. "Sometimes people don't deserve a second chance, Paul. Sometimes they do things that can't be forgiven. What if Derek's not such a wonderful saint-in-the-making as you think he is? I mean, how well can you really know a person like him?"

Paul didn't hesitate. "I know him pretty well. Derek's had his problems, just like all of us have from time to time, but he's got his strengths too. He's a wonderful father, and a man of honor. He's faced his demons and come out on top."

Robert's eyes narrowed. "Could be he still has a few more demons to face."

Before Paul could question him further, Rachel walked into the room. She wore a simple blue dress that was the perfect mix of style and modesty. Both men stood as she crossed to them. The smile on her face cooled Robert's building rage. She was a beautiful woman with no idea what a horrible game she was involved in. For a moment Robert felt uncomfortable and wanted to call the whole thing off. He wanted to explain everything to Rachel and hope that she could forgive him. He'd been a good father and a good husband. Maybe his actions were just a little out of proportion to what had happened....

But then visions rose of Tara and Emily on the cold road with the sheets covering them. He remembered the sound of their laughter, their smiling faces in life, and the gentle caress of his beloved Tara's hand upon his face. He felt the jarring anguish of losing them afresh and knew that he would never be the same man again. That man had died next to his wife and daughter. Derek Morrison would die by his hand only after he had tasted of the pain Robert had suffered.

Robert took Rachel's hand and brought it to his lips. He kissed it gently, and then covered the back of her hand with his other one. The smile on his face was warm, but there was a menace behind it that Rachel could not see.

But her father did.

Paul Mason watched his daughter leave. They did make a more likely couple than Derek and Rachel had, but that had never been a factor before.

Sarah stood at the doorway, watching. Paul came up behind his wife and wrapped his arm around her waist. Sarah waved as they pulled away. Paul couldn't shake the feeling that Rachel was in danger.

"Sarah, I'm going into the bedroom to pray."

Sarah squeezed her husband's hand. "I'll go with you."

"No, you watch Scott. He doesn't need to know anything right now. This can't continue, though. One way or another, Rachel has to make a decision about the direction her life will be taking. This isn't fair to Derek or to her."

He walked toward the bedroom, hoping he could find comfort in the arms of his Creator.

Twenty minutes later Bishop pulled into an empty spot across the street from Marigold's. Derek read the name over the door, and watched as a man in a pressed white shirt and creased black slacks parked the cars as the customers arrived. It was a beautiful place, and it was definitely not the kind of establishment he could have ever afforded to take Rachel to on his salary. As he watched the valet doing his job, he thought about his wife.

I'm not happy with your choice of company, but I hope the food is good. You deserve stuff like this, Rachel. I just wish I could have done this for you myself.

Terrance Gold drove toward Marigold's with his date in the seat next to him. Her name was Janine, and they had been going out for almost two years. Their relationship was a unique one because they would come and go in each other's lives as they pleased. Neither wanted anything more than an occasional night on the town and a casual sleepover afterward. Tonight, however, she was being treated like royalty.

She was dressed in a purple dress that he hated, but it was the only thing she had that seemed really nice. Her large zirconium earrings were too big for his taste, and the fake pearls around her neck really didn't do much for her, but he could put up with them for the night. Her leg pumped furiously in a nervous twitch, and she seemed ready to burst with anticipation.

Terrance gently reached out his hand and placed it on her knee, stopping her jittering before it got too annoying. He winked at her.

"We're almost there, baby. I hope you're hungry 'cause there's nothing but the best for you tonight." He chuckled at the thought that it wasn't going to cost him a cent, but she didn't have to know that.

Janine giggled and looked out the window again.

With a quick glance at a nearby street sign, he turned the corner and prepared for a nice evening meal.

Bishop tapped Derek's arm with the back of his hand. "Hey, you're awful quiet. Don't start getting all depressed on me. It's all gonna work out all right, you'll see."

Derek chuckled sarcastically, still watching the restaurant. "And just how do you know that? Are you able to see the future now?"

Bishop smiled. "No, I'm afraid the Lord hasn't seen fit to let me in on any of those secrets. But I can tell you that it's going to be okay because I know that he's a good God, and I'm praying for you, my friend."

Derek was silent, his face toward the window. Bishop said nothing more, allowing his words to sink in.

Several silent minutes passed, then Derek leaned back in his seat. "Levi, what happened in your life?"

"What do you mean?"

Derek turned to face him. "When we met in Richardson's office this morning, you mentioned that you'd lost your family. What happened to them?"

Bishop's eyes fell, and he took in a deep breath. After a long sigh, his eyes met Derek's as he spoke. "My kids were murdered, Derek … in cold blood."

"Murdered?" Suddenly Derek felt uncomfortable, like he'd gone into a place he wasn't supposed to. "I'm sorry. Did you find the guy who did it?"

Bishop looked out the window at the restaurant. He seemed to be fighting for words. "No." He turned back to Derek. "So you see, I can understand your desire for revenge. I may be a Christian, but I'm still only human. Sometimes I wake up and for a few seconds I expect to hear my kids in the house. Then reality sets in and I realize it isn't going to happen."

"Why don't you get Richardson to find the guy for you?"

Bishop's voice was somber. "Because I honestly don't know what would happen if I ever found him." His hands tightened on the steering wheel. "I just know God would have to help me or it wouldn't be pretty."

116

SEVENTEEN

CHARLIE AND AMY PULLED up to Marigold's and were greeted by the valet who opened Amy's door. After shutting it behind her, he crossed to the driver's side and got behind the wheel. Amy waited for Charlie at the bottom of the stairs leading to the entrance and then took his arm as he stepped beside her. The door was opened for them before they even reached it.

The interior of the restaurant was striking, but only after they stepped into the outdoor courtyard did it become magical. Soft white lanterns outlined the courtyard, and candles on each table provided the perfect atmosphere for a romantic evening. Charlie was pleasantly surprised to find that Robert had reserved a table there for the four of them.

Amy's eyes widened a bit as she saw their table. Pleased at her reaction, Charlie pulled her chair out for her and then took the seat next to her. He wanted to be as close as possible.

She gently touched his arm as she looked around at the muted lights and the starry sky above. "This is like something out of a movie," she whispered. Her gaze locked onto his. "Thank you. No one's ever taken me anywhere like this. It's the most romantic place I've ever seen."

For a moment he was caught up in her eyes. He blinked and smiled. "I'm glad you like it." He knew good and well he was crossing the employer-employee relationship and running hard and fast into dangerous territory, but he no longer cared. In the short time he'd known her, he knew he wanted to talk to this woman for hours, then kiss her forever.

It was their first date, and it was going well.

Robert watched Rachel from the corner of his eye as they drove to the restaurant. Their ride had been a little quieter than usual, and it bothered him.

"Anything wrong?"

Rachel turned to him and stared blankly for a second. Then she smiled and shook her head. "No, nothing's wrong. I'm sorry I'm so quiet, but this is a little overwhelming for me. I've never been to a nice place like this one, and it's a little much. I'm not even sure if it's such a good idea for me to be going out with my boss. I know you said it's just dinner, but I think you know that I'm developing feelings for you that go beyond a 'just dinner' relationship."

Robert glanced at her. "Would you like for me to turn around? I don't want you to feel uncomfortable."

"No. I really appreciate the way you've treated me up until now. I've never met anyone like you. It's just that this is turning so much into a dream for me that I'm a little scared of when I'll wake up."

"Who says you have to wake up?"

When they stopped at the next red light, he turned to her, and they kissed. The car behind them honked its horn, and they both chuckled at being caught. She leaned her head against his shoulder. It felt good, and a part of him wished it could continue.

The other part of him made him casually pat his inside breast coat pocket to feel the small package that rested there. A cold smile crept across his face at the thought of what lay in store for them this night.

"They're here."

Bishop pointed to the restaurant's entrance. Robert's car had just pulled up, and the valet was opening the passenger-side door. Rachel stepped out, and Derek had to fight the impulse to fling open the car door and run toward her. He knew he could take Robert in a fight, but that wasn't what he needed to happen. If he wanted Rachel to see what kind of man she was with, he had to play it smart.

He felt Bishop stir in the seat next to him and saw that the big man had situated himself to grab him quickly if he went for the door. "I'm not going anywhere. I promised to be good, and I will. Besides, I need him to make some sort of mistake."

Bishop patted his shoulder.

Derek's eyes narrowed. "Hey, where's Richardson? Shouldn't he be involved in this caper somehow?"

Bishop laughed. "He is. Trust me. His part is just about to begin."

Robert escorted Rachel into the posh restaurant. Rachel's eyes moved quickly around the room, soaking in every detail. The walls, a muted beige that accented everything, were sparsely covered with tasteful paintings. The maitre d' escorted them quickly to their table. When Rachel saw the outdoor courtyard, she warmed. The sky was clear above them, and the stars shone brightly. It was a beautiful night.

As Robert sat down, Charlie leaned over. "Nice choice of tables, chief."

"Thanks."

Their waiter made his way to the table and took their drink orders. He was a tall man with a goatee and buckteeth. His red hair was slightly disheveled, but his clear blue eyes shone brightly as he spoke. Robert felt slightly uneasy around him for some reason, and he could almost swear something had passed between Rachel and him when he'd walked up to their table.

Careful, you're getting too paranoid. Rachel looks amazing tonight, and the guy noticed, that's all.

Still, he felt better when the man moved away.

The waiter returned with their drinks and took their order for the meal. Robert ordered for all of them and did an excellent job of picking a wine that complemented the meal—though Amy asked for water instead. As the waiter left, Robert glanced at his watch.

It was almost time.

Derek impatiently tapped his fingers on the car's console. He wanted to know what was going on inside the restaurant.

"What are we doing? Shouldn't we be moving in and getting a closer look or something?"

"Just settle down," Bishop replied. "Ian tried to talk you out of coming. This is boring work, but we're just here as backup. The main action's going on inside."

"So all we do is wait until they get through eating?"

"Relax. We have someone inside who's getting a much closer look than we are."

The conversation flowed freely during dinner. All four of them were comfortable with each other, and the rapport between Robert and Charlie began to show itself again. It was obvious that they were more than just coworkers—they were friends who could laugh at each other.

A few minutes before eight, Robert's phone rang. He looked apologetically at Rachel as he answered it.

"Yes? Yes, sir, I remember you. We're working on your project now. Yes, we've just been a little behind."

He covered the mouthpiece with his hand and whispered to Rachel. "I'm sorry. I need to take this call. I'll be right back."

He left the table and went inside. As soon as the door closed behind him, he put the phone back in his pocket. The call had actually been from his computer, programmed to dial his number at the exact minute it had done so and play a prerecorded message he'd created for tonight.

He continued toward the front door. Once there, he situated himself so he'd have a good view of the street and waited. He reached inside his coat pocket and checked once more for the small plastic box. Robert looked up just in time.

Terrance Gold was pulling up to the door with his date.

EIGHTEEN

Robert watched the valet open the door for Gold's date while Gold stepped out of his own side of the car. When they reached the bottom of the stairs leading into the restaurant, Robert turned to face the wall and flipped out his cell phone, pretending to be engaged in conversation. The couple passed him without a second glance.

When they were gone, he moved back to the door and watched for the valet. The boy hurried back just as another car pulled in. Obviously exhausted, the boy slapped the keys onto a Peg-Board beside the door before rushing to help another couple out of their car. Robert locked his eyes on the keys. As the boy drove off to park the new car, Robert slipped outside, grabbed Gold's key ring from the board, and hurried back in.

He went to the men's room and locked himself in a stall, then slid the small plastic box out of his pocket. As he opened it, the overhead lights glinted off the soft wax inside. He flipped through the keys until he found three that looked like house keys, and made an imprint of each in the wax. Slapping the box shut, he dropped it back into his pocket and left.

By the time he reached the door, the valet was just driving off with yet another car. Robert had plenty of time to put the keys back in their place on the Peg-Board before rejoining his dinner guests.

"Did you get that?" Derek asked.

Bishop switched off the camera and set it between them on the seat. "Yeah, I did. I still don't know what I got, but I got it. He was obviously hiding something because of the way he timed those two visits, but I don't have a clue as to what he was doing besides fumbling with that guy's keys."

"What now?"

Bishop settled back in his seat, but kept his eyes glued to the front door. He rested his hand on the video camera, ready to have it working at a moment's notice.

"Now we wait."

Robert returned to his seat and apologized for the delay. The rest of dinner progressed without incident. They all talked for a while after dessert, and then Robert stood.

"Well, if you two will excuse us. It's getting late, and Rachel and I should be leaving."

Charlie looked from one to the other. "So soon?"

Amy punched him lightly on the arm. "Let them go. I'll finally get you to myself for a while."

Charlie looked at her for a moment and then looked up at Robert. "Go. Go. Why are you still here?"

Robert laughed as he signaled for the waiter. The man came up with the bill, and Robert paid in cash with enough left over for a good tip. The waiter's eyes widened as he thanked them and left.

After the valet had left to get their car, Rachel leaned over and kissed Robert on the cheek. He turned to her with a surprised look on his face.

"What was that for?"

She smiled as she hooked her arm into his. "For a wonderful evening. It's been one of the most romantic I've had in a long time."

"The night's not over yet," Robert said as he wrapped his arms around her and kissed her again.

Since childhood, Bishop had always been blessed with natural strength. He'd spent his high-school years in the weight room during free periods and had developed a muscular physique that he still carried. He continued to lift weights as a way to relieve stress, and as a result his arms had grown to the size of some men's legs.

This strength came in handy as he held Derek Morrison down in the front seat of his car.

Derek had stiffened when Rachel kissed Robert's cheek. When Robert had responded with a more intimate embrace, Derek lost control. Only the fact that Bishop had been preparing for it all night kept him from being caught off guard and allowing Derek to escape.

Curses flew from Derek's mouth while he struggled to get free from Bishop's grasp. Finally, he went limp.

Derek watched as Rachel got into Robert's car, and they drove off together. "Aren't we going to follow them?"

Bishop continued to speak in kind tones. "No. Our part is over now. We were supposed to watch the restaurant, and we did. The rest of it is being taken care of as we speak."

"What do we do now?"

Bishop studied Derek for a moment, trying to make sure he was going to be all right. Then he started up the car and pulled into traffic.

"Now we go meet up with Ian."

Charlie watched the candlelight dance in Amy's eyes. He reached out gingerly and touched her hand. She smiled and covered his with her own. With a mischievous grin, she whispered, "Is this where you try to put the moves on me, Mr. Bolton?"

Charlie's eyes widened, and he moved to pull his hand away. "No! I'm sorry. I hope you didn't think—"

Amy's soft laughter broke his tension. "Of course not, silly boy. I just like to see you blush. You're so innocent, and that makes you adorable."

She took another quick sip of her water and turned back to him. "So how long have you and Robert known each other?"

Charlie settled back in his chair, relieved to see the subject change from him for a few minutes. "We've known each other for years. I came to work for him right out of college. I'd been a bad little virus writer, but he helped guide me to where I am today. I'd never have considered running the office myself with any size staff, but Robert had confidence in me. His confidence built mine up, and now I feel pretty good about the way things are going."

Amy smiled. "You should. You're doing a great job. It's obvious he's a good judge of character."

Charlie looked down. "Thanks. I know he seems kind of tough and aloof at times, but if you'd only known him before ..."

Amy's head tilted. "Before what?"

Charlie sat, his eyes still on the table before him, and then began to speak in an almost reverent tone.

"Let me tell you about Tara and Emily ..."

After driving in silence for several minutes, Bishop and Derek finally reached Ian Richardson's office building. They rode the elevator up, and Bishop used a key to let them into the office. It was only after they sat down in the same chairs they'd occupied earlier that day in front of Richardson's desk that Derek spoke.

"So where is he? I sure didn't see him out there around us."

Before Bishop could answer, the door opened, and both men turned to see a stranger enter. The man had red hair and a goatee, and his teeth were in bad need of dental work. He was dressed in a white shirt with a black vest and slacks. Without a word he collapsed into the seat behind the desk and leaned back, propping his feet up on it.

The three men sat silent for a moment as Derek turned to give a questioning glance at Bishop, who was obviously having a hard time holding in laughter.

The man behind the desk spoke. "Laugh it up, big guy. Next time you're the one working up close, and *I'll* sit in the car listening to the radio. Do you realize how much I had to pay the manager to let me in there for that shift?"

Derek looked up to see the man rip off his goatee and take out his upper set of teeth. With a quick flourish, he fanned a deck of cards that had appeared in his hands and began to shuffle them. Derek looked at his hair, and Ian Richardson looked up too.

"Hair spray," he explained. "You can buy it in any color you want, and I felt like being a redhead tonight. Oh, before I forget ..."

He leaned forward and dropped the cards on the desk. Reaching into his eyes, he extracted a pair of blue-colored contacts and put them into a small container. He slid the container into a desk drawer, picked up the cards, and began to shuffle them again, pausing now and then to do a fancy cut or show off a dramatic flourish.

"So what have you two boys been up to?"

Bishop explained what had transpired that evening with Robert's suspicious activities with the keys. Richardson lowered his head in frustration.

"So, he was a Boy Scout at dinner for me, and all you guys see is him playing around with the valet's Peg-Board; is that the gist of it? We got zip. Wonderful. On the bright side, I made over a hundred bucks in tips."

He leaned back in his chair and rubbed his eyes. "We still had someone on the inside. When I get their notes in the morning, we'll have a better idea of what was going on. Maybe they caught the important stuff. Every time I came by that table, they were just talking about computers. Bor-ring."

Derek looked from one man to the other. "Is that it? We end our evening as empty-handed as we began?"

Richardson's head was laid back in his chair, and he spoke to the ceiling. "We'll find out in the morning. I'll give you a call as soon as I read over the notes and let you know where we stand."

Derek felt Bishop touch his shoulder.

"Don't give up hope, Derek."

Derek nodded. He still couldn't believe they'd lost a perfect opportunity to catch Robert Whitney in action. He was beginning to have thoughts that maybe God wasn't on his side as Bishop seemed to think.

NINETEEN

WHEN THEY PULLED UP in front of Robert's house, Rachel eyed the front door and debated within herself what this course of action would accomplish. There seemed to be far too many cons and not enough pros to go through with it, but the night had been magical up to this point. There was really only one way she wanted it to end.

Robert leaned toward her and touched her face. She turned and smiled, but remained quiet. She looked into his eyes and realized that she was falling for this man, but it was progressing way too fast. If she ever were going to put a stop to this relationship, it would have to be now.

"Robert, I've had a great time tonight. The past few days have really been amazing, and I don't know what to say." She glanced at the door again.

Robert placed his finger under her chin and drew her attention back to him. "Listen, all I wanted to do was show you something inside. If you're uncomfortable, just say so, and I'll take you home now. I don't want to ruin this evening for us." His soothing words tore down her inhibitions and defenses and relieved her doubts and suspicions.

"No, I'm not uncomfortable. This is probably the most comfortable I've ever been. I feel like I can be myself when I'm around you."

He smiled and then he got out and opened her door. He put his hand on the small of her back as they walked to the house. When he opened the door, she was amazed. Just inside the living room was a large couch with big, overstuffed cushions that beckoned her to lose herself in them. There was a fireplace along one wall with a picture of a beautiful woman on the mantle. Rachel was drawn to it like a magnet. The woman's smile was generous, and her eyes showed a complete love for the man behind the camera.

"That was my wife, Tara. This is Emily."

He handed her a small photo of a smiling little girl with her arms wrapped tightly around Robert's neck.

His voice cracked as he continued. "She died in the same accident that took her mother. Tara was twenty-nine. Emily was only five. So much life still left ahead of them ..."

Robert stared at the picture. A tear streamed down his face, but no other emotion showed through. After a few seconds he collected himself, wiping his face.

"I wanted you to see them. I needed you to know everything. I love them, and I always will. No matter what happens, there will be a place in my memory they'll always occupy. A part of me will always be empty because they aren't there."

Rachel started to speak, but he raised his hand to silence her.

"But, since I met you that night at Chappee's, I've known that you were special. The first time I saw you sitting alone at that booth, I felt like there was something there. You put me at ease. When I'm with you, it doesn't hurt anymore."

Suddenly it all seemed to make sense. She'd been drawn to Robert because of a growing emptiness she'd felt for a long time. Robert had filled a void in her life that Derek had never been able to. At the same time, she'd done the same for Robert. The feelings they were experiencing for each other—whether real or not—were created more from need than love. They were two hurting people who were tired of being alone. If the relationship lasted or ended tomorrow was unimportant. What was important was just the here and now, and the comfort they could give each other at this moment in their lives.

With her heart pounding, Rachel kissed him. She touched his face and felt the moist trail where the tear had been moments earlier. They held each other and kissed a long moment. In that kiss she felt her inhibitions die away. She didn't want to be alone anymore. Then he pulled her toward the hallway and into his bedroom.

Outside the window of the bedroom looking in, a video camera mounted on a tripod came to life and began to record.

TWENTY

THE NEXT MORNING, DEREK went to the Masons' to see Scott. He had to carry a load that would take him away for a few days, but he couldn't leave without seeing his son.

Sarah answered the door and invited him into the house. He could see the worried look on her face. Before Derek could ask if everything was all right, Scott came bouncing down the stairs and straight to his father. Derek squeezed him and thought he might never let go.

"Hey, buddy, how've you been?"

Scott grinned. "Great. I've missed you, Dad."

Derek gripped his son's shoulders tightly. "I've missed you, too, little guy."

Sarah turned to go, but Derek called to her. "Sarah, is Rachel around?"

Sarah stopped with her back to him and hesitated before turning to face him. She cleared her throat. "Well, Derek, as a matter of fact, she isn't. I, um, think she must have had to get to work early. When I went upstairs to get Scott ready for school, she'd already left."

Derek stared at her for a moment as the truth began to dawn on him. Rachel hadn't come home last night and Sarah had no idea where she was.

"I ... I can take Scott to school if it'll help. I have to head to work anyway, so it's no trouble."

Sarah smiled and nodded. Her eyes, filled with compassion, locked on his.

Derek sent Scott to get his backpack. As soon as the boy left the room, Sarah hugged Derek. "I'm praying for you both, Derek. I believe God will take this situation and turn it around. We just have to trust him."

Derek gave her a weak half smile. "You know, you're the second person in two days to tell me something like that. With all you folks praying for me, shouldn't I be seeing some results by now?"

Before she could answer, Scott ran back to him and took his hand. Derek smiled at his son and then turned to Sarah.

"I'll be out of town for about five days. I'll be home by Monday, but if you need me before then, call the trucking company. They'll know how to get in touch with me."

Sarah nodded. "Be careful."

With Scott leading the way, Derek headed back to his truck. His son talked all the way to school, and Derek tried as hard as he could to listen and participate in the conversation, but his mind was thinking only of Rachel.

Ian sat in his apartment looking at the screen on his laptop. The notes from the night before were open in the e-mail he'd just received. It was a complete dead end. Whitney had acted like the perfect host to his guests, left the table only once for about ten minutes, and then departed with his date.

Ian considered adding that Whitney was a generous tipper, but didn't.

Digging into Whitney's history had yielded some interesting things though. According to his inside contact, Whitney's past hadn't always been so good. He'd started as the literal starving artist, creating freeware programs and posting them on the Internet in an attempt to gain recognition. When he wasn't writing code, he would test his skills in other areas by illegally entering other companies' computers and looking around. Laypersons called this operation "hacking," though it was more technically considered "cracking." If he couldn't get in, he would find ways to get information on systems by calling and impersonating someone from the company's satellite office somewhere, often running into a helpful member of the IT staff who would be only too happy to help a fellow employee. Armed with a new username and password, he'd enter but never touch.

But cracking and social engineering wasn't where the big money was to be made. After a couple of complex database programs and an impressive virtual-reality game sold, he started programming full-time. He opened Whitney Edge Software and became a professional from that point on.

Ian put his head in his hand. He never liked turning up a dead-end for a client—especially when he knew there was something there to be found. He'd continue his surveillance, but he didn't know what he was looking for. Whitney would act as normal as anyone, but then he'd do something suspicious that proved there was more to this whole business than Ian was seeing.

His inside contact hadn't been able to plant the small software program on Whitney's computer that would track his keystrokes and online activities. Whitney seldom left his computer untouched during the day, and even when he did, he kept some amazing security program running on it. And Ian doubted that Whitney would be stupid enough to open a program attached to an e-mail from someone he didn't know.

He walked to a shelf in his living room and pulled down a small cardboard box. Inside were various adapters and plugs. After digging through the jumbled mess, he located the exact item he was looking for and replaced the box. In his hand lay a round plug about two inches long. It was a keystroke logger that would do just as well as the program he wanted installed on Whitney's computer. The downside was this device wasn't like a tidy little program he could run from the safety of his apartment. This hardware had to be installed on Whitney's computer between the keyboard plug and the tower itself.

It would be tricky, but if he timed it right, it could be done.

Walking back to his bedroom, Ian began to work out the details of his plan.

"But I didn't take any advance like that. I don't even own that type of credit card. I don't understand." Chris Rickles wiped his beaded forehead with the back of his sleeve.

For the past five minutes, he'd found himself threatened with a nasty lawsuit if he didn't start paying on the cash advance he'd taken on a credit-card account he'd opened three months earlier. Try as Chris might to deny taking anything of the sort, the man on the phone merely repeated to him his Social Security number, address, and even checking-account number. Chris didn't know what to say.

The man on the line was insistent. "Mr. Rickles, it's on record here. Our systems show that you cashed the check three months ago. By cashing the check, you signed an agreement that stated we can request the entirety of the loan at once if you're consistently late on your payments."

Chris's voice rose two pitches. "But I keep trying to tell you that I didn't take out a loan on a card. I know you have all my information somehow, but I didn't take out any kind of loan, and I don't even have a card from your bank."

The voice on the phone didn't waiver. "Mr. Rickles, I'm trying to work with you here, but if you don't make some form of payment by the end of the week I'm afraid we're going to have to take collection actions. That *will* hurt your credit rating, sir."

Chris swallowed hard and tried to sound calm. "Just how much money am I supposed to have taken out?"

"Ten thousand dollars."

Chris fell onto the couch next to the phone.

"T-ten thousand dollars. I don't have anywhere near that much money."

The voice on the line seemed to perk up. "That's all right, Mr. Rickles. Let's talk about how much you can send for your first payment."

After arguing with the man for twenty minutes, Chris got the information on when and where the check was cashed. It was time to start investigating.

An hour later the phone rang again. This time Chris was a little more apprehensive when answering, and his fears were well founded.

The man on the phone spoke curtly and professionally. "Mr. Rickles, this is Bill down at Addams BMW here in Birmingham. Sir, we need to talk about your account."

Before Chris could recover long enough to explain that he didn't own a BMW, the man started.

It was turning into the worst day of his life.

When Charlie arrived for work, Robert and Rachel were already there. They were both seated in Robert's office, laughing and talking. When they finally noticed him, they waved, and Robert said something that caused Rachel to burst out laughing again.

Charlie headed to his workstation. It was nice to see his boss recovering so well, although he still felt uneasy about it all. But after the wonderful date he'd had last night, there was nothing that could bring him down today.

By the time the rest of the crew arrived and the day was in full swing, Charlie was lost in his work. His mind swam among the lines of code on the screen before him. Amy typed beside him, but managed a quick bump with her elbow on his from time to time.

He leaned toward her. "I had a great time last night."

Amy kept typing. "Me, too. Can I ask you a question?"

"Sure."

"Why didn't you try to kiss me good night last night? You're the only guy I've ever gone out with who didn't at least try."

"Well, I … I guess I didn't want to ruin the beautiful evening by having you slap my face."

"Seriously, why?"

He turned to face her. She stopped typing and returned his look.

"Because you're the first woman I've ever met that I didn't want to take a chance of losing. Because I didn't want to presume you'd kiss me just because you agreed to dinner. Mostly though, it's because I'd like our first kiss to be perfect in every way. I hope I get a chance to show you what I mean someday."

Amy's expression didn't change for a few seconds, then her eyes narrowed, and a smile crept across her face. "You're the sweetest man I've ever known, Charlie Bolton. And you know what's so sad?"

"What?"

Amy touched his hand. "The only guy I've ever dated who didn't try to kiss me good night is the one I've wanted to kiss the most."

Charlie felt the color rise to his cheeks. "Well, does this mean you're free Friday night?"

Amy's melodic laugh flowed between them. "You couldn't keep me away if you tried. Pick me up at eight."

She turned back to her computer. As Charlie turned to his own monitor, she called over to him without breaking the rhythmic typing of her keyboard.

"Oh, and Charlie ..."

"Yeah?"

"This time ... kiss me."

TWENTY-ONE

THE NEXT MORNING, ROBERT arrived at work an hour early. He called Starline Trucking. It was time to let Gordon James know that he hadn't escaped unscathed.

"Starline Trucking, may I help you?" The female voice sounded as perky as ever.

Robert lowered the pitch of his voice. "Yes, may I speak to Gordon James, please?"

"Sure. Just a minute."

Robert heard the line click, and his ears were assaulted with the piped-in strains of some classic rock tune for several seconds while he waited to be transferred.

"Gordon James speaking."

Robert kept calm and continued to disguise his voice. "Mr. James, this is Earl Sparkman at Visa. How are you today?"

"Fine. What's this about?"

"Well, sir, your account is one of many I'm in charge of monitoring, and I notice you've had a number of charges to your account from out of state. I wanted to make sure you'd authorized them. If not, someone may have used your account number. If that's the case, we can close your account and report the card stolen."

He heard James shuffle in his chair. He had his attention now.

"What kind of charges? I haven't used the card lately."

"It appears you've had about five hundred dollars put on your account in the past few days."

He heard James sputter. "Five hundred dollars? I haven't charged anything like that. Cancel the card. I'm not paying."

Robert spoke with a soothing tone. "We can definitely do that, Mr. James. Don't worry about a thing. You're covered with our company for up to a thousand dollars of unauthorized charges, so don't worry about having to pay it back. I just need to confirm some information, and we'll close the account."

James' voice sounded calmer now. "Okay, that's good. What can I do? Do you need me to give you the account number?"

Robert's eyes narrowed as a half grin crossed his face. "Oh, no sir. You should never give that information out over the phone. I just need you to confirm that this is your account. Can you give me your Social Security number?"

Within minutes, Robert had it. He told James that the account was closed and asked him to cut up his card, then hung up. He looked at the sheet of paper in front of him and chuckled.

Turning to his computer, he decided it was time to do some damage to Gordon James' way of life.

Silent and unobserved, a small device on the back of Robert's computer began to take note of everything he typed.

Derek was miserable.

He drove on instinct, his mind on nothing but Rachel and how he could fix things between them. He debated coming clean about everything, but still he couldn't see how that would work. There was nothing that could be done about it now, and all being honest about it could accomplish was to diminish him further in her eyes. She'd accused him of not being a man, and the fact that he'd run away from his problem rather than facing it did nothing to dispel that notion.

Derek came to the same decision he'd reached earlier: He'd have to show Rachel what kind of person Robert Whitney really was. If he could get her to realize that Whitney was just using her, then maybe she'd give her husband another chance.

Why hadn't he heard something? Richardson had promised to let him know the minute they had found out anything. Whitney carefully covered his tracks, but the man had to rest sometime. There had to come a time when he would relax his guard just enough for someone to get through to him.

Derek would be home in two days. By then, Richardson should have at least a little something he could use to show Rachel that her new boss wasn't who he seemed to be.

And if all else failed, Derek knew just the perfect spot to bury Whitney's body where nobody would ever find it.

Terrance Gold finished his coffee and put down his morning paper. Since he wasn't scheduled to work until that evening, he wasn't in any particular hurry. He was still sitting at his kitchen table in his jogging shorts and shirt.

He thought back to the fiasco of a few nights ago when he'd gone to Marigold's for the free dinner he had been promised and found that they'd never heard of him. Things had gotten ugly until he'd pulled his badge and let the manager know that his next trip on Alabama's highways wouldn't be pleasant if things weren't resolved to his liking. The look on the manager's face at that moment still brought a smile to Terrance's face.

He looked around the cluttered kitchen. Adult magazines were everywhere now thanks to the sudden string of them that had magically begun appearing in his mailbox. With a curse, he grabbed the magazines and tossed them into the garbage can until it was full.

When he was finished, he took the trash out and put it in the outside can. The garbage wouldn't run until Monday, but he wanted the stuff out of his house. His instinct told him something was wrong.

He booted up his computer and went online for a quick check on some sports scores. Among the many e-mails he received was one that was headed: *For you from Janine.* Terrance smiled at the thought of her sending him something and opened it. There was an attachment that was named "oursong.MP3." He clicked it, and within seconds an unfamiliar tune began playing through his computer speakers. He frowned, confused about why this unknown song should be considered "their song," and stopped it before it was halfway through.

Must have gotten me confused with some other boyfriend.

Without a second thought, he deleted the file and continued his Web surfing.

The deleted file disappeared from his hard drive, but the small program he had executed by playing it did not. In the background of all his activity, the tiny virus replicated and renamed itself, then began to use a small amount of bandwidth from Terrance's Internet connection.

TWENTY-TWO

THAT NIGHT, IAN RICHARDSON checked his e-mail and went straight to the ones from the logger on Robert Whitney's computer. Whitney had been busy.

Ian looked over every e-mail and printed a few. Most were routine business and various lines of programming code that meant nothing to him. His inside contact knew all about that, so he forwarded questionable parts of the e-mail. He logged information from others, and began a file to present to Morrison. None of it was legal, but Morrison didn't want a court case; he just wanted something to show his wife.

When he finished checking everything, he called Bishop.

"Levi, I think we're finally starting to get somewhere. Nothing concrete yet, but we're heading in the right direction."

The big man's voice was polite, but tired. "Good. Need I ask where you're getting this information?"

Ian chuckled. "It's better you don't know. Your work ethic is a little loftier than mine."

Bishop sighed. "All right. But one Sunday morning I'm dragging you to church with me, and we're gonna fix all this once and for all."

"Well, until that day comes, you just keep praying for me. Besides, if I get all straightened up, I might have to go into another line of work."

Bishop let out a weary laugh. "I doubt it. You'd just approach the job a little differently, that's all."

"Is everything okay, Levi? You don't sound so good."

Silence. Then, "Yeah, everything's okay. Just thinking about Derek and the whole situation and doing a lot of praying. Derek will be back in town tomorrow, and I plan to update him. I'm glad I can give him a little good news."

Ian wondered how Bishop could have such a compassionate heart. "You know, Levi, you're really a great guy. Don't tell anyone I said that 'cause I'll just deny it if you do, but I'm glad you're working with me. You were always the better communicator of the two of us."

Bishop chuckled. "You should hear me preach sometime. Oh, and by the way, I tape every phone conversation, so expect to hear that compliment played back to you someday."

"Get some sleep, Levi."

Ian turned back to the files he'd printed out and started making notes. He knew it would take a few more days of hard evidence, but it would happen.

The noose around Robert Whitney's neck was tightening.

Robert picked up Rachel and Scott at seven for ice cream. Scott had been unusually quiet during the drive, but Rachel had managed to pull him into the conversation from time to time. This was their first outing together, and it was important for her to see how Robert and Scott would interact.

Rachel knew it was far too soon to think of anything permanent in her future, but she was enjoying the present. Things were still unresolved with Derek, and there was a part of her that had started to miss him. The situation with Robert had progressed too fast, and their one night of passion hadn't been discussed. There'd been no attempt by either of them to repeat it. She didn't know if Robert was being a gentleman or was just too shy to talk about it.

The mood in the car changed when Robert started talking about comic books. Scott perked up and began to chatter about various superheroes and things they were doing. By the time they got to the ice-cream shop, Rachel started to worry that his constant talking would wear on Robert, but it didn't happen. For every fact Scott could pull out about a superhero's secret identity, Robert could match it with some obscure villain that was involved with them somehow.

"Superman or the Hulk—who would win?" Robert asked with a smile.

A lopsided grin crossed Scott's face. "Easy ... the Hulk, of course. The madder he gets, the stronger he gets."

Robert raised a finger. "Yes, but what if Superman grabbed him and threw him into outer space? Hulk's got to breathe sometime."

The conversation continued for a while, but Rachel didn't try to join in. She was enjoying this moment. While she never wanted anyone to take Derek's place in Scott's life, it was nice to know that Robert and Scott could get along so well.

When Scott laughed at something Robert said, a pang of guilt hit Rachel. What was she doing? She still couldn't decide whether she should try to reconcile with Derek or give up on their marriage. Since that night he'd barged in on her dinner with Robert, she hadn't spoken to him very much. How was he feeling? How was his work going? She used to know such things, along with the thousands of other little details married people share.

Her chest tightened again as she remembered how her mother had mentioned Derek's stopping by and taking Scott to school a few days ago. It was the morning after she'd allowed her passions to get away with her. She regretted taking this new relationship in that direction so soon. Robert was still kind and cordial as he'd always been, but there seemed to be just a little coldness there she hadn't noticed before. It was like a part of him regretted it as much as she did.

Rachel's eyes continued to jump between Scott and Robert. She weighed the consequences of her actions over the past few weeks and compared them to the years of marriage she'd shared with Derek.

Maybe it's time to talk to him again. I think I'll find out how he's doing.

It was almost as though time had ground to a halt over the past two days for Derek. Every mile on the road seemed to take forever; and even though he'd driven almost all night long the previous evening, it still seemed that home wasn't getting closer.

Richardson had been optimistic when they'd talked on the phone yesterday. He had also called Sarah to see how Scott was, and then called his house to check his answering-machine messages. There were two. One was from Richardson, and the other was several seconds of silence, then the sound of someone hanging up.

He parked his truck at Starline Trucking and jumped out. He left the paperwork for the last trip in the office and then ran to his pickup. He couldn't wait to call Richardson and find out what was going on.

The drive home took less than twenty minutes. He stopped at the mailbox to retrieve the mail from the past couple of days. Among the bills and junk mail, there was a padded mailing envelope with his name and address on it. There was no return address, but the postage showed it came from Birmingham. He put the other mail on the seat beside him and tore open the package. Inside he found a black videocassette with a small white label on it that read: "Enjoy."

Derek's brow furrowed. He pulled into the driveway and headed inside. Stopping only long enough to grab a Coke from the refrigerator, he crossed his living room and put the tape into the VCR.

At first he couldn't really distinguish anything. Then the auto focus on the camera must have come on because shapes began to form. He could tell that whatever he was watching was filmed from outside because he could hear crickets chirping and wind blowing against the microphone.

Through the window, he could see a man and woman kissing. Derek's eyes widened as he recognized the woman. He slid toward the television screen until he was mere inches from it.

Rachel.

Whitney had taken things to an entirely new level of cruelty.

Derek closed his eyes as anger bubbled up. He turned away so he wouldn't see anything else. He turned off the television and walked to the kitchen. The soft-drink can in his hand had felt cool and refreshing at first, but now it seemed to match the coldness of his own soul. He yelled and threw it across the room, watching it explode against the wall.

He wasn't finished yet.

He grabbed the edge of his kitchen table to flip it over, but then he spotted the blinking light of his answering machine. He hurried to it and pressed the play button.

"Hi, Derek." It was Rachel's voice. "I know we haven't talked in a while, but I wanted to see how you were doing. I guess this is pretty stupid of me to call like this, but I just wanted to check on you. I'm sure you're probably out on the road or something. Give me a call when you get back. Okay?"

Derek collapsed on the couch and let his head fall back. He tried to steady his breathing, but it wasn't easy. His first instinct was to call and let her have it, but he realized she was as much a victim as he was. Robert Whitney was very good at what he did. Instead, Derek looked over at the VCR.

Whitney had just made a huge mistake.

Derek now had evidence to show Rachel.

He called Bishop and told him about the tape. Bishop couldn't believe it either.

"What are you going to do?" Derek asked.

"I think it's time for me to go and talk to Mr. Robert Whitney myself."

At midnight, Chris Rickles woke to the sound of screaming.

He stumbled out of bed and scrambled for any kind of weapon he could use. He settled on an old cowboy boot and crept from the room holding it like a hammer.

He narrowed the source of the scream down to the living room. He peeked around the corner to look in.

His computer was screaming.

Chris dropped the boot and cocked his head. He crossed the room and turned down the speakers. He'd left the computer on as he always did, and now the screen showed a small gray box that read: *Do I have your attention?*

He clicked on the button marked "Yes" underneath the phrase. The box closed, and another one opened.

Good. Now watch carefully—this will be fun!

Below the words, his file system opened. Before he could move, files began to delete themselves. He saw that the most important and personal ones were the first to go. He punched buttons on the keyboard in a desperate attempt to stop it.

It did not respond.

He moved the mouse cursor again to find something to click, but every time he got near the window, it would jump to the other side of the screen. Within seconds, his hard drive was almost blank. It was obvious that it had been deleting files long before he got there.

Then the words changed again.

Still with me? Excellent! This is where it gets interesting.

A small box opened, and Chris gasped. The computer had been connected to the Internet for some unknown period of time—and it had been busy.

His printer began to spit out screen captures of various Web pages. First was his bank's Web site showing his checking account had a negative balance of two thousand dollars. Next, he found the Web site for his savings account that showed a zero balance.

His heart thudded against his rib cage. The next sheet was a DMV Web site search for his license number that pulled up several traffic violations he'd never seen before. Web sites from each of his credit cards listed delinquent accounts turned over to collections agencies, and then he found that the finance company that held his mortgage showed his account also six months delinquent and his house on a pending repossession list.

Chris couldn't breathe. As each page poured from the printer, his stomach tightened. Finally, the printer spit out three more pages and stopped. Chris gingerly reached for them, and saw that they were from national Web sites that did background checks and people searches. Three Web sites had searched for his name, Social Security number, and current address.

Somehow, he'd become a wanted man in two states, and a deadbeat dad—even though he had no children.

Then he saw the screen change again.

You've been a bad boy, haven't you? Now pardon me while I clean up this mess ...

A loud grinding noise screeched from the computer tower. As Chris stood in shock, the computer screen went blank, and everything was silent.

He had been in the room for less than three minutes.

He scrambled to the phone and called his bank's toll-free number to check his account balance. He entered the same PIN number he'd used a thousand times before, but the recorded message confirmed what the computer printouts had stated.

He collapsed on his couch, still holding the printouts. He was stunned and had no idea what to do next. As soon as the businesses opened in the morning, he'd call to check the DMV and SSA himself, but he didn't hold high hopes for what he'd find. The meager amount of cash he kept on hand wouldn't last for long, and he had no way to get to the rest of his money.

As impossible as it seemed, his entire life had just been rewritten.

TWENTY-THREE

THE NEXT MORNING, ROBERT noticed his computer was responding a little slower than usual. Anyone else probably wouldn't have detected the slight difference, but Robert had become so accustomed to his machine he could detect the slightest sign of a virus or other problem. A thorough virus scan returned negative results, so he moved to the next level of troubleshooting: hardware.

He went to the supply closet and pulled out one of the extra keyboards he kept there. As he knelt behind his tower to unplug the old one, he found the keyboard plugged through an adapter of some sort. Robert recognized it immediately. Someone had been gathering information from his computer, and he had no idea how long it had been going on.

He looked around the room. The others were at their own workstations tirelessly programming. Rachel was also at her terminal, concentrating on a spreadsheet.

Maybe they were innocent—but then who else would have access to his computer?

He sat back in his chair and tried to think. If he disconnected the logger, then whoever was getting the information would notice and possibly try something different. Maybe this time they'd do something he couldn't catch.

Common sense told him the only way the data could go out would be with his e-mails. He would notice any other information dumps as soon as they happened. That being the case, he could track the program down in his computer and see where it was going.

When he had that knowledge, he could send the snoop a very special surprise.

For the remainder of the day, he would work on his terminal as usual, but he would use his laptop for his "extra projects." And when the logger sent its file for the day, there would be something extra going with it.

As Rachel was going over the financials for the company, the phone rang. She cleared her throat as she answered. "Whitney Edge Software, how may I direct your call?"

"Rachel?"

She froze. She hadn't heard the voice in a long time, and it seemed strange to hear it now.

"Derek?"

There was a pause. "Hey. How've you been?"

Rachel glanced back toward Robert, who was typing away on his laptop. "I'm fine"

"Good. Listen, I won't keep you because I know you're at work. I wanted to see if you'd have dinner with me tonight. I have something I really need to show you."

Rachel fought to control the knot that was building in her stomach. "Derek, it's nice to hear from you, but I don't know if it's such a good idea to—"

"Rachel, please, it's important."

His words seemed to carry such an air of sincerity. Rachel couldn't remember the last time she'd heard him like this. "Derek, if you're trying something, I can tell you now I'm not going to buy it. We've been through this too many times."

"I'm not trying anything, I promise. I just need to see you. Just this once, and then I swear I'm gone forever if you want."

"Okay, Derek, if it's important. When and where?"

"Tonight, six o'clock. I can pick you up at your parents' house."

"No, I'll meet you at the restaurant." Rachel felt that her words might be a little harsh, but she didn't want to make things too easy at the start.

There was a pause. "All right, I'll meet you at Antonio's at six, but I need to show you something after dinner. It's actually why I'm suggesting we get together, so I'm telling you up front about it. I'm not trying to put any moves on you or anything, really."

"All right, I'll see you there tonight."

She started to say good-bye, but he spoke first. "Rachel?"

"Yes?"

"It's great to hear your voice again."

Before she could reply, he hung up. She gently replaced the receiver. Resting her head in her hand, she picked up a pen and tried to concentrate on the spreadsheet before her. Somewhere in the room, one of the computers was playing a collection of instrumental MP3s that floated through the air and filled the space with a peaceful feeling. Every face was intently gazing at the monitor before it, and she could hear the rhythmic tapping of the keyboards in front of each one. Occasionally, Amy whispered something to Charlie, but the rest of the programmers were silent.

Rachel turned to look at Robert again. He was now dividing his time equally between his laptop and his desktop workstation. He was truly a handsome man, and he'd treated her well, but there was something wrong. For some inexplicable reason, she'd begun to feel she couldn't trust him. Since that night at his house, things had cooled between them, almost as if he'd made his conquest with her and was growing tired of her. And now she regretted how fast their relationship had progressed. She'd been hurt and lonely, but had acted more like a hormone-driven teenager than a woman.

She turned to face the front again. Returning to work on the spreadsheet before her, she found her mind drifting to dinner.

Charlie completed an invoice for a project Tom and Jonathan had finished earlier that day. It was going to be a nice sum, as both men had worked tirelessly in getting it done in record time. They were now on separate projects, and neither seemed worried. Jonathan had remained as aloof as always, and Charlie still didn't completely trust the man. There was something about him that didn't sit right.

Tom, on the other hand, was as jovial and happy as ever. His workstation up front appeared to be his favorite place on earth, and Charlie was glad. He'd found that giving an assignment to Tom was tantamount to telling the customer the job was finished.

As for Amy, well, what could he say? She was at least his equal in hacking together complex code, and she never seemed to feel pressure as a deadline approached. If a customer called with a tech-support question—no matter how ignorant it was—Amy was always willing to talk to them.

Robert was coming on strong now and giving everyone a run for his or her money. He had his hands in everything they did and wanted to know every single thing that went out. He still wasn't quite the same as he used to be, but he was back and ready to work. That made Charlie feel better.

Charlie e-mailed the invoice to Rachel to be sent out. He hated to admit it, but having a full-time bookkeeper had come in handy and took a load off him. He hadn't supported the decision to hire her initially, but he was glad Robert hadn't listened to him.

Rachel came up to his desk and dropped two small packages on it. "These are for you," she said with a smile. "Did you win something on eBay again?"

Charlie turned them around to read the return label. "No, this is something better."

Reaching into his pocket, he pulled out his Swiss Army knife and cut open the top box. Inside, placed carefully in neat rows, was a series of small rectangles of paper. He pulled one out and handed it to Rachel.

The bright red logo reflected the light from the fixtures above.

"'Whitney Edge Software,'" Rachel read aloud. "'Charlie Bolton, Head of Product Development.'" Whistling, she handed it back to him. "Not bad."

Amy stopped typing long enough to intercept the card before it reached Charlie's hand. "Well, well, sounds like you're moving up in the world, boss." With a wink, Amy slipped the card into her pocket. "Never know when I might need to get in touch with the big man."

Charlie shook his head and stood. Picking up the other small package, he walked to Robert's office. "Hey, chief. Got a sec?"

Robert looked up from his computer. "Sure. Have a seat."

Charlie put the package on Robert's desk and sat back in an empty chair nearby. "Check it out, O Great One."

Robert cocked an eyebrow. Opening the package, he saw the neat rows of business cards inside. He pulled one out and nodded.

"'Robert Whitney, President/Senior Software Engineer.' Boy, sounds pretty important."

Charlie pulled out a small stack of cards and slid them into Robert's shirt pocket. "We have gone professional, my friend. It's time for us to look that way. You keep those handy for prospective clients, all right? And you don't even have to do any of the work; you just need to send them to me."

Robert laughed. "All right, I can tell when I'm slowly being ousted. At least my name's still on the company logo."

Charlie stood. "For now." He gave Robert a "you never know" look, and returned to his desk.

Amy stepped away from her workstation as Charlie put his cards away. He watched her leave the room, then glanced over at her monitor. He knew she was working on a software patch for CyberCross and their "Barney the Battlin' Beaver" game Robert had created a couple of months ago. Her screen indicated that her computer was compiling code, so he thought it best to leave it alone. As his hands moved to his keyboard, he bumped Amy's optical mouse and saw the screen change.

If that was just a screensaver, then what's she working on?

He looked at the monitor and began to read. He didn't have to finish it to know exactly what he was looking at.

Without a word, he got up and walked toward the back of the office, following Amy.

Robert used his laptop to log into the Web-based e-mail he'd created for his clandestine activities. There were only two messages, but they were both good news. Chris Rickles was now officially out of the picture, and Terrance Gold's computer was filling its cache with the things Robert wanted it to. And through it all, he was untouched—and untouchable.

He logged out of the account and decided to do some research on keystroke loggers. He wanted to know who was watching him. Had someone found out what he was doing? And if so, what were they going to do with the information?

Robert had been using an anonymizer for his Web activities. The anonymizer was a program that allowed him to surf the Web invisibly. Most people never realized that their every movement on the Internet was easily traceable. Every Web site they visited, every picture they viewed, every form they filled out—all could be easily pulled up later by someone with the right tools. Even erasing the computer's history wouldn't stop them. Only something like the program Robert was now using would safely mask their "footsteps" on the Web. And every time Robert logged off, the computer erased everything in its cache and every temporary file stored anywhere on it. There was only one directory on Robert's laptop that was never touched by the program, and it was encrypted so securely that anyone entering an incorrect password twice would automatically format the hard drive. He had thought of everything.

He went to an online surveillance store and browsed their computer equipment. He saw a picture of the exact adapter currently residing on the back of his computer and wrote down all the relevant information about it.

Charlie found Amy in the back room. She was bent over the laser printer installing a toner cartridge.

"Hey there."

Amy jumped. "Whoa! Don't go sneaking up on beautiful women like that. You almost gave me a heart attack."

Charlie smiled and looked down at the printer. "Having problems?"

Amy glanced at the cartridge in her hand and shrugged. "Not really … just changing this sucker out again."

Charlie nodded and waited. Both of them stood in silence for a few awkward seconds, and then Amy grinned. "Did you need something, or were you just coming back here to scare me?"

Charlie pursed his lips and reached for the toner cartridge. "Oh, I was printing up an invoice and noticed the computer saying the printer was offline. I came back here to fix it, and there you were."

Amy gave him a funny look and pulled the cartridge back slightly. "Well, I guess I should have been faster. I'll have it changed in a jiffy. If you want to go start on something else, I'll bring the invoice to you after it's printed."

Charlie stepped forward and took the cartridge from her. "No, that's all right. I've done this a dozen times."

Before Amy could object, he had the cartridge in the printer. As soon as he closed the printer door, it began to whir and take paper from the tray. Charlie turned to see Amy's eyes dart from the printer, trying to act like she wasn't watching it.

"Are you all right?"

She rubbed her palms on her slacks. "What? Oh yeah, sure. I'm just ready to get back in there and finish this code I'm working on."

The printer was spitting out page after page now. It looked like someone else had sent jobs to the printer as well. Charlie pulled off the first few pages as Amy reached for them.

"I'll take those, boss. I—"

Charlie brought the pages close his chest. "What's wrong, Amy? You moonlighting or something?"

Her laugh sounded forced as she raised her eyebrows. "Oh yeah, that's it. It's just something I was working on for you—a surprise. Don't read it now or you'll spoil things."

He looked into her dark-brown eyes. He wanted to ignore what he'd found. He wanted to forget everything and have it all go back to the way it had been just a few minutes earlier. But he couldn't. He had a job to do.

"This is code, Amy. And it's not just any type of code; it's a virus. It's a pretty nasty virus, actually, and I don't think it's something we've authorized for a client. As a matter of fact, from a cursory glance it looks like a stealth virus, and a pretty good one. I should know since I used to write these things in my sleep."

Amy stopped smiling, and her gaze fell. Charlie felt that he was going to die, but he had a job to do.

"Want to tell me about it?"

Amy looked back up at him. "I didn't create it. A friend found it attached to an e-mail that almost wiped out his computer, and I wanted to take a look at it. It's sort of a hobby of mine: I like disassembling viruses to see what makes them tick. I wasn't creating it, I promise. I know I shouldn't have been doing this on company time, but I finished the CyberCross patch and had a few minutes before lunch. It won't happen again. Please, Charlie, believe me."

The corners of Charlie's mouth twitched for a second, and he swallowed hard. His eyes were locked on hers, searching for the truth behind her words. Finally, he found the courage to speak.

"Okay, I believe you."

He saw her shoulders slump. She closed her eyes, and a thin smile played at her lips.

Charlie's face softened. "I'm sorry to be this way, but it's taken a long time to get the company to this point. One bad thing can permanently damage our standing with our clients. Intentionally putting a virus in our software would definitely fall under the category of a 'bad thing.' I hope you understand."

Amy nodded. "It was wrong to do this on company time. It's just that my printer at home is messed up, and I wanted to look at this today during lunch. It's a fascinating virus, and one of the best stealth versions I've ever seen."

Charlie looked at the printouts again. "Well, I'm pretty good at this stuff too. Do you mind if I take a look at it?"

Amy's face brightened. "I'd love it. Two great minds on this thing? We'll have this baby defeated in no time."

They turned to leave and froze. Jonathan stood in the doorway. His face was an unreadable mask. "Are those my printouts?"

Charlie glanced at the papers in his hand. "No, these are mine. We just put another toner cartridge in the printer, though, so yours may still be queued."

Jonathan nodded and turned to go back to his workstation. Amy and Charlie exchanged a quick glance, then Charlie shrugged his shoulders, and they walked back to their desks.

When Charlie sifted through the pages again, he found that Amy's virus code ended after the first five pages. The next seven pages were filled with a whole new set of codes.

This must have been what Jonathan was looking for. I guess I'll get them back to him.

As he stood to find Jonathan, he froze. Staring at the pages in his hand, he felt his knees buckle. His mouth was hanging open. He closed it and swallowed.

He flipped through the pages again and again to be sure of what he was seeing.

Jonathan had been working on a virus of his own.

It made the one Amy was studying look like a joke.

Jonathan's virus was a Trojan Horse. When it was activated, it allowed the hacker complete and total access to every part of the victim's computer. What made this virus especially deadly was the fact that it hijacked the person's modem without their knowledge. They might leave their computer on while they went to work, or shopping, or to bed, and their computer would dial out in silence. It was one of the most complex things Charlie had ever seen, because it had so many commands to execute automatically once it dialed out that it made any human interaction unnecessary. It basically did a ton of things, like visiting particular Web sites, carrying out commands at each one, and downloading certain files and pictures; then it reported the results back to the programmer, and finally erased itself from the victim's computer. By the time they realized something was wrong and ran a virus scan, there would be nothing to find. They'd breathe a sigh of relief and never realize that the damage had already been done.

Charlie managed to take a few breaths and calm himself. Without another word to Amy, he gathered the pages and turned toward Robert's office. He could see that Robert was busy with a phone call, so he decided to get some fresh air. Giving Rachel a quick wave on his way to the door, Charlie left to try and figure out what in the world was going on with his employees.

Robert beamed with pride as he looked at the virus on his laptop's screen. He felt it was the best he'd ever written, and he knew without a doubt it was the most destructive. Now Robert wished he could see the look on the intruder's face.

He moved back to his workstation and typed carefully, knowing that someone else was watching his every move. It was time to put out the bait and see if the watcher would follow it.

TWENTY-FOUR

CHARLIE WALKED TO LINN Park and found a perfect spot to sit on the grass. This was his favorite place to think. In the middle of downtown Birmingham amid the towering buildings on all sides sat one city block that was nothing but grass and trees. It was The Magic City's own budget version of New York's Central Park. Since it was only four blocks from Whitney Edge Software, he'd often found it relaxing to come here and meditate on whatever was bothering him. Whenever a program just wasn't coming along as it should, it was time to go to the park.

He sat leaning against a tall tree near the center of the grass and closed his eyes. So much was going on around him, and it was starting to get to him. His boss was in his own world, leaving him in charge of the company, and his employees were doing things he couldn't explain. He didn't know what to do. The right thing would obviously be to fire them, but he couldn't afford to lose them right now. Since they'd been turning out such consistently good work, they'd added a few new customers to the roster. It was actually time to start hiring more folks and looking for a bigger office, not cutting out half the crew in one sweep.

And then there was Amy. He knew that his feelings for her were well beyond any employer-employee relationship. He had no idea what he was supposed to do next.

He pulled his knees up and rested his elbows on them, then put his head in his hands.

This would probably be so easy for Robert to fix, but I don't want him to think I can't handle things on my own. I'm in charge of this company, so I need to act like it.

His thoughts were so intense that the footsteps barely registered until they were right on him. He opened his eyes and saw a pair of feet. Slowly, he raised his head and looked into the face of the smiling man standing before him, black hair tousled by the breeze. The man crouched down on the balls of his feet with his arms resting on his knees. His deep brown eyes seemed to stare into Charlie's soul. And for some reason, he seemed vaguely familiar.

"Hi, Charlie ... my name's Ian." He held up a small cell phone. "I just got through speaking to a friend of mine, and I understand you may have just discovered a few interesting facts. Before you make any life-changing decisions, you and I need to have a little talk."

Robert looked up as Charlie walked through the front door. He didn't know where Charlie had been for the past hour, but was pretty sure it was the park. It was the only place he would go to in the middle of a busy workday.

He followed Charlie's gait until he sat back down at his workstation and began to type. Amy leaned over toward Charlie, and they whispered something to each other, then it was business as usual.

Robert's eyes narrowed. Of all the people who might be watching him, he'd never considered Charlie—yet of all the people he might suspect, Charlie fit the bill better than any other. He'd been there since before the accident. He'd mentioned several times that Robert had been acting strange lately. He'd seen that screen full of information on Derek Morrison weeks ago. He was usually here alone during lunch hour every day, so he'd have access to Robert's computer.

Why haven't I seen all this before?

Robert decided he'd be more cautious—at least until he figured out who was watching him.

As Robert locked up the office at five thirty, he found his thoughts drifting to Rachel. She'd seemed distant that afternoon. Add that sudden change in Rachel to Charlie's odd behavior, and it really seemed like the world just might be out to get him. Well, it wouldn't be much longer until everything would be wrapped up. After that, things wouldn't matter. If it all worked out as planned—and Robert saw no reason to think it wouldn't—everyone would find out the whole story soon enough. He felt the return of that pang of guilt that came every time he considered how this scheme would hurt Rachel. She'd been a means to an end to begin with, but now he knew her as a person and realized just how great she really was. He pushed her out of his mind. She would hate him when this unsavory business was all over anyway, so why worry about it.

Tonight, he would concentrate on fixing that crooked state trooper once and for all. By morning, Terrance Gold's life would be changed forever. Adding that to the thoughts of what kind of week Chris Rickles must have had made Robert laugh.

But before he finished Terrance Gold, he needed to eat.

As he turned the corner to find a place for dinner, he almost collided with a huge black man wearing sunglasses. The man towered over him ominously, and for an instant Robert was afraid that he might have somehow ticked the man off. Instead, the big man smiled as he took off his sunglasses and gently raised a hand. When the man spoke, his deep voice was kind.

"Sorry about that. I wasn't watching where I was going."

Robert stared in silence for a moment at the man's massive arms and chest, thankful that he seemed friendly. "Sure. No problem."

He nodded and kept walking. Robert watched him and shook his head. If that man wasn't somebody's bodyguard or a professional wrestler, he'd missed his calling.

Ian stood across the street, watching. He had no idea why Bishop was here, or what he'd said to Whitney, but Ian didn't like surprises. After what had happened earlier that day with the near-catastrophic slipup that had brought Charlie Bolton into the fold, Ian felt that he was starting to get too many loose ends in this case. That made him nervous.

He crossed the street and followed Whitney from a safe distance. Rather than stand out, he blended in perfectly with the young professionals who worked in the area.

When Whitney entered a restaurant called Delphines, two blocks from where he worked, Ian gave him five minutes before following. There were several people waiting for a table, but Robert was nowhere to be seen. Ian finally spotted him in the dining room sitting alone and reading a menu.

A girl in a tight dress came up to him and asked if he'd like a table. Ian politely declined and instead took a place at the small bar near the front door. He ordered a ginger ale and sat, keeping Whitney in his peripheral vision.

The activity in the place made it easy to stay inconspicuous. If he nursed the ginger ale lightly, it could last him all the way through Whitney's meal. As soon as he saw Whitney ask for his check, he'd get out the front door first and position himself in the shadows nearby. If Whitney appeared to be heading to his car, Ian would take a more circuitous route to his own vehicle. The guy would never realize he was being shadowed.

The door to the restaurant opened, and several more people milled about. Ian thought about the case and how much longer it might go on. Things were coming to a head now. He was getting information from Whitney's computer, and Derek was supposed to show his wife that videotape tonight. Who knew how things might turn out by morning?

He ignored the door opening again until the bulk of the person entering caught his eye. Ian watched as the new arrival scanned the dining room, totally oblivious to his presence, and then walked to Whitney's table. Whitney looked up and noticed the visitor. Then they exchanged a few brief words that Ian had no hope of hearing. Finally, the uninvited guest took the seat opposite Robert and accepted a menu from the waiter.

Ian could only sit there dumbfounded.

Robert Whitney was about to have dinner ...

... with Levi Bishop.

Derek sat at a table in Antonio's and picked at the edge of the table-cloth. He glanced down at his tie and tried to make certain it was straight. He hadn't worn one in so long that it had taken him almost fifteen minutes to tie it correctly. Twice he'd found himself in a cursing fit fighting it, but it would all be worth it if things went as he hoped this evening.

Finally, he saw her.

Rachel entered and her blue eyes found him quickly. She waved and smiled as she approached. Derek had almost forgotten how beautiful that smile truly was. She was breathtaking.

He stood to his feet and self-consciously straightened his tie again.

She glided across the room and took the seat across the table from him. Derek touched the back of his hair to make sure it wasn't sticking out anywhere. He mentally berated himself for not getting a haircut today.

"You look—" he opened his arms— "wow." He felt stupid and tongue-tied like a teenager again, but the quick smile on Rachel's face put him a little more at ease.

"Thanks. You're looking good too, Derek. I'm glad to see you've been taking care of yourself."

Before he could reply, the waiter came and presented the menus. He took their napkins from the table and placed them across their laps. After listening to the night's specials, they both placed their drink orders. Rachel ordered a glass of red wine, but Derek was careful to avoid any type of alcohol. He couldn't afford to fall off the wagon tonight.

He cleared his throat and watched as the waiter disappeared into a back area. "So, how have you been?" It was a stupid question, and he knew it the moment it came out of his mouth.

"Good. Busy. Things have been pretty steady. How about you?"

Derek nodded. "Busy."

They sat in awkward silence for a few moments, until the waiter mercifully returned with their drinks. Derek sipped his iced tea, his mind searching for something to keep the conversation flowing. Small talk had never been his strong suit.

Rachel lowered her glass and dabbed at her mouth with her napkin. When she finished spreading it back in her lap, she sighed. "So, Derek, what did you need to talk to me about?"

Derek took another long drink of his tea and signaled the waiter for a refill while desperately trying to gather his thoughts. He'd practiced this moment in front of the bathroom mirror. "Rachel, I'm sorry. I wanted to say that first. I know that doesn't fix anything or change anything, but I wanted you to know. I messed up in a huge way, but if you knew everything that had happened, I think you'd understand."

Rachel's expression didn't change, other than the slight rise of an eyebrow at his last statement.

"I know what you're thinking, but I'm right—trust me. Anyway, I wanted tonight to be a night when we could really talk and clear the air. What happened between us happened so fast, and it seemed like—"

Rachel raised a hand. "No, that's where you're wrong. What happened between us had been building for quite some time. Things with your job, our personal life, everything else … it all just added up. That little binge you went on after our fight was just the icing on the cake."

"Rachel, please, about that binge—"

"And then you disappeared for days. I mean, Scott and I were gone after that first night, but I did keep calling to make sure you were all right."

Derek rolled his eyes and tried to keep a civil tone, but her constant interruptions were starting to get on his nerves. "I know, I know. What I did then was wrong too, but I—"

Rachel's eyes narrowed. "And another thing: that little display at the City Lights restaurant—"

Derek's face reddened. "Now just a minute. You're a married woman, and you were having dinner with that guy after I'd been gone less than a week. You didn't even give the body time to get cold before you—"

"Don't you dare!" Rachel brought her hands to her mouth at the outburst. Derek glanced around at the other patrons and saw them cut their eyes toward Rachel. When she spoke again, her voice was lowered, but her tone was hard and cold. "Don't you dare judge me after what I put up with all those years we were married. How many times did I sit in the living room crying all night long because my husband was out drinking himself stupid and doing the worst thing in the world he could do to his wife? How many times did you come to me saying you were sorry and it would never happen again, and things would be great for a few weeks—then you'd be back cheating again? And then you think you have the right to judge me just because some man finds me attractive enough to ask me out to dinner?"

Derek hesitated for a moment thinking she was going to continue, but when she kept looking at him with fire in her eyes, it dawned on him that it was time for his rebuttal. He took another quick sip of his iced tea while the thoughts in his mind tried to find coherence.

"All right, I admit what I did looks bad, but if you'll let me explain, I think you'll understand why I was so upset. It wasn't really that you were eating dinner with another man—though that did hurt—it was the man you were actually having dinner with."

Rachel's eyes narrowed. "How can you say anything about Robert? You don't even know him. He's been nothing but kind to Scott and me, and he's never spoken a bad word against you—even after that episode that night. He's been my friend, and I won't hear you say anything about him. He's a perfect gentleman."

"Rachel, you don't understand. Robert's not what you think he is. He's doing things you don't know about."

Rachel pulled the napkin from her lap and bundled it up, apparently preparing to throw it on the table. "I'm not going to sit here and listen to any more of this. If you want to—"

Derek reached across the table and touched her arm lightly. "Rachel, please don't go. This isn't how I pictured this night going. There's so much I want to tell you, but there's obviously a lot you want to say too. I want to listen to you, but I need you to listen to me, too. I wouldn't say these things if I didn't finally have proof. I'm not here to spit out allegations and lies; I'm here to lay out the truth."

Rachel was silent for several seconds, and then she replaced the napkin in her lap. "This isn't how I pictured this night going either. I'm sorry, but I'm hurt, and this is the first time I've had the opportunity to talk to you about it. It all came out at once."

Derek locked eyes with her, willing her to understand. "Rachel, I know you have no reason to believe a word of what I'm about to say, but I really have changed. I'm different."

Rachel eyed him warily. "Not to seem coldhearted here, but I've heard all this before, Derek. We've played this game so many times now it's not funny. You mess up, I forgive you, things are good for a while, then you hit the road for days on end, and ... I just don't know why I should believe that this time is any different."

"I quit my job today."

Rachel's eyebrows went up. "What? What are you talking about?"

Derek smiled broadly. "I did it. I went right in and told Gordon I was through with that crazy business. He wasn't pleased and wasn't afraid to show it, but what could he do?"

"But, Derek, you love that job. It's all you've ever done."

He chuckled. "I know. Isn't that crazy? But I have to tell you, it feels great. I feel so free. And the thing is, I wasn't the least bit scared about doing it. I just knew it was the right thing to do."

Rachel took a sip of her wine. "But what will you do now?"

"Oh, I'll drive a delivery truck around here or something, anything that'll pay the bills but still let me get home every night. I might not make the money I made doing the long hauls, but I could get a weekend job to make up the difference."

He looked into her eyes and saw that his gamble had paid off. He'd hoped quitting the job would prove how serious he was. She was right: The job had been something he'd loved. Despite the long hours and crazy drivers around him, Derek had always loved the open road and his time on it. She'd tried to get him to quit several times, but each conversation about it ended in a heated argument. But today when he'd considered the most extreme thing he could do to show her his sincerity, the answer had been obvious.

She kept staring in silence, as if to read his mind and figure out what was going on in there. Finally, she was listening.

TWENTY-FIVE

Robert LOOKED ACROSS THE table at the huge man engrossed in the menu. He was still a little uncertain as to how he'd ended up with this unexpected guest.

"Boy, everything looks good, doesn't it?" the man said.

"Yes, I eat here often."

"What do you recommend?"

Another table, Robert thought. "Well, steak is good. They have some great seafood, too, but their offerings are seasonal."

The man chuckled. "Well, I know I'm saving room for the sweets. I passed the dessert tray on the way in, and I think I want one of each."

Robert couldn't help smiling. This man seemed so uncommonly genuine and friendly that he made it hard to be upset at him. "I'm sorry, but what was your name again?"

"Please forgive my manners. Sometimes I get so friendly with folks that I forget the important things. My name's Levi."

A gigantic hand crossed the table. Robert shook it and found Levi's grip firm but not painfully so. "Robert."

The waiter arrived for their orders. Robert ordered a New York

Strip steak, baked potato, and the appropriate wine, while his uninvited guest ordered the Kansas City Cut steak, steamed vegetables, and a glass of water.

When they were alone again, Levi spread his napkin across his lap and leaned back. "I want to thank you again for letting me share your table. Nobody likes to dine alone, and I wasn't looking forward to waiting back there in that crowd."

Robert glanced over Levi's shoulder at the waiting area, packed with hungry bodies scanning the room for anyone about to leave. "Yeah, this place fills up fast."

"I noticed you coming out of Whitney Edge Software. Do you work there?"

"Yes. Actually, I own it."

"Good. I wanted to talk to you about possibly helping my church with some computer problems we've been having lately. I was busy today and couldn't get down here until after you'd closed."

Robert settled back. So this was going to be a business dinner after all. Well, that he could handle.

Their drinks were deposited on their table, and the waiter disappeared again like a wraith. Robert brought his wine glass to his lips, but almost dropped it when he looked across the table.

Levi sat with his head bowed, either silently praying or taking a quick nap. Robert assumed it was the former. With a light chuckle, Robert sipped his wine. When Levi lifted his head, he reached for his water and took a quick drink from it.

As Robert set his glass back on the table, he leaned forward. "So, were you praying, or are you narcoleptic?"

Levi laughed. "I was praying. I like to give thanks to the One who gave me this wonderful meal I'm about to enjoy."

"Not to burst your bubble, but I think you should be thanking the chef if you want to say something to the guy preparing the meal. You don't really believe there's someone out there reading your mind just because you end your sentence with 'amen,' do you?"

The smile on Levi's face didn't waver. "Now I have to be honest and say that I've never heard it put quite that way before. You're talking like God is some sort of space alien or something. That's not what's it about at all."

Robert gave a disgusted chuckle and shook his head. "I have no idea what God is. I used to believe in him. I mean, I wasn't someone like you who prayed all the time or anything, but I thought he was out there somewhere helping the little guy out from time to time."

Levi leaned forward. "Used to believe?"

"I haven't totally discounted the fact he's out there, but I don't trust him if he is. He took my wife and daughter from me, for no reason. Maybe *he* didn't take them, but let's just say God didn't jump in there and act when he could have. It wouldn't have taken a lot of effort from someone who supposedly created an entire universe. Doesn't sound like a loving Father to me. My dad was no saint, but I don't think he'd have ever killed anyone."

"That's not the way God is, Robert."

Robert sat back in his seat and crossed his legs. "Enlighten me," he said with a slight wave of his hand.

Levi's face took on an equally serious air, though the kindness never left his eyes. "All right, Robert. Let's talk."

Ian wanted to scream. He had no idea what Bishop and Whitney were discussing, but he knew this conversation wasn't something that would normally be encouraged in a case. For the first time since he'd met Bishop, Ian regretted including him.

Bishop had the ability to communicate with people on a level that Ian could never reach. People trusted Bishop and opened up to him. Not so for Ian. He thought it probably had something to do with the deceptive practices necessary for his profession. Well, not really *necessary* ... but useful.

They were so close now to trapping Whitney, but they could lose him if the boat tipped the wrong way. If he suspected anything at all, he might become so paranoid that he froze up or changed tactics altogether. As it was, he was starting to make mistakes because he was so confident he couldn't be caught. And what had possessed Whitney to send that videotape to Morrison? Once Morrison got through talking to his wife and showing her that tape, there was really no other way it could go. Whitney had messed up, and there was a huge chance he might do it again. Ian hadn't been able to check his laptop so far today for the latest information coming from

Whitney's computer, but he had a pretty good idea it would be interesting.

And now Bishop pulls this bonehead move.

Ian rubbed his temples and cursed himself for not realizing sooner how personal this business would become to him. Knowing his past, he should have seen it coming. Still, Bishop had come out of it so changed for the better that it was almost scary.

Ian had trusted his life to this man on many occasions, and he owed him at least the chance to explain. Realizing that there wasn't much more he could do there, Ian paid for his soft drink and stood to leave.

When he turned to the door, his eyes bulged in horror. He spun back around and sat with his back to the door. One look into the mirror behind the bar gave him a full scope of his situation.

Standing in the doorway was a broad-shouldered man well over six feet tall. His brown shirt stretched tightly across his expansive chest outlining the muscles beneath it. The man's sport coat was formfitted also. It was obvious this guy could probably bench-press a Volkswagen. His thick brown hair was moussed back, and his demeanor suggested he knew how good he looked.

The pretty redhead on his arm looked bored. This was their first date. Ian knew it because he had just given the man's wife evidence against him for divorce two weeks ago.

Fred Spencer.

Ian didn't figure Spencer would want to buy him a drink if he saw him.

The way Ian saw it, there were two possible scenarios. First, Spencer wouldn't know him from Adam. Even though he'd given the information to Spencer's wife, he'd never actually dealt with him looking like this. The last time Ian had actually spoken to him, he'd presented himself as a lawyer and, learning of his short temper from his wife, he'd tried to intimidate the man into saying something that could be used in court. The recorder he'd been wearing was going to make his job easy.

Unfortunately, that wasn't the way it turned out. Spencer wasn't exactly vocal that day, but he had managed to smash his fist into the wall as Ian ran from his office, motivating Ian to dress up like a homeless person and go Dumpster diving the next day. It seemed to be the safer course of action, though the three punks he'd met proved him wrong.

So even if Spencer didn't know who Ian was, he might remember his face as someone he didn't like. Of the two possible scenarios, this was the least likely to work out in Ian's favor.

Or Spencer and his date might be seated without event, in which case Ian could exit unnoticed. A second glance into the mirror shot that one down too. Spencer was now holding one of those plastic coasters that flash when a customer's table is ready. He and his date found a seat across the room from Ian. One good look in the mirror, and it would all be over. Ian lowered his face into his hands and let out a low groan.

The bartender walked up, obviously wondering what had changed his mind about leaving. Careful to keep his face tilted away from the mirror, Ian quickly ordered another ginger ale.

There was no way to get across the room to the door without being noticed. He was just going to have to wait until Spencer and his date got a table. He hoped things were going better for Bishop.

Levi leaned forward. "First of all, God didn't 'take' your wife and daughter. I've never been able to stand hearing someone say things like that. He didn't 'need another rose in his heavenly garden,' or 'want another angel and choose your loved ones.' Those are all things said by people who are ignorant of the true nature of God. God's not some cosmic sniper picking off folks at random just for the fun of it. Neither is he some spoiled child who snatches up people and tosses them aside like toys he no longer wants to play with. That's not the nature of God at all."

Robert said, "That's the way my wife's pastor put it. If anyone knows about God, I'd be inclined it would be someone like that."

"Oh, life's not perfect—and you'll never hear me saying it is—but it's wrong to blame God for every disaster in your life. You've got to get that picture out of your mind, Robert. God doesn't hate you."

Robert gave a cold chuckle. "Well, it sure doesn't look like I'm on his top-ten list of favorites."

"There are problems in the world," said Levi. "Let's get that out of the way. Most of the time, when I try to talk to someone about

God, they inevitably try to throw things like that in my face. The 'if God is so good then why does he allow so many bad things to happen' questions are good ones, and there are no clear answers. If you can accept the fact that good and bad both happen, and it's not just God picking on some and loving others, then you can get past the first hurdle to accepting God's love."

Levi pointed a finger at Robert. "'For he maketh his sun to rise on the evil and on the good, and sendeth rain on the just and on the unjust.' That's found in Matthew chapter five, verse forty-five, and it's something Jesus said. Jesus was the Son of God, so that makes him a pretty good authority on the subject. At the time he said that, sunshine and rain were considered a blessing. He was saying that God blessed all people, good or bad. It's another example of the boundless love God had for us in sending his son to die in our place even when we weren't worth it."

Robert's eyebrows rose. "Then what's the point of serving him? If you don't get preferential treatment every once in a while, it doesn't seem like too good of a deal."

Levi smiled. "That's another good question. Your thinking is only natural because we're raised as 'what have you done for me lately?' kind of folks. We seldom do anything for anyone without expecting something in return for it, so why should we count God out of that list? But the entirety of the Bible points in a different direction. Rather than asking 'what will you give me if I do this for you?' like a spoiled child, we should take on the attitude that Job had when he said of God, 'Though he slay me, yet will I trust in him: but I will maintain mine own ways before him.' You know what that means? Job was saying that no matter what God did to him—even reducing him to the point of death itself—Job was going to keep on serving him. Now we're blessed in that we know the truth about the whole encounter. We understand from the beginning of the book it wasn't God doing those things at all. God was allowing them to happen to test Job, but God's hand wasn't turned against him."

The waiter arrived with their steaks. Levi took a bite of steak and vegetables before continuing. "I don't have all the answers in life. When you've looked upon lives devastated by the evil and corruption of this world, you realize that there are just things you're never going to understand here."

Levi made a slight sweeping gesture with his hands. "In this room alone, you have folks who have been abused, lied to, cheated on, molested, and hurt in a dozen other ways. You have people here who've lost spouses, children, parents, and friends to circumstances that can only be termed 'bad timing.' A man crosses the street at the exact instant a car is passing whose driver is busy changing radio stations. Neither sees the other until it's too late.

"We could go on for hours, Robert. Every person in this city has at least one instance of something going horribly wrong in his or her life. Would you like to venture a guess as to how many of them blame God for it? Would you like to venture another guess as to how many of them might have brought the problem on themselves from things they did? How is it God's fault when we break the rules he set up for us?"

Robert leaned forward. "You still haven't answered my question, Levi. What good does it do you to serve God when he doesn't even do anything to protect his own?"

Levi's expression grew serious. "Let me stop you right there. First of all, I told you that I serve God because I love him—not because I'm expecting something in return for it. God has blessed me in so many ways I can't begin to list them all, but he does that from his own goodness. I didn't earn so many brownie points that I get a free trip to heaven. As a matter of fact, there's nothing I could ever do that would make me good enough. My sins were forgiven, and I was made clean by what Jesus did on the cross. That was a free gift to me—and you, too. Just because I became a Christian didn't mean I wasn't ever going to have problems."

Levi leaned forward. "But I will say this much: There are two advantages I have when those problems come. First, I have a God I can pray to who will hear me and will either deliver me from my situation or deliver me *through* it. My Bible tells me in Romans chapter eight verse twenty-eight that 'all things work together for good to them that love God, to them who are the called according to his purpose.' That means all things—no matter how bad they seem. It doesn't mean those things are good, but that God makes the best of any given situation for us.

"Second, I have an assurance and a hope that no matter what may happen to my body, my soul is forever in God's arms. To me, that's the best assurance anyone could ask for. When Christ saved me, he changed me for the better. I was a horrible man in a horrible situation, but I was delivered and changed in one moment. It doesn't happen like that for everyone, but it did for me."

Robert sneered. "What kind of problems could you have had? I lost my wife and daughter to an idiot driver right in front of my eyes. They were as innocent as they could possibly be, and they weren't paying for anything they'd done. There were a dozen cars around that truck, and he could have hit any of them, so why were they chosen? Do you have any idea what it's like to watch your family die right in front of your eyes?"

Both men were silent for several seconds, and then Levi took a drink of water and reverently set it down. He closed his eyes and let out a long sigh. When he spoke again, his voice was barely above a whisper.

"Yes, Robert, I do."

Ian continued to sip his ginger ale, casting an occasional glance toward Fred Spencer and his date.

Come on, what's the holdup on that table for two? Can't you see the very big man is hungry?

Quick movement in the mirror caught Ian's eye. He looked up to see Spencer stand and turn to speak to his date.

Then he started walking toward the bar.

Ian closed his eyes and continued to rub his temples.

Please don't let him see me. Please don't let him see me. Please don't let him see me. Please don't—

He felt Spencer trying to squeeze in between him and the man beside him.

"Hey, can I get a Long Island tea and a rum and Coke?"

Ian shifted in his chair to put more of his back toward the big man. He decided it was time to risk a glance in the mirror. He looked up ...

... and found Spencer staring back at him from the glass.

For a moment, Ian thought he was safe. For a brief second,

Spencer seemed not to know who was sitting next to him. Then that second was gone, and a flash of recognition crossed his face. His eyes narrowed, and his nostrils flared.

"Hey ..."

A vise grip clamped into Ian's shoulder as he felt his entire body being spun around to face the man. Spencer lowered his face closer.

"*You.*"

Ian shot a quick glance toward Bishop's table. Neither man seemed to have noticed the situation developing just a few yards away. That was good.

Looking back at Spencer, Ian grinned. "Hi, Fred. How's the family?"

Staring at him with a malicious sneer, Spencer grabbed the front of Ian's shirt and pulled him to his feet. "Outside."

Ian was steered toward the door. Looking over his shoulder, he said, "Has anyone ever told you what a brilliant conversationalist you are? You have this incredible mastery of the English language that can only come from years of careful saturation in the written word."

With one shove of his huge hand, Spencer pushed Ian outside. The crowd waiting near the door scattered at the sudden exit.

Spencer took off his jacket and tossed it to a thin man with glasses who was standing near the door. "Hold this." Turning back to Ian, he began to circle his arms to loosen his muscles. "My soon-to-be ex-wife found out about my money somehow. I remember your sneaky little face coming in and causing me trouble right before her lawyer called."

Ian's eyes widened. "Would you believe it was just a case of really rotten timing?"

Spencer shook his head as a cocky half grin took shape. "I'm gonna hurt you in so many different ways ..."

Ian looked at the crowd around them. Their faces told him that they were enjoying this unexpected entertainment. None of them made any kind of move to stop it. He was on his own. He closed his eyes and shook his head with a sigh. "Well, let's get it over with then."

TWENTY-SIX

IAN STOOD SMILING AS Fred Spencer lunged at him. At the last instant, Ian fell to one knee and threw a straight punch into Spencer's abdomen. It should have taken the wind out of him and ended the fight quickly.

Instead, it was like hitting a brick wall.

Ian rolled to the side as Spencer reached for him. He was on his feet again and backing away before Spencer could turn all the way around. His hand began to throb as he shook it.

Spencer threw another hard right, but Ian stepped toward him and caught his extended right arm at the wrist. Using Spencer's own momentum against him, Ian allowed the force of the punching arm to spin him around. He brought up his left elbow and slammed it into the side of Spencer's head.

But he still wouldn't fall.

Spencer shook his head a couple of times to clear it, and then sneered. Before Ian could move, Spencer grasped his shirtfront and jerked him toward him, shoving a knee toward his groin. Ian twisted at the last second, taking the brunt of the knee on his hip, but it still hurt like crazy. Lights exploded behind Ian's eyes as he fought to stay on his feet. Spencer jerked him back to a standing position. As the giant pulled back his fist, Ian sent an uppercut into the man's armpit and into the nerve cluster there. Spencer's grip loosened. Ian grabbed the big man's wrist and twisted, bending him forward to keep the arm from breaking.

Ian didn't hesitate now. He kicked Spencer's left leg behind the knee. As his knee hit the asphalt, Ian spun and slammed a back kick into Spencer's face. The giant went down.

Ian noticed the crowd. They'd become progressively rowdier with every second of the fight. Now they were attracting far too much attention, and he needed to get away before the police arrived.

He looked up just in time to see the door to the restaurant open. Towering over the exiting procession was Bishop. A look of surprise came over his face as he recognized Ian. Then he looked down and saw Fred Spencer sprawled on the ground. Before he could react, Robert Whitney came from behind him and took in the scene. Ian turned away and walked off in the opposite direction. He wasn't sure whether Whitney had seen his face or not, but he knew that Bishop had.

Ian knew he was going to hear about this incident later.

Derek waited beside his truck as Rachel pulled into the driveway. Her insistence on meeting him at the restaurant forced them to take separate cars. It wasn't the way he'd have liked it to happen, but at least she was still coming to meet him.

As she parked behind his truck, he moved to open her car door. She watched him warily as she brought out her small purse.

"My, aren't you just the perfect gentleman?"

Derek gave a slight nod. "Yes, ma'am. I try my best to impress."

They walked to the door while Derek gave everything a quick mental once-over. He was pretty sure he'd cleaned the place extra thoroughly, but he wished he'd gone over everything again before dinner.

As soon as Rachel stepped inside, he could tell that she was impressed with the cleaning he'd done. It may not have been spotless, but it looked good enough for her. The butterflies in his stomach disappeared.

"My goodness, I'm amazed. I have to say I was expecting to see stuff everywhere, but you've got the place looking almost decent."

Derek beamed with pride. He was thrilled he'd made such a good first impression. If she realized he'd changed in this respect, then perhaps she'd be more willing to accept his change in other areas as well.

He gently took her purse to put it on the hall table. It would still be within her reach, but he'd made it clear he wanted her to stay. His hand brushed hers as he took it. They stayed like that for a moment, staring into each other's eyes. He felt the familiar stirrings inside as he fell into her incredible blue eyes.

Somehow, he found his voice. "I'm glad you like it." He placed her purse on the small stand in the hallway. "There we go, all safe and sound."

He turned to face her again and cleared his throat. "Um, well, would you like anything to drink?" He moved past her into the kitchen and jerked a finger toward the refrigerator.

Rachel shook her head and walked into the living room. She took a seat at one end of the couch and put a throw pillow on her other side, effectively walling herself into a small space. The action was deliberate, and it hurt him. She was making sure he understood there were lines he could no longer cross with the same ease he'd once had. He considered what could happen if they couldn't work things out. He might never get the chance to hold her or kiss her again. They might become nothing more than acquaintances. How would he ever come to accept that? He hoped he wouldn't have to.

She had to know what Robert Whitney really was.

And that meant she had to learn what her husband really was.

First, he'd have to expose Whitney. Then he'd have to tell her everything so she'd understand his motivation. Now that he no longer worked for Gordon James, the truth didn't matter. He felt liberated when he'd hung up the phone after quitting. He was sure he'd feel even more liberated after getting the lies off his chest.

"Rachel, there are some things you need to know. It would be easy for me to ignore the real reason for this visit and pretend that nothing ever happened, but I can't do that. You've got to know the truth."

The expression on Rachel's face betrayed her confusion. "All right, I'm here, just like I promised. Obviously this thing that you have to show me is very important to you, so show me."

His stomach was rolling, but he knew she had to know the truth.

This is it. Once I start this tape, there'll be no turning back until everything's out in the open.

Derek thought about Bishop and what he'd do at a moment like this. Derek didn't feel that he was on good enough terms with God to ask for any help, so he left that recourse alone. He pushed the tape into the VCR and sat in a chair across from the sofa.

"Rachel, I want you to understand I'm not doing this to cause either of us any more pain. We've both had our fair share of that. I'm doing this because I think it's the only way you'll believe me when I tell you the whole story about Robert."

At the mention of his name, Derek saw a coldness touch the edges of Rachel's mouth. She was obviously upset that he was bringing Robert back into the conversation, but he hoped she'd give him the chance to explain it all.

Derek pulled a large manila envelope from beside his chair. "This was waiting for me in the mailbox when I got home yesterday. You can see it doesn't have a return address or anything, and the only thing inside was a videotape labeled 'Enjoy.' The postmark is from here in Birmingham."

Picking up the remote control, he turned on the TV and hit the play button for the VCR. The video began, and Rachel squinted toward the screen. Derek watched her rather than what was playing, unable to bear to see it again. For a few moments she appeared confused as to why he would be showing her this video.

Then recognition dawned on her face.

Her eyes widened, and her mouth opened. Derek felt nauseated, but kept telling himself it was for the greater good. She had to see this tape to understand what kind of man she was dealing with.

"What ... w-where did you get this?" Her voice quivered as she spoke.

"I told you, it was waiting for me in the mail when I got back from my last haul." Derek hated himself for having to humiliate her like this.

"Turn it off ... please." Rachel bowed her head and covered her face with her hands. Derek felt horrible, but he knew he couldn't stop now. He switched off the television and turned back to her.

"I'm sorry, Rachel. If there had been another way, I'd have taken it. I don't think you would have believed me if I'd just told you what was on that tape, though."

He slid from his seat to kneel before her. He gingerly touched her shoulder, and she exploded into his arms. She laid her head on his shoulder, weeping into his neck. Derek held her tightly and patted her back.

When she spoke, her words were muffled against his neck. "I'm sorry. I was confused and lonely, and I let my feelings get away from me. I ..." Rachel could say no more and fell against him, as if releasing a huge weight that she had been carrying for weeks. She shivered in his embrace.

"Now do you see?" Derek whispered. "Do you understand what I've been trying to protect you from? He's been using you to get to me."

Rachel pulled back and looked into his face, her arms still resting on him. "Why? Why would he do something so ... horrible?"

"He's crazy, honey. He's obsessed, or driven mad by revenge, or something."

Her eyes fell as she tried to process everything he was saying. He wanted to keep going while he had the advantage.

"I hired a private investigator to watch him, and we've uncovered some pretty strange habits." Derek hesitated, realizing that he was about to get into some very dangerous territory. "We ... we followed you to Marigold's last week."

Rachel's arms drifted from his shoulders. Her tears dried. "You did *what?*"

"We followed you there. Ian—he's the investigator—found out about your dinner plans. He said they were going to go and see if Robert tried anything. I wanted to go, and Bishop—he's this preacher who helps Ian—said it was all right as long as I didn't freak out and go for Robert or anything."

Rachel sat back, her eyes locked on Derek. She was still listening, but Derek could sense a cold wall forming between them again.

"So let me get this straight, you were stalking me?"

Derek closed his eyes and shook his head in frustration. "No, nothing like that. We were watching Robert. I needed something to show you so you'd believe me about how crazy he is."

He paused, waiting for her reaction. She was staring at the floor now, silent.

"You should see some of the stuff he did, Rachel. I mean, he went outside and messed around with some guy's keys. I have no idea what that was all about, but we videotaped it and—"

Suddenly, her eyes shot up to his. "You what?"

"We videotaped Robert grabbing the keys and—"

Rachel straightened, her body moving to the edge of the couch. "You were there … with a video camera?"

Derek grew impatient. Why wouldn't she let him finish his story? "Yes, but I don't have that tape here. I'm sure I can get it from Bishop if you'd like to—"

She pointed at him and then at the television. "You were there to videotape Robert and me at dinner, and then a few days later you just happened to get this 'anonymous' videotape of what happened at Robert's place later that same night?"

Derek saw where she was going with this. "Now wait a minute, are you saying that I—"

She snatched the remote from him. "I want to see that again … I just realized something."

She pressed the play button, and the video picked up where it left off. Derek didn't look, but Rachel was entranced by what she was seeing. She turned up the volume, and the sound of crickets and the wind poured from the speakers. After several seconds, she turned back to him.

"Just as I thought. This was filmed from outside, Derek. Why would Robert go to the trouble of setting up a camera outside when it would have been easier to film it from the same room?"

Derek hesitated. Then a solution to the same question he'd been asking himself since receiving the tape began to take shape. Unfortunately, he hadn't figured it out in time. "To make it look like someone else was filming it."

Rachel shook her head. "I almost believed you. To think I trusted you and gave you the benefit of yet another second chance, and you were setting me up. You were manipulating me the whole time."

Derek jumped to his feet. "Now just a minute, how can you turn this around to look like my fault? I suppose I somehow forced you to do what you did that night?"

Rachel stood up and pushed past him toward the hallway. Grabbing her purse, she turned back to face him. "You're sick. If I ever see you anywhere near Robert or me again, I'll call the police. Do you hear me?"

Derek took a step toward her. "I can't believe you're actually still falling for his lies after what I've just shown you. What are you, stupid or something? Or are you such a tramp that you can't wait to get another shot at him and don't want to admit the truth?"

Rachel moved with lightning speed to cover the distance between them. Her hand was a blur as she slapped his face.

Without thinking, Derek backhanded her.

They both stood in shock for a few seconds as Derek's mouth fell open with the realization of what he'd done. Rachel's face was hard as stone, even as tears began to fall anew down her reddening cheek.

When she spoke again, her voice was strained.

"I hate you."

"Rachel, I—"

But she was already out the door and running to her car.

Bishop stood looking up toward heaven as if expecting an answer to drop from the sky. They were in Ian's apartment, with Sam watching their every move from the kitchen. Ian had arrived first. Bishop hadn't been far behind.

Ian was lying on his couch trying to rest. He raised his hand. "In my defense, I didn't start the fight. He dragged me outside, and I had to protect myself."

Bishop bent down and pointed at him. "You couldn't have just walked away? I mean, you were outside, there were no chains on you; why didn't you just leave?"

Ian paused. "All right, I'll admit that I didn't consider that option. I don't really think he'd have let me go, but you're probably right. I could've at least tried."

Bishop turned and walked to the kitchen. Sam scurried out of his way. "I was so close, Ian. He was almost at that point of realizing how foolish and dangerous all this has been—I could see it."

Ian sighed. "I'd prefer not to cause an argument with another very large man tonight, but may I remind you that we're professionals and this isn't some evangelistic outreach? I need the goods on Whitney, and his soul is the least of my concerns. I was paid to deliver information to my client that would allow him to prove the man's true intent. That's all. I know that Whitney's got something big happening in the next few days involving some guy named Terrance and another man named Gordon. I need to try and stop him before he hurts someone else. At the moment I have nothing of any interest other than a computer virus of obvious malicious intent. I need more."

Bishop returned from the kitchen with a bottle of water and took a seat opposite Ian. "Look, Ian, I realize that this is just another case to you. And I know you don't agree with my methods sometimes, but I've never gotten in the way before, have I? God has allowed me to reach some people that were truly in need of his love, and I'll tell you right now that Robert Whitney needs the love of the Father right now. He's not totally gone yet, Ian. There's still this part of him that's wrestling with his actions."

Ian closed his eyes. "Let me guess, you could see it in his face."

Bishop looked away. "No, from his words and actions. There's bitterness there, and a lot of hurt, but there's not so much happening that he can't walk away from it. I just need the chance."

The weary PI sat up. "You realize that if I didn't know you so well and didn't owe you so much, this would be over? I couldn't throw you out because you're as big as my recliner, but I could sure ask you to leave in no uncertain terms."

Bishop chuckled. "I understand. And I've never let you down before. I'll help you stop Robert before he hurts anyone else, I promise. I'd just like the chance to reach him before it's too late. I've been in that pit, Ian, and I know how he feels."

Ian ran his fingers through his hair. "Yeah, I know you do. How about just keeping me informed next time you decide to pull a surprise visit like that?"

Bishop smiled warmly. "Done. Now, will you do *me* a favor?"

"Sure. What?"

"Will you try to handle situations without fighting?"

Ian raised his eyebrows and gave a tight smile. "Can't promise anything, but I'll try."

Bishop clapped his hands on his legs and stood. "Good enough for me."

"Hey, let me ask you something. How come you're the one with all the muscles, but I'm the one who always ends up in all the fights?"

Bishop said, "Maybe it's because I'm the one with all the brains too."

The phone rang. Ian groaned and covered his face with his hands. "Would you mind getting that? It's probably Fred Spencer wanting a rematch."

Bishop shook his head and headed for the phone. "I told you not to fight."

Ian shrugged as Bishop answered it on the second ring.

"Hello?"

Ian peeked through his fingers and saw Bishop stiffen. It was not a good sign. Bishop glanced toward Ian. "He's right here, Derek. What's wrong? You sound upset."

Ian studied Bishop, trying to gauge what was going on. Levi continued to listen, and Ian saw him grimace.

"Calm down. You've got to calm down or you're going to make a horrible mistake."

A pause.

"I know that you're confused right now.... No, I didn't have any idea that would happen ... but I told you things might not be what they seemed. I—"

Another pause—longer this time.

"Derek, listen to me, I can be there in a few min— No, you don't need to do that. That's just exactly what ... Stay there. I'll be right—"

Ian saw Bishop flinch. "Derek? Derek, are you still there?"

Bishop closed his eyes and slowly put the phone down. Ian watched him warily.

"Something wrong?"

Bishop looked defeated. "Yeah, things just got a whole lot worse."

TWENTY-SEVEN

Robert sat in his SUV, the darkness covering him like a blanket. Ahead he saw several houses in various states of illumination. Most were dark, their inhabitants slumbering in blissful ignorance of what was about to happen. One in particular held his rapt attention. He glanced at his watch. It was almost ten.

The front door to the house opened, and a tall black man in a gray uniform stepped out. He shut the door behind him and checked it to make sure it was locked. With one sweeping glance over the neighborhood, he climbed in his car.

Robert studied the man, as much out of concern as out of a desire to keep his mind off the contents of the box in the passenger seat beside him. He knew that what he was about to do was wrong, but he also knew it was the only justice this man would ever face for what he'd done to Tara and Emily. That thought made what he was about to do a little easier. He'd called from his prepaid cell phone earlier in the day to see if Terrance Gold was at work. The lady answering the phone had been very helpful with Gold's schedule for the night. Why shouldn't she be? She thought she was talking to Gold's cousin.

Robert watched the car drive off. After waiting ten minutes, he pulled the box into his lap and got out of the SUV. He quietly closed the door and surveyed the surroundings to make sure no one was watching. He'd parked his SUV up the street where there were no streetlights. Now he wished he'd gotten closer. There were three brand-new keys in his pocket, made from the wax impressions from Gold's keys he made that night at Marigold's. One of them would undoubtedly be the key to the front door.

He jogged to the small porch of Gold's house, the keys ready in his gloved hand. The only other possible problem would be if Gold had an alarm system. If that was the case, the plan would have to be altered slightly ... but that wouldn't save Gold. He inserted the first key into the lock and turned.

Nothing happened.

Without hesitation, he pulled it out and moved to the second key. The keys jiggled lightly as he moved, but he didn't think it was loud enough to catch the attention of anyone who might be passing by.

Still nothing. The doorknob would not move.

Taking a deep breath, Robert pulled the key out and moved to the last one. His hand shook as it moved the final key to the lock. If this didn't work, he'd have to get creative.

With a fluid movement of his wrist, he turned the knob.

He opened the door and stepped inside. Without turning on any of the lights, he closed the door behind him. For a moment he was in total darkness, then he switched on his penlight, and a small beam of red light pierced the blackness.

He crept through the living room, careful not to touch anything. Even though he was wearing gloves, he knew that any item knocked out of place could alert Gold to the fact that he'd had an intruder. It was hard to avoid touching everything, however, given Gold's poor housekeeping habits. There were boxes everywhere, along with various magazines and books strewn about haphazardly.

As Robert turned a corner to go into the hallway, his foot caught on something. He twisted as best he could to keep from damaging the box in his hands. Nothing must happen to it. He slammed onto his shoulder with a thud and felt the side of his head smack on the hard wood. With a curse, he laid still, trying to catch his breath. He checked the box and breathed a sigh of relief. It was intact. Finally, he gingerly touched his skull. No blood, but there would be a knot there tomorrow.

Robert groped around for his penlight. He considered turning on the hall light but thought better of it, lest someone should see the lights from outside and get suspicious. His hand brushed magazines sprawled all over the floor. He'd tripped on a stack of them, and now they were everywhere. He'd have to clean them up before he left and hope Gold wasn't too careful about the way he'd left things.

Fighting a rising panic, Robert finally touched something against the wall. He relaxed a little as his fingers closed around the familiar shape of his penlight. Pushing the button to turn it back on, he picked up the box and moved cautiously down the hall. He passed a bathroom before finding his goal.

Terrance Gold's bedroom.

Like a ghost, Robert crossed the room and laid the box on the bed. A quick assimilation of the surroundings showed him the best place to put it. He saw Gold's computer on a small table near the window and smiled, knowing what was going on inside it at that moment.

Five minutes later, Robert had deposited the box, replaced the stack of magazines, and was back in his car. He pulled out the same cell phone he'd used earlier and made one final call on it as he drove away. After repeating the information to the person on the other end of the line, he rolled down the window and threw the phone away. Two miles farther down the road, he tossed out the copies of Gold's keys.

In his mind, he crossed Gold's name off the list. Only two names remained now.

Soon there would be none.

Derek raced down I-20, feeling the blood surge through his veins. His mind replayed the events of the past hour again and again. He went over everything that had happened in a desperate attempt to find out what had gone wrong. He'd thought that showing Rachel the video-tape would drive the final nail in Robert Whitney's coffin, but as usual the scoundrel had somehow turned it all back against him.

It seemed the man was always two steps ahead of him. It was frustrating to Derek because it was almost as if Whitney could read his mind and knew what to do to head off his plans.

The wind roared into the open window of the truck as he drove with no destination in mind. The cars passed by him like blurs, but he was no longer concerned with getting a ticket or even hurting anyone with his reckless driving. Nothing mattered anymore.

It was all his fault, and he knew it. He let out a string of curses as he beat his fist against the dashboard in anger.

If I'd just told her everything to begin with, then this wouldn't be happening. I mean, she wouldn't have understood why I lied about it, but at least she would have known the truth. But I guess either way it wouldn't have been pretty.

Derek's thoughts continued to torment him as he drove through the darkness. He'd tried so hard to do the right thing. Richardson and Bishop seemed perfect for the job, and they'd said they had evidence coming in, but he had yet to see it. And it looked as if Rachel would never believe any of it anyway. Even if he did somehow manage to get it to her, she'd just think he had made it all up.

He'd tried so hard to change. He hadn't had a drink in three weeks, a fact he was proud of considering the downward spiral he'd been on right after the accident. He'd quit his job to stay closer to home. But nothing was good enough. When it all came crashing in on him, he still couldn't control his anger. The real Derek Morrison had come out again.

Derek could still see the look on Rachel's face the second after he'd slapped her. It was as if a light went out. The entire night he'd seen the return of that old fire and spirit he'd fallen in love with years ago. It was as though the separation had been good for both of them, and they were ready to start all over again. Then, in one moment of anger and frustration, he'd lashed out at her and killed whatever feelings for him she might have had. He still couldn't believe it had all gone so wrong.

He saw an exit coming up so he pulled off the interstate and parked on the off-ramp. He dropped his head onto the steering wheel and tried to think. His eyes were shut so tightly that he thought he saw flashes of light. Then he opened his eyes and found that he still saw them.

The flashing blue lights cut through the night around him. Derek groaned as he reached for his wallet. He had no idea how fast he'd been going, but he had the feeling this little roadside stop wasn't going to be cheap.

Glancing in the side mirror, he saw the state trooper exit his vehicle and walk cautiously toward him. The trooper was a tall black man, and when he spoke, his voice sounded familiar.

"May I see your license and proof of insurance please?"

"Sure." Derek passed the license and small sheet of paper to the officer and waited. His mind raced, trying to place the voice. He knew this man from somewhere.

Derek waited as the trooper used his flashlight to read the license. He paused several seconds before turning the light on Derek and then back on the license again.

"Mr. Morrison? Do you remember me?"

Derek tried to get a good look at the man, but still couldn't place him. "I'm sorry. You're very familiar to me, but I'm afraid I can't place you."

"My name's Terrance Gold. I was the officer who worked the accident on I-20 you were involved in a few weeks ago. I remember your name from the accident report."

Slowly it dawned on Derek. "Yeah, I recognize you now. I'm sorry I didn't remember you, but I was in a pretty wild state of mind that afternoon."

The officer nodded as he passed the license and insurance card back to Derek. "That's all right, I understand. Your trucking company was ... rather generous. I think we can let this incident slide."

Derek wasn't about to inform him that he no longer worked for Starline Trucking. Instead, he accepted the proffered items and thanked him.

The trooper leaned in Derek's window. "I'll never forget the way that man looked at you. Did you ever have any problems out of him?"

Derek looked ahead, debating how much information to give out. "Yeah, the guy's made my life a nightmare. I don't think you could begin to imagine everything he's done."

Derek told the officer everything, starting at his first dinner with Rachel and ending with the events of earlier in the evening. He was careful to avoid a confession of wrongdoing in the accident, trying to remember exactly what he'd told the trooper that day. The man's face went from indifference to confusion to disbelief and finally ended with a smoldering anger that made Derek uncomfortable. After he had finished talking, there were several seconds of silence. Then the trooper shook his head and sniffed.

"Hard to believe. I don't see how you took all that. If it'd been me, I would've had to hunt him down and settle it a long time ago."

Derek nodded. "Yeah, well, I guess I should have. I just didn't realize how sneaky and underhanded this guy was. He does things that seem so innocent, but there's something bad coming with them. Something weird happens to you, and you just pass it off as coincidence, but then you find out that all along it's part of something he's doing."

The officer stopped then and seemed to consider something. His eyes drifted past Derek as though he was in deep thought, then they narrowed, and he locked his gaze on Derek's again.

"Do you remember the date of your accident?"

Derek's eyebrows went up as he considered it. "Well, not exactly. It was a few weeks ago … maybe a month?"

The trooper's nostrils flared as his mouth set in grim determination. Again, he looked past Derek as if studying something miles away. "That would be about right."

"About right for what?"

Officer Gold looked back at him. "Nothing. You should seriously think about things, Mr. Morrison. Sounds like the man's messed up your life. I wouldn't take that if I were you." Gold pulled a business card from his shirt pocket. "Here's my card again. Call me sometime if you need any … help."

Derek watched the man walk back to his car and get in. After a few seconds the flashing blue lights atop the vehicle flickered off, and the car pulled away. The trooper's words echoed in Derek's mind.

A few minutes after midnight, Robert pulled into his driveway. His mind was still on the things he'd done a couple of hours earlier at the trooper's home. By morning, Terrance Gold would pay for what he'd done, and justice would be served. Robert thought about it all and wondered where the satisfaction was that he thought he'd feel when it was all said and done. He didn't find the fulfillment he'd imagined finding.

He exited the car and shut the door quietly behind him. The front of the house was dark, which was odd since Robert was sure he'd left the front light on. He looked up at the fixture and saw that the bulb was missing.

Who in the world would steal a light bulb? Were some of the neighborhood kids playing some sort of—

The hair on the back of his neck bristled as he realized that things weren't right. There was a sound behind him—

Something slammed into the side of his face. The force of the blow sent him spinning around and onto the grass. As he tried to push himself up, he felt another blow smash into his side just below his rib cage. It lifted him up and flipped him over onto his back. As he spun, he saw a man's boot.

Before he could focus on the assailant's face, the man swung down from overhead. There was a fleshy *whap,* and Robert felt that his guts would explode. The man moved again, and something collided with the side of Robert's head. He feebly raised his arms to protect his head, as an impact came with such force that he felt certain they would break.

With a momentary respite, Robert tried to roll over onto his side and into a fetal position. He felt blow after blow being rained down upon his back and legs. There was a brief pause, and Robert heard the man groan with the exertion of the next hit. The object hit Robert's left leg with a loud *thwack.*

The intruder pushed him onto his back and shoved his hand on Robert's mouth to stifle his cries. There was intense pressure on his chest as the man knelt on him. Forcing his eyes open, Robert could only see a shadow above him; the silhouette of a nightmare coming to drag him to hell for what he'd done. The attacker lowered his head so close that Robert could hear him breathing hard from the physical exertion he'd been through.

The man slapped him several times. "Are you awake, Whitney?"

Robert's arms came up to claw at the hand covering his mouth, but his strength was gone. He heard the man chuckle and felt drops of sweat falling onto his face.

"You should have left well enough alone. I'm sorry about what happened to your family and everything, but that's the way life is. Sometimes it's great to be alive, and sometimes it stinks. You have to learn to roll with the punches."

Robert felt the pressure on his chest as the man pushed up to stand. Blood flowed into Robert's eyes, burning them. He could vaguely see the man pulling back for one final hit, and knew that his life was over.

I'm sorry, Tara. I wanted them all to pay for what they'd done to you and to Emily, but I've failed. Please forgive me.

As he awaited the killing blow, he heard a distant voice growing louder. It seemed to be shouting something. The attacker heard it too, and Robert saw his head turn quickly to look at something on the other side of the street. Robert heard the man curse, and then he ran off toward the back of the house. Robert heard approaching footsteps and braced himself for another attack. He felt someone kneel down beside him in the grass and heard a familiar deep voice speak.

"Oh, dear Father in heaven. What's he done to you? Can you hear me, Robert?"

His response was weak and barely audible. "Levi?"

"I'm here, Robert. I'm sorry I didn't think to get here sooner though. Help is coming."

Robert coughed and tasted something wet and salty coming up with each ragged breath. Levi gently rolled him onto his side to spit out the blood that was trickling from his mouth. Robert forced himself to breathe in and out, trying to form the words to the question he had to ask before he died.

"Levi?"

"Don't talk, Robert. Save your strength."

"Levi … you still believe God doesn't hate me now?"

Then Robert drifted away.

PART TWO

REDEMPTION

God whispers to us in our pleasures, speaks in our conscience, but shouts in our pains: it is His megaphone to rouse a deaf world.

—C. S. LEWIS (1898–1963)

TWENTY-EIGHT

CHARLIE'S FIRST SUSPICION THAT something was wrong came when he arrived at work and found Tom Watson waiting outside the door. Robert had been getting to work early each morning lately, and Charlie had taken it for granted that his boss would be there to open the door.

He moved to the door to let Tom in. With a brief greeting, he had it unlocked so their day could begin.

A few minutes later, Amy strolled in with a smile. Her brown hair was pulled back into a ponytail with long strands of it loosely hanging beside her face. Today was Friday, and officially "casual day" for her. She gave Charlie a quick wave as she slid in front of her terminal and booted it up.

At Rachel's desk, Charlie checked the answering machine. There were three messages from customers, but nothing from Robert.

Oh well, I guess he's coming in late today, or he's taking the day off. Maybe Rachel will know something when she gets here.

As if on cue, Rachel walked through the door. She noticed

Charlie at her desk and gave him a quick, questioning glance, but said nothing as she put her purse down.

"Hi, Rachel. Have you heard from Robert?"

A look of concern crossed Rachel's face. "No, why? Has something happened?"

"No, I guess not. It's just that he's usually here before me. I didn't know if he was planning on working at home or what."

Rachel reached for the phone. "Maybe I should call—"

Charlie put his hand on hers and gently put the phone's headset back on the cradle. "Not yet. He might be sleeping late today. We'll give him until ten or so to show up, then we'll call and check on him. I'm sure everything's all right."

Rachel didn't look as if she believed him, but Charlie could tell he'd won the argument. "I guess I'd better get started on answering our messages."

Charlie turned and headed back toward his workstation. A quick glance showed him that Tom was busily at work. Jonathan's seat remained empty. Another latecomer today. Both men had projects due by the end of the day, and Charlie hoped Jonathan got there soon.

As he slid into his chair, the phone rang. Rachel spoke for a moment and then forwarded the call to his phone. Charlie answered it, expecting another customer with a last-minute change to their order.

"This is Charlie."

"Charlie, it's Ian Richardson."

The smile disappeared from Charlie's face immediately. He sat up straight, turning slightly away from Amy. "Um ... what ... what can I do for you?"

"Charlie, something's happened. We need to talk."

Terrance Gold arrived home a little after nine. As he pulled in, he noticed an unfamiliar white van parked down the street, and for some reason it bothered him. He'd call it in to headquarters if it were still there when he left for work that evening. His neighborhood didn't get many visitors.

His eyes felt heavy from his long shift the night before; but, as was his custom, he didn't go to bed right away. His mind was always busy processing things when he got home, and he found that the best thing he could do was just fix some breakfast and try to find a game on the sports channel. For a brief instant he thought he saw a shadow pass across his front yard. He checked the window, but saw nothing. Shaking his head at the sudden bout of paranoia, he turned to go to the kitchen.

As he reached the kitchen table, he noticed that the stack of magazines in the hall was different. He only knew so because the top magazine had been the last thing he'd seen as he'd walked out of his bedroom before leaving work. The cover photo was that of a blonde actress from a failed lifeguard series on cable. Now he was looking at some redhead posed provocatively with a blank stare. Instinctively, Terrance reached for his pistol.

Without moving his head, he cut his eyes back and forth to try to see if anything else was wrong. Nothing looked out of place, but he didn't relax. Quietly drawing the weapon from its holster, he moved toward the hall. His steps were noiseless as he reached the bathroom and glanced inside.

He looked down the hall at his bedroom door. It was open just as he'd left it, but someone could be in there waiting for him. As he passed the stack of magazines, something on the floor beside it caught his eye.

Two small white rectangles of blank paper.

Bending at the knees, he carefully reached down to pick up one of them, all the time keeping his face toward the bedroom, scanning for movement.

He brought the paper up to get a better look. As he touched it, he felt something on the back. Turning it around, he realized what he was holding.

A business card.

In raised letters, Terrance read:

Whitney Edge Software.

At the bottom right-hand corner of the card was a phone number, and above it, a name.

Robert Whitney, President/Senior Software Engineer.

A cruel smile grew on Terrance's face. As he stood, he pocketed the card and looked back down the hall toward the bedroom.

As quietly as possible, he chambered a round into his Beretta semiautomatic.

Suddenly there was a loud pounding at his front door. Before he could react, he heard the door crash in and shouts coming from the living room. He turned the corner, pistol in hand, and found four men in black outfits, all heavily armed and scanning the room. All four men saw him at once and brought their weapons around to bear, their laser sights painting red blurs across the walls as they raced toward him.

"What the—"

"Gun!"

The back door behind Terrance exploded inward. He turned quickly to see two more men taking a combat stance on either side of the doorway.

"Police! Drop the weapon, now! Drop it, or we'll open fire!"

Terrance's mouth fell open in astonishment. "What is this? What are you—"

"Drop your weapon!"

Terrance spun toward the front door again. In the process of turning, he brought his pistol up slightly.

It was a huge mistake.

There was a loud popping noise, and he felt something slam into his chest, knocking him off his feet. He fell back onto the kitchen table, the sudden burden causing it to flip over. As it tilted under his weight, he slid to the floor.

I've been shot! They shot me!

As soon as he hit the floor, he rolled into the hall. With men at the front and back doors simultaneously, they had unintentionally put themselves in a crossfire. They couldn't fire at him without risking one of their own being hit.

Ignoring the pain in his chest, Terrance crawled forward and into his bedroom. Slamming the door shut behind him, he collapsed against the wall. He could hear the sounds of careful footsteps in the hallway as the men closed in on his position.

"What do you want? Why are you doing this?" His voice was raspy, and he was finding it difficult to catch his breath. Terrance ripped open his shirt to look at the bulletproof vest underneath it. It had stopped the round before it broke the skin, but the impact had undoubtedly broken a rib or two. If they'd waited five more minutes, he'd have been out of uniform ... and dead on his kitchen floor.

A voice from the hall shattered the silence. "Throw out your weapon and come out with your hands up. If we have to enter, we will use deadly force."

Terrance was panting now. "There's been a mistake. I'm a state trooper. There's been some kind of a big mistake."

"We know who you are, Officer Gold. There's no mistake. Now throw out your weapon and surrender."

Terrance was confused. What was going on? He scanned the room for something that might help him.

Then he saw a strange cardboard box on the other side of his bed.

He knew it hadn't been there when he left. Struggling to his feet, he crossed the room and opened the box. His mouth fell open as his pistol slid from numb fingers.

The contents of the box made him gag.

Suddenly, he understood everything. The mysterious packages he'd been receiving, the magazines that had come from nowhere, the boxes of detestable things that were sitting in his garage waiting to be burned—it all led up to this.

And just as he understood why it had all been happening, he understood who had done it. The business card he'd found in the hall had confirmed it—though it would never stand up in a court of law.

He heard the sound of the door splintering. Men poured into the room and tackled him. He felt the agonizing pain as they jerked his arms behind his back to snap on the handcuffs. He saw the looks of revulsion in their faces as they stared into the open box by his bed— the box they had found him stooped over and looking into as if it were the most important thing in the house and the one thing he'd come to protect.

And everything fell into place.

Robert Whitney had paid him back for the paltry sum for which Terrance had sold his family.

And Terrance couldn't help but laugh about it all.

He was still laughing when the police drove him away.

Derek's head throbbed as he lay on his bed. His sleep had been fitful the night before, but he'd finally drifted off around dawn to a fairly sound slumber. Now he was staring at the ceiling, trying to figure out what had awakened him.

The answer came a few seconds later with a furious banging on his front door. He could hear the muffled sound of someone calling his name. Groaning, Derek slowly sat up and swung his legs off the bed. With his feet flat on the floor, he put his head in his hands to try to give his body time to wake up. The noise at the door continued.

"All right, already. I hear you. I'm coming, okay?"

Forcing himself to his feet, Derek grabbed a T-shirt and slid it on, along with a crumpled pair of jogging shorts he found on the floor. He stumbled down the hall toward the insistent knocking and yelling coming from his front door. Taking a quick look out the peephole, Derek saw Ian Richardson banging on the door with Levi Bishop behind him calmly saying something to him.

Derek began to unlatch the door. "Hey, guys. What's with all the noise? Didn't you see what time—"

As soon as he had the doorknob turned, Richardson slammed into the door, forcing it open. Derek's stunned expression was replaced by a grimace of pain an instant later as Richardson flew into him, grabbing the front of his shirt and throwing him into the wall. Derek's head bounced off the wall behind him, and his headache intensified a hundredfold.

"Hey, what—"

Richardson yelled into his face. "What did you do? Huh? What did you do?"

Derek reached up to pull Richardson's hands from his shirt, but found the vice grip impossible to break. "What are you talking about?"

Richardson's hand shot up so fast that Derek only saw a blur before feeling the impact on the side of his face. "I'm through playing games, Derek!" In one quick motion, Ian pulled Derek forward and to the side. Derek felt his feet blocked by Ian's leg and found his body going airborne. The hard floor rushed up to meet him as he slammed onto his back. The air exploded from his lungs. When his head hit the floor, he felt as though he was going to black out.

Ian was on him like a cat. He pulled Derek up by the shirt and slapped him again. "I want answers, Derek. We were supposed to be a team and take him down legally. What made you lose your stinking mind last night and go after him like that?"

Derek looked over Ian's shoulder and saw the hulking figure of Bishop enter the room. The big man stared into Derek's eyes and then put a huge hand on Ian's shoulder. "Ian, not like this. This isn't the way to get answers."

Ian's heavy breathing calmed slightly, but his eyes never left Derek's. Finally, he released his grip and stood up. Derek stayed on the floor, looking up at the two men. He reached up to rub his jaw as he cleared his throat.

"Would one of you mind telling me what in the world's going on? What am I supposed to have done?"

Ian threw up his hands and turned away. "Would you listen to this punk?"

Bishop extended a hand to Derek as he glanced at Ian. Derek took the proffered hand and felt himself pulled up slowly. "There's been an incident. Ian thinks you're involved."

Derek put his hand behind his head, feeling tenderly for a knot. "Well, what happened?"

Bishop looked deeply into Derek's eyes as if trying to read his soul. "I need to know what you were doing last night, because everything's going to point to you as the obvious choice of a suspect. Don't lie to me, Derek, because it's all got to come out in the open now. I want to help you as much as I can."

Derek felt his heart sink.

Charlie, with Amy and Rachel in tow, burst into the front door at Medical Center East. He searched the entry area, looking for the elevators. Rachel brushed past him and headed across the huge lobby. Amy grabbed Charlie's arm and pulled him along.

When the elevator opened on the fourth floor, Rachel was out the door and gone before Charlie had taken a single step. He and Amy almost had to run to keep up with her. He watched her head turn back and forth, scanning the room numbers for their destination.

Finally, he saw the room number Ian had given him. "Rachel, there it is," he said, pointing across the hall.

Rachel entered the room, and Charlie heard her gasp. When he made it to the doorway, he saw her standing there covering her mouth with her hands. She turned away and began to sob. Amy wrapped her arms around her. "Shhhhh, it'll be all right. It looks worse than it is; that's what the doctor said." With a quick glance at Charlie, she led Rachel out of the room.

When he could finally see the bed, he realized why she was so upset. Robert's left arm was wrapped from the elbow to the hand in a thick white bandage. Gauze encircled his forehead. His face was swollen and bruised, and his lips looked cracked and dry. Charlie knew from talking to the doctor on the phone that Robert's hospital gown and bed sheets hid the worst of his injuries. His ribs were wrapped tightly where they were bruised, and one was cracked. His back had taken a severe amount of punishment as well. The miraculous thing was the lack of broken bones. Though things looked bad, they could have been much worse. Apparently his attacker had been stopped just short of his true intention. He'd only tried to incapacitate Robert long enough to finish him off. That was a scary thought to Charlie, because who in the world would want to kill Robert?

Robert lay silent beneath the covers, asleep and medicated to help him deal with the pain. Charlie slipped into the chair next to his bed and waited. He felt sorry for this man. Robert had lost his wife and child a few months ago, but he'd managed to pull himself out of the depression Charlie was afraid he'd succumb to forever. Then business picked up, and now they were better off than ever. Robert had even managed to find a woman who cared for him deeply, and while Charlie had initially been leery of the idea, Rachel had turned out to be just what he needed to help him snap out of his doldrums.

And then, in one day, life reminded Robert that it didn't like the thought of his being happy. Charlie had no idea what Robert did after hours now, but he knew his boss didn't deserve anything as horrible as what he had experienced last night. He hoped the police found whoever had attacked him in such a cowardly way and put him behind bars for a long time.

There was a sound at the door, and Charlie looked up to see Rachel coming back in, still holding Amy's hand for emotional support. Charlie stood and motioned for her to take his seat, but Rachel shook her head and moved instead to stand next to Robert's inert form. Amy stepped next to Charlie, and her hand slid into his. Charlie squeezed it gently and felt her rest her head on his shoulder.

Rachel's fingertips traced a line along Robert's exposed right arm, finally allowing her hand to cover his. Her left hand reached to caress Robert's face, but she stopped before touching him.

They stood that way for a long time, none of them speaking for fear of waking Robert. A nurse came in to check the IV drip and administer another injection into it. Charlie followed her into the hall and used his cell phone to call and check on Tom and Jonathan.

"Whitney Edge Software," a cheery male voice answered.

"Tom? It's Charlie. How are things there?"

"Hey, Charlie. Things here are fine. How's Robert?"

"He doesn't look too hot, but he should be all right. How are things coming with you guys? Getting your projects done?"

There was a pause. "Well, Charlie, I'm doing all right myself, but Jonathan's another story."

Charlie glanced toward Robert's room, and then lowered his voice. "What do you mean?"

"Well, umm, see, he never showed up."

"Did he call?"

"Nope, haven't heard from him."

Charlie rubbed his forehead trying to think. "Well, I guess it's some kind of emergency. Just keep answering the phones as you can, and don't be afraid to let the machine pick up if you're busy. Amy and I will be back as soon as possible, but Robert's not awake yet. I'll call you later to check on things."

"Sure. I can handle everything here."

As Charlie ended the call, his mind raced.

Where in the world is Jonathan? Does his absence have anything to do with that weird computer virus he was working on?

Before going back to the room, Charlie stopped off at a refreshment station on the floor and brought back two soft drinks for the girls.

As he passed the Coke to Amy, he whispered, "Still no change?"

She shook her head. "No." She motioned toward Rachel. "But she's doing better. I was a little worried there for a minute."

Amy tapped him on the arm. "How about you? How are you feeling?"

Charlie gave her a pained smile. "Well, at least he's alive. Hopefully he'll be all right. Most of the injuries were apparently inflicted to keep him still long enough to finish him off. Fortunately, help arrived before that could happen. I still don't understand why, though. Hasn't he gone through enough already?"

Amy's arm wrapped around his waist, and she hugged him. Charlie closed his eyes and tried to make sense of it all.

An hour later Ian Richardson sat behind his desk idly shuffling a deck of cards. It was a habit he'd picked up long ago to help him organize his thoughts. He considered each card in the deck as a random piece of a case, and by shuffling the deck he was moving the pieces around until they made sense. Fanning the cards toward himself, he saw the suits and colors scattered throughout the deck. Just like the case he was now working on.

On the desk in front of him sat a simple juice glass. To the casual observer, it would seem unimportant, but it was vital to the events of the past twenty-four hours. Ian had "borrowed" it from Derek's house that morning when they'd visited. Soon he would put it to good use.

With one studious look at the pasteboards, he turned them face-down and began to shuffle again. While his mind worked over everything he'd seen and heard up to this point, his fingers moved almost of their own accord. Each action appeared unrelated to the next, but with every separation of the cards, they fell into a specific point in the deck.

"All right, let's consider everything," he said, speaking to the empty room. "Someone tries to run Derek Morrison off the road, so he says—though I have my doubts now. In the process it causes him to run over another car carrying a man's wife and daughter. So, for whatever reason, Derek was involved in the wreck that killed Robert Whitney's wife and child."

He cut the deck again.

"For some reason, Robert seems to think that Derek did it on purpose, so he goes after Derek and his family."

Ian dovetailed the cards and continued shuffling.

"Besides being an excellent tipper, Robert's brilliant and creative. He finds ways to get back at Derek without making it look like he's getting back at Derek. He even has Derek's wife fooled."

He closed his eyes and did several one-handed cuts of the deck.

"Robert is so clever that it's impossible to catch him doing anything or trace it back to him. He's going to get away with it all … then he sends a compromising videotape. That's a pretty bold move, any way you look at it."

Without looking at his hands, Ian cut the cards into four piles interlaced between his fingers, then in one quick motion had them all together again.

"Derek tries to talk to Rachel and work things out. Rachel works for Robert. Rachel doesn't believe Derek about the origin of the video, and they have a big argument."

Ian began a quick overhand shuffle.

"Derek has all he can take and drives off to find Robert and dish out some good old-fashioned street justice, except Derek denies any part of it. Even says he has …"

He slowed as he began to sit taller in his chair.

" … a witness."

Ian ribbon-spread the cards faceup on his desk. Without exception, ace to king, every suit was in perfect order.

TWENTY-NINE

Visitor."

Ian stood by the officer, looking into the small cell at the slumbering form on a cot. The form rolled over, and Ian found himself staring into the face of a tired-looking black man in his midforties. The man wore an orange jumpsuit with "Birmingham Department of Corrections" on the back. He sat on the edge of the cot and looked at Ian warily.

"Officer Terrance Gold?"

The man squinted as if trying to place Ian from somewhere. "Who're you?"

"My name's Ian."

"You a lawyer?"

"Thankfully, no. My father would've never forgiven me."

"Then we don't have any reason to be talking to each other." Gold began to lie down again.

"It would be in your best interest to talk to me, Terrance."

An obscene gesture was his only reply.

Ian continued. "You're in some serious trouble here. I think I know who did this, and I'm pretty sure I can guess why. I'd appreciate it if you could confirm some things for me, though."

The man spoke over his shoulder. "What's in it for me?"

"How about helping out a fellow human being? I'd like to stop the guy who did this to you before he does something worse to someone else. I can do that with your help. I might even be able to prove your innocence in what they're accusing you of."

There was silence for several seconds, then the man rolled over and stood. His weary eyes locked on Ian's as he walked toward the bars. Gold grabbed the bars and spoke in a low voice. "I know who did this to me. I also know the law can't hold me here forever. When I get out, you won't have to worry about him doing anything worse to anyone else. That's a promise."

Ian tilted his head. "Come on, Terrance. I have friends here, and I've seen what they're holding you with. Your house and garage were filled with some rather disgusting material, but what they found in your bedroom—"

Gold pushed his head forward as if trying to shove it through the bars. "I know what they found in my bedroom," he hissed through clenched teeth. "I saw what was in that box before they busted in on me. I've never seen that stuff before. Those were children in those pictures, man. You realize how sick I'd have to be to collect stuff like that? And do you realize how *stupid* I'd have to be to keep that sort of thing in the middle of my bedroom floor for anyone to see? They've got circumstantial evidence. It won't hold up in court."

Gold threw several unkind words in Ian's direction and turned to walk away. Ian did not move but spoke in a calm voice. "How about your computer, Terrance? How do you explain what they found on it?"

Gold froze in midstep. He spoke over his shoulder. "What are you talking about?"

Ian kept his tone even. This was where he could start bargaining. "I guess you haven't heard about that yet, have you? It's been a busy few hours for the guys. While you've been sleeping, they've been cataloging evidence. They found some pretty nasty things on your computer. It appears you've been visiting some ... shall we say inappropriate Web sites. The things they found on your hard drive will be more than enough to hold you for a while. It appears that someone wants it to look like this has been a rather long-term hobby of yours."

Gold moved back to the bars. "How would you know about all this?"

"I told you, I have friends here. I do favors for them, they do favors for me."

Gold's eyes narrowed. "You a reporter?"

Ian had to chuckle at that question. "Not by a long shot. All you really need to know about me is that I'm a man of my word. You answer a few of my questions, and I'll do what I can to help prove your innocence. Helping me will actually do the work for you."

"Man, forget you."

"You know what happens to a sex offender, Terrance? The rest of your life your face will be all over the Internet for anyone to see. You'll have to register yourself before you move into a new neighborhood, and you can't live or work within fifteen-hundred feet of a school or day care. People are going to look at you from the corner of their eyes from now on."

Terrance swallowed hard but said nothing. Ian knew he'd won.

"If someone set you up like you say, they picked the most damaging way to do it. This is something that'll never go away without help."

Gold studied him for several seconds. "What do you want to know?"

Ian pulled a copy of an accident report out of his pocket and passed it through the bars to Gold. "A little over a month ago you worked a traffic accident on I-20. A woman and child were killed. The woman's husband saw the whole thing and contended that it was a deliberate act of the truck driver. The trucker contended it was another vehicle that ran him off the road. The husband has spent the last several weeks wreaking havoc on the guy's life as an act of revenge."

Gold glanced over the report before handing it back to Ian. "How'd you get a copy of this?"

Ian folded the report and put it back in his coat pocket. "The trucker hired me to catch the guy in the act. This was one of the things he gave me to prove his case."

Gold shrugged. "So?"

"So, the trucker mentions to me this morning that he'd talked to you last night. I looked at the report again and found your name on it. I went to see you and found some ugly yellow crime tape around your place. Your neighbor kindly informed me the police carted you off with several boxes. Now, I like to consider myself a clever man, but it wasn't rocket science to figure out where you were. And here I am."

Ian smiled at the man, but didn't receive a smile in response. "Anyway, I'm going to ask you a few questions, Terrance. I can promise you two things before you agree to answer them. First, it'll be in your best interest to tell me the truth. A dishonest answer might make you look better, but it won't help clear up this mess."

The man sneered at him. "And the other thing?"

Ian's smile disappeared. "The other thing is that I can tell when you're lying. I'm an excellent judge of people, and I promise you I'll catch you at every little fib. I'll give you one freebie because I know you're going to be dying to test me. Any more lies after that, I'll walk, and you're on your own. I can find the truth; it will just make it easier for me if I have your cooperation."

The two looked at each other for several long moments before a half grin slowly formed on Gold's face. "You're one cocky little man, aren't you? All right, I'll help you. I'll tell you what you want to know, and then you straighten things out for me." The grin died on Gold's face as he slowly brought a finger up and pointed it at Ian. "But I'm gonna make *you* two promises. First, if you double-cross me and forget our deal, I'll handle this guy on my own when I get out of here—and I will get out of here."

Ian nodded. "And the second?"

Gold's voice turned cold. "After I'm through taking care of him, I'll find you and take care of you, too."

"Watch me lose sleep."

Gold sniffed. "Now, what do you want to know?"

When he entered Robert's room again, Charlie's stomach jumped.

There, standing by Robert's bed, was a giant. The man must have heard the two of them enter, because he looked up and appeared to be scrutinizing them. After a moment's hesitation, a huge smile crossed his face. Rachel was standing on the opposite side of the bed and finally noticed them.

"Hey guys, I'd like you to meet someone. This is Levi. He's a friend of Robert's."

A massive hand reached out to shake Charlie's. The man kept his voice quiet, trying not to disturb Robert. "How are you? I've heard a lot about you, Charlie. Rachel's been telling me how you guys stayed with her this morning."

Levi's grip was firm, but it was obvious that he wasn't trying to hurt Charlie. All the same, Charlie was glad when Levi let him go.

"Not trying to sound rude here, Levi, but how do you know Robert? I'm afraid I don't remember him mentioning you."

"I haven't known him that long. We met last night when I invited myself to dinner with him so we could discuss business. He was kind enough to share his table with me."

Charlie eyed him skeptically. "You met him last night?"

Rachel spoke up. "Levi is the one who found Robert and stopped the attacker last night. He was there with him when the paramedics arrived."

This explanation did nothing to allay Charlie's growing suspicions. "Oh really? You just happened to be there when that guy attacked him?"

Levi kept the friendly smile on his face. "Providential timing."

Charlie looked down at Robert. "Any change?"

Rachel shook her head. "No, but he should be waking up soon. The pain medicine makes him sleepy, from what the nurse told me."

Amy glanced at Rachel. "You need to eat something. I know you're worried about Robert, but ..."

Rachel didn't take her eyes off Robert. "No, I'll be all right."

Levi reached across the bed and gently touched Rachel's arm. "Why don't you at least get yourself something to drink in the cafeteria? There's nothing more you can do around here right now."

Rachel spoke again, though with less conviction this time. "I want to be here when he wakes up."

Levi's voice was soothing. "I'll stay right here with him until you return. If he wakes up before you get back, I'll let him know you're here. He'll understand, Rachel. He wouldn't want you wearing yourself out."

Charlie watched silently as Rachel looked into Levi's eyes for a moment, then nodded a little. Bending over Robert, she kissed his forehead and whispered something. Then she straightened up and looked at Levi.

"I'll be right back."

"Don't worry about him. I won't let anyone bother him."

As Rachel moved toward them, Amy put an arm around her and led her toward the door. Charlie took one more look at Levi, who winked at him. The muscular giant towered over Robert's still form like a guardian angel. Even if the guy who attacked Robert last night was still out there, Charlie had no doubt that Levi would make sure no one bothered Robert.

And Charlie felt sorry for anyone who might be stupid enough to try.

"First things first: Did you doctor that accident report?"

Gold's face turned hard. "I don't like that question."

"I couldn't care less. Answer it anyway."

"What do you mean?"

"I mean did the things you put on that report really happen the way you put them? Or did you do anything to it that could make this Robert Whitney want to get back at you for it?"

Gold huffed. "Why would I do something like that?"

"I don't know … maybe you didn't. Or maybe you had a really good reason. You ever accepted a bribe before, Terrance?"

Gold's eyes narrowed. "No."

Ian hesitated a moment, then nodded. "Okay, that was your freebie. You lie to me again, and I walk."

"You callin' me a liar?"

"Yeah, and I hope it's not a habitual problem. Do it again, and you'll damage our fragile friendship."

Gold glared at him for several seconds, then gave him another half grin. "All right. Yeah, I've taken a bribe before. It's not something I do every day or anything though. I'm not like those guys you see in the movies with stashes of cash hidden in their house."

"I believe you—besides, I saw the police report on you. I know what you've got stashed in your house, Terrance."

Gold's hands balled into fists, but Ian ignored the action. "Next question: Did someone bribe you to change the accident report in any way?"

"Maybe I need a lawyer here."

Ian shrugged. "Suit yourself. I don't have time to wait for him though. You just fix it all on your own."

Ian turned to leave, but Gold reached through the bars and grabbed his sleeve. "All right. We'll just keep this between ourselves."

"Whatever. Now answer my question."

Gold rubbed his hands on his pants, possibly trying to dry off his sweaty palms. "Maybe."

"Fair enough. I'd like to know who did it because I have the feeling that Whitney's probably got something planned for them too, but I can't force that info out of you. At least I have a motive now for Whitney. Now, what really happened out there? I know what the trucker told me, and I know what your report says, but what's the truth?"

Gold eyed him warily. "This stays between you and me?"

"You have my word. I just want to understand what's really going on here. I don't like being used—and I have the feeling I've been strung along for a while now."

"There was no other vehicle. Yes, there was a witness—but I think he was for sale, if you know what I mean."

Ian looked over Gold. "Yeah, I know what you mean."

Gold seemed not to notice the veiled insult. "Anyway, there were two other witnesses. Both of them were close enough to see what happened. One was even in the other lane almost past the eighteen-wheeler when it swerved toward the other car. Those two along with Whitney made a pretty convincing case. That trucking company was in the perfect position for a huge lawsuit—and they'd have lost. I've seen this kind of thing before, though, and I know what some of those companies will do to keep things smooth for themselves. I made it fair for both parties. I gave my contact information to both men. It's not my fault Whitney didn't make an offer. I'd have rather worked it in his favor, but a man's got to do what he has to do."

Ian listened for another five minutes while Gold told the whole story. When he had no more questions, he thanked Gold and started to walk away.

"Hey," Gold called after him. "I meant what I said. You lie to me, and I'll find you."

Ian whirled around and stormed back to Gold's cell with a smirk on his face. He whipped his empty hand palm forward toward Terrance. Gold flinched, as with a quick motion a business card seemed to materialize out of nowhere and appear in Ian's fingertips. Ian flicked the card through the bars at Gold.

"Here's my card. If you get out of here, and you're feeling brave and stupid, you call my office. They'll know how to get in touch with me."

Gold's nostrils flared. "Yeah, I got a feeling you and me will be seeing each other again."

Ian said, "I can honestly say I'm looking forward to it."

When Robert opened his eyes, there were several things he expected to see: total blackness, indicating that he'd ceased to exist after death, or perhaps a bright light at the end of a tunnel, a sign he was still existent. He'd even seriously considered the possibility that he'd wake up surrounded by blazing fire and screaming demons.

Instead, he found himself looking at the same face he'd seen before passing out.

Robert licked his dry lips. Levi reached for a cup on a small table next to the bed and poured some water into it. He brought it to Robert's lips, and Robert drank greedily, enjoying the cool sensation as it flowed down his throat.

"Thanks."

"You're very welcome."

Robert glanced around the room, trying to acclimate himself to his new surroundings. "Have you been here the whole time?"

"No. I came here with you last night in the ambulance. I stayed until they got you settled in, and then went home to get some sleep. I got back here around lunchtime. I had some things to check on before I could get here."

"Thanks for coming. And thanks for what you did last night. You saved my life."

"I'm just sorry I didn't get there sooner."

Robert closed his eyes for a moment, feeling his body slowly come back into focus. A dull, throbbing pain was beginning to sharpen into a headache, and his whole torso seemed to hurt. "Can I get an aspirin or something?"

Levi looked around until he found the nurse call button. Within seconds a nasally voice asked what was needed.

"My friend is awake and would like an aspirin, please," Levi answered.

Robert thanked him and closed his eyes to rest them. Then a thought came to him. "Levi, what were you doing at my house last night, anyway?"

Levi's mouth opened a little, and he appeared to be searching for an answer. "I ... um ..."

Just then the door opened, and a pretty nurse walked in with a small plastic cup in her hand. She smiled at Robert and seemed startled by his gigantic visitor. She recovered quickly. "I hear someone's not feeling too well."

Robert lifted his hand. "That would be me."

The nurse gave him the medicine, her eyes darting toward Levi several times during the exchange before she left.

Robert took a deep breath as he waited for the pain to go away. "I think she's scared of you."

Levi responded with a deep, rich laugh. "Maybe. I'm just glad we didn't meet in the parking lot. I have a feeling she'd have been reaching for the pepper spray."

Robert chuckled. He stopped as lances of pain shot through him, taking his breath away. Levi touched him, and Robert heard the big man softly pray. Robert was too weak to fight him off, but the way he was feeling he'd accept any kind of relief he could get. When he finished the prayer, Levi patted his arm.

"Rachel's here too, Robert. She's been by your bed all morning. She's getting something to eat right now."

"She's a sweetie."

Levi's eyes never left Robert. "Yeah, she's very special. She's been through some hard times this morning, and I don't think she could handle it if something else bad happened."

Robert looked up at him. There was something behind his words that made Robert think he knew more than he was saying.

There's no way he could know anything. He just met me last night, for crying out loud.

"Do you have any idea who did this to you?" Levi asked.

Robert closed his eyes to concentrate. He could remember flashes of things, a cruel voice condemning him, but nothing definite.

"I'm afraid not. I can't remember much. It all just sort of seems like a blur or a series of disconnected images. The voice was definitely familiar, but I couldn't swear as to who it was or anything."

Levi gave him a tight smile and nodded. "I didn't get a good look at him either."

Robert felt the bandages around his chest and reached up to touch the one that circled his forehead. "Any idea what the guy hit me with?"

"A Louisville Slugger. I don't know if there were any prints on it or not. He dropped it when he started running. The police have it now, I imagine."

Suddenly the door opened, and Rachel walked in. Her face seemed to light up when she caught sight of Robert. She rushed to him and kissed him. As she gently stroked his cheek, guilt and shame for what he was doing to her washed over him like a tidal wave.

"I thought we'd lost you," she whispered.

"Nah. I just wanted a day off."

Rachel laughed, apparently more out of relief than anything else. There was a light knock on the door as Rachel's father walked in, followed by Charlie and Amy.

"Hey there, chief," Charlie said. "How are you feeling?"

"I've been better. Why aren't you at work?"

Charlie replied without missing a beat. "I sold the business this morning when you didn't show up. Amy and I are on our way to Aruba now, but we wanted to say good-bye first."

Robert smiled and looked past Rachel. "Hey, Paul. How's Sarah?"

"She's good. She had to stay home so she could pick up Scott from school. She wanted me to tell you that she'd be praying for you, though."

There was a chirping sound, and Levi pulled a cell phone out of his pocket. He looked apologetically at everyone as he noticed the number on the small screen. "I'm sorry about this, but I need to take this call." He hit a button on the phone and brought it to his face. "Just a minute." Then he turned to Robert. "It appears you have enough visitors to keep you occupied for a while. I'll come back later to check on you again, all right?"

"Sure, Levi. Thanks for everything."

"No problem." Pulling out a small business card, he put it on the table beside Robert's bed. "My home number and cell number are on there. If you need me or just feel like talking, give me a call." He shook hands again with Charlie and Paul, and then gave a quick wave to Rachel and Amy as he stepped toward the door.

Bishop waited until he was in the hall before talking on the phone again. "Sorry about that, Ian. I had to excuse myself."

"No problem. Can you talk now?"

Bishop continued walking down the hall toward the elevators. Some of the nurses gave him an evil look as he passed and motioned for him to turn off his cell phone. "Yeah, I'm on my way out the door. What's up?"

"We may have ourselves a serious problem," Ian answered. "I had a delightful chat with Trooper Terrance Gold just a little while ago. Charming fellow. He's promised we can get together again when he gets out of jail."

"Jail? What's he doing in jail?"

"Long story. Apparently Derek wasn't the only one on Whitney's hit list. I know of at least two more folks Whitney could have gone after, but that doesn't mean there weren't more."

Bishop stepped into the elevator and pressed the button for the lobby. "So Derek could truly be innocent."

"Whitney has other enemies, but I'm not sure they know he's the one behind their troubles. Gold is absolutely certain Whitney framed him, although I don't know why he's so sure."

Ian was silent for so long that Bishop thought he'd lost the call. "Ian? Are you still there?"

When Ian answered, his voice betrayed the fact that he was struggling with his next words. "Yeah, I'm here. There's ... there's one other thing I haven't told you. I just found out about it myself about a half hour ago. It's actually the main reason for my call."

Bishop stepped out of the elevator and walked toward the lobby door. The sunlight that poured in through the glass didn't warm him at all. "What's wrong?"

Ian seemed to have a hard time finding words. "This morning, when we were at Derek's house, I lifted the glass he was drinking. I needed a sample of his fingerprints."

"How in the world did you do that without my noticing?"

"An old magician's trick. I can pick your pocket too, if you'd like me to show you sometime. I needed the glass, and I didn't need my taking it raising suspicions."

"What did you find?"

Ian answered quickly. "Remember my friends in the police department? Well, I gave them the glass and asked them to match the prints on it with the prints on the baseball bat used to beat the tar out of Whitney. When I went to see Gold in jail, I gave him a copy of the accident report to handle and he grabbed my sleeve at one point, and that gave me a set of his prints to compare."

Bishop shook his head. "You realize how questionable all that is, don't you? Any halfway decent lawyer is going to get that evidence thrown out of court in a heartbeat."

"I know, I know. I actually wanted to prove Derek's innocence so we could narrow down our list of suspects."

Bishop made it to his car and got inside. He started it up to let the air conditioner turn on, but he didn't begin to drive yet. "So what did you find?"

More silence. Then Bishop heard Ian sigh. "They match, Levi."

"What?"

"The prints on the bat match the prints on the glass. Derek's our man."

Bishop sank back into his car seat and closed his eyes. "He said he was innocent."

"I know how much you like the guy, Levi, but proof is proof. I lied to the guys at the police department about why I needed the prints identified, so he's still clear for the moment. That'll change soon though, I'm sure."

Bishop felt betrayed. "I need to talk to Derek."

"That's another problem. I'm here at Derek's house now, and he's not home. It appears our boy has disappeared."

THIRTY

CHARLIE ARRIVED BACK AT the office a little before five. He and Amy had agreed that she would stay with Rachel while he locked up and let Tom go home. Charlie had enjoyed spending the afternoon getting to know Rachel's dad. The man seemed very loving toward his daughter. To hear Robert talk about it, Paul didn't care very much for him—yet he'd seemed so genuinely concerned all day that it made Robert's initial impressions seem wrong.

When Charlie walked into the office, he was greeted with silence. He glanced over at Tom's workstation and found it empty. "Tom? Hey, are you still here?" Charlie walked to Tom's monitor to see if he'd left his computer on. It was already shut down for the day.

"Hey, Charlie." The sudden noise made him jump. Tom walked from the back holding a small stack of papers. "Sorry I didn't hear you come in." He crossed the room in a hurry and shook Charlie's hand, almost pulling him away from his workstation. "How's Robert?"

"Fine. How are things here?" Charlie glanced back toward the workstation. Tom stepped discreetly in his line of vision and continued to lead him toward Rachel's desk.

"Hey, I handled it. You had some mail come in, but I don't think there was anything in there that can't wait until Monday. We had a call from Duke Library Systems wanting to know about the status of their program."

Charlie glanced over the mail. "What did you tell them?"

Tom held up his hands. "Hey, that's not my project. Jonathan's handling that one. I told them to call back Monday."

Charlie threw the mail back on Rachel's desk and looked toward the back of the office at Jonathan's workstation. "Still no word from him?"

"No, I never heard back from him. You know how strange and quiet he is. I'm sure he'll be back first thing Monday morning."

"Yeah, maybe." Charlie wished he knew what was going on. He could tell something was bothering Tom. He was starting to get edgy. "Is there something wrong, Tom?"

The smile faded as Tom's eyes fell. With a sigh, he brought his hand up and rubbed his forehead. "Well, I guess you're going to find out about it sooner or later. I really messed up."

"What do you mean?"

Tom walked back to his workstation. "Well, when Duke called, I could tell they were a little anxious. I finished my work early and wanted to try and help Jonathan finish it up. Unfortunately, when I tried to log into his computer and check the progress of his work, something bad happened."

Charlie didn't like the sound of that last statement. "Define 'bad.'"

"Let's just say you don't need to try and log into the system right now. Apparently there was some sort of virus in our network. It was dormant until something happened to trigger it. For my life, I honestly don't know what I did."

Charlie slid into the seat at Tom's workstation. He booted up the computer and watched as the login screen appeared. He knew the username and password he'd given Tom, so he had the login fields filled out in seconds.

But the computer would not let him in.

He tried again, thinking that he might have possibly hit a wrong key somewhere in the password.

The computer said that the password was incorrect and would still not let him in.

Charlie glanced over his shoulder.

"It gets worse," Tom said.

Charlie decided to log in as the administrator with all privileges for the account. He put in his username and the password he'd chosen for the master account.

The password was not accepted.

How in the world can I be locked out of the admin account? I'm the only one with that password, and I should be the only one who can get into it.

Charlie tried again, but was still unsuccessful. A theory began to form, and though he dismissed it at first, it soon became too persuasive to ignore.

Someone in the company had locked him out of his own system.

Jonathan could have done it yesterday after I left. He could have waited until after we had all logged out and then changed everything before leaving. But why? On the other hand, Tom could have done it after we all left this morning. He had all day long to work on it, but what would he be hiding?

Whatever the reason, one thing was certain: No matter who had done this, it wouldn't keep him out of his system for long. A wicked smile crossed Charlie's face. This was the kind of challenge he enjoyed, and he hadn't had one in a long time.

Bishop walked into Starline Trucking and found it in chaos. As soon as he opened the door to enter, he heard raised voices in a heated argument. The receptionist sitting behind a battered metal desk groaned. A scratched and dented nameplate proclaimed that her name was Cindy, and it looked as if it had seen as many hard times as she had. Finally, Cindy acknowledged Bishop's presence and spoke with an exasperated tone.

"Can I help you?"

Bishop tried to seem friendly. It was obvious this woman was having a bad day, and judging from the sounds coming down the hall, so were several other people. "Yes, ma'am. I was wondering if I could see Derek Morrison please?"

Cindy cast a furtive glance down the hall and lowered her voice, leaning toward him. "Derek doesn't work here anymore. He quit yesterday."

The voices down the hall escalated in volume. Bishop could clearly make out several words now, mostly profanity. "Sounds like things aren't going too well this evening."

Cindy rolled her eyes. "Yeah, you could say that. We've been having some problems with our computers lately, and today it all came to a head. That charming man you hear screaming obscenities is my boss, and the other man trying to deny his lovely comments about his mother is our computer guy. They aren't seeing eye to eye at the moment."

Bishop's eyes widened at one particularly brutal outburst from down the hall, then a door slammed shut. A frazzled-looking man barreled into the front room. His face was a deep crimson, his eyes fixed straight ahead. Behind him, another man came blazing in like a hurricane. His shirt was wrinkled, and his tie hung like an open noose around his neck. A vein throbbed on his forehead, threatening to burst.

Shirt-and-Tie yelled, "Don't you turn your back on me!"

Red-Face turned and screamed back, "I'm sick of listening to your complaints! I told you I wasn't right for learning those stupid computers, Gordon!"

The one named Gordon got right into the first man's face. "Well, it's too late now, isn't it, Larry? I tell you what, you fix the blasted thing, or I'll find someone else to take your place."

The one named Larry leaned into Gordon's face until they were so close it looked as if they were going to crush each other's noses. "That's what I've been trying to tell you for three months. I don't know what I'm doing, and it's not my fault we're having these problems."

"We bought you all those books to read."

"Well, I guess you just wasted all that money."

Cindy cleared her throat loudly, and both men seemed to realize they had an audience. Gordon looked at Bishop and then glared down at Cindy. She merely smiled and waved a hand toward Bishop. "This gentleman is looking for Derek," she said, her voice polite and professional.

Gordon's eyes widened, and then a strange thing occurred. The scowl left his face, he seemed to attempt to control his breathing, and he straightened his tie. To Bishop's surprise, he actually smiled as he walked toward him. "So, you're looking for Derek?"

"Yes, I am."

Gordon was very close to him now, still smiling and talking cheerfully as well. "Are you a friend of his, or is he in trouble?"

"I'm a friend who's trying to make sure he's not in trouble."

Gordon looked away and chuckled. "Well, would you do me a favor if you find him?"

"If I can, I'll be happy to."

Suddenly, Gordon exploded in another outburst. "Tell that no-good, lazy piece of human garbage that if I ever see him again, I'm going to rip off his head and spit down his throat! Nobody leaves me hanging here—and after all I've done for him!"

Bishop raised a hand. "Now, there's no need to yell."

Gordon turned back to Larry again. "What are you standing around here for? Get in there and fix those computers."

Larry looked almost ready to reply, but instead he turned on his heel in a huff and disappeared into a nearby office. Bishop saw him pick up a thick book from his desk before slamming the door shut.

Gordon watched until the door was closed, then turned back to Bishop. He brought a finger up and pointed at a spot between Bishop's eyes. Despite their obvious size difference, Gordon didn't appear to be the least bit intimidated by his uninvited visitor. He looked down at Cindy and yelled, "What are you sitting around for? Don't you have work to do?"

She shrugged. "What's there to do? The computers are down."

"So file something."

"What do I have to file?"

In one fluid motion, Gordon swept her in-box off the edge of her desk, scattering papers everywhere. As the pages fluttered to the floor, he said, "File that." With one final disgusted glance at Bishop, he stormed back down the hallway.

Bishop's righteous indignation was flaring up inside. He wanted to go down to Gordon's office and turn the man's entire desk over for spite. Fortunately for Gordon, that was not his way. Instead, he took a deep breath and knelt down to help Cindy gather up the papers around her desk.

"I'm sorry if I caused you this trouble," he said.

She shook her head. Her back was to him, but Bishop thought he saw her wiping tears from her face. "No, it's not your fault. We've been having problems with the computers here for a few weeks now. I guess it just got to be too much for Gordon, that's all. He's usually not that bad."

When they had collected everything, he put the stack back on her desk. She kept her head down and slightly away from him so he couldn't get a good look at her face. Not wanting to embarrass her, Bishop stepped back and gave her room to compose herself.

"Well, I've taken up enough of your time."

Cindy looked up at him and smiled. Her eyes were indeed watery and slightly red. "That's okay. Sorry I couldn't be more help."

"Thanks again, Cindy."

When he got into his car, he stopped to offer a quick prayer for her.

Charlie was disappointed. Whoever had locked him out of his system was indeed good at slinging code. They'd written a virus into the system that changed the password every single time someone tried to log in. Basically, there was no way anyone would have ever been able to get into the workstations again—not even the one who created the virus. It had been created to be foolproof, and it would have sabotaged the company to the point that months of work could have been lost.

Of course, whoever it was had underestimated Charlie Bolton.

Charlie had sent Tom home so he could work without distraction. It had taken thirty minutes to find the virus, destroy it, and re-create the passwords to get into the system. It was the best workout he'd had in a while, but he'd been hoping for more and actually had to admit he was a little disappointed.

One thing was certain: Whoever planted the virus had no intention of ever coming back to work again. There were six people in the office, counting Charlie. One was in the hospital now and had not even come to work that morning—though Charlie had to admit that Robert could have put the virus in the system last night. One appeared to have little working knowledge of computers, and really had no reason to hurt the man she apparently cared for deeply. Charlie knew that he himself hadn't done it. That left three possibilities.

When Charlie finally got into Tom's computer, he started to pull up the history. Suddenly, he heard a familiar tapping noise coming from the tower. The hard drive was being erased.

Acting on instinct, he unplugged the computer to halt the destructive program. He had no idea whether the program was local or on every machine. The only way to find out was to check each machine individually.

Finally, Charlie decided to test the program on another machine. He logged in at Jonathan's workstation. Everything was fine for almost two minutes. Then he heard the tapping noise and saw files being deleted on the screen. Before it even started, he had the machine unplugged.

The malicious program was system-wide. That meant he'd have to hunt it down on each machine and destroy it. But first he had to find a way to get into the machine without activating the program.

Now he had a challenge.

And despite the difficulty and near impossibility of what he was about to face, Charlie smiled.

"Excuse me? What did you say?"

Charlie looked down at the phone in disbelief, as if he could see Robert's face reflected in it. Robert was awake and talking now, having just finished a dinner of lukewarm chicken and vegetables. His call had broken the intense concentration Charlie had been locked into.

"I want you to bring me my laptop so I can get some work done around here," Robert said. "It's on my desk. I mean, I hope you're coming back for a visit tomorrow … if so, you can bring it then."

Charlie laughed, holding the phone with his shoulder while trying to reach the files on his computer in a roundabout way to avoid the virus. "You are a piece of work, mister. Last night someone plays stickball with your body, and tonight you're worried about finishing a project. I'm not sure, but I believe our customers will be kind enough to grant you an extension due to the extenuating circumstances."

"Look, humor me, okay?" Robert replied.

Charlie shook his head and chuckled. "Why don't you take a couple of days off? Hopefully you'll be out of there by Monday night, and then you can concentrate on other things."

"Just bring me the stupid computer!" Robert's sudden outburst shocked Charlie into stunned silence. After a few awkward seconds, he heard Robert sigh. "I'm sorry. I'm just not feeling well, and I let it get the best of me. Can you please just bring me the computer? I won't be on it long. I just have some things to take care of, that's all."

Charlie nodded, still numb from the past few seconds. "Sure. I'll bring it by in the morning." He glanced up as Amy walked into the office. "I have to go. You take it easy tonight."

"Thanks, Charlie. I appreciate it. I'm really sorry about the way I acted, okay?"

"I understand," Charlie said. "Just take your meds and sleep like a baby. You'll feel better in the morning."

After saying good-bye to Robert, Charlie told Amy about the conversation. She propped herself against his desk as he spoke, her perfume caressing his senses with her closeness.

Amy said, "Robert's not usually like that. Something's not right."

Charlie had to agree. "Maybe Robert's just not feeling well. I mean, the guy got his head knocked around quite a bit last night. He's lucky whoever it was didn't kill him."

Amy stared straight ahead. "Not lucky … blessed." Then she clapped her hands on her legs. "Enough talk. You were supposed to take me for a quick bite of dinner. Instead you're here working on something; so what's got such a stranglehold on your attention? You've got me pretty intrigued with whatever problem you have brewing back there."

Charlie decided not to fight her about it now. In the back of his mind, a little voice nagged him that she might actually be the one responsible for the mess. He tried to push the thought away, wanting to think the best of the woman he was quickly falling for.

Terrance Gold stood outside the city jail and breathed the free air. Like Richardson, he had friends here too. His lawyer had managed to get him out on bail, and now he was ready to get as far away from this place as possible. He got into his car and started it up, his mind on one thought.

Revenge.

Robert Whitney didn't know it yet, but he was a walking dead man.

THIRTY-ONE

ROBERT WATCHED AS THE news anchors droned on about minor stories and sports scores, but he wasn't interested in any of that. He was looking for one story in particular, and he hoped he hadn't missed it. His body begged for more pain medicine and sleep, but he wouldn't allow himself the pleasure until business was done.

Rachel sat silent at his bedside, staring ahead. She was lost in some deep train of thought, but she hadn't shared any of it yet. He knew he needed to seem concerned, but he hated the thought of missing the one news story he'd been waiting so long to see and hear. Finally, he decided to try to break the ice while keeping a careful ear open for what was on the screen.

"Is everything all right? You seem so quiet."

Rachel looked up at him and gave him a tight smile. He could see genuine pain in her eyes. She was going through something hard for her right now. Suddenly what was on the television didn't seem to matter as much to him.

Watch yourself, Whitney. You can't afford to fall for this woman. Remember the real reason you hired her.

But even as he thought the words, he felt little conviction of their truth. As much as he'd tried to avoid admitting it, he still had feelings.

"I'm fine," Rachel said. "Don't worry about me. I'm just thinking about some things, that's all. I'll work it all out."

The commercial on television ended, and Robert watched the news anchor reappear. His face was serious, giving a hint about the tone of the story to follow.

"Local police this morning arrested a state trooper on child-pornography charges. Kim Hall has the story." The screen changed to an exterior shot of Terrance Gold's house. Yellow police tape was stretched across the front yard, while several policemen carried some ominous-looking boxes out the front door.

Then the camera cut to a pretty redhead standing across the street from the now-deserted house. "This morning police raided this home in Trussville," she said, gesturing behind her. "While the details are still sketchy at this time, we do know that several officers were seen carrying out boxes earlier today. One source we talked to confirmed that the boxes were filled with adult material of every type imaginable. At least one of those boxes contained offensive material involving minors. Just minutes ago a computer was also removed as evidence."

Robert's eyes narrowed as his heart raced. *Come on, tell his name. What are you waiting for? That's the most important part.*

As if reading his mind, she continued. "State trooper Terrance Gold was arrested this morning and taken into custody on child-pornography charges. He was released this afternoon on bail pending his trial."

The reporter continued to drone on with more detail, but Robert's mind was locked on that last statement she'd made.

Gold was out.

Don't get paranoid. There's no way he could know you were involved. And even if he figured it out, there's no way he could ever find you. He'd expect you to be at home or at work or something. You're safe.

But Robert couldn't believe his own reassurances. He was in danger now. He'd struck and expected Gold to be held for quite a while, but apparently the trooper had friends who pulled strings. He was on the streets, and probably pretty ticked off.

Ordinarily this wouldn't have been a problem. If Robert had still been able to get around easily, he could have moved the final part of his revenge on Gold up a bit. Instead, he was helpless here in the hospital with no way to orchestrate anything without at least his laptop.

Robert rubbed his eyes with his good hand and tried to think of what to do next. He had no idea how, but he had to defend himself a little while longer. There were still two people who had to pay for what they'd done. Nothing could happen to him until then. Derek would be the last, and after he paid, it would all end—forever.

"Robert?"

He blinked several times, snapping out of his reverie, and smiled up at the source of the interruption. "I'm sorry, did you say something?"

Rachel raised an eyebrow. "Actually, I said something a few times." She pointed toward the television. "Can we turn that off please? It's a little disturbing."

Robert turned his attention to the television again. The anchors were on to a story about a bloody battle somewhere in the Middle East. "Sure. Sorry about drifting off like that." He hit the button on the side of his bed, and the screen went dead.

"It's all right. How are you feeling?"

"I've felt better. My head's beating like a drum, and I feel like I could sleep another two days. But I'm lucky, from what I understand. It could have been a whole lot worse—and much more permanent."

"Don't think about that. Who was your overly muscular friend who was here earlier?"

"He's a pretty interesting fellow. Had dinner with him last night. He's a preacher who believes that whole 'God is good' bunch of nonsense."

Rachel leaned forward. "He got you thinking about your wife and daughter?"

"Yeah, I let him talk about how good God is, and then I asked him to explain my situation."

"And what did he have to say?"

"That's the strange part. He didn't try to justify it or explain it away as part of some greater good like my former pastor did. Instead, he just admitted there were some things we could never understand.

He was adamant that God wasn't the one who took my family, though."

"That's easy for him to say. He hasn't been through the things you have."

Robert turned to her. "Actually, he has in a way. He's been through worse."

"How can he believe in God after all that? And even if he does, why would he want to serve a God who allows things like that to happen?"

Robert leaned back on his pillow. "I have no idea. For me, everything has to make sense. I'm afraid I'm not much of one for accepting things for no reason and moving on. I need order. Everything should fit nicely in its box, and nothing should be out of place or unexplained. Levi's not like that though. It just seems like he looks beyond the moment and on to the end result. He's perfectly willing to accept pain right now because he seems to think that it's all going to work out for him later." He looked over at her. "How can anyone do that?"

Rachel had no answer. She appeared just as confused as he was.

Robert closed his eyes as a wave of pain overwhelmed him. Try as he might, he couldn't stifle a groan that erupted from deep within.

Rachel stood up and reached for the nurse call button.

"Hold on." He grabbed her hand to stop her. "Not yet. When they give me those painkillers, it puts me out like a light. I want to talk to you a little bit more."

"Well, that's sweet," Rachel said, smiling. "But it's time for you to take another nap, okay?"

Robert nodded his agreement before settling back into his pillow. "Thanks. And thanks for being here. I know you have to leave soon. By the way, how are you going to get back to the office to get your car?"

Rachel squeezed his hand. "I've got that under control. I'll take a cab back."

"Be careful."

"Don't worry about me. Nothing's going to happen."

The nurse came in carrying a small paper cup of pills a few minutes after Rachel called her. Robert took them and settled back, trying to remain still so the pain would pass. When he was almost asleep, he heard Rachel stir. He opened his eyes a little and watched as she got up, went to the tiny closet holding his clothes, and rummaged around in it. She pulled something out and closed the door quietly.

Then, without a word, she left.

Charlie stood behind his computer as Amy sat at his desk. They'd opted to pick up Chinese food while he explained the situation. He'd decided to go with his gut feelings about her and tell her everything. It had been the right move.

After another five minutes of questioning, she said, "I think I can beat this."

"How? Every workstation is set up to crash the minute we try to get inside."

Amy winked at him. "Trust me. I'm as smart and resourceful as I am beautiful."

Then you're an absolute genius.

She stood and started pulling boxes of Chinese food from the bags. "First we eat, then I show you how amazing I truly am." Holding up a small white box, she wiggled her eyebrows. "Now, who's up for sweet-and-sour chicken?"

As they were about to dig into their dinner, there was a knock on the door. Charlie looked up and tried to see outside into the darkness. "Who in the world could that be?"

Amy shook her head. "Maybe it's Rachel."

The knock returned, and Charlie stood. "Could be." But as he got closer to the door, he could see that it wasn't Rachel at all. A tall black man stood at the door. Charlie spoke through the door without opening it. "Yes?"

The man looked past him into the room. "Is Robert here?"

Charlie shot a quick glance to Amy and then back at the man. "No, he's not. Is there something I can do for you?"

The man shuffled through his pockets and pulled out a small business card that Charlie recognized immediately. "My name's Terrance. He left me his card, and I was hoping I could talk to him."

Ian walked through the door to his apartment and tossed his jacket onto the couch. Sam was waiting in the kitchen by his bowl. His tail thumped against the floor as Ian rubbed his head in passing.

"Sorry, but I didn't bring you any scraps. You'll just have to settle for plain old dog food tonight."

Moving into the bedroom, Ian booted up his laptop and connected to the Internet. Within minutes he'd downloaded all of the incoming e-mail messages from Robert's computer. There were no new ones from today for obvious reasons, but there were a few marked with yesterday's date. Sam trotted into the room and jumped on the bed, getting comfortable.

"All right, let's see what you were working on before somebody made you their personal piñata, Mr. Whitney." Ian opened the first message and began to scroll through it. Five seconds later the laptop froze up.

"What in the world?" Ian punched a couple of buttons, but found the actions ignored.

A message popped up on the screen.

Ready to Play?

Beneath the words a timer appeared and began to count down from ten.

"Oh, that can't be good." Ian tried to type in a few commands, but his limited knowledge of computers held no answers for a situation like this one. That was what he had his team for. He was good at getting information, Bishop was good with handling people although unintentionally intimidating some folks, Linda kept the place organized and running, and the computer stuff was handled by—

The timer reached zero, and the message changed.

Shredding All Data on Drive C.

A progress bar beneath the message slowly began to fill while Ian heard the hard drive rattling as it was accessed.

"Stop it!" He began trying to type feverishly, hoping that something he did would have some sort of effect. It didn't.

The progress bar continued to fill. Ian grabbed the plug and jerked it from the wall, but the laptop instantly switched to battery power. He cursed and tried to find a way to take the battery out. By the time he located it, the progress bar was at 40 percent. He slid the battery out, and the screen went blank.

Looking at the battery in his hand, he exhaled sharply. "Well, that was uncalled for." He stood and tossed the battery on the bed near the resting dog. "I think I can take that little episode to mean that Whitney found my toy. The well has officially run dry—and it took my laptop with it." He opened a box on the floor filled with printouts. "The good news is that Daddy was smart enough to make hard copies of everything."

His cell phone buzzed. "Hello? Hey, where have you been? Never mind. I need you to fix my laptop tomorrow ... some kind of virus or something. No, I believe it's pretty much toast, but I've seen you work wonders before." He listened to the excited voice on the other end of the line before continuing. "All right, you do what you've got to do. We're on a very limited time frame now. Sounds like you've been busy today, so let's finish this, and it's my treat at the restaurant of your choice—provided the place has a value menu of some kind."

Ian hung up. After a second he remembered another call he needed to make. Looking through his phone's address book, he found the number he needed and placed the call.

A tired voice answered. "City lockup."

"Yes, I need to check on the status of a prisoner please."

Less than three minutes later, Ian was out the door.

THIRTY-TWO

HE WALKS THROUGH A *field with his wife and daugh-ter. In one hand he holds a picnic basket filled to the brim with food. In the other he holds the tiny hand of his little girl. He hears her laughter as it floats on the breeze gently blowing around them. He gazes over at his wife and sees her beautiful smile. She catches him staring at her and blows him a playful kiss. They all move slowly, as if underwater, but with no effort.*

He finds the perfect spot in the middle of the field and sets the picnic basket down. As he picks his daughter up and spins her around, his wife spreads the blanket out and prepares the sandwiches. The pink ribbon that holds his daughter's ponytail bounces up and down with each toss. Finally, he puts her down, and her contagious giggling starts up again as she initiates a game of tag. He runs after her, keeping behind so she can win the game.

His wife calls to them. He scoops up his tiny daughter and puts her on his shoulders as he walks toward the outstretched blanket upon which his wife is sitting. The girl squeals with delight at his every step. As he lets her down, she wraps her tiny arms around his neck and speaks softly into his ear.

"I love you, Daddy."

He pats her back and holds her close. "I love you, too, baby."

As soon as she touches the ground, she finds her spot on the blanket and begins to munch on her sandwich. He kisses his wife's hand. They eat together and laugh. The gentle breeze cools them. Birds sing in the woods all around them.

"As soon as this is over, we head for the zoo." His wife's eyes get big as she looks to their daughter. The little girl drops her sandwich and begins to clap, a huge glob of grape jelly still sticking to the edge of her mouth.

He smiles and looks toward the horizon. His smile vanishes. In the distance, dark-gray clouds gather. They roll in quickly, as if pushed by some horrible unseen force. He puts down his sandwich and stands.

His wife speaks behind him. "What's wrong?"

He gestures toward the clouds and turns to her. "Looks like a storm is rolling in fast. I hope it doesn't mess up our trip."

She looks past him. "Oh no, where did that come from?"

The sun disappears around them as the gray blanket of clouds covers the sky. Lightning flashes, and thunder rumbles above their heads.

He steps away from the blanket, trying to get his bearings. "We need to get out of here and back to the car. It looks like it's going to get rough in a few minutes."

His daughter continues to eat her sandwich, oblivious to the danger hovering overhead. She begins to sing a lilting melody that threads its way through each thunderclap.

"Jesus loves me this I know …"

He takes three more steps away, his mind disoriented. He spins around, but can find nothing familiar about this place anymore. A rising sense of dread overwhelms him. "We need to get out of here."

"Robert!"

He turns at his wife's cry and sees her still sitting on the blanket. Her face is a mask of terror as she reaches to him. Behind her, his daughter continues to sing as she finishes her sandwich.

"For the Bible tells me so, little ones to him belong …"

He tries to run to them, but his legs refuse to respond. He is glued in place. He can do nothing but feebly stretch his arms toward them, trying in vain to pull them to himself.

"Tara … Emily … run!"

His daughter waves to him now as she sings.

"They are weak ..."

Suddenly, the clouds part, and a massive hand slams down upon them from above. The ground shakes with the force of its impact.

"Noooo!"

His legs begin working again, and he runs toward the gigantic hand crushing his family. He beats upon it and tries futilely to pull up the fingers. It will not budge. A tiny wisp of something flutters from under the hand. He circles around, trying to find some way to move the horrible burden. As he reaches the other side, he sees what had caught his attention.

A pink ribbon tied to a small ponytail.

He cries out at the top of his lungs as thunder rumbles around him and lightning flashes above.

"Why are you doing this to me?"

Robert gasped as his eyes flew open. He fought for breath while his heart hammered in his chest. Reaching up with his good hand, he found his face wet with tears. His mouth was dry, and his tongue felt as if it were stuck to the roof of his mouth. His head throbbed as he wiped his cheeks.

The room was dark, illuminated only by a dim light behind his bed that allowed the nurses to come and check on their patients without awakening them. He closed his eyes, fighting desperately to regain control of his shaking body.

"Are you all right?"

Robert squinted, trying to focus on the source of the voice from the darkness. "Who's there? Is that you, Levi?"

"Who's Levi?" The figure stepped forward into the pool of light.

Terrance Gold.

Robert used every ounce of self-control to keep his expression neutral. "Who are you?"

Gold chuckled. "That's good. Who am I?" He spaced the words out, pausing between each as if savoring the feel of them upon his tongue. "Who ... am ... I?" Smiling, he shook his head and put a hand on the bed. "You are something else, you know that?"

Robert's mind raced, trying to think of a way out of this situation. He knew he had to play it cool for now—at least until he knew what Gold had found out. "What are you talking about? Do I know you?"

Gold laughed and shook his head. "I'll say this much for you: You're a cool customer. I'd believe you were innocent and apologize before leaving, if not for a couple of things. You see, I've been getting packages for the last few weeks that had some bad stuff in them. I found out earlier this afternoon that, according to the police, all those things were charged on a credit card of mine—a card I didn't open. I called about it after I got out of jail today, and apparently 'I' opened it almost three months ago."

Robert hoped his act could hold up. "So?"

"All right, I'll lay this out for you. Whoever opened that credit-card account knew a whole lot about me. I'm a secretive person, and I don't give out much information about myself to anyone—not even my girlfriend. Whoever did this had to be pretty smart, and had to have a wicked mind."

Robert fought to sit up. "You should take better care of your personal information. Identity theft is the fastest growing crime in America right now."

Gold's hand moved like lightning, grabbing Robert's leg at the shin and squeezing. Robert grimaced as pain ripped through him. Gold released his grip, but kept his hand resting on the injured leg. "The game's over, snake. There's no use playing dumb anymore."

Robert's voice was strained. "I don't know what you're talking about."

Gold reached into his pocket and extracted a business card. The red writing on it was visible even in the dim light. It was the one Charlie had created for him. "I found this in my house. Look familiar?"

Robert tried to focus his mind through the pain. He must have lost the card from his shirt pocket when he fell in Gold's hall. "You can't prove anything. Those cards are freely available at my office."

Gold's eyes widened. "Oh, I know all about your office. I went by there a little while ago and found out where you were." A malicious smile crept across his face. "Did you know I was shot when they broke into my house to arrest me? Do you have any idea how much that hurts?"

"You look pretty healthy to me."

"Yeah, that's what happens when you wear a bulletproof vest. It'll stop most of the bullets from going in, but it's still gonna hurt like crazy when they hit you."

Gold brought his other hand into the light. Something glinted in the dim light. "Amazing what you find in a hospital, isn't it? I found an unlocked supply closet near a nurse's station, and this little jewel just popped into my hand."

Then Robert could make out what Gold was holding.

A hypodermic syringe.

Gold continued, his voice droning on hypnotically. "You ever watch them as they prepare to give someone an injection? They always hold the needle up and make sure there's no air bubbles in there anywhere. Air bubbles are bad. They can actually make a person's heart explode."

He moved next to the bed, his hand covering the nurse call button. "Now just imagine how big an air bubble I can make with an empty syringe."

Robert struggled against him in the desperate hope of making enough noise to get help. A quick blow with his good hand brought the satisfying sound of Gold crying out in pain, but instead of making him back off, Robert only succeeded in making him madder. Gold took a half step back, and then fired off a hard punch to Robert's bandaged head. Robert screamed, and darkness began to close in around the edges of his vision. As his eyes rolled back in his head, he felt consciousness slipping away and peaceful oblivion beckoning.

Suddenly, there was a sharp crack, and his face began stinging. He could hear a distant voice. "Oh no, don't even think you're passing out on me. I want you awake and knowing every bit of what's coming."

Robert feebly swatted at the painful intrusion to his rest, but a few more hard slaps brought him back to full attention. There was no way he could fight off Gold. Robert tried to prepare himself for what was coming. He tried to imagine what it would feel like when his heart exploded in his chest. He hoped it would be quick and painless. He felt something like a bee sting prick his neck.

"You ruined me, little man. Even the guys I work with don't believe I'm innocent. I'm on suspension. My name and face were all over the television today, and I can only imagine what the papers will be saying tomorrow." Spit rained on his face with Gold's words. "My own mother doesn't want to talk to me. My girlfriend left a message on my phone telling me we were through. That wasn't any big loss, but it's the principle of the thing, you understand."

Gold positioned his fingers on the syringe and leaned close to Robert. "Any last words before you go to meet your evil master in hell?"

Robert tried to form a coherent thought through the maelstrom of pain in which he was swimming. He licked his lips and spoke with a cracking voice. "I won—and there's nothing you can do to change that."

Gold chuckled. "You won a battle, little man. Eventually everyone will forget what happened today, and life will continue on for me like before. I will win the war."

Robert steeled himself for the inevitable. He thought about closing his eyes, but he wanted to face his death like a man. He wished he could work up enough saliva to spit in Gold's face as he prepared for his execution, but he couldn't. Gold leaned forward ...

Then he disappeared.

He seemed to be sucked into the darkness behind him. Robert thought he was hallucinating and brought his hand up to the space that had been occupied by Gold just a second before, but he wasn't there.

He heard struggling from beyond the pool of dim light around his bed. There was a flash of light as the door opened and then the sound of running footsteps. Slowly, a silhouette rose from the foot of his bed.

"Are you all right?"

The familiarity of the statement caused a momentary panic inside Robert's chest, but then the figure stepped into the light and he saw his rescuer.

Levi stepped forward quickly and slipped the syringe from Robert's neck. "I came by to see how you were doing and saw him leaning over you. For a second I thought he was a doctor, but then I heard him talking about you going to meet your evil master in hell, and I knew that couldn't be good."

Levi pressed the nurse call button and began to ask Robert if he had been injured. Within seconds a voice said, "Can I help you?"

"Yes, you need to check on this patient."

"Is there something wrong, sir?"

Levi began to show signs of irritation. "Just come in here and check on him. I'll explain everything when you get here."

"We'll be there in a few—"

"Now!" The tone of Levi's voice left no room for discussion. Robert had the feeling the next thing he'd do would be go to the nurse's station and physically drag one of them to the room.

Robert's mouth was dry. "I don't think you made a new friend."

Levi smiled. "I'll apologize later."

"What'd you do to Gold?"

Levi poured him a glass of water and held it to him, fixing the straw so that it touched his lips. "I showed him the error of his ways. He took off before we could finish the discussion."

After a deep drink, Robert settled back into his pillow, feeling his heartbeat settle down. "He'll be back."

Levi looked toward the door. "Not if he's smart."

THIRTY-THREE

RACHEL PULLED UP TO her parents' house and sat in the car staring at the front door. She didn't want to go in, but she knew she had no choice. Scott and all her earthly possessions were inside, so there was nothing else to do but go in and face her father. She had thought things through carefully and knew exactly what the next step would be—and that he wouldn't like it.

She stepped out into the darkness and quietly shut the car door behind her. She knew it was far too early for her parents to be in bed, but there was a chance she could slip inside unnoticed and start packing. She was ready to move on.

"Rachel."

The sound of her name startled her, and she had to stifle a scream as the stillness of the night was broken. She'd been lost in her thoughts and hadn't even heard him sneaking up on her.

"What in the world are you doing here, Derek? Were you trying to scare me to death?"

Derek stepped into the dim glow of the front-porch light. "I'm sorry. I just wanted to catch you before you went inside. I've been waiting here awhile. I need to talk to you."

"I think enough was said last night, don't you?"

When he spoke again, his voice was quiet. "I'm sorry about last night. Things went really wrong, and I never meant it to be that way. I was just trying—"

"I know what you were trying to do, Derek, and it didn't work. I'd never have imagined you'd sink that low."

"Rachel, I promise you I didn't make that tape. I know it looks that way, but I honestly had nothing to do with it." Derek closed his eyes for a second and took a deep breath before continuing. "I know how things look, but I need you to trust me. I would never hurt you on purpose."

"Derek, did you attack Robert last night?"

The question appeared to stun Derek. His mouth hung open, and his eyes fell. He seemed to be searching for an answer.

Or an excuse.

His eyes lifted, and he stared at her blankly. His lips parted with his jaw working nervously. Finally, he squeezed his eyes shut and brought a hand up to rub his face.

"I'm moving in with Robert, Derek."

His head shot up. "What? What are you talking about?"

"I didn't have to tell you, but I wanted you to know. I think it's for the best. He's hurting, and he needs someone there to take care of him while he recovers."

"He's not what he appears to be, Rachel. I know things look bad for me, but I promise you he's the one being so deceptive. He's playing you, and when he's finished whatever it is he's doing, he'll leave you hanging high and dry—or worse, he'll use you to the point that you feel like you want to die ..." Derek's eyes fell again as his next words slipped from his lips. "... like I do."

Derek began to walk away, speaking softly to himself. "That's the answer. That's it. I don't know why I didn't see it before. I can't beat him, but I can rob him of his victory. How much fun will he have gloating when there's no one to appreciate what he's done?"

Rachel's eyes narrowed. "Derek, are you all right?"

Derek waved her off and walked back into the shadows. A few seconds later, she heard his truck start up and saw its headlights explode through the night. The truck pulled away with an almost reverent air. She watched until the taillights disappeared in the distance. She felt an overwhelming sense of loss wash over her, and she wanted to break down and cry again. But she decided that there would be no more tears for Derek.

Charlie had just popped the last bite of egg roll into his mouth when Amy walked out to her car. A few minutes later she walked back in carrying what looked like a black suitcase.

"You moving in?"

"Nope. Just brought in some stuff to help fix our problem." Amy opened the case and pulled out something that looked like a small voltage regulator with two wires sticking out of it.

Charlie managed to get a glimpse inside the case and saw several other strange-looking devices inside. "What in the world is in that suitcase?"

"It's a computer forensics kit."

Charlie tilted his head, trying to comprehend what she'd just said. "You keep a computer forensics kit in your car?"

"Doesn't everyone?"

Within seconds she had the cover off his computer tower and was attaching the wires to the hard drive.

"What are you doing?"

"Getting the information off the hard drive without activating it." She didn't look up. "I'm basically reading the contents like a book. Hope you didn't have any secrets you were trying to hide."

Before Charlie could reply, Amy snapped her fingers. "Got it. The only thing I'm going to be able to do is transfer the information from your hard drive to another one—minus the virus. It'll take a little time, but we can do that to the whole system and shouldn't lose much."

"How long will that take?"

Amy pressed a button on the yellow box and set it on the desk. Numbers on a digital readout began to count up. "Unfortunately, this isn't a quick process. I mean, for one computer we'd be all right, but we're talking five workstations and the main server in the back room. Each workstation has a huge hard drive—some have more than one—and we can't localize the virus yet because it appears to be on every computer. We'll disconnect everything from the network and go one station at a time."

Charlie walked to Robert's desk "Then I guess we should start with Robert's laptop next, even though it's not plugged into the network. I'm supposed to take it to him tomorrow, so I want to make sure it's clean before it does something weird there. The last thing he needs is something else to worry about."

Amy picked up the suitcase and walked into Robert's office, taking a seat behind his desk. She set the laptop in front of her, but didn't turn it on. Next, she pulled the tower for the desktop computer from under the desk and began to disconnect the cables to it.

"I don't know any of his passwords to get into his system," Charlie said.

She opened the black case she'd brought in and extracted a flat silver metallic box. "No problem. I'm going to be looking directly at the information itself. Besides, I have a few programs on this external hard drive that I always bring along for just such an occasion. They'll get me any passwords I need. There's nothing on this hard drive I can't get to."

"I don't know of anything Robert wouldn't want you to see, so that's fine. He does that so no one can get into the programs he's writing. Just make sure there's no nasty code on there waiting to destroy the information, and I'll be a happy guy."

Amy smiled and pulled the tower out to take off the cover. "Well, let's see how happy I can make you."

Derek lay in the back of his truck looking up at the stars. He'd found the perfect secluded spot to park, away from the city lights and sounds. It was a spot he and Rachel had used regularly during their dating years. It was where it had all begun for them, and he could think of no better place for it all to end. A large paper sack filled with various drinks he'd picked up from a liquor store sat beside him. His plan was simple: Since he didn't own a gun, he'd drink himself into oblivion with the help of some of Rachel's sleeping pills.

Reaching into his pocket, he pulled out his keys and threw them into the woods nearby. "No sense in taking a chance of hurting someone else if I decide I want to drive off later," he said to no one. Settling back in the bed of his truck, he looked at the stars above and thought how beautiful they were. There was so much about them he'd always loved, even though he didn't know the names of any of the constellations. The nighttime sky looked like a giant black ocean speckled with diamonds, and he'd loved looking at it since he was a kid.

"Wow, didn't I blow it? I had so much going for me, and I blew it. All I had to do was be honest with my wife. All I had to do was take a nap in my truck at the truck stop and then head out. I'd have been a little late, but at least no one would have been hurt. How did it all go so wrong so fast?"

Without shame, he cried. His words were spoken to the night with no anger, just a simple resolve to settle things once and for all. He almost felt that the stars were looking back at him, wanting to answer him. Or maybe it wasn't the stars … maybe it was Someone else.

"Hey, God, are you there? I just wanted to say thanks for giving me such a beautiful night tonight. I can only think of one other thing more gorgeous than these stars, and she'll never talk to me again. I couldn't have asked for a better scene in which to close my eyes for the final time."

Sitting up, he reached into the bag and pulled out one of the bottles. He held it in his hands but did not open it. For some reason he felt compelled to keep talking, to finish the conversation he'd begun. "You still there, God? I forgot to say thanks for giving me such a beautiful wife and a great kid for the short time I had them. I mean, Rachel and I had our moments when things got ugly, but the good times were so much better than the bad. I really had it pretty good, and I'm sorry I messed it up."

He licked his lips and opened the bottle in his hand. The acrid odor wafted up to his nostrils, and he could feel the familiar tendrils of the liquid comfort pulling at him. But still he did not drink. Something wasn't right. He couldn't stop talking. The more he talked, the better he began to feel.

"I wish Bishop was here, God. He'd know what to say. He talks to you a lot more often than I ever did. Sorry about that, too, by the way. I should have lived a better life ... should've gone to church more often. Maybe that would have made things better. Should've tried to get to know you a little more. My mistake."

He looked down at the bottle he held in an iron grasp. "Oh well, spilled milk and all that stuff." He brought the bottle to his lips. It was time to finish it.

But then he felt such an overwhelming feeling of sorrow envelop him that he almost choked. His body began to shake as he cried out for help.

"I'm so sorry, God. I'm so sorry for every mistake I've made. I'm sorry for the way I've totally messed up the life you gave me. I'm sorry for everything I did wrong that hurt my family and you. I don't know how to do this right, but I'm begging you—please forgive me." As the tears continued to fall, he felt something sweep over him. It was a feeling he hadn't had in a long time.

Peace.

He didn't know what to do. He didn't want to move for fear the feeling might disappear, but somehow he knew it wouldn't. He felt that it would never leave him again. He needed to find Bishop. Levi would know what he needed to do next. Pouring the bottle out into the grass beside the truck, he tossed it back into the bag and jumped out of the back of the truck. As he opened the door and began to slide into the driver's seat, he remembered what he'd done with his keys. Reaching across the seat, he opened the glove box and pulled out a small flashlight.

For some reason the thought of searching for the keys didn't bother him. He decided to use the time to talk to God some more. He had a lot of years of silence to make up.

Terrance Gold sat in his car in the hospital parking lot. His eyes were glued to the front door, watching for the large man who'd stopped him in Robert's room. Terrance's first impulse had been to get in the car and drive away as fast as possible, but when he saw that no one was chasing him, he decided that was unnecessary. Instead, he moved his car so that he could get a good look at the front door. That was the only way out now that visiting hours were over, so he knew the man would have to leave that way. The parking lot was emptying, which worked to Terrance's advantage.

He replayed the entire scene in his mind again, cursing himself for taking too long. He'd tried to drag it out and make Whitney suffer, but now he saw that it had been a mistake. Hindsight was twenty-twenty, though, so the best thing to do was learn from the mistake. He'd just be waiting for Whitney when he went home from the hospital. As for the man who'd stopped him, Terrance guessed that he wouldn't be expecting another visit in the same night.

Finally, his persistence was rewarded. The man walked through the double doors and into the parking lot. He turned away from Terrance's car and headed in the opposite direction. That put the man's back to Terrance—and made him an easier target.

Reaching into the backseat for an empty beer bottle, Terrance opened his door. He got out and shut the door as quietly as possible. Crouched low, he moved between cars on a path he hoped would allow him to intercept the man before he got to his vehicle. Terrance had no idea which vehicle was the one the man was looking for, so he didn't know how long he had to reach him.

Better not take any chances. I'll move fast and get him when he's reaching for his keys.

The man stopped and looked around again, apparently having forgotten where he'd parked. Terrance ducked down and watched through the windows of the SUV he was hiding behind. The man smiled and began to move with purpose. He'd found his car. This new path would take him right past Terrance's hiding place. It would be a simple thing to step out once he'd passed by and attack him.

Terrance switched his grip on the bottle and held it by the neck. His plan was to hit the man over the head with the bottle, stunning him and breaking the bottle at the same time. Then he'd take the jagged remains of the bottle and teach the guy a lesson. Messy, but effective.

Sliding down the car, he sank into the shadows and waited. He heard the man's approaching footsteps and smiled to himself as he thought of what he was about to do.

Then the footsteps stopped. Terrance could feel his heart hammering in his chest. He fought the impulse to jump up and fly into the man, knowing he'd lose the advantage of surprise. After a minute he heard the footsteps again. Terrance tightened his hold on the bottle and moved forward on the balls of his feet, preparing for the ambush.

When the man passed by, Terrance counted to three and slipped from between the cars. Finding the exact point on the back of his head to hit, Terrance moved.

"Now that wouldn't be nice at all."

He whirled around at the sound of the voice behind him.

Ian Richardson stood there watching, his hands in his coat pockets.

Suddenly he understood. Terrance sneered. "This was all a big setup, wasn't it? You lure me into the parking lot, then the two of you gang up on me and take me out. Too scared to do it one on one like a man, huh?"

Richardson laughed. "First of all, Mr. Mental, how in the world was I supposed to know you'd be stupid enough to wait in the parking lot? Second of all, from the conversation I had with Bishop on his cell phone before I got here, he didn't need my help to pound your sorry head into the floor before, so why should he need it now?"

Richardson held up a finger. "One final thing—and here's the cool part ..." He pointed past Terrance, who was too suspicious to look immediately. Turning his head slowly with his eyes still on Richardson, he gave a quick glance in the direction Richardson had been indicating. The large man had gotten into his car and was driving away. Terrance looked back at Richardson, his eyes narrowed slits.

Richardson raised his eyebrows as he slid his hand back into his coat pocket. "I told Bishop to go home. I want it to be as easy on you as possible."

"You touch me, and I'll arrest you for attacking an officer," Terrance said with a cruel grin. He hefted the bottle in his right hand and took a step forward. "So what you need to do is just take your beating like a man, and we'll call it even."

Richardson nodded toward Terrance's hand. "You come at me with that bottle, and it's self-defense."

"What bottle?" he replied, swinging his hand back and preparing to slam the bottle into the side of Richardson's head.

Rachel pulled up to Robert's house and turned off the engine. Scott was asleep in the front seat next to her. Things had been busy for her lately, and she'd almost neglected him. She felt horrible about that, but now things would be different. From now on they'd both be spending more time together with Robert. Maybe they could start a new family and give Scott some stability in his life again.

Reaching into her purse for Robert's keys that she'd taken from his hospital closet, she slipped out of the door as quietly as possible. Once on the other side of the car, she gathered her son in her arms and walked toward the front door, key in hand. Opening the door, she found the living room and gently laid the sleeping child on the couch. Several papers were scattered around the room and covered the kitchen table.

This place needs a woman's touch, she thought, gathering up a few pages. *I'll just try to organize things a little so it's not such a mess when Robert comes home.*

As she moved some of the papers around, her eyes fell on what was printed on them. At first she couldn't believe what she was reading. After a few minutes she felt her legs grow weak. She lowered herself to the floor and picked up another page. After several more minutes there, she got up, went to the kitchen table, and began to scan the contents of the papers spread out on it. Her chest began to constrict as she realized what she was seeing.

Terrance grabbed Ian Richardson by the front of his coat and pulled him closer, shifting his weight slightly to put more force into the blow he was about to deliver with the bottle.

But his blow never landed.

Richardson's right hand came up quickly and reached over Terrance's hand that held his shirt. He grabbed Terrance's thumb in a vice grip and twisted. Instantly Terrance felt pain explode from his hand and wrist, and he released Richardson's shirt. Following through on his hold, Richardson continued the twist until Terrance went down to one knee.

"I could break your wrist right now, or I could take it a bit further and make that thumb useless to you for the rest of your life," Richardson said, his voice still soft and even. "Fortunately for you, I'm not one to enjoy hurting people." He released his grip, and immediately Terrance felt the pain in his hand starting to subside. He stood to his feet again and glared at Richardson.

"You got me once because I got cocky. It won't happen again."

Richardson just shook his head. "Walk away, Terrance. It's not worth it."

Terrance snorted and drew the bottle back again. As his arm came down, Richardson's hand came up. He grabbed Terrance's right hand at the wrist and slid smoothly underneath it, pulling it behind Terrance in one fluid motion. Then he leaned forward and whispered in Terrance's ear, "Drop it and go home."

Terrance swung his elbow around to hit Richardson's face, but the movement worked against him. He felt excruciating pain from his right shoulder as something popped, and then lights exploded into his vision. He screamed and fell to his knees again. This time he had no fight left in him at all. Richardson released his arm and stood in front of him.

"I'm sorry, Terrance. I really am. You shouldn't have moved like that when I had your arm behind you. Your shoulder's dislocated ... but you're in a hospital parking lot. That means they can fix you up inside as good as new in just a little while. Once the swelling goes down, you'll be all ready to stalk people in deserted parking lots again in no time."

Terrance's arm was useless. He stood to his feet and spoke through clenched teeth, fighting to keep the pain from his voice. "You ... are ... under arrest ... for assaulting ... an officer of the law."

"It was self-defense, and you know it."

Terrance allowed himself a smile, speaking between deep breaths. "That's ... your side of ... the story. Who do ... you think they'll believe?"

"They'll believe their own eyes. They can't argue with what they see." Richardson looked up at the light pole they were standing under. As Terrance followed his gaze upward, he saw what he meant.

A surveillance camera was mounted near the top, pointed directly at them.

Terrance's gaze fell back on Richardson's face. "I tried to get you to walk away," Richardson said.

With stars in his vision, Terrance stumbled toward the hospital door.

Charlie watched as Amy sat busily typing away on Robert's laptop. He stood amazed as Amy fixed what he could never have hoped to fix in such a short amount of time—especially considering the fact that he didn't have a clue as to how to use anything from the computer forensics kit.

"Whatcha thinkin'?" Amy asked.

"Just watching," he replied. "Looks like you really know what you're doing. Mind if I ask how you learned to use one of those kits, and what you're doing carrying one around with you?"

Amy stopped typing and looked up at him. "There are a few things about me you don't know. I used to work for the police doing computer forensics. When they raided a perp's home and took his computer, it was my job to check it out before they turned it on. You'd be surprised at the security some of those guys have. Nasty stuff. Programs that shred the hard drive if you enter a wrong password, and things like that. But even the best security can be bypassed with the right equipment."

Charlie raised an eyebrow at her. "You're a cop?"

She laughed. "No. Used to work with them, but never had a badge and gun or anything. I'm still one of the good guys."

Before Charlie could come up with something witty in response, the screen on the laptop changed. Amy took it all in within seconds. When she spoke, her voice was full of awe.

"Whoa. What in the world?"

Bishop stepped from his car and turned toward his front porch. He hadn't expected to be out so late, so he hadn't left a light on. Now the darkness that covered the porch seemed foreboding. Being stalked through a parking lot had made him a little paranoid.

As he reached the porch, he saw something move in the darkness to his right. He turned quickly, fists tight in preparation for whatever was about to happen. His mind flashed to a day in his past that had been similar.

"Wait, I'm on your side." It was Derek's voice, but he sounded different. He stepped into the dim light that came from across the street, and Bishop could see a look in his eyes he'd never seen before. "Can I come in?"

Bishop opened the door and stepped aside, gesturing with his hand. "Absolutely," he said. "I've been looking for you all afternoon, Derek. Where have you been?"

When Derek turned to face him, the change was apparent. Something had happened while he was gone. "Sorry about that, Levi. I did a lot of driving and thinking today. I also had a pretty bad run-in with Rachel."

Bishop motioned for Derek to sit down on the couch and then pulled up a seat across from him. Derek told him everything that had happened during the day. Then a huge grin spread across his face as he talked about his experience in the back of his truck. Bishop laughed.

"Ah yes, isn't it wonderful how he answers prayers?"

Derek nodded. "I knew I had to come and find you. This is what you were trying to tell me about the whole time. What now, Levi? What comes next?"

"Now," Bishop said with a smile, "you learn." He stood up and walked to a bookshelf nearby. He scanned it for a second, then pulled out a small book and handed it to Derek. "That Bible's yours from now on, and I want you to underline some verses I'm going to show you. I'm going to talk, you're going to talk, we'll ask questions and find answers in that book."

And as he sat down, Bishop watched Derek reverently open to the first page.

THIRTY-FOUR

ROBERT CARRIES EMILY IN *his arms. Her laughter fills the air around them. Her tiny arms are wrapped tightly around his neck, and he squeezes her in a bear hug that brings a squeal of delight from her.*

"I love you, Daddy."

He smiles and closes his eyes, feeling her next to him. "I love you, too, Em."

He gently lowers her to the ground and feels arms encircle him from behind. He feels the familiar sensation of Tara's head resting against his back. He turns to face her and pulls her close. "Hey there, gorgeous. Where have you been?"

She smiles up at him. "Here and there, thinking of you the whole time."

He laughs, then looks at her. "I've missed you, beautiful," he says, gently brushing a lock of hair from her face.

She smiles. "I've missed you, too."

Suddenly he feels Emily tugging at his sleeve, and he turns to her. Taking her tiny hand in one hand, and Tara's in the other, he walks with them. After several steps, Emily pulls her hand away and runs ahead a little. Robert turns to his wife—

His entire body jars from the impact as he slams into an invisible wall. Tara keeps on walking as if nothing has happened, but he cannot go forward. He yells out to them. Nothing comes from his throat. He beats helplessly against the air, watching his wife and daughter move farther away.

Finally, they turn to face him. Their eyes fill with sadness as they realize he's not coming with them. Tara raises a hand and turns to go. Emily gives a short wave before turning to follow her.

"Tara!"

Robert's eyes flew open. He could feel his heart hammering in his chest, threatening once again to explode. The sheets felt damp with his sweat.

"Robert?"

Forcing his eyes to focus, Robert turned toward the source of the familiar voice.

Charlie came to the bed. "It was just a dream, man."

Robert looked past him and saw the sunlight streaming in from the window. It was morning. He'd made it through the night. Looking back at Charlie, he nodded.

Charlie looked at him with concern, but Robert noticed something else in his eyes. It was as though Charlie was studying him, trying to read him, and Robert disliked the feeling.

Something's happened. He knows something.

He forced himself to smile. "Did you bring my laptop?"

It seemed to Robert that Charlie almost flinched at that question. Charlie reached down beside the bed and pulled up a black case. "Right here, chief. I'm ever the faithful servant."

"Is something wrong, Charlie? You seem a little … distracted."

The two men stared at each other for several seconds, then Charlie reached back to the chair he'd been sitting in and pulled up a file folder stuffed with papers. He looked down at it as if debating whether or not to continue, then took a deep breath. "Robert, I'm your friend, and I've been so for years. You took me right out of college and gave me a chance to do something that I loved. Then the … accident happened, and you even trusted me enough to put me in charge of running the business. I've tried to do the right thing with all that I did there."

Robert adjusted his bed so that it brought him to a more upright position. "Is this about a raise? You've done a great job, Charlie. I appreciate your hard work there."

Charlie gave him a pained smile. "Well, that's where we have our problem. Yesterday we had a little incident at work. It's a long story, but a virus was let loose in our network."

Robert pushed himself up with his good arm. "What did we lose?"

"Nothing. Amy had a hidden talent we knew nothing about, and she saved us. It took all night to get it purged from the system, but by about three this morning we were clean."

Robert relaxed. "Any ideas?"

Charlie sniffed and shrugged. "Amy started doing cleanup. Eventually she was able to trace the exact file that started all the problems."

Robert forced himself to remain calm. "And so it was … "

"It was a file on your machine, Robert. Tom was trying to help finish a project Jonathan was working on. He tried to access the file across the network but hit your node instead. The result was a nasty little virus named Armageddon that was designed to destroy any machine that intruded on it. I assume you did that to protect our source codes from outside eyes and you'd never considered someone inside the company trying to access it. We ended up facing your wrath, and I have to say I'm impressed with what you did. If not for some quick thinking, we'd be looking at a room full of expensive paperweights this morning."

Robert shifted uneasily. "Sorry about that, Charlie. I'd been having some problems with someone trying to hack into my computer lately, and I wanted it stopped."

"I really wish you'd told me about that. We could have set up more secure firewalls or something. I mean, honestly, what you were unleashing was serious. If someone had managed to get your virus on the Internet, it could have shut down thousands of businesses within just a few hours. You should have at least told me that you were protecting your stuff that way."

Robert nodded. "You're right. I'm sorry."

"It's not what we lost that surprised me … it's what we *found*. I had to make sure the virus was out of every computer on the network. I'd never have made it into your machine without Amy's help."

Robert's voice grew cold. "You went into my machine? What were you thinking?"

"Just trying to do my job, boss. I didn't know the origin of the virus, and I had no idea what we were facing." Charlie lifted the file. "Like I said, I'm your friend. I want to give you the benefit of the doubt in everything, but I need your help to understand some things." He handed the file to Robert. "I need you to explain this stuff to me, because it sure doesn't look good. One could almost think you were doing something underhanded here."

Robert stared at the folder. "What's this?"

Charlie seemed to be pleading with Robert now. "Please tell me that I'm misunderstanding the whole thing. Please tell me that you didn't know who Rachel's husband was when you hired her."

"What are you talking about?"

"The list on your computer. You had four names on it, and Amy found info on three of them. The last name was Derek Morrison. I noticed Rachel had a Scott Morrison listed on her paperwork as a dependent. A little more digging, and we were able to put two and two together for certain."

Robert opened the file. A quick glance told him it was all there. Somehow they'd gotten into his personal files and cross-referenced them with information from some online news source. There was too much in the file for Robert to ignore.

He'd been caught.

He looked back up at Charlie and thought for a moment. Finally, he knew what he had to do.

"All right, Charlie. You're right. I guess it's time you knew everything."

Gordon James sat fuming behind his desk. He hated computers anyway, and now this system had gone so crazy that he'd been forced to come in on a Saturday to try to get it all straightened out. The printouts in front of him were a complete mess, and according to his last reckoning, the books were now short somewhere in the neighborhood of thirty thousand dollars. In his entire career with the company, he'd never seen anything even remotely approaching that kind of shortage. The money seemed to have come in, and yet it wasn't there.

He closed his eyes and rubbed the bridge of his nose. There was no doubt the corporate office would be coming down hard on him soon. When they got wind of what had happened, there'd be trouble. To make matters worse, he had no idea how long they might have known about it. The company polled the sales figures each weekend to the corporate office via dial-in. How long this shortage had been going on was anyone's guess.

He stood and picked up his lucky coffee mug. He'd bought the mug on his way to work one morning. When he got home that night, his wife had left him and filed for divorce. Since that day he'd always considered it his good luck charm.

He walked out of his office and toward the cramped area where the coffeemaker and vending machines were located. Two men in dark business suits were in the hall waiting for him.

Gordon gave them a quick once-over. "Can I help you?"

"Gordon James?" the taller of the two men said, reaching into his pocket and pulling out a black leather wallet.

Gordon eyed them warily. "Yeah, that's me. What do you want?"

Before the man could reply, another figure entered the hall. The man wore an expensive business suit with absolutely nothing out of place on him. Gordon recognized him immediately and couldn't stifle an involuntary gasp.

Thomas Strand.

The owner of Strand Industries and a dozen other companies—including the Starline Trucking line.

In all the years Gordon had been with the company, he'd never met the man face-to-face, but he had seen his picture often in company newsletters and in the large portrait that hung in the lobby.

"Mr. Strand, sir?" Gordon hated how weak his voice sounded, but he felt more worried now than ever before in his life.

Strand stood a good six inches taller than Gordon as he looked down at him. "Did you feel you weren't being paid enough?"

Gordon was confused. "I-I'm afraid I don't understand what you're talking about."

"You were clever, I'll have to give you that. Your computer virus had us scrambling for days."

"Virus? What are you talking about?"

Strand chuckled and shook his head. "Playing dumb all the way to the end, eh? Whatever. You should know I've paid to have everything researched before I got here. You must really think I'm stupid, James. Did you think I wouldn't notice more than thirty thousand dollars missing from the books here?"

Gordon raised a hand. "Mr. Strand, I can explain. We've been having some computer problems lately and—"

Strand snorted. "Yeah, I imagine you have. Let me guess: The money just mysteriously disappeared, right?"

"That's exactly it. The guy that takes care of our computers here really doesn't have a clue as to what he's doing, and—"

"And you're sure the money's here somewhere, but you just don't know where."

Gordon smiled. "Absolutely, sir. Boy, I don't mind telling you I was worried when I saw you here, sir, but I'm glad to know that you understand."

Strand sneered at him. "Oh, I understand. You see, last night, we found the money."

Gordon almost collapsed in relief. The tension he'd been feeling had kept his insides knotted up, and now it all was gone. The money was back, and he could relax. "I'm so glad to hear that, sir. I knew we couldn't be that short. As a matter of fact, that's why I'm here today."

"Did you wonder why *I* would be here, James?"

"I ... I guess I hadn't really given that much thought, sir."

Strand pulled a gray PDA from his pocket and tapped its screen to turn it on. "I don't get to actually see someone's face as they're caught very often. And no one steals from me and walks away unscathed. All the money is in one place, safe and sound. Unfortunately, I have to leave it there for a few days, but it will be mine again."

Looking up from the PDA, he said, "Exactly what is your checking-account balance as of today?"

Gordon shrugged. He'd never been one to keep exact amounts. He'd never actually balanced his checking account, preferring instead just to keep an eye on his deposit slip every other week to make sure there was enough money to cover whatever bills he had coming up. "I'm afraid I don't know, sir. I haven't checked it recently."

A condescending smile was on Strand's face as he spoke, turning the PDA so Gordon could see the screen. "Well, let me enlighten you as to your balance as of yesterday." Gordon stared at the display and couldn't stop his mouth from dropping open.

The PDA showed a balance of $30,162.44 … more money than he'd ever seen in his life.

Strand jerked a finger back at the two men behind him. "These two are here for you. Next time you try embezzling from your employer, don't deposit it all at once—and use some other account with a fake name or something. You practically gave yourself to us."

The man holding the leather wallet opened it, and Gordon saw the badge. He heard a loud crash and looked down to see the remains of his coffee mug on the floor at his feet.

His luck had run out.

Derek opened his eyes and took a moment to acclimate himself. For a few seconds, he couldn't place where he was; then the memories of last night returned. He'd been talking to Bishop until it was close to dawn, then Bishop had offered his couch to Derek, and Derek had been happy to take it. He couldn't remember a time when he'd slept better than he had in the past few hours. The knot in his stomach was gone. He had a sense of peace and confidence that everything would work out for the best, as in the verse in Romans chapter eight that Bishop had read to him.

He caught the rich aroma of sausage cooking and got up. He found a bathroom, rinsed his mouth with water, and took a shower. Putting on his clothes from the night before, he ran his fingers through his wet hair to push it out of his face, then stumbled into the kitchen. Bishop was at the stove standing over a skillet sizzling with sausage patties. Fresh biscuits sat on a pan nearby, and scrambled eggs were in a bowl on the kitchen table. As Bishop moved another smoking patty of sausage onto a nearby plate, he noticed his guest and smiled.

"Good morning. I tried to let you sleep as long as possible, but my stomach was rumbling too much to ignore it."

Derek smiled and sat at the kitchen table. "Thanks. It all smells delicious."

Bishop sat the plate of sausage patties on the table. "One thing about living in the South no one can deny: We know how to make breakfast. How'd you sleep?"

"Better than I have in a long time. It's amazing. Everything feels so different—yet I know nothing's changed."

Bishop sat a mug down in front of Derek and filled it with coffee. "That's where you're wrong. Things have changed. *You've* changed."

As Derek sipped his coffee, he noticed for the first time that there were three plates at the table. "Expecting company?"

"I invited someone to have breakfast with us this morning. I hope you don't mind."

"Not at all. Who?"

Before he could get an answer, there was a knock at the door. Bishop raised a finger and stood. "That will be our guest. Would you mind filling another coffee cup?"

Derek watched Bishop leave the room. He got up and found a mug hanging on a small wooden holder on the counter. He heard Bishop talking as he opened the door, but he couldn't catch the voice of their new visitor. When he had filled the mug, he turned to go back to the table with it.

Rachel was standing there.

Bishop moved past her and took the cup from Derek's hand. "I'll take that. Rachel, why don't you sit here and make yourself comfortable?" He motioned to the chair next to Derek's.

Derek still hadn't spoken, but found himself drawn to her eyes. She was the most beautiful woman he'd ever seen. All the rage and anger he'd felt before at their last meeting was gone. He wanted to hug her, but he was afraid to move for fear of scaring her off.

She looked at him with a quick smile and then sat down in the proffered seat. Bishop gently laid a hand on Derek's back and guided him toward his own chair. When they were all seated, Bishop folded his hands and said, "Shall we bless the food before we commence with the rather lengthy discussion that will be forthcoming?"

"Any questions?"

Charlie stood in mute astonishment. What he'd just heard made the room seem to spin. He looked hard into Robert's eyes to see any sign of remorse for the things he'd just described, but saw none. This wasn't the man he'd known all these years. The accident had claimed more than just the lives of his wife and child—it had killed something in him as well.

When Charlie spoke, his voice was low. "You ... you don't feel the least bit bad about any of this? You destroyed the lives of at least four people—five counting Rachel."

Robert shook his head. "You're getting this all wrong."

"Getting it all wrong? You methodically destroyed the lives of four people you blame for Tara and Emily's accident. You framed two, destroyed one altogether, and I can only guess what you'd planned for Derek Morrison."

"No, you couldn't."

Charlie was silent for a moment. "That's not what I meant, Robert. The fact is that you've taken a situation best handled by the authorities and turned it into your own personal chess game. Good grief. Do you realize how many laws you've broken?"

"Do you think I care? Tara and Emily died, and no one else seemed to care about the truth. They took my family from me, and then they all walked away laughing in my face about it. Did they face justice? No. They got away with it. Is that fair?"

Charlie shook his head. "No, it's not. I can't begin to imagine the pain you went through in losing Tara and Emily. I loved them both very much, but I know that my love doesn't begin to touch what you felt for them. And no, it wasn't fair for all that to happen to them—or to you—but that doesn't excuse what you did, Robert."

Charlie turned and walked toward the window. "You have to come clean about all this, Robert. You can't destroy people's lives like this and then just walk away. I mean, with the exception of Derek they probably have no idea what they're paying for. Where's the justice in that?"

Robert chuckled. "I don't care whether they know now what they are paying for or not. They'll know someday. Until then, they can rot in the filth of their own sin."

Charlie turned and took the file from Robert. "I don't know who in the world you are now, but I know what I have to do."

Before Robert could say a word, he was out the door.

"The car was near me and I ... I ... swerved just a little. All I wanted to do was scare them, but the next thing I knew the car was spinning out of control, and then it ... it ... went under me. By the time I could stop, the car was crushed."

Derek could see Rachel starting to cry. Bishop was still sitting there silent and unmoving as he continued. "I got out, and there was this man there by the car, screaming and crying and trying to get into the heap of metal that was left. It was—"

"Robert." She startled him with her answer. "I know, Derek. I know all about it now." She opened her purse and pulled out several sheets of paper. On top of the stack was a copy of the accident report.

He stared at it for several seconds before looking back at her. "When—"

"Last night. I found out a lot of things, actually. You were right about Robert, and I was so mad at you that I ignored you. I'm so sorry I didn't try harder to find out what was wrong to begin with."

Rachel reached out and gingerly touched his hand. Her touch sent electric fire through him as he gently interlaced his fingers with hers. They sat looking at each other for several long seconds.

Finally, Bishop broke the silence. "Well, what are you waiting for? Kiss her."

With a nervous chuckle from both of them, Derek came out of his seat and onto his knees in front of her. "I'm sorry, Rachel. I should have trusted you to understand. I should have just talked to you. And there's so much more you need to know ..." She silenced him with a finger to his lips, and leaned forward to kiss him.

The taste of her ... the feel of her ... he'd missed it all. He kissed her as he had never done before, wanting nothing more than to know she'd be there forever.

He heard Bishop laugh nearby. "Praise the Lord," he whispered in his deep voice. "God is so good."

And at that moment, Derek couldn't agree more.

Robert stared out the window in his room. Charlie had stormed out three hours ago, and Robert had no doubt that at the very least he'd talk to Rachel and let her know what was happening. She'd never want to have anything to do with him again.

It had all gone wrong. His weeks of planning and careful preparations were now wasted as everything came crashing down at once. Even the fact that he knew without a doubt at least two people on his list were paying for their transgressions didn't ease his frustration. The only one that really mattered would get away.

He reached down and hit the nurse call button. Within seconds, he heard, "Can I help you?"

Robert looked down at the black case that held his laptop computer. "Yes, I was wondering if it would be possible for someone to step in here and help me for a moment please."

"Yes, sir."

"Thank you." Robert settled back into his bed and closed his eyes, thinking of how he'd word the e-mail he was about to send. It was important to get it just right.

A few minutes later a nurse stepped into the room and helped him situate the computer atop the stand on which his food was served. After she left, he slid the wireless card out of the case and into a vacant slot on the side of the laptop. Cell phone use wasn't encouraged in the hospital, but he had to make one call later to send the message he was about to compose.

Ten minutes later, it was done. He dialed out and sent it to his mail server with a delayed delivery instruction. The message wouldn't be sent out for two days, and by then it would be too late to do anything about it but mourn.

His body ached, but the pain had subsided somewhat. With effort, he was able to pack up the laptop. He began to flex his legs and arms as much as he could. He no longer had an extended time to heal. Ready or not, he'd be leaving the hospital on Monday.

And by Monday night, it would all be over.

THIRTY-FIVE

CHARLIE OPENED HIS EYES on Sunday morning to excruciating pain in his neck. Slowly, he lifted his head from his kitchen table where he'd fallen asleep the night before. The papers from Robert's file were scattered all over the table. He rubbed his eyes and the back of his neck. After waiting several moments for the pain to subside, he gave up and decided to try something different. After a long hot shower he began to find some relief.

He was torn between what he knew was the right thing to do, and what would be the best for Robert, his closest friend in the world. Yes, Robert had lied and had become someone far different from the man he'd known for years, but there had been just cause. A man watching his family die had to face problems as a result. But how far was too far? At what point did justifiable revenge become sadistic torture? But Charlie knew that if he did nothing about what he now knew, he himself would be considered an accomplice to Robert's actions.

Stepping out of the shower, Charlie put on a faded UAB T-shirt and jogging shorts and walked back into his kitchen, ignoring the mess on the table and heading straight for the refrigerator.

No need to try to think on an empty stomach.

As he began to search through the feeble groceries on his shelf, his phone rang. Before he could reach it, there was a knock at his front door. Ignoring the second and third ring of the phone, he went to the door and opened it, planning to answer the phone after finding out who his visitor was.

"Hello there, Charlie."

Charlie stood stunned. *Man, I definitely should have answered that phone first.*

The phone rang twice more before going silent as Charlie faced his visitor. It was the last person in the world he expected to see.

"What in the world are you doing here?"

Jonathan smiled. "In the neighborhood … thought I'd drop by … that sort of thing. Can I come in?"

Charlie shrugged and stepped back, allowing him to enter. "Missed you at work Friday."

Jonathan nodded as he walked straight to the kitchen. "Got any coffee?"

Charlie arched an eyebrow. "Guy disappears from work without so much as a good-bye and then shows up on his employer's doorstep two days later wanting coffee … this should be extremely interesting." Digging through his cabinets, Charlie was able to find some Folgers and a filter for his machine. After it started brewing, he turned to see Jonathan staring intently at the papers strewn across the kitchen table. He crossed the room in an instant and scooped them up and back into the file folder. "And nosy, too."

Jonathan laughed and sat down. His beard was as unruly as ever. Looking around, he nodded appreciatively. "Nice place. Love what you've done with it. Hard work, I'm sure, but nicely done."

Putting the file on top of his refrigerator, Charlie walked back to the table. "Have we been drinking this morning, Jonathan? I don't believe I've seen you this talkative since … well, ever."

Jonathan laughed and leaned back in his chair. "Sharp as a tack and witty as ever. You know, you really took a lot out of me."

Charlie returned to the coffeemaker and poured them each a cup of the fresh brew. Placing the mug in front of his visitor, Charlie sat down across the table. "What in the world are you talking about?"

Jonathan took a sip of coffee and closed his eyes, seeming to savor the taste. "Oh, that's good." Putting the cup down, he looked back at Charlie, his green eyes glinting devilishly. "I'm talking about the fact that you were quite a challenge, Charlie. I never really knew if you believed or not, but by the way you're looking at me now, I'm thinking you probably never suspected a thing."

Suddenly, Charlie understood. "Oh, you mean about who you're actually working for?"

Jonathan's smile died away. "You know about that?"

"Yes, I know you're working for Ian Richardson. He said you guys were trying to investigate another employee of mine on the possibility of his reverse-engineering some programs. I don't think Tom's doing that though. I believe he's a little too inquisitive for his own good, but otherwise he's honest."

Jonathan shook his head. "You still don't get it. You're still clueless." Settling back in his seat again, he said, "The story about investigating an employee of the company is true. The employee you're referring to, however, is the wrong one. Yes, I'm working for someone else—but I wasn't there to investigate Tom. I was there to watch Robert."

Charlie's eyes bulged. "You knew about Robert? How could you have known?"

Before Jonathan could answer, there was a frantic knock on the door. Charlie gave Jonathan a quizzical look before standing and crossing the living room to answer it. When he opened the door, Amy brushed past him waving her cell phone and almost ran inside.

"I tried to call you, but you didn't answer. Is he here?"

Charlie closed the door behind her. "Hello to you, too, gorgeous. If the 'he' you're talking about is Jonathan, then yes, he is. He's in the kitchen, and in a very talkative mood."

Walking straight to the kitchen, Amy stood over Jonathan's seated form and glared down at him. "Have you told him yet?"

Jonathan looked past Amy to Charlie's confused face, then back to her again as he shook his head.

"Then tell him—now."

Jonathan spread his hands in mock surrender and then looked back at Charlie with a smile. "You might want to sit down, sport."

Charlie looked at Amy. Her eyes fell as they met his, but she nodded slightly. Feeling uneasy, he moved back to his seat and gripped his coffee cup with trembling hands. "Tell me what?"

Jonathan smiled. "I've been involved in this for a long time, Charlie. I couldn't have done this without you and I honestly mean that when I say it." He slowly took another drink of his coffee.

"Oh, and my name's not Jonathan ..." Reaching up, he pulled what looked like a top plate of dentures from his mouth, but Charlie could see that they were only a false front set. A gleaming row of teeth lay hidden behind them. Before Charlie could react, Jonathan reached into each eye and pulled out a contact lens, revealing two dark-brown eyes. Finally, he reached up and pulled the unruly brown hair from his head, exposing the thick black mane underneath it.

" ... it's Ian."

Derek and his family enjoyed a festive lunch with Bishop and his parishioners after their Sunday-morning service. Bishop had even taken the time to explain in greater detail the finer points of his sermon. Rachel sat silently listening to the preacher's every word, and Derek wished now more than ever that he could know what she was thinking. He wanted her to find the same peace he'd felt two nights ago after being on the verge of suicide. Try as he might, he could never articulate the feelings and emotions he was experiencing.

By the time lunch was over, and they'd all said their good-byes, they seemed a little more subdued than when the meal had begun. It was almost as if each member reflected once more on the goodness of the God who would forgive them of their mistakes and love them anyway. Derek hated the thought of leaving the gathering, but he knew it was time to go.

"Well, I hope to see you three back again next Sunday," said Bishop. "What God has begun in you must be nurtured, Derek. Remember what we talked about."

Derek nodded. "I remember. We'll be there."

Rachel and Scott both hugged Bishop and turned to wait for Derek. "Honey," Derek said, "will you two excuse me for just a minute? I need to talk to Levi about something."

With a quick glance back at her husband, Rachel took Scott by the hand and smiled. "We'll be in the car. Take your time."

Derek watched them leave. "In all the excitement, I guess I forgot to talk about the other thing. How much do I owe you for the investigation?"

Bishop gently put a hand on his shoulder. "Derek, I'm not the one you need to talk to about that. Ian is the man who gets paid for his services. Everything I do, I do for free and for the opportunity to minister to someone in need. You can talk to Ian tomorrow, but I have a feeling he'll probably cut you a pretty good deal. He actually had a lot of fun on this particular case because it was such a challenge to him—and he loves challenges."

"So where is Ian today?"

Bishop chuckled. "If I'm not mistaken, he's visiting a friend."

If Charlie hadn't been sitting, he would have fallen down. He watched dumbstruck as Ian continued to remove the rest of his disguise. The fake beard was next to go, with pieces of spirit gum still sticking to his chin.

Finally, Charlie found words again. "You were working for me the whole time?"

Ian nodded, a lopsided grin on his face. "Good one, eh?"

"But that day in the park, you were at work."

"Yes, but you left before me. I took off 'for lunch' right after you walked out the door, changed in my car, and found you. I'd been watching you during your walk so I couldn't lose you."

Charlie closed his eyes and rubbed his forehead. "But you were at work when I came back."

"Correct again—because I left you in the park in deep contemplation. You must've walked around a bit afterward too, I think. Whatever you did, it gave me time to get back to work. Fortunately, it didn't take a lot to become Jonathan."

"But why?"

Ian raised a finger. "Now that's where it gets a bit more complicated. I needed to keep an eye on Robert. It was what I was being paid to do, and I always believe that the easiest way to do something is to get as close to the subject as possible. Don't get me wrong, I pretty much stalked Robert all the time—but I needed to see what he was doing when he thought nobody was looking. It also gave me the opportunity to plant a keystroke logger on his machine one day while you were at lunch."

Charlie looked at the remnants of Ian's disguise on the table and said, "What in the world kind of private investigator are you?"

Ian shrugged. "Shall we say I'm a little … unorthodox?"

Suddenly a new revelation dawned on Charlie. He turned to Amy. "You knew. When you came in here … you knew. How?"

Charlie heard Ian speak even as he kept his eyes glued on Amy. "I have another confession to make, Chuck—as if you haven't had enough already. I'm not very good with computers. I needed someone to do the work for me, and to be there in a capacity I wasn't capable of handling."

Charlie's eyes remained on Amy as he asked over his shoulder, "What do you mean?"

"Well, as good as I am, I don't think I'd make a convincing enough woman that you'd fall for me and take me into your confidence."

Charlie felt knots twist in his stomach.

Tears began to flow down Amy's face as she broke the painful silence. "It was my job to get close, Charlie. Ian and I would work shifts, so to speak. He'd watch Robert, while I got to know you. I did his programming at night after work and gave it to him to present to you during the course of the next day. It's the way we've always worked."

Amy wiped her face before continuing. "But you were such a nice guy, Charlie. You were so unpretentious and real. Right away, I knew you were someone I could grow to care about deeply. The problem was that at first I didn't know whether I could trust you."

Charlie blinked. "You didn't know if you could trust me? What in the world are you talking about?"

Ian said, "We didn't know who the bad guy really was here, Charlie. I found out during the course of my research that you were a close friend of the family. You were also a computer genius every bit as capable of destroying someone's life electronically as your boss. I knew one of you was up to no good. I just didn't know which one of you it was—if not both of you together."

Amy said, "But eventually I saw that you were oblivious to what was going on. You were still defending Robert and trusting him, even as a part of you was starting to recognize the truth and wanting to deny it." She came up to him and gently touched his chest. "My feelings for you are real, Charlie. I didn't want to hurt you. That's why we're here today. I wanted you to know the truth about everything." Her eyes cut to Ian and narrowed, her jaw set. "But this isn't the way we were supposed to go about it."

Ian shrugged. "Hey, he wouldn't have believed me any other way."

Charlie stepped back and turned to Ian. "So why now? Why should you tell me all this after it's over?"

Ian said, "Two reasons. Number one, Amy's making me. But number two is because I want you to come and work for me. I like you, Charlie boy, and I think you'd be an incredible asset to the team. Amy's got the programming thing down to an art form, but you know the down-and-dirty side of it all—the finer details of hacking and social engineering."

Charlie stared incredulously at both of them. "Are you insane? You lie to me, you use me, you take my feelings and laugh at me behind my back, and then you want to hire me?"

Ian said, "No, no, no, you misunderstand. It's not hire exactly. It would be more of a pro bono kind of thing at first, but then we—"

"I never laughed at you behind your back, Charlie. Since that first night we went to dinner with Robert and Rachel, I knew my feelings for you were strong. I could have stayed at arm's length ánd still got what I wanted, but you were so special and—"

Charlie snorted. "I'm sure. How many times have you gone through this little act together? I guess now you two head to a bar somewhere and have some drinks and laughs, eh?"

Ian said, "Well, actually, I'm not much of a drinker myself—and Amy never touches the stuff, some sort of religious thing."

"Get out."

Charlie's words were so low and cold that neither Amy nor Ian moved at first, but merely cast a quick glance at each other. Realizing that they weren't going to go, Charlie grabbed Ian's arm and yanked him out of the seat. "Get out!"

As Charlie shoved him toward the door, Ian spoke over his shoulder to Amy. "He's not taking this very well. I'm sensing a little hostility here."

When he had the door open and Ian on his porch, Charlie turned to Amy. "Well? What are you waiting for? Go!"

Amy took at tentative step forward and reached for him again. "Charlie, I—"

"Go!"

Amy stepped out the door and turned to look at Charlie again. Her hurt expression almost made Charlie want to apologize, but the humiliation was too much to ignore.

Ian said, "So we should just come back later then?"

Charlie slammed the door in their faces and turned back to his living room. In the dead silence of the house, he collapsed onto the couch and slipped into deep thought.

PART THREE

THREE

REQUIEM

God may forgive you, but I never can.
—QUEEN ELIZABETH I (1533–1603)

THIRTY-SIX

ON MONDAY MORNING, DEREK woke up early and sneaked into the kitchen. As quietly as possible, he pulled out the pans he would need to fix breakfast for his family. Since they were all unemployed at the moment, no one had to be anywhere at any particular time except Scott, who had to be at school at eight. That meant that Derek would have the day to spend with Rachel. He'd never realized just how special such moments truly were.

The soft patter of footsteps behind him alerted him that he'd been discovered. He turned with a smile to see Scott standing in the doorway still dressed in his pajamas.

"Whatcha doin', Daddy?"

Derek put a finger to his lips and winked. "I'm fixing a surprise breakfast for Mommy and you."

The boy's eyes grew wide. "Cool. Can I help?"

"Absolutely. Why don't you get the forks and napkins out and put them on the table. We have to be quiet, though, so we don't wake Mommy, okay?"

Scott nodded and scurried across the kitchen to the silverware drawer. Derek pulled out an egg pan and decided to cook his famous ham and cheese omelet. He knew Rachel would like it, and Scott could always have a bowl of Cocoa Puffs if nothing else.

"Big day at school today?" Derek asked while pulling three glasses down from the cabinet so Scott could reach them.

"Not really, just more of the same old stuff. Can I stay home with you and Mommy today?"

"Good try, but no. You have to go to school so you can get into college and land a good job and make lots of money someday."

"I always have to go to school." Opening the refrigerator door, he pulled out the container of orange juice and struggled to bring it to the counter as Derek stepped behind him to pull out the ingredients for the omelet.

"You'll appreciate it someday, buddy, I promise. When you're older and driving around in your Porsche, you'll be glad you went to school and got so smart."

After several minutes of talking about other things, Scott turned to his father and cocked his head slightly. "Daddy, I'm glad you're back."

Derek put down his cooking utensils and knelt in front of his son so they were face-to-face. "I am too, Scott. I've missed you." He hugged him and kept him close for a long time before breaking away. "Now, why don't you go wake up Mommy and tell her breakfast is getting cold?"

"Mommy's already figured that out."

Derek and Scott both turned to find Rachel standing in the doorway, a crooked grin on her face. She was still dressed in the T-shirt and shorts she had slept in, but her hair was brushed, and Derek could tell she'd taken some time to fix herself up before coming out to greet them. She looked radiant.

"Looks like you boys have been busy," she said as she came to Derek and wrapped her arms around him. He never wanted to leave that embrace again. "Mm, I like it here," she purred.

Derek kissed the top of her head. "Why don't you stay here for a while?"

After a tender kiss, she said, "I'd love to, but somebody has to get to school."

Scott sat down at the table and began to dig into his bowl of cereal. "I know."

Rachel smiled and sat next to her son. "Well, how about after school we all go see a movie?"

Scott's face brightened. "Really? Which one?"

"Your choice—within reason."

"Yeah!" Scott became so excited it was hard to get him settled back down again long enough to eat.

Derek watched his family. Rachel turned to him and winked. That simple action sent electricity through him.

I never thought I'd see us all together like this again. It really is a miracle.

He put the omelet in front of Rachel and sat down beside her. Taking her hand in one of his and Scott's in the other, he led them in a prayer of thanks for their food and for the day.

Robert walked through the stone garden around him, forcing his feet to take each step. He limped slightly from the beating, but he would not let that deter him. He'd left the hospital earlier that morning, determined that nothing would interfere with his plans for the day. He didn't allow his eyes to focus on the names carved in rock and marble around him. Instead, he concentrated on his destination.

Amid the gravestones in Cedar Hill Cemetery, only two held any significance to him. He had not been here since the day their caskets were lowered into the ground, and he had purposefully avoided coming back since then. He had been afraid that seeing this place would force him to feel something, to possibly become human again. He couldn't allow that to happen. He needed the hate to fuel him, to make him hard. The things he'd done were merciless, and he could never have imagined doing them before that day.

Finally, Robert reached the two gravestones. The words were simple, but they caused a stirring in his stomach somewhat akin to nausea. He had been right to stay away; he was feeling again.

He looked at the larger stone and read the name carved into it.

Tara Nicole Whitney.

Seeing the name instantly brought her smile to his mind. He was flooded with memories of their first kiss, of the way her hand felt in his own, and of a thousand other intimate moments they had shared. The stirring inside him grew.

Below her name were the dates of her birth and death. The two dates were far too close to each other. She'd died much too young.

What he saw etched into the stone beneath the name and dates caused his breath to come faster. It was a phrase he had requested carved into this monument as a promise and a fact. It was the creed that drove him on even now.

Beloved wife, never forgotten.

Next to the grave was a smaller gravestone. The name upon it caused the emotions inside Robert to pound against the walls he had built to protect himself.

Emily Dawn Whitney.

Underneath the dates of her birth and death—also far too short a span of time—were the words he had chosen.

Precious daughter, light and joy.

As the memories of her laughter overwhelmed him, he lost the inner battle he'd fought since coming here. Tears streamed down his face. He stood silently staring down at the graves for several minutes. Finally, he spoke.

"I'm sorry I haven't come before. It's not that I'd forgotten you—I could never do that. I've thought of you both every day since you left. There's been no life without you."

He moved forward and knelt between the stones. His fingers traced the name of his beloved bride.

"I miss you so much, Tara. I miss our lazy Saturday mornings of sleeping in and talking until lunch. I miss holding your hand on a sunny day and feeling the breeze blow around us. I miss the cards you'd send me just to tell me you were thinking of me. I miss the way you'd light up whenever I'd bring you flowers. I'm so sorry I didn't think to do that more often.

"You were everything to me, Tara. You were the love of my life, and I loved you more every single day. You balanced me out and gave me a center in the middle of the craziness of day-to-day life. There was no stress you couldn't erase with a touch and a kiss. There was no anger you couldn't dissipate with that wonderfully sexy laugh at one of our little inside jokes. You meant so much to me, and I don't think

I ever really let you know that. I always thought we'd have tomorrow. I never considered for a moment that there'd come a day when I'd wake up and you wouldn't be there."

He leaned forward and let his forehead rest on top of the stone. The tears trickled from his face and down the gravestone, disappearing into the ground at its base. His chest began to heave as his words grew in intensity, becoming louder with each sentence.

"You weren't supposed to go. Didn't you know that? You made me a promise on our wedding day. You promised me you'd be there forever. You promised we'd grow old together. Everyone heard your vows to me. You have to keep your word, Tara. You always kept your word."

The hand resting on the gravestone balled into a tight fist. A low groan originated from deep inside him and began to build. Finally, it erupted from his throat as he threw back his head and screamed into the sky.

"Why? Why did you take them, God? Was it so horribly bad that we were happy? Is that what ticked you off? Did it make you angry that we were so in love? What's your problem? Why do you hate me so much? What did I ever do to you?"

Again he screamed. He yelled until his throat was raw. Then he waited in silence, still staring up toward the heavens.

But there was no answer.

Closing his eyes, Robert slowly lowered his head and tried to regain control of his breathing. His heart pounded in his chest with such fury that he could feel his body shake with each surge of his pulse. He opened his eyes and turned again to his wife's grave.

"You wouldn't understand what I'm about to do, and why. There was never any malice in you, and you couldn't possibly conceive the things that are about to happen. I don't even think you'd know me now if you saw me, and I know I'd be ashamed of who I've become if you did. But this is the only way, Tara. It has to end like this. I'm sorry."

Leaning forward, he closed his eyes and gently kissed the first letter of her name, forever written for others to see. Then he laid his cheek against the cold stone and whispered so softly that no one else could have ever known he'd spoken.

"Please forgive me."

Gathering his emotions, he stood. His eyes moved to the smaller gravestone, and his lips began to tremble.

"Daddy's coming, baby. It won't be long now."

Before he could lose control again, Robert turned and walked away. With each step, the fire began to build inside him. He wiped away the tears, and none took their place. He'd made his peace, and now it was time to finish things.

As he opened the door to his car, he glanced back at the two stones. For the first time, he acknowledged the other words that were engraved next to his wife's name. He had ignored them completely before, but now he read them gladly.

Carved beside Tara's name on the large stone was one other name.

Robert James Whitney.

He smiled and felt a small tinge of relief. He would be glad when this was over and he could finally rest with his family again.

Scott Morrison was outside for afternoon recess. He didn't like school very much, but he knew he'd be going to a movie with his parents right after school, and that made the day better.

He found a quiet spot away from the other kids and started to dig. His plan was to dig a tunnel all the way through the yard and to his desk. That way he could sneak out of class during the day and come straight outside with nobody seeing him. He looked up at the school and saw that it was pretty far off, but that didn't stop him. He'd seen some guys do the same thing in an old war movie he'd watched with his grandpa a few days ago, so he knew it could be done. Casting a quick glance toward his teacher to make sure she was still reading her book, he tore into the dirt.

Suddenly a shadow covered him, and he knew he'd been caught. He looked up expecting to see Miss Horton, and found that it was Mommy's friend Robert—the one who knew so much about Superman. Robert knelt down beside him, looking toward the teacher then back again.

"Hello, Scott."

THIRTY-SEVEN

THE RINGING PHONE WOKE Derek from his nap. He hesitated for a moment, thinking Rachel would get it, but then he noticed the sound of running water and realized she was in the shower. He rolled over and fumbled with the headset, almost knocking the phone off the nightstand.

"Hello?"

An urgent voice responded. "Mr. Morrison? This is Miss Horton, Scott's teacher. Did you pick Scott up early from school today?"

Instantly awake, Derek sat up. "No. My wife's getting ready to come and pick him up now. Why?"

"He's missing, Mr. Morrison. I took all of the children outside to play, but when it came time to go back in, we couldn't find Scott anywhere. I got several teachers to help look for him, but he's nowhere to be found. I thought possibly you'd picked him up early today and neglected to mention it to me. I—"

Derek slammed down the phone and bolted from the bed. He banged on the bathroom door. "Rachel! Scott's missing from school!"

"What?"

"I said Scott's gone! He's not in his class, and his teacher can't find him! I've got to go!"

He heard the water stop as Rachel scurried from the shower. When she opened the bathroom door, he was already dressed and heading for the front door.

"Don't even think of leaving without me. I'll be dressed and ready to go in a few seconds." Rachel hurriedly began to dress. "Where is he, Derek? You don't think Robert ..."

Derek paused at the door and looked back at his wife. He didn't answer, but he had a sick feeling he knew the truth.

By the time they reached the school, the teacher was outside waiting for them. Derek saw several adults combing the area and the wood line near the school grounds. Miss Horton waved to them. She appeared frantic.

Rachel rushed up to her. "What happened?"

"I'm sorry about this. I don't know where he could have gone. We were all in the playground area, and I was watching them. But when it was time to come in, he wasn't there."

Derek said, "Did you see anybody out here wandering around when you first came out? Maybe a male, early thirties, black hair?"

"No, I didn't see anyone. We did find this a few minutes ago, though." She pulled out a white envelope and handed it to him.

Derek turned the envelope over and read the scrawled handwriting on it.

For Derek Morrison, father of Scott Morrison.

He tore the envelope open and extracted the single sheet of paper inside. When he opened it and began to read, he felt his blood chill.

> *Derek,*
>
> *If you're reading this, then you know about Scott. Sorry to do it this way, but it's the last avenue open to me. I had such a beautiful plan laid out for you and me. Unfortunately, some bad luck has changed all that for me. I've been forced to improvise.*
>
> *It sure looks like you won, doesn't it? You killed my family and got away with it, got yours back, and succeeded in*

alienating me from the last few friends I have. Congratulations.
Unfortunately for you, I made a promise that you'd pay, and
I meant it.

I have Scott. I don't want to hurt him, but I will if you
don't come to the Joiner Storehouse on Twenty-sixth Street at
five o'clock. Not to seem melodramatic, but come alone and
keep your mouth shut. This is between the two of us.

We end this tonight.
Robert

Derek's throat was dry. He felt fury building up inside as he reread the note. How this could have happened, he didn't know. How it would end, he no longer cared, as long as Scott was safe. He just wanted it all to be over. Robert would haunt them forever until he had his revenge. To protect his family, Derek had to make a choice.

"What does it say?" Rachel asked.

He passed her the note and turned to go. It was almost three now, and it would take him roughly forty minutes to get to the storage facility. That gave him a little time to prepare. And despite Robert's demand, he *would* tell someone what he was going to do. He owed them that much.

Charlie tried to concentrate on the code he was writing, but it was no use. The office was quiet. He'd gotten so used to people filling the room that it seemed like a tomb now. He'd made up his mind that he would finish the projects they were contracted to do, and then he'd leave. While the idea of starting his own company appealed to him, the money necessary to get it going wasn't available to him just yet. Besides, the only client pool he had was the one he'd created with Robert, and no matter what had happened between them over the past two days, he didn't want to hurt him.

He looked at the empty workstation beside his and thought about Amy. He missed her smile. He had no idea what his next course of action should be. One part of him wanted to forgive her and see if they had a future together, but another part of him was afraid she'd been using him the whole time and would only hurt him again.

As he sat lost in thought, he received a notification on his screen of a new e-mail. Hoping it was from Amy, he pulled up his e-mail program and looked at the new message.

It was from Robert.

He hesitated for a moment, trying to decide whether to open it.

Oh, grow up. It's not like he's going to send me some killer computer virus or something. The letter size is too small for anything but a few paragraphs. What can it hurt?

Just to be safe, he scanned the message with his antivirus software and found it clean. He clicked it and watched as it filled the screen.

Hi Charlie,

First I wanted to apologize for deceiving you. I know you must feel like some pawn in my game, but nothing could be further from the truth. This was always about the four people on my list and me. I tried to do everything while leaving you oblivious to it all so you'd be innocent later. You've always been my closest friend, and I didn't want you involved. It really was for your own good.

I put this message on a schedule so you won't receive it until four o'clock on Monday. I don't know what time you'll end up checking your messages, but I wanted you to know before you found out on the news later.

You see, I'm going to kill Derek Morrison.

I guess I always knew it would come down to that. I knew it when I was standing on the highway looking down at Tara and Emily. I promised them then that he'd pay, but I never intended on just hurting him. I wanted him to suffer, and then I wanted him to die. I also know I have no reason to live anymore either. I can't fill the void Tara and Emily left, even though a part of me has tried. There's nothing left.

That being said, the company is yours. You're smart enough and talented enough to keep it running and make it better than it ever was. I apologize for making this message so abrupt, but you'll find everything you need to know in a safe deposit box in the bank across the street. The key is in my top desk drawer, and the box is in your name. I set it up weeks ago.

The documents inside it include my will, which gives you everything I own. I ask only that you make sure I'm buried next to my wife and child. There is a sufficient amount of cash in the box to cover the burial expenses. If you sell my house, you should have enough money to keep the company up and running while you get situated.

Take care of yourself, Charlie. You're gifted with an amazing talent for programming, and I know you'll do well in life. Thanks for your friendship.

Robert

Charlie read the message in stunned silence, but it only took seconds for him to recover enough to plan a course of action. He pulled up Rachel's employment record and found the phone number she'd listed there. If he could tell her what Robert had planned then there was a good chance she could warn Derek. Since Robert had set the message to arrive at this precise time, it had to mean he didn't think Charlie would have a chance to stop him.

But Robert had underestimated his business partner.

"You've done some stupid things so far, Robert, but I'm not about to let you do this. I'm mad at you, but even you don't deserve this."

He grabbed the phone and prayed there was still time.

The Joiner Building on Twenty-sixth Street in Birmingham had been an important place in the early sixties. It was a seat of commerce for the area and a hub of activity every day of the week with offices of important people on each of the five floors. As the city grew, it moved away from the area, and the businesses in the building no longer felt safe. By 1984, only two offices were still being rented on the ground floor, with the rest of the building falling quickly into disrepair. At the end of the year, the remaining two tenants moved on.

The building remained empty for more than a decade until someone had the idea of remodeling it. Each of the offices was turned into smaller storage rooms, the entire building was repainted, and the historical Joiner Building became the modern Joiner Storehouse.

After a half-dozen break-ins and two muggings of people coming to pick up stored items, the modern Joiner Storehouse became an empty shell for the second time in its existence.

That was where Derek found himself today.

He stood outside the building and looked up. The few parking spaces still afforded the building were empty. He was completely alone; and somewhere inside there was his little boy. Derek knew it was his fault that Scott was even involved in this sordid affair, and he was just as ready as Robert was for it to all end here and now.

Walking to the front door, he saw shattered glass around it. The door moved when he touched it. He stepped inside and searched for any sign of his son. The lobby area was empty, looted long ago for anything of any value. An elevator stood directly before him, but Derek had no intention of going near it—even if the building had had the power to run it. Instead, he found a stairwell and carefully began the ascent. As he rounded the first set of stairs, he found a message spray-painted on the wall.

Top floor–R.

Looking up the stairwell, he could see a faint light at the very top. He continued his climb and found candles placed at regular intervals on the stairs to provide enough illumination to see the area clearly.

"Robert?" Derek's voice echoed through the quiet building. "Scott? Scott, Daddy's here."

He strained his ears to hear anything at all, but he heard nothing. The creaking steps beneath his feet warned of their years of neglect and protested his sudden burden upon them.

"Dad?"

The voice was faint, but Derek caught it. It was coming from one of the upper floors. Ignoring the danger of the weakened stairs beneath him, Derek raced upward.

"Scott?"

"Dad?"

Derek heard Scott's voice again, but this time it seemed to be coming from the floor below him. He stopped between the second and third floors, trying to catch his breath. Eerie shadows danced along the walls from the flickering candles.

"Scott? Where are you?"

"Dad?"

This time the voice was directly above him.

"Dad?"

Now it sounded as if it was coming from the lobby.

"Scott? What's going on? Where are you?"

"Dad?"

Derek hesitated for only a moment. This time he was certain the voice had come from the top floor. He raced up the final steps and burst through the doorway. He stood at the beginning of a long hallway with at least a dozen closed doors on each side. More fat candles lined the hallway, and light poured in from a window at the end of it. His nostrils caught the faint smell of gasoline.

"Scott! Scott, are you—"

Then it all made sense.

Robert Whitney stood at the far end of the hallway.

THIRTY-EIGHT

W HERE'S MY SON?"

Robert merely stood there smiling coldly. "I haven't hurt him. I told you I wouldn't as long as you came."

"Dad?" Scott's voice came from the room beside him. Derek raced for the door and found it locked.

"Scott? Scott, it's Dad. Are you all right?"

No answer.

Derek glanced down the hallway toward Robert, who stood observing the entire exchange. "Give me the key."

"Break it down."

"Fine." Derek slammed into the door several times. Because of its age, he saw results. His shoulder began to hurt with the effort. After he had hit it three more times, the door gave way, and he burst into the room.

It was empty.

"Dad?"

Then he pinpointed the source of the voice. A small silver box lay at his feet. He picked it up and walked back out into the hallway.

Robert was still standing in the same spot, hands in the pockets of the black overcoat he wore.

"Ingenious little device, isn't it? A wireless speaker. Twenty-four rooms in the top four floors of this building, twelve on the ground floor, and one of those little beauties in each— including the room Scott's in right now. Quick math tells you that that's over a hundred possible hiding places, not counting the storage closets sprinkled here and there. One room houses my laptop computer. It's controlling all of the speakers via a wireless network using a program I created. Remote-controlled chaos."

Derek looked at the small object in his hand. There was no way he could hope to break down all those doors, but there was no reason to. Throwing the speaker on the floor, he began to walk toward Robert. "You're going to tell me where he is, Robert."

Robert stood his ground. He pulled a hand from his coat, and Derek could see a small remote control in it. "You touch me, and Scott's dead. There's no way you can get into all those rooms fast enough to find him."

Derek froze in his tracks. The distance was too far. He could never reach Robert before he did whatever he'd planned to do. He needed time. "So what now?"

"We're here to finish this, Derek. We're going to end it the only way it can, and the way you knew it had to." Robert slowly slid his hand back into his coat pocket. The sun was setting outside, and the only light of any significance in the hallway now came from the candles dispersed on the floor. Robert seemed almost to gather the shadows around him like a cloak.

Derek heard Scott's voice again calling for him somewhere in the distance. A few seconds later, it came again, this time from the same floor he was on now. Robert gave a crooked grin, obviously enjoying Derek's torment. Trying to ignore the maddening cadence of his son's cries, Derek said, "Robert, please let Scott go. I'm here just like you asked. You said he'd go free as long as I showed up."

"Scott will be fine. I wouldn't get any pleasure from hurting him or Rachel. I just used them to get to you. It was all going so well too; then I got jumped one night, and in a single weekend everything I'd worked for fell apart at once." Robert looked around the hallway as

Scott's voice echoed around them. "This was ultimately how it was going to end, it's just a matter of it all happening a bit sooner than expected. By the way, are you the one who attacked me the other night?"

Derek looked down and sighed. "Yes. I was at the end of my rope and couldn't stand the thought of losing everything and not being able to do anything about it. Believe it or not, it actually made things worse. It seemed like everything I did made things worse. I even planned to kill myself the next night, but something happened. I'm a different man now."

The ethereal call of Scott's voice around them made the place seem almost like an evil fun house. The sun was gone, and the only light was from the candles. It was almost as if even the streetlights outside were too weak to penetrate the darkness.

"A different man now? I guess that means I should just forgive and forget and let us both get on with our lives. You go live with your wife and son, and I'll go sit in the empty shell of my house. We'll call it even. Is that what you mean?"

Derek took another step toward him. "No, that's not what I'm saying at all. As a matter of fact, Rachel and I discussed it today. I'm going to the police with what really happened. I'm going to go face up to what I've done. I was just hoping I'd get a chance to talk to you first."

"Let me guess: You're sorry, and you hope I'll forgive you. Am I right?"

Derek took another small step. "Robert, I—"

"Derek, if you come any closer to me, Scott won't appreciate it." Robert brought the small remote out again and held it up.

"Dad!"

Derek spun around. This time the voice had been different. It was stronger, and had an urgency that made him feel that he had to act.

And he knew exactly which room it had come from.

"Scott! I'm coming!" He ran for a door two rooms down. He braced himself and slammed into it with all his strength. The doorframe gave way, and he fell into the pitch-black room. His nostrils still detected a whiff of gasoline.

"Scott?" Derek crawled around the room on hands and knees feeling for his son. He had to get him out before it was too late. He searched the room in a panic. His fingers brushed the floor as he pushed his way deeper into the darkness.

He heard the sound of footsteps behind him, then stars exploded into his vision, and the floor rushed up to meet him.

Robert stood over Derek's still form. He hefted the metal rod in his hand and prepared to hit him again, but there was no need. Derek was unconscious.

He turned and walked back out into the hall, dropping the rod. He descended the stairway to the fourth floor. There were no candles on this floor, as he'd wanted Derek to come straight to the top and not take time to investigate this one. Three gas cans were lined up in a corner for the next part of his plan.

Robert entered one of the darkened rooms and closed the door behind him. He was finally alone. Everything he'd worked so hard for was now coming to pass. He could just walk out and leave Derek here to die a painful death, then he could go to Tara's grave and kill himself, as he'd always intended. Then rest would come for him too.

His fingers wrapped around something in his pocket. He pulled out the scrawled drawing Emily had made for him, along with a photograph of Tara, Emily, and himself. The girls were on either side of him, their cheeks together. What an amazing family. And now they were gone.

It was strange, but he just didn't feel the cathartic satisfaction he'd been expecting with Derek's death. It wasn't that he had imagined Tara and Emily suddenly popping up alive in front of him in exchange for Derek, but he had thought it would have at least partially eased the pain he was feeling.

Instead, he felt the same emptiness overwhelming him.

What's going on? This is what I've planned for and dreamed about since Tara and Emily died. Why doesn't it feel as good as I thought it would?

In the back of his mind, he could feel condemnation attacking his senses. His wife and daughter would never have wanted him to avenge their deaths this way. They would have been appalled by the man he had become.

And in truth, so was he.

He'd used and betrayed a woman who'd never done him any harm. He'd committed several felonies by using his knowledge, intelligence, and skills to destroy three other men's lives and identities. He'd even resorted to kidnapping Scott so Derek would come after him when things fell apart.

And now he was finishing it all off with the cold-blooded murder of the man he held responsible for the death of his family. And the sad thing was that the family he was punishing the man for would never have wanted it this way.

There was still time.

He could still act and change what he had become.

Glancing back at the picture in his hand, Robert closed his eyes and wept.

"You are one sick puppy, you know that?"

Robert jerked at the sudden intrusion into his reverie. His eyes shot to the figure in the doorway.

Terrance Gold.

One arm was in a sling. The other held a pistol pointed at him. "You got some sick stuff goin' on here, man. I mean, I thought you'd gone to a lot of trouble to get me, but now I feel jealous." He glanced up at the ceiling. "You sure slapped that guy down good. So what happens next? I saw the gas cans. You gonna torch him?"

"What are you doing here?"

"The trucker called me."

"I didn't realize you two were buddies."

"We ran into each other a few nights ago. He called today to ask for my help as an officer of the law and wanted me to keep my mouth shut. Guess he didn't know I'm not currently working for the state anymore, thanks to you."

Robert chuckled. "And I'll bet you didn't share that little piece of information with him, did you?"

Gold raised an eyebrow and sneered. "Nah, it slipped my mind." He stepped into the room, the pistol still steady on Robert's chest. "I couldn't get to you at the hospital, but there's nobody here to save you now."

"So what are you going to do?"

Gold slammed the barrel of the pistol across Robert's face. Robert staggered back, stunned. He tried to put some distance between them, but Gold rushed forward and hit him again. Robert fell to his knees as another blow came down.

He lay on his back, his vision blurred. Gold stepped into the hall for several seconds, then walked back into the room holding one of the gas cans. "I just got through dousing the upstairs. Now I've made a nice little trail up to your door.

"You know, Robert, there are very few ways to die more painful than burning up in a fire. It's slow, inescapable, and you feel every agonizing second of it. You pray for death long before it actually overtakes you. I like this even better than the needle."

Gold was silhouetted in the doorway. Suddenly, a flash of light exploded in front of him. He slowly brought the lit match up until his face was illuminated. Then with an evil grin he flicked the match into the pool of gas.

THIRTY-NINE

SOMETHING WAS BURNING.

As Derek opened his eyes, he could smell smoke. He lifted his head and saw flickering lights on the hallway outside. But this light was much brighter than the dim candlelight he'd seen before.

And then he saw why.

Like a scene from a nightmare, the hallway exploded into flame.

"Scott!" Derek tried to ignore the imminent danger in which he suddenly found himself and used the growing light to scan the room around him. He scrambled to his feet and ran to several large boxes near the back wall. He could feel the heat on his back as he began to push the boxes away. The top ones felt almost empty and were easily tossed aside. When he got to the bottom one, it didn't move. There was a substantial weight in it.

He tore the box open. Despite the flames at the front of the room, the interior of the box was still dark. He reached inside and felt his knuckles slam into something hard.

A cement block.

Then his fingers touched a familiar object at the bottom of the box. He gripped it tightly and brought it up to his face. It was another one of the wireless speakers he'd found earlier. He'd been baited into the room. Derek turned toward the door to find that the doorway was now blocked by the rising blaze.

He watched in stunned silence as the flames engulfed the room.

Terrance stopped before he reached his car and looked back up at the building behind him. He could see light from the small windows on the top two floors. Soon the fire would consume the entire structure.

He'd considered saving the trucker, but then thought better of it. If Morrison hadn't wanted to hurt Whitney, then he would have become a liability when he saw the fire. No, it was easier to just clean up the whole mess at once.

There was nothing more to keep him in Birmingham anyway. His job was gone; his reputation was forever scarred here. No, it was time to start fresh somewhere else.

Laughing to himself, he got in his car and drove away.

Snapping out of his terrified stupor, Derek glanced around the room. There was nothing to work with that he could see. Everything was going up in flames quickly. Empty boxes lay scattered near his feet, along with the open box holding the—

Suddenly Derek knew what he had to do. He reached into the open box and lifted out the cement block. Smoke filled the room, making it hard for him to breathe. He moved to the wall and knocked on the Sheetrock. The walls had been put in to separate larger offices into smaller storage rooms. This meant that the sturdier walls had been taken out and replaced with thin walls made of little more than Sheetrock and framework. He just had to find the right spot. Quickly, he started tapping on the walls.

Finally, he heard a hollow thud and knew he'd found a place between the studs in the wall. Coughing and with his eyes burning, he slammed the cement block into the Sheetrock. The flimsy wall gave way. He pulled the block back and slammed it in again, this time a little lower. With another hit, he'd made a space large enough to get through. Shoving his head through the hole, he breathed a lungful of fresh air.

After he'd squeezed the rest of his body into the room, Derek stood and got his bearings. Light filtered in from the hole, allowing him to see the door. He had to find Scott.

Opening the door, Derek looked down the hall for Robert. The hallway was in flames. Derek burst into it and began to bang on doors as he passed by them. "Scott! Scott, where are you? Can you hear me?"

He shook his head and stopped. There was no way he could search all of the rooms in this building before it burned down. Only Robert knew where Scott was, and that meant he had to find Robert.

Smoke filled the hallway, making it hard to see. Derek's lungs and eyes burned. "Robert! Robert, I'm out! You didn't get me! Come on, try again!"

"Dad!" Scott's voice rang out from one of the rooms down the hall. A few seconds later the same voice answered from several doors farther down. It was all a horrible game.

Come on, Robert. I need you to find me. I have to believe that you wouldn't leave Scott up here to die alone, so if you're on one of the lower floors, then that's where Scott's got to be.

Derek ran to the stairwell at the end of the hall and jumped down the stairs two at a time to reach the fourth floor. The stairs creaked out their objection with his every step, but he ignored them.

The fourth floor was also burning. Derek moved cautiously into the hallway. The ceiling above crackled and snapped, losing its war against the flames. He tried the first door on his right and found it unlocked. It swung open easily.

It was empty. The next room was unlocked; as were the next three doors he tried. Apparently Robert hadn't planned on his getting down here to check on anything.

Each room was as deserted as the one before. He moved as fast as he could, dancing around the flames that were everywhere.

Reaching the far end of the hallway, Derek heard a cough. Eyes watering, he kicked the door open and then jumped back as fire rushed toward the sudden influx of air. Shielding his face with his hands, he looked through the flames and saw Robert on the floor near the back of the room. The fire slithered toward him like some hideous flaming serpent.

"Robert! Get up!"

Robert turned his head toward him, and Derek could see blood on the side of his face. The dazed look he gave him told Derek he didn't yet realize the danger he was in.

Derek looked into the room. A small table stood in one corner. A laptop computer sat on it, its display showing several small boxes that lit up randomly. He could hear Scott's voice with each one that lit up.

"Robert!"

Robert continued to lie there. Derek stepped back as far as he could, then ran forward and dove over the flames. He slammed into the hardwood floor a few feet away from Robert. His shoulder throbbed again, but he knew he couldn't stop now.

He grabbed Robert and shook him. Robert's eyes opened, trying to focus. Finally, a spark of recognition appeared when he saw Derek.

"You should have run while you had the chance, Derek."

"Where's Scott?"

Robert laughed, coughing. "You mean you haven't figured it out yet?"

There was a loud crash in the hall and a brilliant flash of light. The ceiling had begun to collapse.

Derek turned back to Robert, pleading now. "Please, Robert, where's my son?"

"You don't get it, do you?"

"Get what?"

"Rachel has him."

Ian pushed his Mustang for everything it could give him. The streets of downtown Birmingham raced by in a blur. Bishop sat in the passenger seat next to him, while Amy and Charlie were holding on for dear life in the back.

"Anyone catch a street sign back there?" he asked.

"I think we're getting closer," Charlie replied. "Rachel said the note she saw mentioned the Joiner Building on Twenty-sixth Street. We passed Eighth back there, if I'm not mistaken."

"How long had she had the note?"

"She said she'd just found it when I called. When did Derek call you, Levi?"

"About twenty minutes ago. He wouldn't tell me where he was going, though. He just told me to keep an eye on Rachel. Robert's note to Charlie made it obvious that he's through with the subterfuge. The game's over. He's ready to end it."

"I'm just glad you called us," said Amy. She gently placed her hand on Charlie's.

He glanced at her, but didn't remove his hand. "I didn't know what else to do. I hoped you guys at least had an idea of what Robert had planned."

The loud ring of Charlie's cell phone caused everyone's already frayed nerves to jump.

"Hello?"

After a moment of silence, Charlie spoke to Amy. "It's Rachel."

"Hey, isn't it a little late for sunset?" said Ian.

They all turned to look at what he was talking about. The horizon held a faint red glow. As they got closer, they saw the flames.

FORTY

RACHEL HAS HIM?"

Robert pushed himself up on his elbows. "Think about it, Derek. This has never been about your family. This has always been about you and me. Rachel and Scott were pawns to get to you. I never wanted to hurt them."

"Rachel doesn't have Scott. She wouldn't do this to me." Derek slowly stood and backed away from Robert.

"Do what to you? You think she's in on this or something? Please, Derek, tell me you have a little more trust in your wife than that." Standing, Robert dusted himself off. "I called her right after you entered the stairwell and told her where Scott was. He's in a day-care center about three miles from your house. He thought he was on a little vacation with me until his mommy came to pick him up. He has no idea of what's going on."

Robert looked down and noticed a piece of paper on the floor near his feet. Emily's drawing. He picked it up and opened it, his face somber. "My little girl made this for me. It was the last gift I ever got from her." His voice trailed off. He gently folded the paper and put it in his pocket.

"So Scott's really not here?" asked Derek.

"No. I never intended to hurt them … just you. You were the one who took my wife and child from me. You were the one who emptied my life forever. You were the guilty one. But now for some reason it doesn't seem to matter anymore."

Derek closed his eyes and breathed a sigh of relief. "Thank you. Thank you for not hurting them because of me. I'm the one who deserves to be punished, and I'll gladly pay for what I've done."

There was a loud crack, and the light in the hall flared up even brighter. "Looks like you and I will both be ending it together after all," said Robert.

Derek jumped back over the flames and into the hall. The heat and smoke made him cover his face, but not before he caught a glimpse of what was before him.

A wall of flame blocked their way to the stairwell.

"Is there another way out of here?" he asked.

Robert leaped over the flames to stand beside him. "This old building has one stairwell, and it's down there," he said, pointing past the fire. "The only thing down this way is that old elevator, and you'd be better off taking your chances with the fire than with that thing."

Derek looked down the hall to the closed elevator doors. They were on the third floor. There was a possibility that he and Robert could make it out.

"Come on," he said, grabbing Robert's arm. "We're getting out of here."

Robert jerked his arm away. "What are you talking about? Why should you want to help me? Have you forgotten who I am? I'm the guy who almost cost you your marriage, your job, and your life."

"My job is no big loss, I promise you. My marriage is going to survive, thanks to a miracle from God. And I'm not quite ready to give up on my life just yet either—or yours. We can still get away. We've got to at least try."

Derek ran toward the elevator door.

As Ian pulled in front of the Joiner Building, he could hear Bishop beside him calling 911. Flames were pouring out of the top of the building, and he could see light dancing on the third-floor windows as well. It would be burned to the ground long before the firefighters arrived. If Derek and Robert were in there, their only hope of help had just arrived.

"Charlie, you come with me," he said. "Amy, you stay here and tell the firemen the situation when they arrive. Tell them there's definitely one man in there somewhere, possibly two. As soon as Bishop gets off the phone, tell him what we're doing."

Without another word, he bolted from the car and ran toward the front door. He could hear Charlie's running footsteps behind him. They burst through the door and into the empty lobby area.

"Stairs," said Ian, motioning to one side of the area. "The top two floors are burning, which means the blaze wasn't started down here. If Robert had Derek down here somewhere, he wouldn't set the top of the building on fire first; he'd start at the bottom and work his way up. We need to check the top and work our way down."

As they ran toward the stairwell, Ian could see it was well lit from above. When they entered it, he saw why.

The entire stairwell was ablaze.

Ian glanced at Charlie, who was staring up in awe, and said, "This is not good."

It was a terribly beautiful sight. Flames filled the area above them and lit it up like a gigantic pillar of fire. For a moment Ian thought back to his Sunday-school days and remembered Moses saying that God appeared to the Israelites that way at night. Seeing this smaller version of what they surely saw, he had a new understanding of the wonder they must have felt at seeing it.

A huge crackle overhead grabbed Ian's attention. A section of the stairs broke off and began to rush down toward them. Reacting on instinct, he grabbed Charlie's shirt and pulled him out of the stairway with him. The flaming steps crashed behind them, shutting off the stairwell completely.

"Th-thanks," Charlie said, coughing.

"Eyes open." Ian stood and moved away from the intense heat pouring from nearby flames. Smoke began to billow into the lower lobby. If Robert and Derek were in this building somewhere, they only had a few more minutes to live.

And Ian knew that if he didn't come up with a way to find them and get out of here soon, then so did he and Charlie.

"What are you going to do?" Robert asked.

"If I can get this elevator door open, we should be able to climb down to the bottom floor and get out the front door—if it's not on fire too. Barring that, at least we can get down to the second floor and possibly break out a window and jump. We'll stand a better chance of surviving a two-story drop onto the asphalt than a four-story nose-dive. The tricky part is getting the door open."

Robert brushed past him and shoved his fingertips into the door's seam. He pulled, and Derek could see a small opening begin to form. Without waiting for an invitation, he grabbed one side of the door and pulled. Within seconds it was open.

"How in the world did you do that?" Derek asked.

"This place is falling apart anyway. Vandals destroyed most of this stuff years ago. But this way is just as suicidal as the stairs."

Derek looked down the elevator shaft. Along the wall just a few feet away was a ladder that extended down to the bottom floor. It would be easy to reach it and climb down. He turned back to Robert. "Why do you think that's suicidal? It looks like an easy climb."

"It's not what's below you that's the problem," Robert said, pointing up the shaft.

Derek looked up and saw what he'd been talking about. He was looking at the underside of the elevator car itself.

And there were flames flickering along the top of it.

"If that thing breaks lose while we're climbing down, we'll be dead before we realize what's happening," Robert said. "On the other hand, if it breaks first, it'll block off this way completely—even up to the second floor."

Derek looked behind them at the growing blaze. "Then I guess we'd better be fast on our feet," he said, reaching around the door and grabbing the ladder.

Before he could talk himself out of it, he stepped out into thin air.

Robert watched Derek move around the shaft door and onto the ladder. He glanced up at the elevator car and shook his head.

What a stupid time to decide I want to live.

Derek was already down several feet, so Robert grabbed the ladder and stepped out on it. It felt hot under his hands.

He was between the third and fourth floors when he heard a loud groaning of metal above. Looking up, he saw that the flame on top of the car had intensified. It was moving along the side of the car, burning anything flammable. Glowing ash and debris fluttered down around them as they climbed down. The ceiling above the elevator was aflame also.

"Derek, since you and God have gotten so close lately, you might want to start asking for a favor."

A loud pop like a shot echoed through the shaft.

Glancing down, Robert saw that Derek was almost at the bottom of the third floor. "Can you open that door and jump in?"

"I think so, but we might be able to make it to the ground floor."

There was another loud pop, followed by two more. Flames poured in from the open fourth-floor doorway from which they were leaping.

"Go!"

Then Robert heard a scraping noise, and the ladder began to shudder.

A bright light grew from overhead, and he looked up just in time to see a large piece of flaming debris coming straight for him. Before he could react, it hit his right shoulder, and his arm went numb. It dropped uselessly to his side. He shook frantically, trying to dislodge the burning wood before it reached his face, but he couldn't use his left hand to swipe it away because it was the only thing holding him to the ladder. The heat intensified until he could take it no more. Derek was yelling something to him as he released the ladder and brushed the wood away.

And then he felt a rush of heat and wind as he fell.

FORTY-ONE

SMOKE FILLED THE BUILDING with a black cloud, and both Ian and Charlie had tears streaming from their burning eyes. Glancing around, Ian banged on the elevator door. "We've got to get this thing open. This is the only way we have to get up to wherever they are."

"Do you think they're still alive?" Charlie asked, coughing.

Ian tried to get his fingers into the door opening. "I don't plan on quitting until I find out one way or another. But if this doesn't work, I'm out of ideas."

He tried to get the door open, but couldn't get his fingers wedged in deep enough to get a grip. "Come on, come on!"

He felt a huge hand rest on his shoulder and heard Bishop's deep voice. "Excuse me."

Ian stepped aside as Bishop dug his fingers into the door slits. Suddenly, all three men heard a loud thump behind the door.

"What was that?" Charlie asked.

Ian shook his head. "I don't know. Bishop, can you get it?"

Bishop grunted with exertion. A small crack formed where the door began to open, and it was all they needed. Ian and Charlie grabbed opposite doors and all three pulled together. Within seconds they had the door open wide enough to step through.

And then they saw the bodies.

Robert lay on top of Derek at the bottom of the shaft three feet below. Both men lay motionless on a growing pool of crimson.

"Dear God in heaven." Bishop dropped into the shaft. Ian jumped down after him and turned to Charlie. "Stay there."

He heard Bishop praying as he checked each man. Bishop yelled out, "Call an ambulance!"

Charlie nodded and stepped back, grabbing his cell phone.

Ian noticed the flaming debris around and looked up. Four stories above, he saw the burning elevator. "Bishop, we're going to have to move them."

"We can't. They don't need to be touched until the paramedics arrive."

"*Now*, Levi." Bishop turned toward him as Ian pointed upward. "That thing's coming down."

Bishop's gaze fell back to the men on the floor as if trying to find some other course of action. Finally, he closed his eyes and sighed. "All right, but let's be careful."

Ian put his hands on both sides of Robert's head to stabilize it as Bishop lifted him off Derek. The big man offered words of comfort as he did so, but Robert didn't respond. They moved with him together to the doorway. The crackling sound of burning wood over-head was like the ticking of a time bomb. Then there came another loud crash in the distance.

"We'll put him up there, and then get Derek," Ian said. "This thing's coming down fast."

As they reached the door, Charlie stepped up with Amy. Ian had to yell to be heard over the loud creaking of the building as it protested its imminent demise. "What are you doing in here? Never mind. Here, Amy, take Robert's head, and don't let his neck move any more than you have to. Get him out of here."

Bishop handed Robert's still form to Charlie and then turned back to Derek. Ian moved with him and felt for a pulse. "He's bad, Levi. I don't think he's going to make it."

The preacher spoke to Derek as he cradled him in his arms. "Don't let go yet, Derek. We're getting out of here. Rachel's waiting for you."

Bishop struggled to reach the elevator door. Ian saw that the three-foot step up they'd have to take was going to be tricky. Sudden brightness over his head made Ian look up again. A large piece of flaming wood was coming down—fast.

"Levi, move!"

Ian fell to his hands and knees in front of the doorway to form a human step for Bishop to use. Without hesitation Bishop followed Ian's hurried command and was through the doorway as the wood crashed to the ground behind him.

Then Ian's stomach fell as he heard a loud roar. For a second he thought the elevator was finally falling, but then the reality of what he was hearing hit him.

The ancient building was finally admitting defeat in its war against the fire.

It had begun to collapse.

He looked up as a curtain of flame fell toward him.

Charlie and Amy didn't stop with Robert until they were all the way out of the burning building and across the street. After laying his former boss on the ground, Charlie looked back and stood mesmerized as the flaming building filled the night sky with light. He could feel the heat pouring off of it.

Charlie caught movement near the front door and ran toward it. As he drew closer, he could see Levi walking as fast as he could with Derek in his arms. When he reached him, Bishop nodded over his shoulder, his eyes watering from the smoke.

"Ian's still in there."

Charlie raced toward the inferno. The heat almost knocked him off his feet. In the distance he heard the sound of approaching sirens.

In the lobby it took a moment to acclimate himself to the surroundings. Things had changed drastically. Entire sections of the building were now piles of burning rubble. Common sense told him that he was going to die if he stayed there, but he knew that Ian had no other help coming.

Finally, he was able to get his bearings and head toward the elevator shaft. When he was almost to it, he stopped.

Fire was pouring out of the door of the shaft. As far inside as he could see, the entire thing was one huge blaze. If Ian was still in there, then he couldn't possibly have survived.

Loud coughing to his left caught his attention. Ian was on the floor, his clothes smoking. Charlie ran and knelt beside him. He heard a huge crash behind him.

"Ian? Are you all right?"

Ian continued to cough, but nodded. "I'll live." Charlie helped him to his feet, and they turned toward the front door, only to find it blocked with debris.

The building creaked and groaned above them under the strain of the flames. Charlie glanced around, but there were no other exits.

They were trapped.

FORTY-TWO

ROBERT FEELS THE BURNING *in his shoulder. The fire near his face gropes hungrily for him. His right arm is useless, and his other holds him to the ladder ... but the fire calls to him. His survival instinct takes over, and he reaches to push the fire away. As he does, he feels himself falling.*

For a moment there is almost a peace about it. A part of him knows that he will die and that he is not ready, yet another part of him welcomes the end of his suffering. A single word flashes through his mind: hell. He is in hell, and it is where he will spend eternity. Nothing can save him from it.

Then as the air rushes over his body, he feels two arms wrap around him. A voice whispers in his ear—Derek's voice.

"Gotcha."

They fall together ...

And he feels the impact cushioned by Derek's body.

Robert opened his eyes. His head hurt, and his ears were ringing. As his eyes focused, he saw that the sky was strange. It was night, and yet it wasn't. He raised his head to search for the source of light.

The Joiner Building.

But how did he get here? The last thing he remembered, he was in there. He was trapped with flames all around him ... flames everywhere—including on him. Then he fell, and Derek ...

Firefighters rushed toward the building. Amy stood near them, hands at her mouth as she looked inside.

Then he saw Derek lying nearby, apparently unconscious.

Helpless.

Robert began to crawl toward him.

His body hurt, and the sudden pressure on his already bandaged hand made him crumple to the ground. Fighting with his one good hand, he got to his feet and struggled toward the fallen figure ahead.

Derek's breathing was shallow. Blood was all around him.

"Derek?"

Derek's eyelids fluttered slightly, his eyes focusing on nothing. Robert moved into his field of vision. He saw recognition on his face.

"Why did you do that? Why didn't you let me fall?"

Derek swallowed. His lips moved as he tried to force words from his mouth. Robert bent down, placing his ear next to the dying man's mouth to hear the words he whispered.

"Forgive ... me ... sorry for ... your family."

Robert turned his face toward the dying man. Derek's eyes stared unseeing into the night sky.

And for a reason Robert couldn't comprehend, he felt such sorrow that he cried. His body shook with sobs as he fell back and tried to move away from Derek, as if his impending death was somehow contagious.

The blaring of approaching sirens grew louder as he rose unsteadily to his feet and stumbled away into the night.

"I am wide open for suggestions." Ian was bent low, trying to breathe whatever clear air he could find in all the smoke.

Charlie stood speechless beside him. Ian was pretty sure the kid had already given up.

But that wasn't his way.

"Come on, Levi," he said under his breath, "I am gonna be so ticked off if you let me die."

As if in answer to his prayer, a part of the ceiling fell four feet from them. Both men jumped back in surprise. Somewhere above them, another section of ceiling crashed. The building crackled as the flames reached for them.

And then Ian had a horrible vision. A gigantic figure shrouded in black leaped through the flames and stood before them.

It was Death.

And it had come for him.

It reached out a hand … and called him by name.

"Ian! Come on, man! Let's go!"

Taking a good look at the specter before him, he recognized it. It was Levi, covered in a coat of some kind to keep the flames off him.

"Took you long enough," Ian said. "Let's go, Chuck." He turned to find Charlie sprawled on the floor, overcome by smoke. Before he could move, Levi picked up the fallen man and was heading toward the door.

Torrents of water began to pour inside. Within seconds a small pathway had been formed through the flames. Levi charged through, carrying Charlie as if he weighed less than a bag of groceries. Ian, still bent low, plowed through behind him.

Rachel studied the directions on the paper again. Scott sat in the backseat, playing with a toy. He was blissfully unaware of what was going on, or that he'd been kidnapped earlier. He had been playing with several other children when she found him at the day-care center, just as Robert had said she would. Now it had taken her forever to find this place.

As she drew closer, a glow on the horizon caught her attention. Something was on fire.

"Oh, no."

"What's wrong, Mommy?"

"Do you remember what Grandpa taught you about praying?"

"Yeah."

"Then do it now," Rachel said as she floored the accelerator.

Flashing lights were everywhere. When she was still several hundred yards away, she saw the building burning.

Her hands were shaking as she gripped the wheel. "Dear God, no ... please no. Please don't let this happen."

She was blocked by several fire trucks about a block away from the site of the fire. Rachel glanced back at Scott and toward the building again. She needed to be out there, but she didn't know whether her son needed to see what was happening or not.

"Cool!" Scott's eyes were wide as he finally noticed the commotion around them. "What's going on?"

"Stay in the car," Rachel said, opening her door and stepping outside. Even from this distance, she could feel the heat from the blaze. She ran past the fire trucks.

When she rounded the first truck, she got her first full look at everything. She tried to take it all in, but it was a scene from a nightmare. A few firemen were running around, but most appeared to have given up on saving the building. Across the street, paramedics worked on several bodies lying on the ground.

And then she saw her husband.

"Derek!" She rushed to the fallen man's side and collapsed on the ground next to him, her hands hovering over his body, afraid to touch him and cause him more pain. Blood was everywhere, trickling from his mouth and several cuts and gashes on his face. His clothes were filthy, and he smelled of smoke. She watched the paramedics work on him, but the looks on their faces told her they didn't have much hope.

"Derek?" she said, trying to keep her voice strong.

His eyes fluttered open. "Rachel?" The word was barely audible.

"I'm here, baby. I'm here."

He fought to smile as he focused on her. "Hey."

She gently touched his face. "Hey."

He spoke through ragged breaths. "Sorry ... for what ... happened between us. Wish I could ... change things."

Rachel placed a finger on his lips. "Shhhh. We can talk later." Despite her resolution to remain strong for Derek, she began to cry.

Derek moved his head slightly to push her finger away. "We had ... good times, didn't we?"

Rachel nodded. "A lot of them."

His tongue touched his lips to moisten them. "Love you."

"I love you, too. Now please rest. We'll—"

A single tear trickled down his cheek as he sighed. The ragged breathing stopped, and he was still.

Rachel sat staring at him for several seconds, then gently laid her head on his chest and held him close.

FORTY-THREE

Rachel stood at the foot of the grave. She'd come here every day for the past week, trying somehow to make amends for what had passed between them in their last weeks together. They'd lost so much time; and by the time they finally got everything back on track, he was gone.

She thought about the difference she'd seen in him during those last few days. He'd truly been a changed man, and there was no way of knowing how their life would have turned out.

"Well, baby, I'm here again. You probably thought I'd be late, but I've really been working on being more punctual. I'm starting classes next month, and I know you'd want me to be there on time for them. You tried your best to provide for us. I hope to make you proud of me."

Movement in her peripheral vision caught her eye. The leaves in a nearby grove of trees stirred, and she studied them before turning back to the grave. Her body shook as a chilly autumn wind blew past her. "Scott misses you. He put his football up on the shelf over his bed and won't let me touch it anymore. He says that's just for the two of you. You meant so much to him—to both of us—and it's gonna be hard without you there."

Finally, she could fight it no longer and began to cry. "Oh, Derek, I'm so sorry. I'm sorry for what I put you through, and I'm sorry that I made you feel like you couldn't talk to me. If I hadn't gotten so angry with you, then you'd have never been mad enough to have that accident. Our lives would have been so different. I can't help but feel it's all my fault. Please forgive me."

She walked over to the headstone and knelt beside it. Gently, she placed a single rose at its base.

"I remember the good times, baby. They're all I remember now."

She kissed her fingers and touched the mound of earth. Her eyes closed, then she stood and took a step back. She turned to go and gasped.

"Sorry if I scared you."

"No, it's all right. What are you doing here?"

Bishop walked to the grave and stared down at it. "I called your mother to check on you two. She said Scott was still in his room, and that you'd come back here again. I just wanted to see how you're doing."

"I'm alive. That's the best I can hope for, I guess. I just came to visit Derek."

Bishop nodded. "He's not here. You know that, don't you? His body may be down there, but his soul is …"

"… in a much better place. I get it. I've heard that before."

Bishop turned to her. "I wasn't going to say that. I was going to say that his soul is with God now—literally. Derek gave his life to God, and death wasn't something to be afraid of anymore."

They both stood silent for a moment, then Rachel walked over to stand beside Bishop and looked down at Derek's grave. "He was a good man, Levi. Things got to him for a while, but he was always a good man."

"We all make mistakes, Rachel. Derek was a great man. I saw that the first time I talked to him. Everything he said and did that night was about you and how it would affect his family. You and Scott were the most important priorities in his life. He died a changed man, but his love for you only grew stronger because of it."

The breeze carried the scent of roses as they turned to walk away.

Robert watched from the safety of the tree line as they left. Rachel had almost seen him when he'd first arrived, and the sudden appearance of Bishop didn't help anything. Now he knew he had to be more cautious. He waited five minutes before walking into the sunshine and toward the grave of Derek Morrison.

He stared at the fresh pile of earth. The hole had been filled only a week earlier, yet even now there were signs of grass attempting to grow through it. A single rose lay at the base of the gravestone.

He had finally worked up the courage to come. After he had stumbled away from the fire, he'd hidden in a cheap motel for a few days to recuperate. He'd been careful to stay out of the public eye, even though the television news hadn't said anything about him relating to the fire. Apparently Levi hadn't told the police about his involvement, and any evidence of his being there had gone up in flames.

Now he was here ... and he didn't know why.

Glancing over his shoulder to be certain he was alone, Robert turned back to the grave and stared, almost trying to see into the ground to the man deep below. He replayed their last hour together, examining in detail every action and every word that had passed between them. Still he had no answers.

Finally, in frustration and anger, he said, "Why?"

"No greater love has any man than to lay down his life for his friends."

Robert knew the source of the unmistakable voice behind him. "I thought you were gone."

"I figured you could use the company too," Bishop said.

"You saw me?"

"You were watching Rachel, but you didn't even know I was here until I walked up to her. If she'd been paying attention, she'd have seen you too. You really aren't that good at skulking about."

"So what now?"

"I just wanted to talk to you for a bit."

"It's not fair. He prays a little prayer and gets to walk away scot-free after killing my wife and daughter. How does that make sense?"

"Derek didn't walk away. Just because people give their lives to God doesn't mean their pasts are erased. Their mistakes are still there waiting for them when they get off their knees. There are always consequences, Robert."

Levi stood next to him. "As for killing your family, that was never intentional. He made a horrible mistake, and he knew it. He tried to run from it, but in the end he was ready to face up to it. He just never got the chance."

Neither man spoke for several seconds. Finally, Robert sighed and looked up. "He was a hero. You don't know what happened in that shaft, do you?"

"No. Why don't you enlighten me?"

"I fell off that ladder, three stories up. I was going straight for the concrete, and I knew I was going to die. I also knew I wasn't ready for whatever was waiting for me after death, but there was nothing I could do about it. Derek must have figured he couldn't hold onto me if he grabbed me, so he let go of the ladder and wrapped his arms around me. He became a human air bag for me."

Robert looked up into Bishop's face. "You know what's so strange? He sounded genuinely happy when he caught me—like he didn't know he was about to die."

Bishop said, "It wasn't that he didn't know he was about to die, he just wasn't afraid of it anymore. He'd found there was something more to life than living in shadows and lies. He was going to come clean about what he'd done, Robert. He just didn't have the time."

"I destroyed his family, but he forgave me and tried to save my life. What is that, Levi? Why would a man do that?"

"A man did that two thousand years ago for all of us, and the ones who know him learn that it's nothing to lay down their life when called upon to do it."

Laying a hand gently on Robert's shoulder, Bishop said, "Want to hear about it?"

Later that night Charlie knocked on Amy's door, his heart pounding. This would be a big night for them—if he could pull it off. He was wearing a polo shirt and shorts, decidedly less formal and more comfortable than the way he was dressed on their first date.

She answered the door looking as radiant as ever. She wore a T-shirt and shorts, with colorful sandals on her feet. Her hair was pulled into a ponytail.

Charlie stepped inside and took her hand. "You look amazing. Are you ready for your surprise?"

She narrowed her eyes and tilted her head slightly. "You've got me a little suspicious here, big man. What exactly do you have planned?"

"I just wanted our first official date to be special. Things have been crazy lately, and this is my chance to make up for the dinner I cancelled on you." He pulled her out of the apartment and waited as she locked the door behind them.

"Now why am I dressed like this, may I ask? I'm usually a little classier for my dates."

Charlie winked. "You'll see."

He opened her car door and waited as she slid inside. Within minutes, they were on the road.

"Where are we going?"

"You don't want to ruin the surprise, do you?"

Amy laughed and patted his leg. "No one's ever done anything like this for me before. I'm excited." She looked at him with a beautiful smile.

Charlie glanced over at her. "Hey, we're almost there. Now, close your eyes."

With one last playful glance, she did so. He stopped the car and went around to open her door. Careful to make sure she didn't hit her head or stumble, he led her along several feet until they reached their destination. Then he let go of her hand and said, "Now, open them."

Her eyes widened as she took in the scene around them. They were in Charlie's front yard. A blue plastic wading pool with cartoon fish and sea horses on it was filled with water in front of them. Several floating candles were burning inside. The ground around the pool was covered with sand for at least six feet on all sides. Seashells were sprinkled here and there on the sand.

Charlie reached behind the pool and pulled out a small CD player. After he pressed the play button, the sounds of crashing waves and seagulls began to fill the air. He set the player down and walked over to her, taking her hands. "You said you wanted to dance on the beach. I'm afraid I can't take you there right now, so I thought I'd try to give you the next best thing."

He pulled her close and began to sway with her. She snuggled into his chest. He could hear her sniffling. She pulled a hand free to wipe her eyes, then took his again. After several minutes of moving in silence, she looked up at him.

"Thank you."

Instead of replying, Charlie leaned down and kissed her.

It was their first kiss, and it was everything he'd imagined it would be.

FORTY-FOUR

CHARLIE WALKED INTO WHITNEY Edge Software the following morning and stopped in his tracks.

Robert was sitting in his office.

"Um, hey there, chief."

Robert looked up from his computer and gave him a pained smile. "Surprise."

"To say the least."

"Yeah." Robert stood. "I went through a lot when Tara and Emily died. There was a lot of hatred inside me, and I reacted wrong. I did things that I would have never imagined doing before, and I hurt people in ways I'd never thought possible. I became an entirely different person."

Charlie sat on the edge of his desk. "I noticed."

"I just want you to know that I'm sorry. I want to set things right again, if possible."

"What did you have in mind?"

"I've spent the morning checking up on some ... projects I had going the past few weeks. I want to undo the things I've done."

"So how can you fix things?"

"Well, I wrote a second virus this morning and sent it into Starline Trucking's computer network. It should've straightened out their books. I also mailed some printouts to the police that will prove the bank records for Terrance Gold were falsified. I didn't tell them who did it, but it should be enough to prove he was innocent of the charges they had on him. The only thing I have left to do is fix the things I did to Chris Rickles. I was just about to start when you walked in."

Charlie expelled a deep breath and stood. With a quick nod and a crooked grin, he said, "So what are we waiting for? Let's fix the little guy's life."

As Robert turned to go back to his computer, Charlie noticed the Bible on his desk. "New reading material?"

"A gift. A friend told me I should read it."

"Let me know how it turns out."

"I will. I promise." Robert stopped typing but didn't turn around. "You know, Charlie, once the police find out everything I did, I'm going to be in some serious trouble. I'll probably be out of touch for a while. Will you keep things running here until I get back?"

Charlie felt his eyes begin to water as he considered the future awaiting his friend. "Yeah, I'll keep it all going. Hey, I'll have it running a lot better than you did, that's for sure. You won't recognize the place."

"You'll have to hire some help."

"I think I can convince Amy to stick around for a bit, and I still have Tom. I'll grab a couple more good folks and we'll be fine."

Robert turned to face him now. "Thank you. I don't know why you stuck around, but thank you."

A million snappy comebacks flew through Charlie's brain, but none truly conveyed the meaning he wanted. Instead, he nodded and pulled up a chair next to Robert.

The two of them together at a computer, working to solve another problem.

And maybe just for today, it was like old times.

Bishop stood in the empty sanctuary of his church, praying for his congregation. He heard the door open and close behind him, but he didn't stop until his prayer was over. He turned to find the one person in the world he'd never expected to see in this place.

"Well, well, the prodigal son has come home."

Ian raised a hand. "Don't get your hopes up. I just came to talk." He plopped down into a nearby pew and leaned back. "Big crowd Sunday morning?"

Bishop slid into the row in front of him. "It was nice, yes. I could have used one more."

"You never give up, do you?"

"I serve a God of miracles."

Ian chuckled and looked away. "Haven't seen you since Derek's funeral. I never got to thank you for saving my life in that fire. Charlie and I would've been dead if it wasn't for you."

"I care too much about your soul to let you go before you're ready."

Ian turned to him and pursed his lips. Shaking his head, he sighed and stood. He patted Bishop's shoulder and stepped out into the aisle. "There's definitely something different about you, big guy."

When he reached the door, he spoke over his shoulder. "I have something big. Linda called and gave me the details. Sounds pretty interesting, but I could use some help. Amy's a little ... preoccupied right now. Any chance you could ..."

"I'll be there after lunch."

Ian nodded. Sunlight filled the church as he opened the door and stepped outside.

EPILOGUE

Ian LISTENED TO THE footsteps echo off the walls of the parking deck around him. It was late and he was tired of waiting for the man. He hoped he could stay hidden in the stairwell long enough for what he had to do.

Two weeks had passed since Derek's funeral, and life had almost settled back to normal for everyone in his small agency. Linda had managed to send enough money to Rachel anonymously from the agency to help her get started in her night classes. Levi checked on both Scott and her on a regular basis, and she'd even begun attending his church. Amy was helping Charlie keep Whitney Edge Software afloat, and Ian seriously doubted she'd be coming back to work for him anytime soon. He could see it in her eyes—she was in love.

He was in Montgomery, almost a three-hour drive from his apartment in Birmingham. Tonight was personal and he wasn't making a dime off of it. He considered this a favor, though he couldn't say to whom. Maybe this was just something he needed to do for himself.

Jingling keys greeted his ears as the man neared a dented blue Camaro that had seen better days. He passed under a light, clearly illuminating his face and verifying this was the person he was after. Ian reached in the darkness and felt the comforting shape of his cell phone. He pushed a button and waited three seconds before he stepped from the shadows.

"Hey there, Terry."

Terrance Gold spun around and froze as he saw Ian. Recognition dawned on his face, and he shook his head. "Don't know when to leave it alone, do you?"

"I missed your sense of humor."

Gold looked around, most likely seeing if there were any witnesses to what was about to transpire. "How'd you find me?"

Ian walked toward him. "I have friends. One of them found out about your job as a night watchman here. Not the most glamorous stint in the world, but I guess it pays the bills."

Gold sniffed, his eyes still roaming around the empty parking deck. "What do you want?"

Ian stepped past him and sat on the hood of Gold's Camaro. "Can't a friend just drop by to say 'hey'?"

Gold was wary, but Ian could see a confidence building in him again. He'd expected an ambush, but Ian had come alone. "You're here about the fire, aren't you? Thinking you can blackmail me or something?"

Ian nodded. "Something like that."

"Whitney turned me in, didn't he? I saw on the news where they only had one fatality at the fire. Guess he escaped after all 'cause Derek never saw me there."

"Well, Robert told me everything that happened, but I convinced him not to go to the police. I told him we'd be much better off keeping this to ourselves." Ian rubbed his fingers and thumb together.

Ian said, "Why'd you do it? Why'd you set that fire?"

Gold smiled. "That man made my life miserable. He messed up a good thing I had going, and I wanted to pay him back."

Ian shook his head. "But why try to kill Derek too?"

"I talked to the boy on the phone and he just wanted me to help take Robert into custody peacefully. He didn't want the man hurt. But I did. Besides, he could place me there later."

Ian didn't say anything. Terrance had stopped fidgeting and was settling down. His hand casually drifted to the gun strapped to his belt, then past it.

Gold said, "So what now? How much to keep you quiet?"

Ian thought for a moment. "How much did Starline pay you to lie about the accident report?"

Gold looked at him warily. "Why?"

"Just wondering so I can come up with a fair price. Remember what I said about lying to me? Better be honest."

"Five grand."

"The woman and her daughter were only worth five thousand dollars?"

Gold sneered. "Hey, Whitney wasn't offering me a dime. If he'd gotten into it, it might have been interesting."

"That should do it then." Ian stood up. "Don't you think so?"

"What?"

A voice answered. "Yes, I believe we have what we need. We'll be waiting for him with open arms."

Gold looked down at the cell phone strapped to Ian's belt.

Ian saw him staring and tapped the phone. "Don't you just love these speakerphone options on cell phones today? Terrance, I believe you know Captain Tim Doyal, don't you? Tall ... rugged ... honest."

Gold said, "You can't use any of what I just said."

"Actually, Terry, in the great state of Alabama it's perfectly legal to tape a phone conversation and use it in court—so long as at least one member of the party knows about it." Ian winked at him. "And Captain Doyal knows." He pulled the phone from his belt and whispered a quick thanks to Tim, then hung up. He stood a few feet away from Gold, and it was almost impossible to keep from laughing at the look on Gold's face.

"You just cleared up a little confusion back in Birmingham. We didn't know for certain who really started that fire. Robert told me what happened, but unfortunately you decided to rabbit on us and I had to track you down."

"How much is he paying you?"

"Robert? Nothing. I'm doing this for Derek. He was a much better man than you, and he died because you started that fire."

Gold's cold stare bore into Ian. "I should've finished you in that parking lot. I should've found your friend and finished things with him, too."

Ian thought about the ambush Terrance had tried to set for Levi in the hospital parking lot. If he hadn't been there and seen the man creeping between the cars, Bishop might have walked right into it. The mental picture of his friend cut up—or worse—sickened him. He turned to go. "There'll be an arrest warrant out for you within the hour. I'd just turn myself in if I were you."

Gold drew his gun and grabbed Ian's shoulder. "I'll kill you, you—"

Ian whirled around, his left arm encircling Terrance's where it held him. He lifted up slightly, forcing Terrance off balance to keep from breaking the arm at the elbow. Ian launched a vicious punch to Gold's solar plexus. The gun clattered to the ground. Before Gold could collapse, Ian pushed him back over the Camaro's hood, his forearm crushing into Gold's throat. Gold's trapped arm squirmed in Ian's grasp. His eyes were wide with astonishment and fear.

Ian fought to control the rage building inside him. "You listen to me carefully 'cause I'm only gonna say this once: Turn yourself in and face the music. May not be fun, but that's life."

Gold was gasping now, desperately clawing at Ian's arm with his free hand. Ian leaned into him heavily once, and Gold raised the hand in understanding.

Ian stared deeply into the man's eyes. "And if you ever—*ever*—try to hurt Levi, I'll find you. I found you here and I can track you anywhere. And when I find you ..." Ian lowered his face to within inches of Gold's "... I'll make you disappear. No one will ever know what happened to you, and no one will ever care. Understand?" Gold moved his head slightly to acknowledge him.

In one fluid motion Ian released Gold's arm and neck and moved back. He picked up the Beretta, ejected the clip, and disassembled the gun with military precision. Terrance rubbed his throat as he watched each piece fall to the floor. When he was finished, Ian kicked the small cluster of parts, sending them in several directions.

He walked backward toward the stairs. "You've got twenty-four hours to do the right thing. If you don't, I'll be coming for you—and it'll hurt."

He descended two flights of stairs to the level where he'd parked his car. Five minutes later he was back on I-65 heading north.

Ian knew now what had driven him to track Terrance Gold and clear Robert of the arson charge. It was Derek, even though Derek never really seemed to like him that much. There was something about him. In the end he'd tried to set things right. Levi said Derek would've wanted to forgive his enemies. He'd have wanted to help Robert as much as possible because he'd found the same peace Levi had.

Derek had finally found rest.

And as he drove toward home, Ian hoped that someday he would find it too.

AUTHOR'S NOTE

Identity theft is one of the fastest growing crimes in America. While many people are secure with their thoughts of antivirus software and firewalls, much of identity theft is not done by talented computer programmers. It's done through the practice of social engineering called "phishing." Basically, they try to trick you into divulging information about yourself or your company by appearing to be legitimate in their inquiries. The greatest protection program you have on your computer is only as good as the person at the keyboard. Social engineers no longer have to spend time guessing passwords. All they have to do is call someone, act like they're from their company's IT department, and get the helpful stranger to give them the little details they want. One compromised account in a company's network is all it takes to get just about anything.

Everything Robert did in this book is taken from actual social engineering tactics currently used by identity thieves. However, in order to keep this from becoming a how-to manual, I changed key practices at certain points in the story and left out something vital in each. One key ingredient is missing from the scenarios to make them work: either additional preparation, legwork, or something similar.

Every computer virus created in the book is based on a real one.

Current statistics say that most people will be the victim of identity theft at some point in their lives. And before you say this could never happen to you, I'd encourage you to download a spyware detecting program and run it. You'd be surprised to find what's lurking in the background of your own hard drive right now.

Special thanks to Tim Abel and Eric Wilson, two very gifted writers, for their help and encouragement.

I'd love to hear from you!
You can contact me by e-mail at Brian@BrianReaves.net.
Download a free readers' discussion guide from my Web site,
http://www.BrianReaves.net.